Books by J. D. Evans

Mages of the Wheel Series

Wind & Wildfire (Prequel)

Reign & Ruin

Storm & Shield

Siren & Scion

Ice & Ivy

Mountain & Memory (TBD)

Fire & Fate (TBD)

MAGES OF THE WHEEL BOOK FOUR

Ice & Ivy

J. D. EVANS

Ice & Ivy is a work of fiction. Names, characters, cultures, places, events, and incidents are of the author's imagination or used in a fictitious manner. Any resemblance to actual persons, living or dead, or actual events is purely coincidental.

Published by Whippoorwill Press LLC 2023
North Carolina, United States

ISBN: 978-1-951607-12-8

Cover Art—Tatiana Anor
www.artstation.com/tanyaanor

Cover Design—Eric C. Wilder
https://www.ericcwilder.com

Hardback Case Design—Raven Pages Design
https://www.ravenpagesdesign.com

Interior formatting & design—Terry Roy
www.teryvisions.com

Editing—Michelle Morgan
www.fictionedit.com

Whippoorwill PRESS

To my mom, who showed me all the hope, wonder,
and magic contained in a seed.

Tero
Corsan Republic
Corsyra
Marceo
Aklion
Eannea
Isla Sora
Rieta
Haenna
Tyrus
Sun Sea
Nasiye
Menei

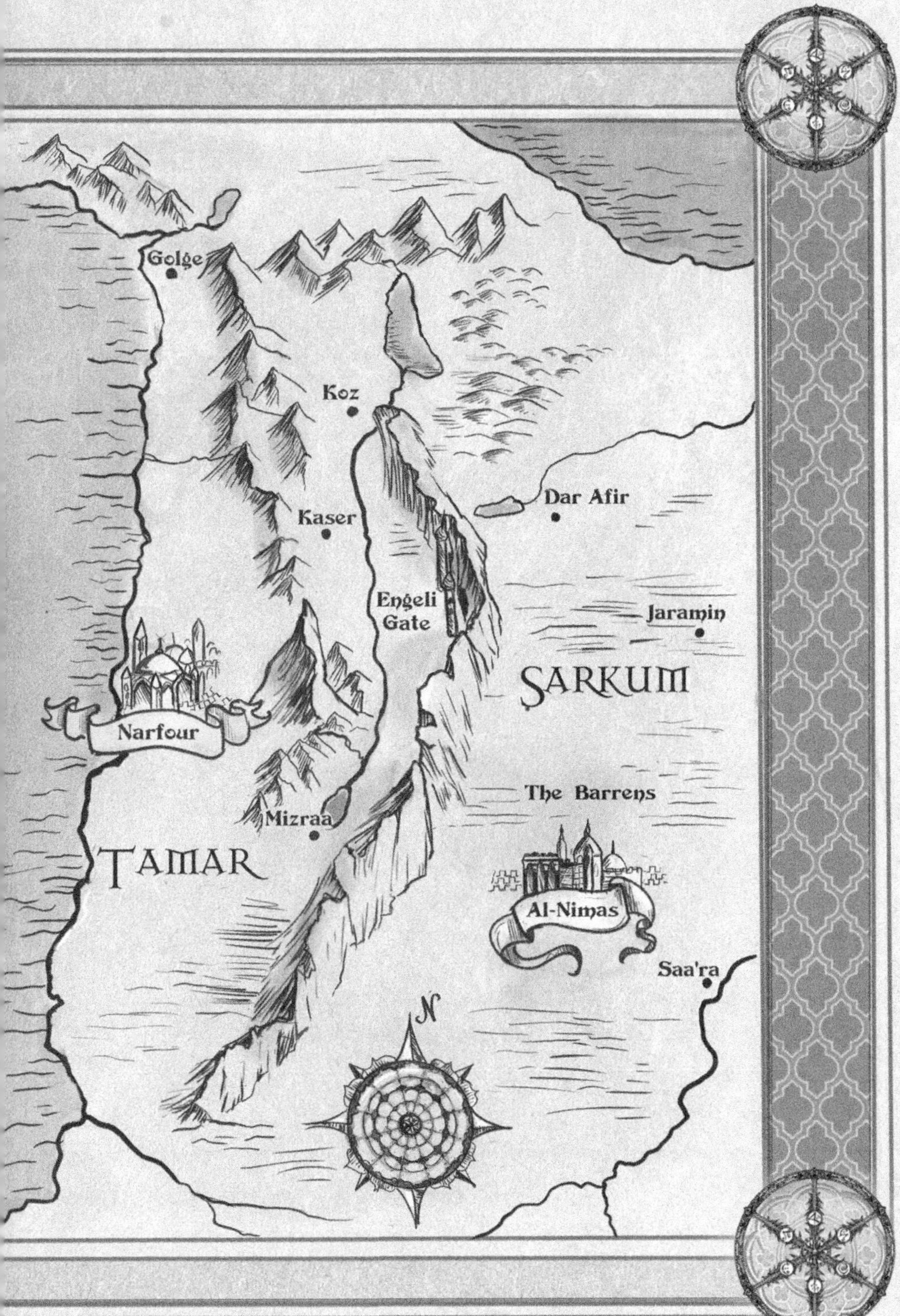

Golge
Koz
Dar Afir
Kaser
Engeli
Gate
Jaramin
SARKUM
Narfour
The Barrens
Mizraa
TAMAR
Al-Nimas
Saa'ra
N

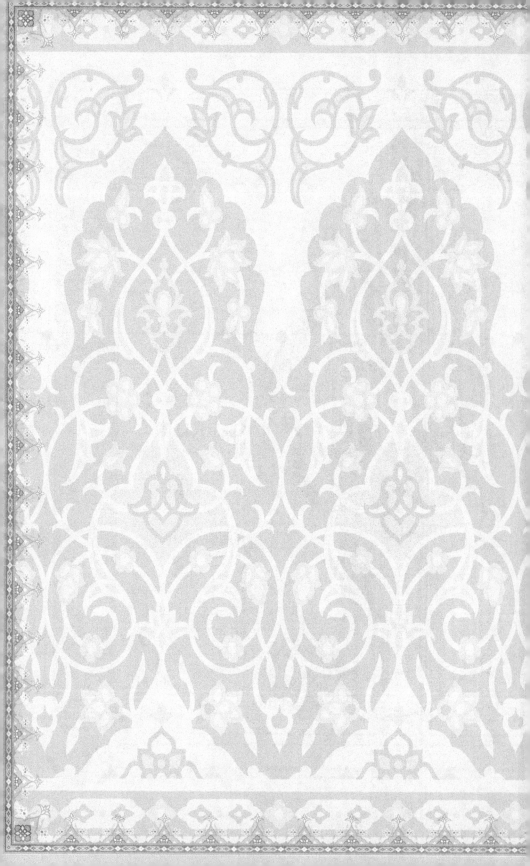

Poem of the Wheel

4th

In Circle endless, birth to death
The Wheel spins the world
All await magic's breath
Seeds in slumber curled
To rise through twilight
Into the sun
To stretch out root and leaf so bright
Until our Turns are done

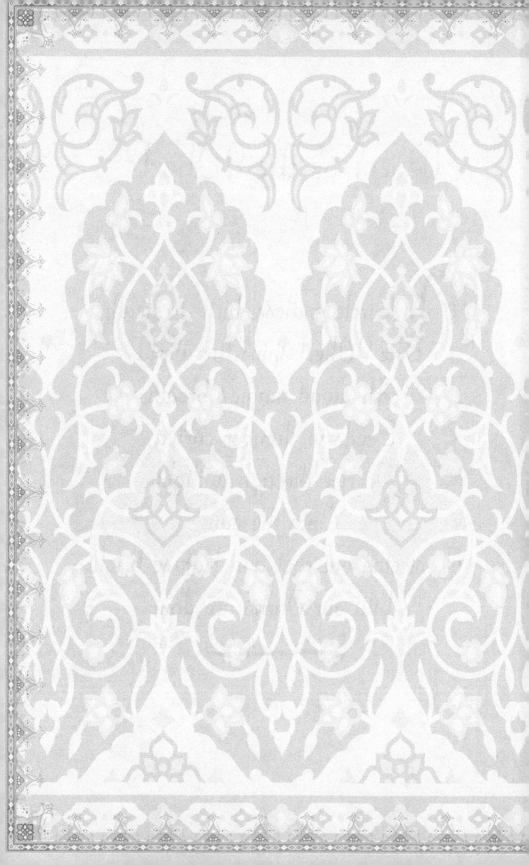

One

He crumpled the letter in his fist as it disintegrated to ash, its carefully inked, coded letters warping and curling. He held his hand out the window of his office and unfurled his fingers. The grey specks drifted into the light breeze. That was the third shipment this season. The letter speculated it was the more agreeable weather of early summer that brought out bandits. But there was no news of other merchants being targeted with such zeal. No. Whoever this was, they knew exactly what was in the wagons they were destroying. This was not thievery, this was war.

"They've arrived, Grand Vizier," Cemil said from the doorway where he stood sentinel. Behram did not look at him, but out his window, his gaze tracing a path to the edge of the Air District. The boundary between the lowborn and the highborn had shifted in the intervening Turns. But his gaze was drawn like filings to magnet. The house still stood, though it was owned by a distant relative now. He could not actually see it from this distance, but its silhouette was forever burned into his memory.

As she was. As she had been. Before they'd let her die, let her succumb to the wasting disease of those she had no business serving. He dropped his hand to the windowsill, fingers clutching at the wood, the aggravating prick of splinters driving her from his mind. She never strayed far away. Haunting him in death as she had in life.

Voices drifted from below. He was in no mood to deal with any of them today. But needs must. These loose ends needed snipped, or they would fray his carefully woven plans. He tugged the window closed, then turned.

"News?" Cemil asked from the doorway, eyes fixed on him. Glittering. Fire and gold. Rage burst and died in Behram's chest, the smoke of its demise fueling a smile. Every day a reminder of all those who had wronged him. Taken from him. Used him. Cemil the worst reminder of them all.

Besides Omar. Sultan, and deceiver. Thief. A selfish, afflicted child who could not see past his own wants to what his people, what Tamar, needed: a firm hand, to keep the magic strong and undiluted. Someone who knew how to pick allies, and enemies. Someone who had the spine to maneuver pieces into place, whether by coercion, or force.

Behram suspected Cemil saw all that in his expression, all the thoughts, the calculations. Just as Behram had been able to read his own father. Cemil was being shaped the same way Behram had been, through hammer and anvil, fire and forge. But he was crumbling under the pressure of it. That was no surprise. Zehra had been weak in every way. Her decisions only reinforced her failings. How could her son be better than that which whelped him?

"Another mule has died." He would normally not speak of it out loud, even in code, but both Banu and Mahir were present to notify him of any listening spells. He rounded his desk. Cemil backed out of the doorway as Behram approached. His son stank of alcohol, as usual—though it took an impressive amount to put the man out of his senses. The fire in him burned strongly enough to take the bite from the alcohol before it affected him. Cemil was good at pretending to be drunk, when it suited his purposes. He was steady in posture and words, for now.

"Shall I investigate? Or have them halt production until we can identify who—"

A snapped spark across Cemil's neck made him hiss then he silenced. He knew better than to speak such things aloud.

"That is what they want," Behram said, "and I will not be manipulated by specters I cannot see."

"I can reinforce the escorts."

Behram nodded once. "Bring me someone with answers." He wanted one of these bandits so he could find out who knew enough of his plans to target his shipments before they had even left Tamar.

"As you wish." Cemil punctuated with a vicious smile as they moved for the stairs that led to the first floor. They descended through the invisible barrier of Mahir's dampening spell. Momentarily it filled Behram's ears and mind with cotton, but he adjusted quickly to the lack of ambient noise.

The two Viziers inside the dampening spoke amicably enough, but the tension they hid from each other was obvious to Behram. The conversation ceased as they stood and bowed to him.

Cemil sank onto the far end of a couch, resting an elbow on a pillow, and effectively disappeared from everyone's notice but Behram's. A talent of his, to fill a room with his presence or disappear from it as he willed. It would have been an invaluable resource to Behram, if it were not so unpredictable.

The Viziers sat. Then Behram. Mahir set down a tray of refreshments, then bowed and retreated to the edge of his spell.

"Welcome, my friends," Behram said, his gaze on the swirl of his coffee as he stirred the sugar he added. "To what do I owe the pleasure of your company?" The question was a formality. He knew exactly why they had requested to meet with him. It was Enver Balik, grasping at power. Behram regretted that he needed the man at all, or rather, needed someone with influence in the Northern valley, and especially, access to its roads.

"We have concerns," Enver said, lifting his coffee but not drinking.

Behram tapped the diminutive gilt spoon against the rim of his glass and set it on the table. "Please." He gave a tight smile.

"Another warehouse was set fire to." Enver set the coffee back in its saucer. "This one containing the grain meant to pacify my villages south of Golge. Right now, all they can hear is Sirhan Yavuz's honeyed promises of supplies from the Sultan. The Council will not follow you if your minions are burning the city at their feet. It took nearly half a Turn to acquire that grain."

"Do not concern yourself with that," Behram said. These vandalisms of his property in Narfour were growing tiresome. He had not yet discovered if they were related to the attacks on his shipments. "The grain will be replaced."

In Tamar, most grain was provided by farmers in the Northern valley, from holdings belonging to Sirhan Yavuz. His supplies were dwindling, though, thanks to this Sarkum-born Blight, which had devastated agriculture in half the valley.

Behram had access to relationships with Menei, and the grains that still grew plentifully in its fertile river valleys. As it stood, he would soon be the only source of grain into Tamar. A fact he was leveraging to bring himself more support in the Council, and access to routes to Golge and beyond. Those routes required Enver Balik to be an ally, which Behram was willing to pay dearly for. Within reason. But Enver was not overly gifted with reason.

"If you are not careful and quick, it will be Mutar Charah who replaces it, and steals the support of the Northern Viziers out from under you." Doruk Caliskan sighed. "Her ties with Menei are stronger than yours. Soon, she will have control of the Merchant Guild from you as well." Doruk was one of Behram's oldest allies. They had grown up in the Council together, had been united by their shared grudges against the Sabri family. They were not friends, but as close to equals as Behram would begrudge anyone.

"Control of the Merchant Guild is for me to worry about." Behram flicked a look at Cemil, who avoided meeting his gaze. He had yet to punish his son for acting on his own, failing to do as he was asked with Mutar Charah. The boy was half slave to his alcoholism, and it made him bold and petulant, as it had that day, undoing what Behram had done out of pique. But Cemil would have a chance to redeem himself soon.

"It is not her grip on the Merchant Guild that concerns me, Grand Vizier," Enver said, "but that her discovery of Third House mages in the Republic, and yet another Charah, has stirred belief that the Sultana will indeed be able to stand a full Circle. The moderates in the Council are beginning to lean." He was the only Vizier with enough territory to challenge Sirhan Yavuz. Enver knew his holdings were invaluable to Behram. They encompassed the only roads leading out of Tamar that did not require passage through the Engeli Gate.

"*Mages* is a generous word for their parlor tricks. And only two," Doruk said. "Whatever support that has granted her will be fickle, easily snuffed out when that weak magic amounts to nothing. And the Charah they brought with them is more liability than ally. Who knows how long their herbs and tinctures will hold him."

Behram hummed his agreement, but Enver plowed forward in his track, trying to steer the conversation toward his own end. "These vandalisms and protests—are they yours? And to what end?"

Giving even the tiniest mote of information away could be deadly. Enver was a pawn, not an ally. A tool Behram needed for his plans, but useless beyond his singular purpose. Still, the man must believe he had sway in their exchanges.

"They are a useful distraction for now," Behram answered.

A small uprising of fire mages held little threat. They would be quelled or shipped off to the army in Sarkum before they endangered him or his plans. And if they stripped one or more of the city Viziers of their holdings or power, it would be one more hound brought to heel to add to his collection. One more voice turned in his favor in the Council when he swept in to assist.

And the Princess Sultana too preoccupied with her father's decline and the failure of her champion in his civil war. In fact, it would be best to leave them to their minor infractions until they had attacked some of his known allies before the princess turned her suspicions on him as some sort of ringleader.

"With the latest arson, the other Viziers will not wish to put stock into stored grain that can be burned by malcontents." Doruk leaned forward to retrieve a triangle of flatbread from the tray of mezze, which he proceeded to rip into pieces. "We need a local source, or the appearance of one." The crumbs scattered between his feet, pale against the crimson rug beneath his boots. He chewed thoughtfully, the smacking of his lips the only sound for an eternity.

Behram rubbed his thumb and forefinger together as he waited, a drop of flame running and flattening like a bead of something viscous between his fingers.

"The Southern valley is still generally free of Blight," Enver said, following Doruk's example by taking a piece of flatbread and swiping it through the generous helping of labneh. "And largely unrepresented on the Council."

Ah. And he had come to it. Behram pinched the flame in his fingers out. Enver had been attempting to make this gambit for nearly a Turn.

Behram leaned into the cushions behind him, taking pressure off the ache in his hip, and waited. He had known he would have to deal with it eventually. "Bardakci Pasha is uninterested in a Council position, and I see no reason to force the matter, when I am perfectly happy to relay his vote."

"You have not lived up to a single one of your promises to me," Enver said. "No grain. Not so much as a meet with Bardakci Pasha." He tossed his half-eaten piece of flatbread back onto the dish. His smug smile pricked Behram's fragile patience. He must have something now, a bit of leverage he thought would aid him. "I begin to wonder if the man even exists?"

Cemil coughed a laugh. Behram did not look at him. "He exists."

"Then bring him to the Council. Having a spokesperson for Mizraa in your pocket would give faith to your supporters that you can hold up your promises to keep people fed without having to rely on Menei, as Doruk suggested."

Doruk met Behram's stare, eyes tight at the corners.

"You speak of things you do not understand—"

"No, you do not understand. I want land in the Southern valley. I want the grain you promised my holdings. And if you continue to do nothing"—Enver leaned forward—"then I will ensure the Council, the Sultana, and all of Narfour know that their esteemed Grand Vizier is a Wheel Breaker."

Fire lit through Behram's veins. But he sat still, holding his expression neutral as he sorted Enver's threat. Off to his left, Cemil leaned his elbows onto his knees, one hand casually moving to the hilt of his sword, the grip hidden from Enver by his body. His gaze lit on Behram's face, waiting.

Doruk launched to his feet. "How dare you fabricate lies about the Grand Vizier!"

"Lies?" Enver laughed. "The fact he has hidden a life debt for nearly three Cycles is no lie. You are a Wheel Breaker, and the Council, Narfour, all of Tamar, will gladly turn on you as the cause of their troubles."

"Is this true, Grand Vizier? Do you owe a life debt?" Doruk looked at him.

Behram pressed his lips together to stop the sneer. A life debt to a meddlesome peasant and his snot-nosed child. Even if he had yet to repay their clumsy efforts, that was surely not enough to cause any real Unbalance. How had Enver known? The accident had happened in Mizraa. Only a few, those closest to him, knew the true cause of his limp, of his scars.

Someone had betrayed him.

He flicked a look at Cemil, who raised an eyebrow. No. He could not. Mahir and Banu would not. There was nothing to give it away. Nothing…

Cold fire replaced the burn of temper in Behram's chest. He blinked, a slow control of his expression. The first lesson his father had taught him was to never allow anyone to see a reaction beyond control. It did not matter what that reaction was, anger, fear, pain… the moment they recognized it, the battle was lost. They owned some power over you.

"What debt do you owe?" Doruk asked, thick brows furrowed over his beady eyes.

"It is *called* a life debt," Cemil sneered, "is it not? Someone saved his life."

Doruk's face reddened, his distended cheeks turning splotchy as he glared at Cemil. He was Behram's closest confidant on the Council. Not a friend, certainly, but someone who shared his grudge against the Sabris. Now he understood that he was not as close to Behram as he had thought.

Behram cast Cemil a look of reproval and Cemil shrugged, relaxing back into the seat.

He could not bring Osman Bardakci to Narfour. He was under Behram's control, but not infallibly so, and his placement in Mizraa was necessary to the smooth running of these blasted shipments. Bringing him to Narfour would upset that enterprise and cause more problems than it solved.

But how to solve this immediate one? A junior Vizier who thought too much of himself? And the life debt. How a Vizier, the Grand Vizier in fact, a noble and powerful mage, could possibly be expected to pay homage to filthy, barely magic-touched farmworkers was a thorn that had pricked at him every time he felt a pang in his leg or saw his scars in the mirror.

He should have eliminated them the moment he had healed, but that fool Osman had made the man overseer of his operations. Behram had never determined if the move had been deliberate to defy him, or simply business.

If Osman had ever managed to produce any more children, this dilemma could be solved with a marriage. Marry Enver Balik off to a daughter of Mizraa and be done with his whining.

Marriage.

Behram stood, limping away from the other three to stand in front of the fountain at the base of the stairs.

"Are you going to answer me?" Enver demanded.

Osman had no daughters. But that peasant did. He had an entire litter of brats. And had he not written to Behram about it? He spun and mounted the stairs, followed by Enver's shout for attention. It was met with Cemil's low voice, though it had a lilt of jest in it. Behram heard nothing else from Enver. Cemil could be intimidating when he wished to be.

He continued into his office and yanked open the drawer where he kept correspondence.

Yes. Behram withdrew the letter, its envelope stained with two dirty fingerprints. The words were formed in a shaky, unrefined scrawl, the letter dated more than a Turn past. Rereading the request for a marriage for his daughter, Behram squinted, forcing his memory to churn. The family were Second House, if he recalled. The girl would have some nominal water powers. He folded the letter closed and replaced it in the drawer, then sat down at his desk.

He pulled a piece of paper from a stack and thumbed the stopper from his inkpot. He dipped the quill, thinking.

A peasant girl disguised as a noble daughter would make the perfect wife for Enver Balik. When they were married, and Enver had found out his folly, it would be too late, he'd be shackled for life. Divorce was also a breaking of the Wheel, and no Vizier could afford the shame and loss of political power that came with such an unthinkable act. By then, he would be completely under Behram's control.

It would also finally remove the thorny weight of his life debt in one move. Osman would have to go along with the plan. What else could he do? If anyone accused Behram of planning the deception, he would simply put the blame on Osman trying to gain influence in the Council. It was long past time to rid himself of Osman as well and put a new proxy in place at Mizraa. Enver Balik would do for such a purpose. His impotent attempts at scheming suggested he had just the right amount of selfishness to be easily controlled.

He was penning his response to the peasant's letter, when Cemil entered the room.

"Tell Enver I have considered his *offer* and believe I have found a suitable solution," Behram said as he swept a flourish through his signature and set the quill back in its rest. Cemil raised an eyebrow when Behram looked up at him. "And summon Banu. I have something for her to deliver to Mizraa."

Two

IHSAN SLIT THE LENGTH OF A leaning, blackened stem of wheat. The fetid stench of the Blight, now familiar because so much of the land around them had succumbed, tainted the air he breathed. He tried to ignore Mathei Attiyeh staring over his shoulder. But it was difficult, considering the man was wearing the most purple shade of purple ever to accost Ihsan's vision, and kept making thoughtful noises with each of Ihsan's movements.

Behind them, Kuhzey paced, slapping at the desiccated plants with a stick, his restless boredom unnecessary proof that he was a poor pick for bodyguard. Ihsan pivoted just enough to peer at the boy over his shoulder. He cocked an eyebrow as Kuhzey executed a turn, slumping back the way he had just walked, tracking a flattened path through the field, his bony shoulders hunched, his head bowed and unkempt curls flopping in his face, mouth knotted in displeasure. Dust puffed beneath his feet, the current drought and lack of living plants turning the once-rich soil into a wasteland.

Mathei clucked his tongue. "Well done, Kuhzey, keep up the good work," he called cheerfully. Kuhzey turned his back on them, his fingers working through a rude remark Ihsan almost missed. He was a steward after all, not a soldier or guard. Though no one, not even Ihsan, thought much of Kuhzey as a steward, either.

"I saw that," Ihsan warned. Kuhzey marched a bit farther away.

"Why him?" Mathei muttered to Ihsan. The destruction mage's dark curls were plastered to his forehead, though the heat did not seem to trouble him. Of course Sarkum was his home. Or had been.

"Because I do not enjoy small talk." Ihsan glanced sidelong up at Mathei, whose eyebrows rose but he said nothing else. There were many similarities between Mathei and his sister but looks were none of them. The destruction mage was tall and attractive enough to warrant attention from most, while his sister was small and plain-faced. Though she made up for that in attitude, attitude which her brother shared.

Sweat trickled down Ihsan's back as he turned his attention to the sky, pale blue and depressingly clear of anything more than a teasing tuft of clouds. Summer was, without a doubt, the worst season in the Turning of the Wheel. And though it was not truly summer yet, it mocked him with its imminent arrival.

He could not bear the heat on his skin, warming him, burning him, lighting his scars and his memories on fire. He couldn't remember what it felt like to be warm and happy. The two would never come in tandem for him again. And even if Sarkum's late-spring heat was drier than Narfour's, swaddled by the ocean's dampness, Ihsan sensed the summers would be dreadful.

It was worse out here, away from the camp and the shade trees and cool water that fed Saa'ra. Crouched in a rotting clump of what had been a season's worth of wheat, there was nothing to distract him from the mocking sun. Except company he did not want.

Sarkum was where the Blight had started. Though from what he'd seen during this futile sojourn, it was the same in Sarkum as in Tamar. He dropped the stalk and stood. Silly of him to think he could be useful in this manner. Naime had not sent him here for plant samples anyway.

He had been sent to serve, more or less, as a carrier pigeon.

She had deployed him in lieu of his feathery predecessors so she could speak directly to Makram without the risk birds bore of being intercepted. But Makram was away, overseeing reinforcements he'd deployed to the siege on Al-Nimas. Elder Attiyeh could not pinpoint when Makram would return, and so they had waited. Idle and hot. For two small turns.

"What do you know of the Blight in Sarkum?" Ihsan asked Mathei. "How did it spread? Where did it begin?"

"So you do desire small talk, after all?" Mathei smirked. When Ihsan only stared blandly at him, Mathei waved his hand to dismiss the joke. "It began Turns ago. In small, isolated pockets near Al-Nimas. In the last few Turns, it began to spread in earnest. In a large crescent swath from Dar Afir through the farmlands surrounding Al-Nimas, and radiated outward like sepsis from a wound. No crop resists it." Mathei kicked at a rotted clump of wheat. "As Tamar has learned."

It had spread into Tamar and decimated the Northern valley crops of winter grain. The discontented opinion of most was that it had been brought into the valley by refugees. Yet, despite it beginning to appear in Narfour, the Southern valley remained uniquely untouched. Refugees had traveled there as well. If they were the cause, then why was Mizraa still producing? Another question for which he had no answer.

"Ah. Your nursemaid has discovered your absence," Mathei said dryly, staring past Ihsan toward the road they had taken from Saa'ra. Ihsan turned to see Aysel riding toward them like a miniscule thunderstorm.

Every attempt Ihsan made to do anything other than sit uselessly while waiting for Makram's return had been stopped by Aysel, who had proved to be more boarhound than person, dogging his every step, denying him any opportunity to leave the safety of Saa'ra. He had not had issue with the First House Charah until Naime requested she serve as his personal entourage for the trip. He would rather risk dismemberment by enemy soldiers or bandits than endure her coddling of him one more moment.

"Blighted Void," Ihsan swore. Mathei grinned in glee.

Aysel reined her horse to a stop beside them, kicking dust up into their faces as she did. "Why do I feel as though this is all your fault?" She swung down as she addressed her brother and flipped her braids over her shoulders.

"Me?" Mathei pressed a finger to his chest and adopted an outraged expression. "I was merely keeping the Sehzade company."

Aysel made a mocking face. "How generous."

"I am, yes," Mathei said. Ihsan wouldn't call it generous that Mathei had followed him and Kuhzey out of Mizraa talking the entire way, unconcerned that no one was answering.

Aysel looked at Ihsan. "I was told to keep you out of danger. Why are you making that impossible?"

"I do not appreciate being henpecked like a child in gowns," Ihsan said. "Nor spoken to in such a manner."

Her face twitched as if she controlled an expression. Knowing her, it was an eyeroll. "And I do not appreciate having my time wasted by having to chase you down. Or putting my brother in danger." She cocked a hip and folded her arms over her chest.

"Leave me out of your spat," Mathei said.

"What am I supposed to tell the Princess Sultana when you get yourself killed or kidnapped? 'He tromped out into an unprotected field in the middle of a war'." She paused, then added in afterthought, "Sehzade."

"Attiyeh Charah," Ihsan muttered in reprisal.

The rider behind Aysel caught up, pulling her horse alongside Aysel's. She was a young woman Ihsan had only ever seen in the company of Amara Mutar. Built like a whip, slim and lithe, she had a look in her eyes that held that particular mix of apathy and a belief in one's own unique wisdom that only those in their teens could manage.

Kuhzey appeared at Ihsan's side as if conjured there. He stood a bit taller as he cast a glance in Kiya's direction, which she ignored.

"If you had not run away from Saa'ra this morning, I would not have had to track you down like a stray goat to tell you that a scout arrived. Makram will be here this afternoon."

Kuhzey shifted closer to Kiya, unsubtly, as she dismounted and gathered all the horses together. She was two Turns older than Kuhzey, which was practically a Cycle when it came to interest and maturity. Especially in his case.

Mathei muttered in exasperation as he stepped to Kuhzey's side, put a hand on his shoulder, and steered him away from the rest of them. Aysel and Kiya appeared surprised but lost interest quickly. Ihsan didn't know if he wanted to allow Mathei to give romantic advice to Kuhzey. The last thing Ihsan needed were *more* reasons for Kuhzey to be distracted.

"Shall we?" Aysel extended a hand in invitation toward the road that led back to Saa'ra.

IHSAN SAT ON A CRATE in the command tent, scrubbing at the remnants of Blight ooze on his hands with a rag. Mathei had a hip propped on the map table, arms folded as he took in the changes Makram had made to the position of troops and numbers. He had a dizzying talent for switching between flippant humor and intense focus and back again with no warning.

Makram stood in the center of the tent, one hand on top of his head, the other on his sword, with an expression like a parent on the fence between amusement and chastisement. Ihsan knew that look well. His father had worn it near constantly.

Aysel fumed beside Makram, arms crossed over her chest and feet set apart. If she expected him to scold Ihsan, it looked as if she would be disappointed. Ihsan did not find Makram especially intimidating. His decency was obvious in too many little ways, and of course the large, obvious way. He had given up title, homeland, and what family he had for the woman he loved. Now he was even less fearsome, shrouded in the dust of travel and a pall of exhaustion. He'd grown a beard and his hair was unkempt, not tidily braided and wrapped as it had been before he departed Narfour. Though, no doubt Makram was still a terrifying sight to his enemies when in the flux of his power.

Rather than suffer through whatever admonishing speech Makram pieced together, Ihsan stood. "Shall we get this over with? It is a wonder the water I brought for the summoning has not evaporated in this Wheel-forsaken heat." It wasn't a wonder at all. He'd been maintaining a sheath of ice around it for two turns, a small, yet not insignificant task.

Makram's mouth twisted to stop a smile. "Might I trouble you for a few moments to tidy myself up, before presenting to the Sultana, Sehzade?"

"She will only be able to see your form, not your details. You might save yourself the trouble." He tossed the fouled rag onto the crate behind him. "She is aware you are at war, and having a modicum of intelligence, would assume you may not look as polished as you normally might. The only thing likely to distress her is the beard."

Makram reflexively touched the beard at its mention. "You do not think she will like it?" He grinned. Charm came as easily to Makram as violence, though Ihsan found the charm more difficult to stomach.

Charm was such a lie, and there were too many lies in Ihsan's life. Too many sympathetic smiles, too many forced, awkward conversations. Pleasantries. Too many times people tried too hard not to look at the scars. Then as soon as his back was turned they whispered, when they thought he couldn't hear, said if his power had not been transformed by his accident he would be the most powerful water mage in all of Tamar. Save Mutar Charah, of course. They said he was ruined, physically, mentally, and magically. *What a shame*, they said.

"Whatever you require, Agassi. I am at your service." Ihsan gestured magnanimously with one hand as he sat back down. Aysel exhaled in disgust.

Makram raised an eyebrow. "I wouldn't wish to keep you longer than I already have. We can conduct the summoning when you are ready."

"Kuhzey," Ihsan ordered. The boy was outside the tent, most likely pining after Kiya, or just as likely contemplating his navel. There was little predicting the vagaries of the boy. Ihsan did hear a shuffling. "Get the water." Water that Amara had spelled before he left. He'd kept it in his tent, where it was less likely to be molested by an oblivious soldier looking for a drink. Djar had recounted such an incident from their travel to the Republic, cementing Ihsan's opinion of Amara's Republic smuggler as a bit of a dimwit. Still, it made for a good cautionary tale.

While they waited, Ihsan hoping Kuhzey did not become sidetracked and wander off task, Elder Attiyeh entered the tent.

"Look, Father," Aysel said in singsong, "your favorite son has returned."

"I thought you were my favorite son," the man said, without breaking his stride toward Makram. Aysel spluttered, and Mathei tsked. Makram laughed as the two men clasped arms. "You had me worried this time," Thoman Attiyeh said to Makram, but looked at Ihsan as he spoke. He was nothing like either of his children, both of whom caused Ihsan teeth-grinding irritation within a few sentences. Thoman was subdued and thoughtful, and far less intrusive. All the Attiyehs were intelligent, but Thoman was the type that looked at a person and understood them immediately from imperceptible clues the person was not even aware they provided. He had inferred instantly that Ihsan did not enjoy conversation for the sake of noise to fill the silence, and had been tolerable company in the days since Ihsan had arrived. "What stands at Al-Nimas?"

"We are down a contingent of riders," Makram said. "They went north to the border and did not return. Had I not received your message that the Sehzade had arrived, I would still be tracking them. And will return to the search when I leave again."

"That brings us to half our original numbers of mounted fighters," Thoman said, grimly. The proclamation elicited silence from all present. The three Attiyehs exchanged a look.

"Let us accompany you at least to Dar Afir," Mathei said. "That was the route I planned with Cassian anyway."

Kuhzey lumbered through the door with a heavy, two-handled urn grasped in both hands and hanging between his legs as he waddled to the center of the tent. Ihsan dragged a hand down his face. Aysel, who seemed endlessly fascinated by Kuhzey's ineptitude, snorted in disbelief.

"Thank you." Ihsan stood. "Did you happen to remember the basin?"

Kuhzey's eyes rounded, and he dropped the urn, spinning around to dart back outside. Aysel prevented the urn tipping with a foot, and peered sidelong at Ihsan. In fact all four looked at him, and he picked at a bit of dirt beneath a fingernail. Kuhzey was a mess, but he was Ihsan's mess, and he wouldn't tolerate them speaking ill of him. He was the only one allowed to do that.

After a few moments of interminable silence, Kuhzey returned with an earthenware basin, which he placed on the table, on top of Makram's detailed map of Sarkum and what he knew of troops and battlefields. Then he gave a jerky bow. Ihsan dismissed him with a wave, and stacked an empty crate on top of the one he'd been using as a bench. Aysel brought the basin and set it on top.

Ihsan hefted the urn and carefully poured its contents into the basin. Every drop was precious, each minute trace of Amara's spell significant. It was a simple thing for her to summon his magic to hers through the water, but an iffier endeavor for him to call to her. His magic was always primed to obey hers, but if she was not listening for him, she might not hear his call. He waited for the water to settle to complete stillness.

Makram stepped to his side.

"Are you ready?" Ihsan asked. Makram nodded. Ihsan closed his eyes.

There was a thread in him now. It had always been there, a connection, but he had not seen it, understood it, until Naime had named Amara to the Circle. Whatever was done in that ceremony had powered that thread to brilliance. When he closed his eyes and gazed inward, he could see it, shining, twined around his magic, something that both gave and took. He infused it with his power now, diamond-blue ice, glittering and flashing as it spun away into the void and he whispered Amara's name. The sound of his voice thrummed in the darkness of his mind, in the emptiness around his power.

Moments stretched, marked by his breaths and heartbeat, a cadence like waves.

Then she was there, lighting the darkness, a being of fractures lit by turquoise power. Exquisitely beautiful and painfully powerful. She was shape only, in the void, as his power saw her. He opened his eyes and drew one hand up from the water, like a potter drawing clay, and her likeness rose from the basin, a smaller, perfect copy.

"Our practice has paid off, I see," she said in her musical accent. There was music in everything about Amara, which was not unusual for a water mage. He had thought, after all the events that had transpired with her travel to the Republic and her naming to the Circle, that if he were a different man, he could like her. But for the man he was, she was too much. Too much a reminder of what his power had been and should be still. She reminded him too much of what he missed. The fluidity of his power before. Water that danced to his simplest thoughts, the emotion and sensuality of the Second House.

But that was gone now, stolen, along with everything else, by fire.

"Are you at the palace?"

"As I have been, for turns," she said acerbically, "waiting for your summons."

"Can she hear me?" Makram leaned forward and down to study the small, liquid avatar that stood in the water.

"Extraordinary," Thoman said from behind them. Ihsan did not care for the sudden feeling of being on display. He almost lost his grip on their connection.

"If you touch me, Agassi, she will see and hear you. I must apologize ahead of time though." Ihsan said the last as Makram's hand settled on his shoulder.

"For what?"

Ice spread across his fingers and Makram startled with a grunt.

Amara's likeness smiled serenely. "A pleasure to finally meet you, Rahal Charah."

Makram reached forward in boyish wonder, as if he meant to poke the water figure. Ihsan grabbed his wrist.

"Your power will sever my link," he said, in a tone he thought might sound apologetic.

Makram straightened. "I did not realize the Wheel stretched to Menei."

"I believe the only place it does not reach is Sarkum," Amara said with a stiff smile.

Makram's eyes widened at the jab.

"Just be grateful she is clothed," Ihsan murmured. Aysel snickered as Makram looked at him askance. Before anyone else could speak, Naime appeared. Because Makram was touching him, because the ice of Ihsan's power was crawling up his arm, Ihsan felt it as tension melted away from Makram.

Makram exhaled as though freed from a burden. "My Queen."

Naime smiled, a truer smile than Ihsan had seen from her in some time. Jealousy mingled with happiness, to see the expression on her face. Jealousy that he did not, and never would, have something like that which the two of them shared. He could not risk it. But happiness, at least, for her.

"You are well," Naime said, relief tangible in her voice.

"As I can be," Makram said with an easy smile. "Considering your Charah of Air and cousin bicker like children."

Naime's smile dipped. "What has the Sehzade told you?"

"I've only just arrived back in Saa'ra."

"We do not have long. Mutar Charah informs me the spell on the water will be depleted quickly. There are a number of things I have been afraid to write down to inform you. There is a growing restlessness in Narfour. An uprising in the making." She paused, and tension reanimated Makram, his fingers digging into Ihsan's shoulder. "Attiyeh Charah can give you details I will not have time for, as she is delving into the network. It seems to be primarily comprised of the Fifth House, though we cannot discern who is heading it, if anyone is."

An involuntary shudder cracked apart the ice spreading between Ihsan and Makram, and the thin sheet of it across the basin. Fire mages were, in Ihsan's estimation, responsible for more misery and chaos than any other House on the Wheel. They were like Wheel-forsaken rabbits, breeding in every dark corner available and to be found in every possible occupation, inescapable. Makram cast him a quick glance, then tried to pretend he hadn't.

"You assume they are led by our dear friend?" Makram asked.

Naime gave the tiniest dip of her chin. "But we have yet to find proof, links, evidence of any kind, though Attiyeh Charah has been working tirelessly on the problem. Tell her to sleep."

Now Makram looked at Aysel. Ihsan could not turn his attention from the basin, so could not see her reaction to it.

"There is much conflicting evidence, pointing in too many directions, but one of those directions is Al-Nimas," Naime said, uncharacteristically reticent. Makram huffed.

"It is possible. Perhaps Kinus has developed enough strategic thinking to put together an insurgency. I will investigate it. What are they doing?"

"Small attacks, vandalisms, thefts of supplies that indicate they may be stocking up for a larger attack," Naime said, "gatherings and protests that disperse before the City Watch can be involved and take anyone for questioning."

"Are you in danger?" Makram's question sounded like a drawn blade, and Ihsan had to step quickly away from his touch as the Charah's power bolted awake beneath his skin.

"You must control yourself, if you wish to finish this conversation," Ihsan warned. Makram exhaled then nodded.

"I am fine," Naime bristled. Ihsan and Makram exchanged a look, and their shared humor seemed to rein Makram's power under his control once more. He gripped Ihsan's shoulder again.

"There is more." Naime's voice hitched, even distorted as it was by the water. Ihsan would have liked to warn Makram of this, but there had been no opportunity. "My father is declining rapidly. I fear when he..." No one spoke as she took a single breath for composure. "When he is gone, I fear those behind the fire mage attacks will see it as an opportunity."

"To what end?" Makram asked.

"I do not know, but I must assume it is about me taking my father's seat. That they will seek to make certain I do not. That I cannot, so they can place whoever they wish."

Makram's fingers dug into Ihsan's flesh, but Ihsan did not flinch away. He understood the emotion. It had been a relief that the Sultan had been able to announce Naime as the future Queen Sultana, but without him, even as a figurehead, the words meant little. They faced a revolution. Makram was strung tight, his grip painful, his body tipped forward as if he thought he could jump through the water to her.

"I will return," he said.

"No," Naime commanded. "You are where I need you. If the Republic moves and we are not ready because I have pulled you home too soon, we will have lost just as surely. How goes the siege on Al-Nimas?"

"All I can do is wait to see how long Kinus will allow the city to starve before he surrenders. I do not know which of us is the worse tormentor." Disgust sharpened Makram's tone.

"Can you take the city?"

"Tareck reports that the cost would be too high. We would not have enough soldiers left to hold off an attack by the Republic."

"And how long will it be until *you* starve?" Naime's image pressed fingers to forehead.

Makram did not answer.

"Have Mathei and Cassian gone north yet?" Amara asked while Naime considered.

"Not yet," Ihsan said. Mathei and Cassian, his Suloi companion Peio, and the brother and sister who had returned from the Republic with Amara had wished to wait for Makram's return before they departed. They believed they could bring more Suloi from the Republic into Tamar. Naime hoped there might be a Charah among them. Specifically, the Third House Charah. Hope was not something Ihsan subscribed to, and he wondered what plan Naime had for yet more refugees should the Suloi prove as diluted magically as the three Ihsan had already met.

"I do not want any of these things we've discussed spoken about, even coded, in any missive passed between you and the palace. I hoped

I would not need to hide from my own Council, but I do not know who is involved in this uprising."

Of course she knew. Who else could it be? The complete lack of clues was evidence enough. There was no one in Narfour more careful, more capable of secretly planning and inciting a revolution, than Behram Kadir.

"The magic is fading," Amara said, the gentleness in her voice carried faithfully by the water.

"San," Naime said, "return to Narfour as soon as you are able."

Ihsan nodded.

"Do you have more for me?" Makram asked quickly. The figure of Naime shook her head. She appeared to stare straight ahead, but Ihsan knew she was taking in the watery figurine of Makram on her side, just as he gazed fiercely at hers. They stood silent, and Ihsan wished he could be less intrusive for them, even as a thin flutter of jealousy made his mouth sour.

Naime needed Makram. For so many Turns it had been her and Ihsan, together against everything, bound by family and shared trauma. But what she needed now was a blade, not a shield, the only thing Ihsan had ever been good for. He could not settle himself into a purpose, now.

"Be safe." Naime's words faded like ripples as the image wavered. "Return to me."

"Always," Makram said. The women's figures melted into the basin. He dropped his hand from Ihsan's shoulder and let his head fall back. No one spoke, allowing him a moment. Ihsan wondered if he was ever permitted that, as a commander in a battlefield that spread two nations.

"I'll stay if I can assist in any way," Ihsan offered. "Otherwise, I'll leave in the morning. Keeping watch on the Sultan is taxing for her, even with others of us taking shifts."

"How long?" Makram did not look at Ihsan when he asked, only dropped his chin. Ihsan understood.

Whatever kept Ihsan's uncle tethered to the mortal side of the Wheel, it was fraying. The Omar he had known as a boy was gone, little more than a shell remaining. And wolves circled in the shadows, ready to attack when Naime was at her weakest.

Ihsan let his hands drop from the water. "I cannot be certain."

"Estimate," Makram commanded.

"If he lasts to the Turning of the season, it will be a miracle."

Three

RAIN DRIZZLED, SOMETIMES A HOVERING mist, and at moments a true downpour, as unsettled in its mood as the crowd that gathered in its murky cloak.

Nesrin could almost believe it was the people driving the weather, or the other way 'round, or both. A circle. Perhaps the Wheel wept as they did, for the senseless loss of life that lay, bundled in oilcloth, on the pyres within the circle of villagers. She'd counted the bodies at least a dozen times, a vain attempt to control her own whiplash emotions.

One…two…three……twenty-three.

And worse. Those that could not be counted. Forever missing, from home and heart.

Gone. Their Turns finished. They were sons, some so young they could barely grow the beards their fathers wore. Some grown and fathers themselves. All whose place in the fields, jobs, and hearts of the valley could not be replaced.

"They won't burn in this," Sanem murmured, her voice muffled by the patter of rain on their clothes. She coiled her arm more tightly through Nesrin's, her other arm cinching around the two youngest girls, the four sisters huddling together so they did not have to bear the rain and the sorrow alone. Nesrin's gaze lifted, to the rise of the road over the hill that led north, toward the estate.

Two men stood there, shadowed by the misty rain and the fog it kicked up from the ground, fading into a darkened landscape behind. Both wore oiled ferace of dyed kidskin. Finer clothes lay beneath the ferace than were worn by anyone below them in the field. Bardakci Pasha and Master Ansar. No one was certain if Master Ansar was friend or steward to the Pasha, but everyone gave him wide berth. The way he watched people, as though he wondered what would happen if he lit them on fire, made Nesrin want to flee him any time he was close.

She shuddered, her fingers tightening around the neck of the burlap bag she held. Gifts for the dead. To honor their passing, each villager would contribute a small token. Something to balance their end. Flowers were common. Eggs. Seeds. Lambswool. Anything that represented the beginning of the Wheel's turn.

It was tradition in her family to gift the cones of the Tamar cedar. One for each life lost.

Nesrin still bore the scratches from the branches and bark and the pitch in her hair from her climb to retrieve these the day before. They were the most enigmatic of trees. Their seeds locked so tightly in cones they could only be released when the cone was burned, then the seeds would explode outward and grow in the remains of their forebears. Entire groves of cones would lie dormant for Cycles, centuries, even if the trees themselves died. Until one day a lightning strike or stray spark would ignite them and begin their cycle anew.

There was no more perfect representation of the Wheel in all of nature than in that process. A new beginning from destruction. Birth from death.

The low drone of Beyza's speech ceased. Nesrin dropped her gaze to where the crone stood, eyes narrowed against the rain in a face wrinkled like tea-stained paper crumpled and smoothed a dozen times over. She was the oldest of the village elders, older even than Nesrin's grandmothers. And a dozen times more judgmental. But that was absent today. All emotion but sorrow buried deep within broken hearts.

The wagons bearing the men had arrived two days prior, bodies piled like they were nothing more than garbage, trundling loudly through an entire village gone silent. The village had never been silent. Since the moment Nesrin could walk its single dirt lane with any sort of awareness, it had been filled with laughter, fights, shouts, and songs. The smells of cooking, the playful screech of children. The bray and cluck and bleat of animals.

But with the return of men lost to a war that meant nothing to anyone within its boundaries, the village had hushed. That war had seemed far away, was far away, mere gossip to pass along and shake their heads about. For greybeards to argue theoretical questions over tea. A story in a place no one knew or cared about. More greedy land-grabbing by nobles, rulers who came and went, names that meant little. A thoughtless waste of resources and people during a crop blight. In Mizraa, the name of the ruler mattered little. They worked, lived, and died the same no matter who sat their silver-encrusted backside in the Sultan's seat. The world outside their village might as well not exist.

But now, it mattered. Narfour had demanded sons, and the Pasha had been bound to deliver them from those indentured to him.

The Pasha turned his head, his visage—and words—hidden by the edge of his ferace's hood, and the fire mage beside him gave a curt nod, then smiled. Or sneered. Nesrin did not think the man knew how to smile. He gave her the worst skin crawls she'd ever experienced.

The mage descended the hill, his boots sliding in the mud of the road. Flash rains made the worst sticking, slipping mud. It was always better to walk in the grass after a rain and avoid the roads. But how would he know? Nesrin doubted he spent much time in inclement weather. Nobles could afford to stay indoors and shirk any duties that would require them to test themselves against anything worse than a stiff breeze.

Sanem gave a sniff of disapproval as Master Ansar passed between the people who had moved aside to let him into their circle of grief. The whispers of the onlookers blended into the sigh of the rain as he walked toward the pyres, boots squelching. He took a place beside Beyza, hunched miserably against the rain. Did he mean to assist where the simple Fifth House Aval of the village would be unable to? Wild fire could not burn through the damp, clinging wet of this unseasonal rain. But Wheel fire could.

Nor destruction magic. Nesrin suspected, anyway. She had never seen destruction magic, but her grandmothers had told stories, passed down from their own grandmothers, about how funerals used to be done. Before the Sundering. Before the Wheel broke. Bodies were committed to the earth the way all things returned to it. Bone, sinew, and blood turned back to dust. Fire could do it, though ash was not the same—everything mixed together and transformed. But since there were no death mages left in Tamar, the Fifth House served as the final spoke of the Wheel. The end made in fire.

Those who had family on the pyres approached first. Beyza stood with hands outstretched, palms up, in the same manner that one might greet a mage of higher power. It was symbolic, honoring balance and the spin of the Wheel. The gifts were placed in her hands, one at a time. Beyza leaned forward to touch her forehead to each person as they set their gift in her palms, creating a circle between hands, hearts, and heads. Then each gift was reclaimed by the giver to set at the base of the pyre of their loved one.

The procession moved slowly, the hiss of the rain drowned out by the wail of mothers and wives. Nesrin did not wail, nor did her sisters, or her parents. Their father was too old, and some whispered too favored, to be sent away. And their brother, though he loathed it, was not considered battleworthy. But she did cry, silently. Her tears indistinguishable from the rain on her skin.

As they neared Beyza, Nesrin opened the bag and handed a cone to each of her sisters, then passed the bag behind her to her mother, who distributed the remaining cones to the rest of the family. Beyza's hands trembled beneath Nesrin's when she set the backs of her cupped palms into the elder woman's.

"From dawn to dark. Winter to summer. We walk the circle. We spin the Wheel," they murmured in unison. The words were slurred from Beyza's lips. Even the warm summer rain chilled her wizened body and affected her speech. Nesrin took her own wool ferace off and swept it around the woman's shoulders.

Beyza's gaze flickered over Nesrin's hands, scratched and sticky from her climb to retrieve the cones. Nesrin tried to smile as she took her cone back from Beyza, hiding her scratches against her rain-wet entari. She stepped away, as Sanem moved into her place.

Villagers gathered at each pyre, and Nesrin could, as an acquaintance, leave her gift at any of them. But she chose the empty pyre in the center, behind Beyza. The one that represented the missing. She had a special affinity for the lost, and the forgotten. The lonely.

Her parents and siblings scattered, trying to honor as many as possible. The families of those not brought home huddled in small tangles around the empty pyre. Nesrin knelt in the mud beside a little girl who wept, soundlessly, on her knees. Voices murmured around them.

"...he may be alive," a woman was saying to her husband. "He isn't here. He could just be lost, or injured and unable to return."

Hope was a beautiful, and dangerous thing. Her grandmothers had taught her that. Hope could heal. And it could wound, could stop time around itself so nothing moved forward, like a held breath. She would not tell the little girl that her father might be all right. She would not give her hope that would only wound her over endless Turns. Not that hope, anyway.

"Wherever he is, Defne, the flowers will be more beautiful than ever when they grow," Nesrin said, as she imagined it, a beautiful patch of daisies growing in the remembered horror of a battlefield.

"They'll be perfectly white." She could see them, leaves and petals stirred by a happy breeze and painted in sunlight. "And his magic will return to us."

Sniffing, Defne wiped the back of her hand across her eyes. "He liked red."

"Then they will be red," Nesrin said. In the image in her mind, the flowers transformed to crimson poppies, both poison and succor, very much like the hope she heard in the whispers around her. She placed her cone into Defne's hands, and the girl clutched her fingers around it.

"Thank you, Nessa," she sniffed wetly.

"I liked his laugh," Nesrin said. He had not been the most talkative of men. But he was a hard worker, a good friend of her father, Temel's, and his laugh, when it came, had boomed like thunder. Defne broke into a wide smile.

"He told funny stories."

"Oh, did he?" Nesrin prompted. Defne nodded, but her mirth faded as quickly as it had bloomed and she bowed her head again. Nesrin slipped an arm around her shoulders.

"Defne," a woman said, gently. The little girl startled, squirming out from Nesrin's hug and popping to stand at her mother's side. The woman gave Nesrin a sad, thankful smile as she stroked her daughter's damp hair.

Nesrin had not heard her brother approach, in the rain, but she could feel him at her back. Looming. Trying to shield her from the rain she could not shield herself from like everyone else in her family could. Not a water mage. Not a mage at all. Nesrin continued to kneel in the mud, the rain washing over her and braiding through the grass and dirt in miniature rivers.

"From void," Beyza's voice rang out. The whispers and the sobs quieted. Nesrin could not see Master Ansar move to command his power, but she felt it. The air funneled around her, heat billowed, and flames flumed upward from the pyres. She did not look at any of the others, only the empty one before her, the fire slapping at the rain that tried to quench it.

"To void," Beyza finished as the flames burned. Wood cracked and gave, cloth smoked, and that smoke rose to join the fog of clouds, transporting lifeless breath and wondrous power back to the void.

Rest well. May the magic of the void sing your return, and birthe you back to us soon.

The rain worsened as families tossed their gifts into the fire. All around them, the cones her family had brought made loud, sharp pops as the flames opened them. Nesrin drew a circle over her heart. She watched the empty pyre burn until the flames became insipid, and the rain finally won its battle.

A big hand closed on her shoulder, shifting her from her reverence. She looked up into her brother Metin's face, and he held the hand out for her. She took it and he brought her to her feet.

"Abi," she chided. He was always trying to protect her. "I'm fine."

He opened his ferace, deftly managing the buttons with one hand, and stretched it to provide her with some protection from the rain. As if she were so fragile from her lack of magic that she would melt away. She admonished herself. That was her grief speaking. Grief often spoke through anger. She knew that too.

Or perhaps it was still shock and had not yet crystallized into grief. These pyres were not her family. Or her friends. Yet…they *were* hers. Fixtures in the only world she knew and understood. There would be empty spaces where they had been, in the village, and in her.

Metin led her to where her family had regrouped. Her two grandmothers were still making their way back, stopping to converse and give comfort to each person they knew. Which was everyone.

Now, with her attention freed from the funeral, the biting emptiness of her stomach demanded her awareness once more. A corner of her thoughts, of everyone's thoughts, was dedicated now to food. Where they could find it, how much they had left, who needed the rations the most. Today was her family's day at the mill, to scrape up what bits of grain or flour remained after that convoy of new soldiers from the city had come through and stripped it bare.

Nesrin forced a breath to clear the twisting of panic and resentment away. That was the language of hunger. Desperation. The soldiers were starving too. She imagined the feelings lifting to the sky along with the smoke trails from the pyres. Despite the funeral, the sorrow, and the aching weakness of her body, there was a full day of work ahead. For all of them. The winter had been lean for everyone, the spring worse, as stores were depleted. She was not the only one who listened to the sound of her churning stomach as she tried to sleep. Not the only one who struggled to complete her work in the fields without collapsing. How impossible would it be to fight in a battle with that same gnawing absence of strength?

She glanced behind her, where the families had reluctantly begun to pull away as the pyres burned down. Would the men and boys burning on the pyres have fared better, if their bellies had been full? Their muscles strong from full meals? There was food here, growing in the fields. Untouched by the Blight that ravaged the rest of the valley. Somehow, it had not come to them yet. But that food was not meant for them. It was property of the Pasha, of the Palace in Narfour.

Some had begun to steal. The Pasha turned a blind eye to it, for now. He knew starving workers would do him no good, though Nesrin could not bring herself to believe he cared for them beyond their use to him. He would not be able to remain willfully ignorant for much longer, or the stealing would make a noticeable dent in the crops he was due to ship to Narfour.

"Those two," Metin grumbled, yanking Nesrin's attention back to the moment. His gaze swung away from something. She did not need to look to know. Sanem and Anil. Their sister, beloved eldest of their family, and village darling, mooned after by every young man in the village, had finally fallen in love. The two of them were walking up the hill hand in hand, heads tipped together as they whispered. Their faces reflected the same sorrow as everyone else's, yet beneath that glowed the comfort of having someone to unburden it to.

Anil was everything Sanem was not. Quiet, unassuming, the kind of person who faded into the background. He was steady, and dependable, and would soon take the mill over from his father. He had loved Sanem since they were children. But he had bided his time, waiting until her wild dreams of running away to the city or marrying some traveling merchant had finally calmed. Then he had wooed her with thoughtfulness. Something no other man who had pursued her could claim. He knew she hated the heat and loved a rainy day. He knew how fiercely she loved her family and treated them with special care. He brought her bouquets of her favorite wildflowers, had stolen her to dance in the rain.

That didn't matter to Metin, for whom no man would ever be good enough for his sisters. Especially for Sanem. Beautiful, bright, sunny Sanem. She wasn't just the village's favorite, she was the heart of their family. Nesrin understood Metin's aversion, as the only brother. But in her eyes, Anil was everything she wanted for Sanem, and for herself. A steady, hard worker who adored her. But she would live vicariously through Sanem's happiness, since a pledge of love like that, for Nesrin, was as impossible as ice in summer.

"You're as grumpy as old Beyza. Or maybe just jealous?" Nesrin tapped his ribs with her elbow. Metin rolled his eyes as they strode up the hill. His silence told her old wounds were hurting. Her gaze strayed to his empty right sleeve, shortened and stitched closed by their mother, so the extra fabric wouldn't flap and catch on things as he worked.

Was it worse to be missing something inside…or something outside? Metin thought his prospects were as bad as Nesrin's. But she knew that wasn't true. His pride was abraded by the return of the men he had not been allowed to follow to war. By the people who gave him looks, because he was alive, and their men were not. Anil had not been sent to war, their father had not been sent to war, because they were needed to fill their roles.

But Metin…she could not look at the stump of his arm and not remember the horror that had caused it. So she looked away. Like the coward she was.

"You cannot mean for me to do that," the sound of her father Temel's voice, rising in anger, cutting through the gentle rain, brought both her and Metin to a stop. Metin was moving again before Nesrin had quite focused on what she saw, tugging her with him up the slippery hill. His arm dropped from around her, so the rain drizzled in her face, obscuring the details even more.

Her father faced off with Bardakci Pasha, crumpling something in his big, rough hand.

"You made the request, Master Irmak. I cannot not defy…"

His next words were lost as Temel made an indecipherable sound of denial.

Brother and sister arrived at his side, Metin posturing as though he were jumping into a fistfight—as he had done, on several occasions, because of taunting. Temel brandished a hand at Metin in a wordless order to back down.

"Baba," Nesrin said. She took in the Pasha's face beneath his hood in an attempt to discern what had upset her father. Bardakci Pasha had an interesting face. Not quite handsome or beautiful, as earth mages tended to be. But rugged, and stern. And while she had not had occasion to see him often in her life, she'd seen him enough to have decided his most interesting feature were his eyes. Palest brown. Like jasper, not the usual deeper brown of most people. Not hazel either. There was no hint of green to them, just that golden hue. Peculiar. It made him appear more intense than Nesrin suspected he was. When he looked at you, it was a bit startling. So she avoided meeting his eyes. An easy thing, usually. As a void, she did not warrant his attention in most circumstances.

Only once could she ever remember meeting his eyes. The same day Metin lost his arm.

"You already approved their pledge," Temel said. He did not pull away as Nesrin put her hands on his outstretched fist and pried the crumpled paper loose.

Their pledge.

The workers of the valley did not marry. Marriage was for nobles and their mage-breeding machinations. To divorce was to break the Wheel, one of the few unforgivable offenses in their lives. And love was too fickle a thing to chance breaking the Wheel over. They pledged. Made a promise only to themselves, never to the Wheel.

The paper had mostly been protected by Temel's hand, but the ink was smudged in places as Nesrin ducked over it to protect it from the rain. Somehow, she knew. Knew the misery that waited in the words written in a graceful, flowing hand before she even read them. Temel had demanded his children be literate. Was considered odd for it. This was the first time Nesrin had ever wished she wasn't.

"Nessa?" Metin urged. But she was reading. Rereading. The words falling like brittle leaves, drifting, covering the green hope of her sister's joy. Hope. The sharpened blade which struck only the heart.

Master Irmak,

You asked a boon of me, in remittance of the life debt I owe you. I thought your request more than fair, but have been unable to fulfill it to my satisfaction until now. Happily, I have found a suitable match, one that will provide well for your daughter, and your family, for many Turns to come. I am more than happy to oblige you. Such a simple thing to do for the man who saved my life so many Turns ago.

I have included arrangements for your eldest daughter to travel to Narfour and instructions for Bardakci Pasha to provide the means for her to travel comfortably. Please see to it she leaves as soon as you receive this, otherwise I may no longer be able to promise the match.

Warmest Regards,

Behram Kadir, Grand Vizier

"I expect your compliance." Bardakci Pasha fixed his unsettling jasper gaze on Temel. "The Grand Vizier's courier leaves at dawn, and Sanem will be in the carriage with him. By her own actions, or by mine." The Pasha turned up the hill, striding to join Master Ansar in his carriage, which waited with door swung open.

Just beyond the carriage, at the hilltop, Sanem stood with Anil, his arm slung around her waist to hold her close, a furrow of worry in her brow.

Nesrin's fingers tightened on the letter as she looked at it again, willing the words to say something else, anything else.

The ink ran, drawing black tears down the paper.

Four

Nesrin hugged her empty basket against her belly. The rain had stopped, leaving a mess of mud and gloom in the village. The lingering smoke from the smoldering pyres stained the air with sour tang, making her long for the reprieve of the post-rain smell she loved.

The day held more sorrow than Nesrin could have ever believed possible. A funeral, and a letter that would turn her entire family inside out.

Villagers gathered in a haphazard line in front of her to collect their flour ration for that small turn.

The grain mill was just east of the village and the path to the estate. Its wheel spun steady circles through the canal water, overseen by a dour water mage who lurked on the maintenance walk, glaring at the wheel as if it had insulted his mother. The miller stood just outside the entrance, a stone, arched affair with heavy double oak doors to allow for wagons. Three such wagons stood in queue, with men crawling on and around them like ants. Soldiers, packing bag after bag of the last of the village's flour and grains.

The ration line was at a standstill, neighbors huddling to whisper angry theories as they watched. The miller oversaw the pillaging with arms folded, his normally unfriendly eyes now murderous. But what could any of them do? If Bardakci Pasha was told to give, he must give.

Nesrin couldn't help but notice how young the soldiers were. Some faces still had that bit of youthful plush to them. The ones that had probably been plump babies, their mother's pride. All of them were dressed in earth-brown caftans over tan salvar, belted with more brown, with yataghan and daggers and tiraz on their arms proclaiming their Houses. Newly drafted soldiers. These weren't from Mizraa. They had the fervent look of city-dwellers. Perhaps the sons of rich men, who did not understand what they were doing to the small village they passed through on their way to glory.

"Broken Wheel!" one of Nesrin's neighbors exclaimed to the woman next to him. "There's barely enough left to keep the village until the crops come in this summer."

"*If* they come in this summer," grumbled a friend of Nesrin's father.

A woman pointed at the soldiers. "And all for some distant war no one cares about."

Nesrin held her breath, for it was all true. It was the lean times, the end of the winter stores, waiting for summer's bounty, if it even came. The mill had started harsh rationing because the winter wheat up north hadn't made it this Great Turn. A Blight. From Sarkum, some whispered. It had hit the northern part of the lake, the fruit orchards and farms that raised winter and spring greens, roots, and grains.

The first man spoke again. "It's only a matter of time until the Blight comes here, and you'll take what little we have!"

One did not have to be a water mage, Wheel-tied to emotion, to sense the shifting mood of the crowd. Their distress warmed to outrage. Faces hardening from concern to pinched, drawn brows and clipped words tightening mouths. The soldiers kept their heads down, working faster.

Nesrin knew her village like her own heartbeat. Had learned to navigate its delicate emotions and opinions early, to make friends of the people who might have otherwise succumbed to the superstition and hate that sometimes surfaced in reaction to her lack of magic. The dam was near to bursting.

"We cannot feed the Sultana's army! We cannot even feed ourselves!" After the shout, a rock sailed from somewhere in front of her, striking the back of a soldier so hard he cried out in pain and surprise. The young soldiers halted their work and turned to face the villagers.

The line undulated, clumping into a mob, with people picking up rocks as they shifted.

"Leave us be! What gives you the right to starve us?" one of Beyza's weavers shouted.

The old goat was the head of the Weaver's Guild in the Southern valley, and all girls that were to become weavers spent time at Beyza's home during apprenticeship. She and the other Master Weavers in the village were a silver-haired quail covey, doddering around the village bobbing heads and wagging tongues. Nesrin's mother, Pembe, called them gossips and instigators.

"Thieves!" another weaver crowed and a trio of rocks arced from villagers to soldiers, smacking the wagon, opening a bag of grain, and striking another soldier along the temple. The soldier's bewildered face contorted.

Hands went to swords. The villagers packed tightly together, shifting a step closer. If Pembe were here, or Nesrin's father, or Sanem, they would stop this. They would quiet tempers with their level heads and the respect the village held for her family. Nesrin puffed a breath out. But it was just her.

If you can help, do. Always. Her father's voice. She shifted her basket, wrapping both hands around the handle and dropping it to hang in front of her as a shield, squared her shoulders against the sparkling burn of trepidation, and strode forward.

The crowd parted around her, turning to see who dared to push through them. If it had been Sanem, their anger would cool, quenched by their adoration of her. They only stared in bewilderment at Nesrin, but some of their whispers quieted as she emerged at the front of them and took up a place with her back to the closest wagon.

"You..." She swallowed, then exhaled her tension out. "...should be ashamed." She used Pembe's scolding tone, which worked equally well on mischievous animals and village elders throwing their weight a bit too far.

Nesrin had never seen her quiet an angry mob, though.

She addressed the older villagers present. They would be the ones she could reason with. "Have you looked at their faces? Are these any different than our own? The same we buried only this morning. Taken from their homes and families."

She spun to face the wagon at her back as the villagers murmured to each other, some looking chagrined.

One soldier stood on top of the already-piled bags, towering above her, a stricken expression on his face. "I am sorry," he said.

Nesrin measured him with a look. Tall, gangly, with lank black hair and small dark eyes, she was immediately put in mind of a garden snake. Which were, in general, shy, helpful creatures. She hoped he was, too.

"We did not know you'd had a funeral today. They're hurting for rations on the other side of the Engeli. One group of us went north," he said, "and we came south, to try to find what we could without causing everyone to starve."

"They've nothing left up north!" a woman shouted. "So you'll take all we have? My daughter just had her baby. She won't have enough to feed him or herself."

Cries of agreement, more stories of woe, followed. Nesrin knew their pain.

"Can you not spare the rations we're due?" she asked the soldier. His face twisted, tortured by the question. His gaze swept over the crowd. The gaunt, miserable, angry faces. She feared his answer. The road from Narfour to the Engeli Gate was farther north, beyond the lake. It was a lengthy diversion to come all the way down just for grain, which suggested how desperate they were for supplies.

She also knew the North, especially along the route from the Engeli to the pass and Narfour, was ravaged by Blight. Many blamed the movement of refugees, saying their travel was spreading the Blight. Which meant of course that every man, woman, and child in Mizraa was in a panic about strangers building another camp in the Southern valley. The certain outcome of fear, her father said, was always disaster. Fear made no room in one's mind for reason.

Finally the soldier relented, thin shoulders falling. He slid off the side of the wagon to stand beside her. "Can you ensure they only take what they're due? If they riot and cut the bags—"

"Hayri will make sure." Nesrin nodded to the miller, who sidled warily closer. "Your men can keep them orderly, certainly?" She chanced a smile. The soldier's face relaxed and he nodded stiffly. Hayri pulled his ledger book from where he kept it tucked into his apron.

The villagers mumbled at the exchange. Nesrin faced them again, this time trying her best impression of her father, who had the luxury of assuming he had authority when he spoke. "You may collect this turn's rations from what is available. No more."

"Oh? And what if we decide to take back what's ours, eh?" a man jeered, and another snickered.

"With what? Your rocks and legless taunts?" Nesrin chided. The soldier beside her choked on a laugh. "They have swords and stronger magic. They can pack up these wagons and leave us with nothing."

She peeked at the soldier, who agreed with a nod, though he looked more embarrassed than militant.

He turned and gave some orders in a tone that told Nesrin he was a man more accustomed to being ordered than ordering. The other soldiers formed a blockade around the mill and wagons and Hayri flipped through his logbook. The woman who had spoken about her daughter and new baby came first, giving Nesrin a look of gratitude as she did. Hayri called off her ration and two soldiers hopped up into the wagon to dole it out.

With grumbles, the rest of the villagers followed suit. Her nervousness faded with each person that peaceably collected their share and departed.

The soldiers didn't speak as the rest of the villagers filtered through, until the last had turned down the path home.

"Yours?" the soldier asked. Nesrin looked to Hayri, who also avoided her eyes as he pointed to a quarter bag of flour, half the ration the others had received. Nesrin held her basket out. "Why so little?" The soldier put the burlap bag in her basket.

"Voids." Hayri shrugged. "You can't do the work, you don't get the food that good, hardworking mages earn."

"She should get extra for preventing your mill from getting looted."

"Well, she didn't, did she?" Hayri eyed the soldiers and loaded wagons, then Nesrin with ire before he disappeared into the dank interior of the mill. Nesrin sighed, releasing the tension that had started an ache up the back of her neck.

"Thank you. I hope you will not be punished for giving up some." She hoisted the basket up into the circle of her arms.

"How could they know?" He leaned against the wagon. "That many bags won't win or lose a battle. I've seen men do more damage with a belly full of beer than a belly full of grain. I'm Harun, by the way, from Narfour."

"Oh." Nesrin bowed. His tiraz marked him a Fifth House Aval. Even mages of the barest power were worthy of bows from her. "Nesrin."

"Nesrin." He smiled, shyly. "Here." He took a bag half full of unmilled grain and hefted it into her basket. One of the soldiers standing on another wagon observed the gift and breathed out a rising *oooooo* sound that was swiftly picked up and carried from soldier to soldier. Harun's skin deepened with his blush.

"I can't accept this, but I thank you." Nesrin held the bag out to him, even though she could use it to stretch pilaf far enough to feed her family one extra turn. Every fiber in her, from skin to soul, ached in protest as she held it out, her empty belly burning.

"Without you, no one here would have anything," Harun said.

"We all have a chance to save each other from ourselves. It was my turn, and I cannot take more than my share and turn the Wheel from temperance to greed."

He took the bag reluctantly. "Then I'll repay you another way. If you are ever in Narfour, my mother owns an inn on the pier. Tell her I sent you."

Nesrin smiled wanly. Narfour might as well be Menei to her. She was rooted to this place. Bound by law to the chiflik and its labor. She bowed again, and when she rose he was already climbing into the wagon as it pulled forward, slipping sideways in the mud. She lifted her hand in farewell.

Who knew when the man would get another friendly wave? People in the valley were notoriously closed ranks. And beyond the Engeli… it might as well be the void itself for all Nesrin knew about it. The only things she knew about the world beyond Mizraa was what she could glean from the stories merchants told on their way through, and she knew they were unreliable, the way old Abrahim's stories about the giant vegetables he had grown back in his younger Turns were unreliable.

Still, they were all she had. All anyone in Mizraa had. People didn't leave Mizraa. They were born here, they lived their lives here, they bore children here, and they died here. Bound to the land by laws created after the Sundering War.

Those stories and rumors painted a bleak picture. One where they would soon be overrun with hungry, desperate strangers, bringing their problems with them to ruin the good valley. But all Nesrin heard in those stories was tragedy. Hungry families fleeing something terrible. All they wanted was survival. She had never understood how anyone could close their hearts to that, just because someone was a stranger. But whispering fear nearly always won over even the loudest logic.

The old men of the village said that was what happened when a woman was in charge of things. Too soft to rule, they said. Too emotional. Nesrin's mother Pembe responded to that particular sentiment with her most derisive snort and inquired if the men had been able to find their pants without their wives' assistance that morning. *'So that you could sit out here and gossip while she works,'* she would end with.

The greybeards didn't like Pembe any more than they liked the idea of a Queen Sultana.

Nesrin wondered if the Sultana was like Pembe, practical and effective, or like the old tongue-waggers said she was, silly and spoiled. It would be easy to be silly and spoiled if one lived in a giant palace, with all the space and privacy one could ask for. And everyone having to do what you told them. Someone to do all your laundry and cook all your meals. What did a sultana do all day? Brush her hair a dozen times? Try on all her expensive clothes over and over? Fuss over all her jewels? Dine on all the food the chifliks sent to Narfour?

Well, she would never know. But that was all right. She was happy with a humble place in the world where she could be of some use, with problems she knew how to solve. She clutched her meager bag of wheat and turned to trudge home.

Nesrin clapped flour in her hands and shoved the heels of her palms into the dough. The warmth of the oven at her back competed with the brisker air of the approaching evening, and intensified the humidity that made sweat bead on her brow.

Their little outdoor kitchen abutted the back of the house, which was a long, half cylinder laid on the ground. Like a log split in two down the length. Most nights she shared the duty of cooking with her grandmothers. They had taught her almost everything she knew about anything—how to heal everything from wounds to hearts, how to forage for food that was tasty and not poisonous, how to cook, how to stretch meager rations. How to give, even when it hurt. How to stand on her own two feet. But this, cooking, was her favorite besides healing. She had no magic for water, so she made do with the magic of food, and that was her place.

Nesrin had spent countless days like this, outside of the house while the family argued, or laughed. It seemed fitting.

She was part of the family, but separate. Not by their order, it was simply the way of things. She was a void, who could not do what they could do. So she made do with the small chores, invisibly working in and around everyone else, like a mouse, picking up and carrying crumbs away.

"How could you?" Sanem howled inside. Nesrin flinched. Their father had only just returned from the estate house, to try to bargain with Bardakci Pasha to annul his request for Sanem's arranged marriage. "You sold me."

"I did no such thing," he barked back. "I thought you were miserable here. You were, until Anil grew a spine." His sharp voice held edges of panic, and pain. It was unlike him to say mean things. They had all been so happy for Sanem.

Nesrin wiped her eyes against her flour-coated sleeve. She could not comfort Sanem. She could not fix this problem. But she could fill their bellies, and the rhythm of the work would soothe her own frail emotions. She rolled the dough and reshaped it into a log, which she segmented into pieces.

She tried not to think of what would happen when they were done with this latest bag of flour.

She flattened out the portions of dough into single ovals, then poured a large glug of olive oil from its ceramic jug into a bowl filled with za'atar. She brushed the mixture on with her fingers, then sprinkled each pide with ground lamb she had left over from the night before.

"Get out, you beast!" Nimet, Nesrin's youngest sister, squawked as she elbowed open the back door and tossed a cat out into the kitchen. The cat meowed in disbelief and wended a double wheel around Nesrin's ankles. Nimet slammed the door closed again.

"Buse," Nesrin chided, "I've told you not to go in the house when I am not there." She shoveled the pide onto a wooden peel and deposited three of them into the oven. "Haven't I?" The house was cramped with all seven of them inside, and no one but Nesrin had patience for animals indoors.

Buse hopped onto the edge of her wooden worktable and sat politely. Nesrin swept the remaining crumbles of lamb toward the cat, who took to them selectively, one morsel at a time.

She bent and rummaged for onions and carrots in a wooden bin sheltered in the shade of the kitchen worktable and the shadow of the house.

"Evening, Nesrin," a familiar male voice called from the main road, along which all the indentured families' homes lay in a tidy grid, a candlemark's walk from the vineyard and estate. Anil had arrived. He had a bundle of flowers cradled in one arm, and was smiling brightly as he greeted her.

"Anil!" She dropped the vegetables on the table. He waved and disappeared around the corner of the house before she could warn him. The front door banged closed.

Nesrin's breath shuddered over repressed tears. If she'd had fire or flint, she would have burned the Wheel-damned letter. But defying a noble was punishable by caning at the least. While she'd never heard of Bardakci Pasha enacting corporal punishment, thieves, vandals, and malcontents did have a way of disappearing. What would happen to a servant who burned the summons of a Vizier?

She turned her mind from it and to chopping carrots with determination. A full stomach held a broken heart together, her grandmother always said.

Buse gave a plaintive meow. A gaggle of sparrows had landed behind Nesrin, picking at the bits of meal she always inevitably spilled. Nesrin cast a look of warning at the cat, who flattened an ear in annoyance. He knew not to hunt where she could see. She was all for the natural order, but birds were her particular favorite, and Buse had learned that lesson at the end of a broom and a stern talking-to.

"If you're still hungry, you can be about the mice that have been after the grain stores." Nesrin pointed to the open cellar doors. Buse sneezed, then meandered toward his task.

The wooden door to the house opened again and Temel ducked out. He set an empty stoneware platter on the table, his broad face mottled with red. He smiled tremulously at her, cupping the back of her head in one big, paw-like hand as he kissed her forehead, his beard tickling her.

"How is my favorite child this evening?" He peered into the oven. Every muscle tensed and she squinted her eyes against tears.

"I'm only your favorite because I have the food. Which you will have to fight Anil for now." She thought she did an admirable job of sounding normal. Never lie outright. A water mage could smell it a league away. Deflect, misdirect. "And Metin, when he arrives."

Temel gave a gusty sigh, eyeing the house. Normally, when Anil was there, the sound of Sanem's laughter echoed. Now there was only silence, occasionally broken by a sob. Nesrin continued slicing the carrots and onion and laid them out on the platter.

"Labneh," she ordered. Her father stepped down into the cellar, where the cool earth and her family's water magic kept things from spoiling. Fire mages made heat, water mages made cool, which made them indispensable in agriculture. Everyone had their place.

"I'll be at the big house with you tomorrow." Temel set the crock of strained yogurt on the table and scooped some into the middle of the vegetables. "The Pasha is reviewing accounts for levies."

Temel could not write well or read fast, but he had a head for numbers, which the Pasha relied on, along with the fact that Temel and Pembe Irmak knew absolutely everyone within ten leagues of Mizraa, as well as their entire family lineage. Except Bardakci Pasha's, of course. No one knew anything about him despite the fact he'd been in the valley for many Cycles.

Nesrin pursed her lips. She dusted the labneh with sumac and pushed the plate toward the end of the worktable. Work seemed trivial. Their lives usually revolved around it. But all she could think of was Sanem. The Pasha, heartless as a mountain of stone, would not budge from his order that Sanem would report to the estate house in the morning to travel to Narfour.

"Baba," Nesrin said as she picked up the wooden peel. He glanced at her over his shoulder, having hunched to assess the progress of the pide. She shoveled the pide out of the oven, drizzled more oil on them, and sprinkled more za'atar as her father looked on with a critical frown. To his mind, one could never use enough of the spice blend. When Nesrin finished, he added more to one of the flatbreads.

Their garden grew the most vigorous bed of it in the entire village. Nesrin had to viciously cut it back every Great Turn and dig its roots halfway through each summer. If it weren't completely necessary for the spice blend of the same name, she'd probably burn it to be rid of it.

"Nims!" she called. Her two younger sisters, Nimet and Nuray, marched out of the house. They were ten and thirteen Turns respectively, and inseparable. Her mother and father claimed they had given up thinking of names after Nesrin, and just stuck with N.

"You put too much on, *again*," Nuray said, bravely, her lip quivering as she tucked her russet hair behind her ears before she lifted two of the flatbreads to carry inside.

"There is no such thing as too much za'atar," Nimet said sagely, copying their father, who nodded his approval. Nesrin tugged her sister's russet braids as she turned away. The entire family shared their father's red-brown hair. Nesrin's was the lightest, with some copper streaks in the auburn. A throwback to some trade-route ancestor who had High Northern roots. It was not a unique story in this part of the valley. Before the Sundering War and the Engeli, a southern arm of the Spice Road had gone through Mizraa on its way south and to Menei. Mizraa had once been a trading hub for the wine produced in the valley and the Tamarine dye produced in Narfour.

Temel stepped beside her at the table, and took her hands in his, pressing a brief kiss against her forehead. His bushy brows gathered together over dark eyes, his mouth sinking into a frown. He stroked his thumbs over hers, idly, searching for words that did not come. She turned her hands over in his and squeezed them. He always meant well, even if sometimes he bumbled.

Releasing her hands, he picked at a nick in the table, prying loose a sliver of wood with thick fingers. He had farmer's hands. The same hands her brother had. Big, hard, and callused. They could untangle vines, dig deep furrows, steady and calm a kidding goat, and make a small, fragile child feel safe and protected. But there was nothing they could do for this.

Nesrin swept up flour and crumbs and bits of vegetable and tossed them over the low stone wall. "You could have asked for anything." Her eyes stung and prickled as she tried to keep her voice steady. "Anything in the world. That was the best you could do?"

"Yes, at the time. I wrote that two Great Turns ago. I thought she wasn't happy here. I did not know if he would answer at all."

Not answer? If it weren't for her father and brother, the Grand Vizier would have been dragged to death that day. The man should be grateful until the day the Wheel spun him into the void for good. No one else would have endangered themselves to help him.

Nesrin shuddered, unable to banish the memories of that day. They just said she was too young to understand. She'd been afraid, she'd never seen that much blood before, or actual bone protruding out of a wound, and her memory was confused and fragmented.

"We'll need the money. With the Blight…" Temel's voice trailed off as he curled his upper lip over his teeth to worry his mustache. The words barely covered the heartache in his eyes. Sanem, his eldest. His true favorite. She was the very best thing in Mizraa.

Nesrin untied the apron strings about her waist and rather than hang or fold it, she wadded it up and slapped it on the table. She picked up the remaining pide and went inside.

Serving food to her family was usually akin to tossing a bloodied carcass into a pack of wolves. Tonight, no one even moved when she placed it in front of them. Even her grandmothers, forever bickering over some minor detail of the seasoning, were silent.

"Aren't you going to eat?" Pembe asked as Nesrin wove her way between the table and the wall toward the front door.

"I ate while I cooked," she lied, and smiled when her mother frowned at the baldness of it. There was no lying to Pembe. To any of them. Water mages knew lies the way geese knew north and south.

Sanem was trying to be brave, picking at her food and trying to hold her tears, and Anil had an arm around her shoulders, his own dusky face lit with adoration and anguish.

They were so perfectly matched, both of them *more* because of their love. She could not bear to see their despair and be incapable of fixing it. So she had to leave. Nesrin turned away and ducked out the front door.

She walked. She walked until the sun set and the animals of the light slept, making room for the ones that slunk and pattered. She walked until night began to swell with the promise of day. Bright, glorious day was Nesrin's preference. But she was the daughter of water mages and had never feared the dark, or the cold.

Without magic, she had no affinity for time, or season, though she had her favorites. Now, when deep spring turned to summer. When life began to outrun the winter, bountiful and effervescent, beginning to show hints of flowers and fruit. Midday, when the sun was bright and warm, often even in the winter, banishing the sluggishness of night and the lingering fatigue of the morning. When potential felt highest. When hope blazed.

It had not felt that way today. They'd buried so many. And now they would lose Sanem.

A tear slid down her cheek. Sanem flourished here, where she was princess of her own small kingdom. In Narfour no one would care about her, they would look down on her, a country clod from the valley. They wouldn't appreciate her light, and she would die a slow, wilting death in the city. Nesrin wished her father had asked to marry her off in the city, instead.

Her steps slowed. She stopped and turned halfway around, staring west. The mountain broke the sky in half. Empty black below, star-filled indigo above. Her breath hitched, her thoughts twisting through her like twining ivy. Yes.

They had been much younger when the Grand Vizier had his accident in the fields. Certainly he would not know one of them from the other, who looked so much like each other, if he even knew Temel had more than one daughter. Only their magic distinguished them, shaped their lives. A stranger would know no difference.

Her gaze swung to the estate house, looming in the hazy, pre-dawn light. Then she turned toward her own home, and clenched her fists.

Could she fix this?

She did not have a plan when she took that first step toward home. She had only that feeling, a seed in her belly, sprouting into decision, coiling upward through her chest and gripping her lungs and heart and throat with a desperate understanding. If she thought about what she was doing, if she hesitated, she would stop. Momentum was all she had. So she kept going.

She hurried down the twisting path to the back of their house, to the outdoor kitchen. The day's laundry still hung in the crisp night air.

Nesrin tugged down Sanem's favorite caftan and entari, the ones she wore to village festivals and special occasions. She laid it over the wall, then quietly opened the gate and stepped into the kitchen area. She crouched in front of the worktable and dug two carrots and a mealy apple out of the storage bin and laid them on the table.

Sanem and Anil had oiled the hinges on the back door because most nights Sanem snuck out to meet him. Nesrin opened it with confidence and slipped inside.

Mage orbs were a luxury of fire mages, so Pembe had left a single oil lamp burning for light, and for balance. It illuminated the curtains drawn around where she and Temel slept. Nesrin's sisters were snuggled in a tangle of arms on the mat they all shared, with their grandmother's handwoven pink blanket bunched over them. On the other side of the room, Metin slept sprawled on his belly, drooling onto his pillow. He usually slept with as few clothes as he could manage without traumatizing his family, so his fully clothed state suggested he was responsible for the empty bottle of arak on the table.

She skirted the table in the center of the room as she crept toward the front of the house. With quiet, nimble fingers, she removed three coins from the jar of money they used for trading, to supplement what they provided for themselves. Her throat squeezed, sweat breaking over her face and hands, along with a wash of nausea. Stealing. From people who could not spare it. People she loved more than anything in the world.

Perhaps they would understand. Forgive her, even. She hoped so.

Tears streaked her face. She swiped them away. She would see them again. She would convince the Grand Vizier, or this stranger, this future husband, that her deception was not from malice, but love. She could make them understand, eventually.

But for the time being, she would be alone. Her family could not follow her and expose her intended lie, and she would be unable to return and give the Pasha a chance to correct her disobedience. Could she exist without them? She'd always had them, when there was nothing else.

Metin snuffled in his sleep. Nesrin slipped the coins into the pocket of her entari and stepped to his sleeping pallet. The smell of alcohol wafted up from him, but for once she didn't care. She crouched and drew a threadbare blanket over him.

"I will miss you, Abi," she whispered. Metin, who always stood beside her. As lovable, in his way, as Sanem.

She rose and went to her sisters, stopping at the foot of their shared sleeping mat. The twisted blanket made her fingers twitch, but her sisters slept too lightly for her to re-cover them. Even in sleep, Sanem looked so sad that it galvanized Nesrin. She could not bear that.

"Wheel turn for you." Her voice caught, and she swallowed. She touched her heart with three fingers, then kissed them.

She took a hooded ferace from a hook beside the door as she slipped back outside. There she changed quickly into Sanem's clothes, folding her own neatly on the table. She, Sanem, and their mother had always been similar in size, but now the clothes hung on her, sizes too big on her gaunt frame.

The caftan and entari she had taken were the nicest they owned, but perhaps her family would understand. Maybe they would be grateful, relieved. They'd never resented her. No. Her family loved her, she knew that. Just as she loved them. But there had always been that tension, that unspoken wall between Nesrin and the future.

The void. They wouldn't miss her and the small chores she handled. Not like Sanem. She was beautiful and kind, a gifted Deval just like their mother and father. Just like Metin and Nimet and Nuray.

Broken Wheel, even the poorest, dimmest of farm sons didn't want Nesrin for more than sport. But that was the beauty of it. The sinister spin of the Wheel. The Grand Vizier had offered this marriage as collateral to a life debt. He could not back out, even if the daughter who showed up at his door was a void.

To deny her, he would have to know she had taken her sister's place. Her family were not dimwitted. They would know what she had done, and the consequences of revealing the truth.

Nesrin shoved the apple and carrots into the pockets of the entari along with the coins. When she turned to the gate, Buse let out a plaintive meow from his place on the corner of the table. "*Shh.*" She stroked his soft fur and smiled bravely. "Watch over them for me."

He observed her with a cat's grave expression as she set out toward the estate as swiftly as she could, racing the morning. Her family rose early. She would need to be on her way before they did and before they realized what she had done.

The very last marks of night cloaked her as she strode up the path to the circular drive. She put the ferace on at the last moment, because even the nights were warming as summer approached and the ferace was much too thick for the season. As she reached the house and the first light of dawn paled the eastern sky, she tugged the hood up to hide her face.

The fear would come. It would blossom and grow like stinkweed, consuming her temporary bravery, growing in the loam provided by her doubts and half-formed plan.

This was foolish, and impossible. She rubbed her damp palms against her belly.

The carriage waited near the entrance to the estate, a driver seated on the front, and two people standing beside it. One was Master Ansar, a looming shadow beside a woman Nesrin didn't know. The woman had a thin face and prominent nose, with dark hair pulled severely back into a coil.

Nesrin hesitated, the gravel crunching underfoot as she halted. Master Ansar was not as distractable as Bardakci Pasha. Nesrin held the hood tighter around her head, her shoulders hunching as she forced herself forward to stand in front of him and bow.

"This is Mistress Banu, Deval of the First House," Master Ansar said. "She will escort you to Narfour and the Grand Vizier." He handed an envelope to Banu. "For Kadir Pasha. All the information he requested."

Banu snatched it from his hands. Nesrin remained silent during the exchange. She did not think Master Ansar would know Sanem's voice well enough to discern she was not her sister, but better not to take chances. Master Ansar frightened her, though he had never done anything more offensive to her than leer.

He gestured at the carriage. Nesrin had never been in one before. She'd ridden in wagons plenty of times, but perhaps this would be a smoother ride, less bone-bruising bouncing. There was just enough light now to see the Grand Vizier's crest on the side of this carriage. Carved in relief and painted gold.

"In you get then." Banu fluttered her hand toward the open carriage door. Nesrin itched with nervousness as she climbed inside the dark box, hoping she only imagined the feeling that Master Ansar's stare was burning between her shoulder blades. She held her breath as the air mage climbed in behind her.

"Sit," Banu demanded. Nesrin plopped obediently on the bench which put her back to the wall between carriage and driver.

"Pass Bardakci Pasha's regards along to the Grand Vizier," Master Ansar sneered.

"Perhaps he'll call you back to civilization soon, and you may be relieved of your orders to babysit." Banu swung the carriage door shut as insult twisted the fire mage's face.

Nesrin clenched her hands together in her lap, avoiding Banu's gaze. She was sweating, waiting, stifled by the weight of the ferace and the other woman's stare.

"You're quiet. Good." Banu's voice was smoky and rough. "The less you speak, the better this journey will go."

The carriage shrank around Nesrin.

Banu reached into a pouch at her belt, then withdrew her fingers, her sharp nails dusted with chalk, and traced a sigil on the side of the carriage. She spoke into the glowing rune, announcing their departure from Mizraa. A whip cracked, Nesrin closed her eyes, and the carriage lurched forward.

Five

Ihsan stifled a yawn. Somehow he had slept better out in the wilderness of Sarkum than he had in the safety of the palace. But then, he hadn't slept well in the palace in over a decade. And his nightmares plagued him. That made focusing on the mundane task of audience even more excruciating than it usually was. He wanted to do these tasks for Naime. He wanted to be useful, wanted to ease the burden that grew heavier each day for her. What use was the title of Sehzade if he had no purpose? Naime was called to rule. He was called to…

"Sehzade? Is that agreeable?" Kadir asked.

Ihsan avoided looking at him, instead flicking his gaze up to the two men standing in front of him. Dispute in the Merchant Guild. "You wish for him to pay for the cost of sweeping up goat shit from in front of your shop," Ihsan summarized. Somehow he'd heard the dispute, despite his mind being leagues away from the room. He propped his elbows on his knees and leveled a stare at the ceramics merchant.

His coarse language amused some in attendance and appalled others, giggles and whispered conversations bubbling up everywhere in the hall.

"Is this a matter for the Sultan, Grand Vizier?" Ihsan said without looking at Kadir. "Surely you could have dealt with this without bringing it into audience?" The merchant squirmed uncomfortably as Ihsan glared at him instead.

"Master Fikret is not a member of the Merchant Guild, Efendim, and therefore out of our jurisdiction. And the Tribunals are busy dealing with vandalism and looting."

"Is it also not the jurisdiction of the Grand Vizier?" Ihsan finally looked at the man, ice frosting over the upwelling of fury and repulsion that assaulted him whenever he did so.

"I did not wish to overstep my bounds and make it seem as if I thought you could not deal competently with the simplest of matters." Kadir smiled and tipped his head in a mockery of deference. He did everything he could to bring demeaning cases like this to audience every time Ihsan filled in for Naime.

He closed his eyes. "Master Belgesi will pay to sweep the area directly in front of Master Fikret's place of business. And for Wheel's turn, take the goats a different route. Guild Street, for instance." That would move the problem to the Merchant Guild, so Kadir would have to deal with it. Small victories.

Someone in the audience had the stones to bark a laugh. Kadir banged his staff.

"The Sehzade has spoken on the matter."

The two men bowed and shuffled out of the hall. Ihsan straightened, then leaned backward, his spine cracking as he bent it over the back of the bench.

"Next."

"I bring the next matter for your consideration," Kadir said. Ihsan glanced at him as Kadir motioned to someone in the audience.

Attendees ranged from Council Viziers to minor nobles, merchants, and those with nothing better to do than spend their morning listening to others bickering about goat pellets and property lines. Or marvel at the glamorous life of the only male heir of the Sabri line. Ihsan grit his teeth.

A man stood. Enver Balik, Governor of the land north of Narfour, all the way to the village of Golge. Balik Pasha was supportive of Behram Kadir, though Ihsan was not sure they were allies so much as uneasy partners in a battle to win control of the land and routes in the northern half of Tamar. Ihsan could not recall a time that Enver Balik spoke about anything, in audience or Council, other than to nod along with whatever Kadir had to say.

Enver approached the dais and bowed, his gaze fixing on Kadir. There was the edge of expectation, perhaps even threat, in the look. Ihsan held his expression and body still so he did not let on that he had seen the unspoken exchange.

"I seek approval for a marriage between Balik Pasha and the daughter of Bardakci Pasha."

Ihsan held his reaction in for the space of several breaths. Osman Bardakci was the reclusive governor of Mizraa, in the Southern valley. It was the most productive farmland in Tamar. He had inherited it in a trade with the Altimur family after their fallout with Behram Kadir during his father's takeover of the Merchant Guild, Cycles ago. Bardakci Pasha paid his taxes on time, and reliably shipped crops. He had the best vineyards in Tamar, besides the farmland, and productive orchards as well. His was the only land where Blight had yet to be discovered. It was the most valuable asset any Vizier could claim, currently.

He had never heard that Bardakci Pasha had a daughter, in fact up until that moment he would have said there were no children at all. He'd never sent anyone to the University to train, or to court to learn politics. That he had a marriageable daughter no one had heard of sent purls of conversation through the hall. Ihsan picked at a fleck of paint on the bench, trying to sort the new information.

If Balik Pasha were to marry into the Bardakci family, he stood to eventually inherit Mizraa. Even the future possibility of that was troubling. Sirhan Yavuz was Naime's greatest ally in the Council. To allow a marriage that would nearly triple the size of his competitor would be a blow Ihsan did not think even Sirhan could overlook.

But Ihsan could not simply deny the marriage outright. And he could not deny it on the grounds of creating a competitor for Sirhan, because Kadir's supporters would eviscerate Naime if she appeared publicly biased.

"He wishes to marry his daughter to a Council Vizier without her ever having been to court?"

"It is unlikely there are many, if any, reasonable marriage candidates in Mizraa, Efendim. What else would you have him do?" Kadir answered patiently, as if Ihsan were a simple child. Ihsan ignored the tone. Balik Pasha was younger than Kadir. Still, he was at least forty Turns. Osman Bardakci's daughter was likely much younger. Ihsan was all too aware of how little that mattered to some, most, of the men who decided such things. He did not wish to sentence a woman to a marriage she had no say in, if he could help it.

He would much rather consult with Naime than answer this request out of hand. "We will consider the match and give the answer at audience next small turn," Ihsan said.

Kadir smiled apologetically. The temperature between them, on the dais, and surrounding Ihsan, rose. Cold sweat broke out over his back. Ihsan's scars itched, some ached, as if he were standing directly beside a blaze. "I'm afraid the young woman will be on her way shortly, Efendim. I would hate for her to leave her home and make the trip over the pass only to arrive and be denied what she had been promised."

The heat tangled Ihsan's thoughts and sped his breath. Black wiggled at the edge of his vision. It summoned his nightmares, their formless horrors slinking at the edge of his awareness. He tried to order his thoughts, to slow his breathing. Kadir was doing it on purpose, fully aware of Ihsan's fear. He held on to his composure only by his magic, calling ice into his body, an armor that pushed away the heat.

"He hesitates so he can think of a way to grab power for his cousin," Balik Pasha said with a thin sneer.

"You are bold to stand before the Sultan's seat and ask a boon while insulting the person you ask it of," Ihsan snapped. But Enver's jab had the intended effect. The whispers began. The glances, the discontent. Ihsan silently cursed himself and his lack of control. His panic had cost him the few moments he had to make a decision of his own accord. He could do nothing now but acquiesce. He and Naime would decide on damage control later. Though starting off the day with her disappointed in him rankled.

Kadir's magic pressed into him like a wall of hot metal, slurring his thoughts and raising his temper. Ihsan tried to concentrate on his own magic, on the cold, without letting it break out over his skin and reveal to everyone how flustered he was. Any susceptibility he showed to Kadir, and his bullying, made him appear weak. Manipulated.

"You will present Mistress Bardakci at audience to the Princess Sultana before the betrothal is made official." That was not an unusual ask when it came to a Vizier's marriage. Though it was only a formality. As far as he knew, no marriage had ever been rejected by the Sultan by the time a future wife was presented at court. Still, it was a slim opportunity to find a solution with Naime to fix the mistake he'd been corralled into.

Balik Enver smiled politely and bowed. "Of course, Efendim."

"That concludes audience for today," Kadir said to Ihsan. Ihsan did not have to look at the man to know he smiled, he could hear it in his slithering voice. Though he had not bothered to dampen the heat of his magic despite his victory. Sweat dripped down Ihsan's temple and he froze it in place with a flicker of magic. Wheel, he despised being out of control of his own damned body.

He stood abruptly. "That is all for this turn," he said in dismissal. Then he strode off the dais and down the aisle without looking back. Kuhzey trotted after him, his footfalls drowned out by the upwelling of conversation.

When he was in the Sultan's wing, Ihsan ripped at the fabric belt on his waist, unwinding it with a violent yank. He unbuttoned his entari, shrugging out of it as he arrived at the Sultan's rooms. He was still hot. The sound of flames snapped in his ears. The guards did their best not to look at him as he knocked and entered before being greeted.

Kuhzey closed the doors behind him as Ihsan crossed the room in fast strides. He slung his entari and waistcloth away from him, not caring where they landed. Then he collapsed on a roomy chair in a slouch, hand over his face. He just needed to breathe.

He was so lost in his personal battle with memory that he did not see Naime sitting in her father's chair until she spoke.

"It did not go well today, I presume." There was no accusation or disappointment in her tone. That wounded him even more. That he had failed and she wouldn't even chastise him for it.

"I succeeded in handing Mizraa to Enver Balik," Ihsan snarled into his hand. "Call that whatever you wish."

She made a thoughtful sound. Ihsan scowled, dropping his hand to the cushion beside him. But he kept his head tipped onto the back of the chair, staring at the mosaic ceiling.

"I call it an issue to be dealt with. Can you explain in more detail?" Naime's House gave her logic and emotional control. Ihsan's gave him empathy, and emotions that often overran his good sense.

"Bardakci Pasha apparently has a child no one knows about. A daughter. She is of age to marry, or I assume she is, and it appears that Behram Kadir has brokered an alliance behind the scenes by way of marrying Balik Enver to this woman. He asked for blessing on the betrothal." Ihsan released a breath at the end that finally extinguished the heat that had seemed to cling to him even after leaving Kadir's presence. "They backed me into a corner."

Naime sighed and stood. "You approved it."

"I told him to present her at audience. It was the best I could do. I had no valid reason to deny the request at that moment."

"Do not be so hard on yourself, San. He would never have asked for something like that without timing it completely to his advantage. I do not know if I could have done any better."

Ihsan didn't respond. They both knew that wasn't true.

"I'll spend some time in the records and see if there are any ways to deny him by way of intermarriage."

"No," Samira said. She had appeared out of the second bedroom, where Naime had been sleeping. "I will do that. The last thing you need is something else keeping you awake and draining you."

"I will be awake anyway." Naime settled back into her father's chair and turned her gaze out to the garden. Samira sighed, her eyes finding Ihsan's, full of sorrow and exasperation. He acknowledged the wordless request with a nod.

"Naime. Let us do this task. It was my failure. Allow me to attempt to find a solution."

"You two are as subtle as a boulder in a puddle," Naime dismissed. She rubbed the spot between her brows. "Do we know when she will arrive in Narfour?"

"Kadir indicated it would be soon."

"Have Bashir speak with the City Watch to notify me as soon as she arrives in the city. We can discuss the matter further after we've searched records." She looked critically at Ihsan. "Get some sleep," she said. Then she stood and left to slip quietly into her father's bedroom.

Six

THE TWO DAYS IT TOOK to get to Narfour were the longest of Nesrin's life. The only sounds to break it up were the crack and rattle of the wooden wheels over stones and packed dirt, the creak of wood and metal as the carriage swayed and jolted, and the driver's grumbled nattering at his horses.

Nesrin tried talking once with Banu but received only an annoyed glance in exchange. Banu was one of those people who broadcasted their general discontent in every movement and expression. Some people were forced into misery by Wheel-spun circumstances, and some chose it. Banu seemed like someone who chose it.

The monotony was only broken by a wakeful, shivering night spent curled up in an open-air shelter at the top of the pass while both Banu and the driver snored.

That was the first morning of Nesrin's entire life that she had woken without her family. Without the bickering of her grandmothers as they made eggs and labneh to eat with remnants of flatbread from the night before. They had enough flour for the small turn, maybe more, if they were careful. But they were too hungry to be careful.

Tears welled at the thought of her younger sisters. Her little chicks, following her about, bickering and giggling. The tautness in her chest and throat returned. Before she could spiral more deeply into despair, she looked out the window once more.

A swirl of dust obscured the view for a moment, as the heat of the afternoon sun baked the road they followed. When it cleared, Nesrin saw Narfour for the first time. It spread below and away, north and south, swallowing the foothills of the mountain they descended and tumbling against the sea. The *sea*. Despite the gravity of the moment, and her turmoil, she was suddenly a child again, wide-eyed with delight.

It sparkled. The lake at Mizraa sometimes did the same, in the right light. But this was different. From this distance it was silver glass, just kissed by the new sun. The dark shapes of ships moored in the bay flecked the water. Nesrin had never seen a ship. They must be enormous, to be visible from here. She stared until the carriage took another switchback and her view was dominated by mountainside again.

The city welcomed them with sound first. A low hum that became a clamor as they transitioned from the rough mountain trail to something smoother. Their angle of descent lessened, until Nesrin no longer had to cling to prevent sliding from one side of the bench to the other. The road transitioned from packed dirt to cobbles, making the ride even more backside-bruising than it had been. The sounds, smells, and light billowed in along with the dust.

“There is nothing to see in this part of the city,” Banu groused at the sudden sensory assault.

Nesrin stared. Perhaps there was nothing for Banu to see. Nesrin had thought Mizraa was bustling when a traveling merchant came through, when all the villagers turned out to buy or trade. It was all she could do to stay politely seated, now, instead of cramming her head out the carriage window to drink in the chaos more fully.

The smells were both foreign and familiar. The same scents that welcomed her when her grandmothers cooked, and things she could not name, simultaneously interesting and repellent. The view was alien to her, nothing like the sprawling landscapes she had lived in all her life. Buildings packed so tightly together she doubted she could slide sideways between some of them. Some were so tall she could not see their roofs. People passed the carriage in packs, their voices a steady, underlying buzz, like a heartbeat.

Fear sprouted from her wonder. How could she survive here? What would happen if the Grand Vizier threw her out instead of honoring his offer? If he discovered she wasn't the sister he had agreed to marry off? But how would he possibly discover the truth? Her family would understand the consequences of her lie if they were to reveal her by pursuing, or telling anyone. The threat of imprisonment, or perhaps worse, not just for Nesrin, but for all of them, would mute them and keep them away. Still, while she did not believe that Bardakci Pasha would punish her family for Nesrin's lie, because he could not afford to lose Temel, she had no doubts the Grand Vizier would.

No. That would not do—giving in to the power of her fear. *A flower must grow where it is planted.* Her anneanne had told Nesrin that from the time she was small, before she had accepted that there was no cure for being devoid of magic. She said it when Metin and Sanem were practicing their magic, slinging water and mud at each other and learning runes, and Nesrin could only be victim or audience to their games. *Grow, tatlım. Use the wind and water to grow strong. Do not let it knock you over.* She said it again when the younger girls came into their magic. *A wildflower alone is all the more beautiful for the barrenness from which it grows. A single note more glorious for the silence around it.*

"We'll arrive shortly," Banu said as if every word had to be pulled from her with rope and hook. Nesrin folded her hands in her lap. That would be a relief. Her bottom was bruised and numb. She could now inform Sanem that despite their fancy looks, carriages were no more comfortable than wagons. In fact less so, as there was no way to stretch out comfortably in one, the way they could in a wagon. Nor was there the luxury of a cushioning—if poky—pile of hay to take a nap in on the ride to and from the estate.

Her heart broke open a little more, her nose growing stuffy and her eyes stinging. When she sniffed, Banu cut a censoring look at her, making a little hiss.

"I cannot abide water mages. They are always so…wet." She curled her lip. Nesrin sniffed again, then wiped her nose on her sleeve when Banu seemed affronted by the sound.

Nesrin could not tell if she was meant to answer. Banu obviously had not recognized she was a void. Nesrin was saved from the dilemma by the sudden, creaking halt of the carriage.

The city sounds were louder now that the movement of the carriage over cobbles did not drown them out. Banu did not move to exit, so Nesrin didn't either. The driver eventually yanked the door open.

Nesrin looked from it to Banu, who maintained her scowl. "Get out," the woman snarled, but did not move to do the same.

Nesrin exited without grace, staggering out as her legs, needling from lack of blood flow, wobbled beneath her. They had stopped on a hill, the slope of the cobbled road falling away to the south and west. The city loomed. From the mountain, and in bits and pieces from her window view, it had looked somehow manageable. Now she stood, a seedling shaded and choked by giants. She did not know where to look, her panic sending her gaze one direction, then another, seeking an escape she was blind to. Her breaths drew too shallow and quick to rescue her from the sense of drowning.

"When you've finished gawking?" Banu called from the carriage. She hadn't bothered to step down. The driver had returned to his seat.

Nesrin glanced from the carriage to the house. Could it even be called a house? It was a palace to her. Even the chiflik house in Mizraa could not compare. There were two floors, and the top hosted a balcony facing the front. The view of the city and the sea from there must be breathtaking. Vines draped from pots, cascading to frame the entry door and flanking windows below it. Vivid crimson flowers in the shape of miniscule trumpets adorned the vines. Firecress, though it wasn't a cress at all. Cress could be eaten, like lettuce. Firecress was toxic even in small quantities. The seeds, roots, flowers, and leaves, all. Nesrin absently rubbed the shape of a water sigil between her fingers in a subconscious attempt to balance the fiery warning of the plant.

The plaster was painted in sunset shades, as searing to her eyes as staring at a fire in the dead of night. This entire street was populated by Fifth House mages, if the homes squished to either side were indication. She'd never seen so much red plaster in all her life. They were lavish but tightly packed, with no gardens or green spaces to speak of. Who could even live like that?

"A word of advice"—Banu proffered a smile with all the friendliness of a badger—"never keep him waiting." She pulled the carriage door closed.

Nesrin startled at the sound, spurred to cross the few paces between the carriage and the house. A pair of narrow, ornate oak doors perched atop a brick staircase of six steps, with windows of matching size and curve to either side. When there could not be six there must be three. It was the same in the valley. Doors always coupled with two windows, when windows could be afforded.

The driver cracked a whip and the carriage rolled away. Just as Nesrin spun to look, Banu yanked the curtain of the window closed.

The house loomed, vivid and terrifying. She mounted the steps. As she raised her hand to knock, a crack and scrape signaled someone had opened the door on the balcony above her. Nesrin tipped her head back to peer up at the balcony.

"What have we here?" a male voice, bright with fire, drifted from above. He leaned over the wrought-iron railing, head turned toward her. The brightness of the sky obscured him, but he appeared far too young to be the Grand Vizier. Another servant? Or a son? She swallowed back her apprehension and tried to speak. "Another drudge?" the man suggested in bored tones. "We're overrun at the moment." He gripped the rail and tipped his head back to look skyward. A smell drifted down to her, mingling nauseatingly with the peppery perfume of the firecress. The sour stink of alcohol. He rocked forward, leaning so far over the balcony that Nesrin gasped. He extended a hand and wiggled his fingers and sparks rained down on her. She squealed, batting at the ones that caught on her clothes. "You aren't going to like it here, little mouse. You should leave."

When she looked up again, stunned to muteness, he was gone.

"Oh no." Tiny, singed holes pockmarked her entari. Sanem's entari. Tears bit at her eyes. What an ass. Her father had always said that fire mages couldn't be nice people, it wasn't in their nature.

She reached for the righthand iron knocker, of two, one on each crimson door. But the doors swung inward before she grabbed it. Nesrin nearly toppled backward off the step, slapping her outstretched hand over her heart instead.

"Broken Wheel," the young woman in the doorway breathed. She was Nesrin's age, or close to it. "Filthy." Nesrin recoiled but did not have time to speak before the woman said, "Get inside. You are late, they have already left for the Council." When Nesrin did not move or respond, confused and insulted, the woman let out a harsh sigh and snagged her by the sleeve, wrenching her inside.

An errant vine runner from the firecress caught in Nesrin's hair. She tried to reach to free herself before it pulled, but the woman dragged her into the house, and the runner snapped, part of it still tangled in Nesrin's hair.

"You needn't drag me." Nesrin tried to sound polite, but she thought instead her voice was too shrill.

"We do not have any time for you to dawdle and gawk. You must be made presentable. Come." The woman tugged more sharply as she turned toward a side room. Nesrin only caught a moving glimpse of the main room, marble and sandstone and couches overflowing with jewel-toned pillows. Not even in Bardakci Pasha's house had she ever seen such opulence. She might have imagined it in the palace, but never in a home.

A lump filled her throat. She had made a terrible mistake. She did not belong here.

The woman tugged Nesrin about like an errant pony until they reached a utility room. Two older women rose from a bench against the far wall and bowed. Nesrin was flung toward them and into the middle of the room.

"There is no time for the bathhouse. Wash up and do something with…this." The woman plucked at a tangled lock of Nesrin's hair, frizzed by the humidity. Nesrin grabbed the bit of vine still stuck in her hair and freed it as she gestured to the empty barrel against one wall. A spout jutted from the tan stone above it. There was no handle to manually pump. The master of the house could afford water mages.

"I cannot wash with no water," Nesrin said. The woman's eyebrows shot toward her hairline.

"Sing it." She waved a hand at the spout, as if it were perfectly obvious. Disquiet consumed Nesrin's voice and she stared mutely. Her father had not named Sanem in his letter, had he? Had they known to expect a water mage?

The woman's face contorted, then she grabbed Nesrin's hand. Heat pulsed against Nesrin's skin where it touched the woman's. Her magic pushing for an echo it would not receive. The woman withdrew, her breath exiting in a rush.

"Clean her," she snipped before spinning to leave. The door slammed shut. Nesrin eyeballed the older women, who avoided her gaze, and did not speak. One shuffled to the spout and drew a rune above it, each line a control measure, command, or instruction for force. Nesrin could draw many water runes in her sleep, not that they would do her any good. Water poured from the spout as the woman, grey hair braided and wound about her head, hummed and swayed. The familiarity of that slowed Nesrin's breathing enough to bring some sense back to her.

She looked down at the vine in her hand. Remembering what it was, she dropped it and rubbed her hand on her entari. Her brother had gotten into a patch of it once. His skin had erupted into an oozing rash everywhere it had touched him.

"Is that how people are welcomed here?" She pointed at the vine.

"It is the Pasha's favorite plant," the water mage said, gesturing to the tub that filled rapidly with water. Both women still avoided Nesrin's eyes. The second one had busied herself with warming the water, the fingers of one hand dangling in the tub as she knelt on the stone tiles, sorting through a basket of hygiene items with her other. Combs, brushes, soaps, diminutive bottles of oils. Nesrin had never had more than a rough, torn bit of scrap cloth to wash with and a misshapen comb her father had carved for her to tame her hair.

The fire mage approached Nesrin. Without word or ceremony she began tugging at clasps and laces to take her clothes. Nesrin let out a squawk of protest, but the old woman's hands were sure and strong, manipulating her out of her clothes before Nesrin could sort thoughts to argue. The servant tossed her things in a pile and Nesrin stared at them as she was ushered to the tub.

It was about the size of a wine barrel turned on its side and cut open, meant for standing or sitting. A servant's bath, Nesrin imagined. She'd never bathed with anything but a basin, or in the summer, a dip in a cold mountain lake. And she'd never had warm water.

This was not a bath so much as an assault. The women worked rough and fast, as though Nesrin were stained clothing and not a person. She expected they might bring out rocks to beat against her at any moment. Instead they rubbed her raw with brushes, perhaps trying to remove the stain of sun from her skin. Nesrin might have appreciated the luxurious smell of the soap they used, or the oil they rubbed into her hair, except that it felt they were tearing it from her scalp as they washed, combed, oiled, and braided it.

All of it was scented with Fifth House smells, like cinnamon and clove, black pepper and musk. The potent fragrance made Nesrin lightheaded. She kept rubbing her skin, unaccustomed to the slick, greasy feeling the creams left on her.

The fire mage left eventually, leaving the water mage to rub Nesrin, *everywhere*, with cream that burned in the scratches on her hands and the raw places they had left after their ministrations. Nesrin submitted in silence because what else was she to do? She did not even know where she was. Was this the Grand Vizier's home? They had called him Pasha, so it must be. Certainly it was not her future husband's. Even a Grand Vizier could not convince a noble to marry a farmworker.

When the other servant returned, she carried a set of clothes in shades of turquoise. The sort of clothes a water mage might wear. Nesrin did not know how to allow others to dress her. She and the two women struggled in an awkward dance, while Nesrin tried to be helpful but ended up in their way more than she assisted.

The clothing fit loosely on her gaunt frame, a fact which made the older of the two women, the water mage, cluck in disapproval. She fussed with the clothes, fluffing them about the belt to give more volume in places that hung limp. It might have been more effective to offer her something to eat. Nesrin bit her lower lip, staring toward the ceiling as the woman tugged and rearranged. Tiles of red and orange made geometric patterns.

Finally, the older woman stepped back and nodded to the other, who opened the door to the washroom and gestured for her to exit.

Nesrin did not move at first, looking from one woman to the other, but neither moved to escort her.

"Reyhan will come for you," the water mage said, nodding toward the foyer. Nesrin bowed to them, then returned alone into the foyer. Pale mage orbs she had not noticed when first dragged inside floated serenely around the room, but were unnecessary, as the afternoon sun shone brightly through the front windows onto the ocher plaster and sandstone interior.

She was relieved to be alone, to take a moment to collect herself. She'd met more strangers in these two days than she normally did in a season's stretch. She stared for long moments upward at the ceilings. The plaster that covered them was painted with geometric designs that clashed and yet somehow complemented each other. A nod to the Wheel and its eternal, slow spin toward balance through opposition. She tried to let that reminder calm her, soothe away thoughts of what might await her. Discovery and punishment for her lie.

The main floor where she waited was divided into three spaces by two sets of columned arches. First the entry, then a central seating area that was recessed, and the back of the parlor where a marble-stepped stairway spiraled up to the second floor. The seating area dominated the long room and had stone benches that ran the length of it on either side with cushions made of red velvet. A long, low table sat between the benches, with a fabric runner woven in reds and purples. The bloodred cushions, set off by pillows in various shades of red, orange, and pink, shouted that this was a Fifth House family.

At far end of the room, just in front of the staircase, stood a waist-high fountain. It was meant to balance the house's fire, but despite being the largest fountain Nesrin had ever seen, it was empty of water. She had never encountered something like that, something so blatantly against balance. An empty fountain in a house of the Fifth spoke. It was a wonder the place hadn't burned to the ground. Nesrin shuddered. She much preferred earth and water mages. They were steady, not always in their heads, like air mages could be, not too intense, like fire mages.

She was like a weed seed dropped by an ill wind into a flower bed, standing in borrowed clothes and lies, in a home far too grand for her plainness.

Footsteps descended the stairs. Nesrin wrung her clammy hands. It was the woman who had dragged her inside and left her in the washroom. Reyhan, the water mage had called her.

Reyhan strode with force, her face tight with stress. Her gaze raked Nesrin from head to toe. With quick fingers she adjusted a wavy lock of hair that had already escaped the crown of braids the others had attempted to tame Nesrin's hair with. There were not enough pins in the world, though it did feel as though there were at least that many in the arrangement, stabbing into her scalp.

"Come," Reyhan spoke as she moved past.

"Where?" Nesrin hurried after her.

"The palace."

Nesrin stood, dwarfed by the building before her, a miniscule minnow in a wild stream of people. The consuming desire to run, to disappear, ached in her throat. She did not belong here. Did not know how to ease so much discomfort, physically, from the constriction of such heavy layering, and mentally, from pondering what she had mired herself in.

It might have been more bearable if she were in her own clothes. Comfortable, well worn.

The carriage rolled away from her back after Reyhan disembarked, and without it as backdrop Nesrin felt exposed. Cold despite the already-brutal morning sun. Reyhan nudged Nesrin's elbow as she passed, spurring her to follow. She'd not said a single word in the carriage or even offered a smile but kept her eyes downcast and her lips sealed. Nesrin had half hoped to sway her to be a confidante, but the woman had ignored her every attempt to begin a conversation.

Even with her racing thoughts, the palace's broad, spreading domes, verdigrised and immense, awed her. They walked up a squat, wide set of stone stairs, between two armed guards, and through a set of doors taller and wider than her home in Mizraa.

Reyhan did not even acknowledge the guards, but Nesrin had never seen men in armor and armed. She hunched as she hurried between them. But they were forgotten as soon as she entered the palace. She tipped her head toward the painted ceilings, soaring above the foyer they entered. A few people paused to look at her, likely amused by her wonder.

Reyhan did not stop, focused on her destination. Nesrin had to trot to keep up, a chore in thin slippers and the heavy brocade.

Tiles in a dizzying array of patterns blurred by. Murals and frescoes decorated walls and ceilings of even the most out-of-the-way alcoves. Plush carpets cushioned her steps. They walked through galleries open to sprawling gardens, where birdsong and the perfume of flowers called to her.

Just when Nesrin had begun to wonder exactly how long they might be navigating the palace labyrinth, Reyhan turned down a hall and into an arched alcove. She pulled Nesrin in beside her. Nesrin had glimpsed another long hall, where a handful of men stood, chatting. Reyhan fussed at Nesrin's hair and clothes.

"Please tell me what we're doing here," Nesrin implored when Reyhan's gaze was directed at her hair. Reyhan met her desperate stare.

"I am taking you to the High Council. Where the Grand Vizier will present you as the intended betrothed for Balik Pasha."

"W-who?" Nesrin whispered, unable to speak any louder. The High Council? What did they care about the marriage of a farmgirl?

The other woman's expression sharpened, and she showed her teeth in annoyance. "Your husband-to-be. Is that not why you are here?"

Her husband-to-be. The weight of that settled. She'd been distracted from it by missing her family. By fearing being found out in her lie.

"Pasha?" She blinked when the title sank after the position. "But…" She'd thought a merchant, at the very most. More likely a worker. A blacksmith, or a miller. A fishmonger. Those felt safe. This was unthinkable. It was too absurd.

"There has been a mistake," Nesrin said firmly.

"The only mistake is that your father failed to mention you are a void. And if you do not do as you are told, that deception will be punished." Reyhan's voice hissed in the way a fire mage's tended to when they were riled.

"It was not a deception. I—"

"You," the woman ordered, gripping her wrist, "will not speak unless spoken to. You will not argue, deny, or correct. If you make a single peep, a tic, or breath that contradicts the Grand Vizier, you will find yourself and your lying father in chains. Is that clear?" The words were delivered as facts, not threats, and Nesrin could not sort them as an order or a warning.

Her lungs emptied as the woman pulled her out of the alcove and into the hall. "But I don't understand." Nesrin's voice drew the attention of the handful of men that gathered before two doors were thrown wide.

Reyhan moved her body between Nesrin and the men, her expression furious.

"You do not need to understand. You need to be *silent*." Her eyes, nearly black, were wide, her mouth set hard. Nesrin did not respond, which seemed enough for Reyhan, who turned and strode toward the doors. Nesrin followed, too numb to think.

As they approached, someone called something from the room with the open doors. The men made their way inside, and Reyhan paused, gripping Nesrin's elbow so she would do the same. Voices drifted to them, though she could not see inside the room from where Reyhan had stopped them. It was just chatter, nothing organized, and cut off abruptly.

A single voice came next, though Nesrin's heart was pounding so hard it was all she could hear. Whatever he said spurred Reyhan to movement again.

"Walk in front of me. Do not look anywhere but ahead. When you reach the fourth blue mosaic, bow. Do not rise until I do. Do *not* speak."

"Please. This is wrong. It's a mistake."

"It is too late for that," Reyhan whispered, pointing toward the open doors. "Go, now."

With no other option, Nesrin obeyed. But when she stepped around the doors and saw a long hall stretched before her, filled with benches and men dressed in more jewelry and silk and brocade than she could have ever imagined existing, she stopped. Reyhan jabbed a thumb into her back, nail somehow digging through the layers of fabric to make Nesrin wince.

The High Council. Nesrin's slippers tapped in the silence. She started to glance from side to side, at the gauntlet of Viziers who stared at her. Then she remembered Reyhan's command to look forward. But forward, she saw only two men. One dressed in fire, the other in ice, and her vision blurred with fear and tears. She tried to breathe, to put one foot in front of the other.

That had to be the Grand Vizier, to the left of the dais. Why was this walk so long? Her breathing was too shallow. She drew a deeper breath and blinked her vision clear. So the other was…the Sultan? She tripped. One slipper catching against an edge in the tile, and her stumble caused a stir of disapproving whispers. The heat in her neck and cheeks was hot as sunburn. They could see through her, surely. Through the clothes that were not hers and the soap and perfume. Her gaze dropped in time to witness her steps over a blue mosaic of tile.

What had Reyhan said…the fifth? She had not been paying attention. She had not counted them. It was too late to stop on the one she had noticed, so she continued to the next, but Reyhan hissed a warning. She went too far. Her teeth clenched as she halted and bowed.

In the next moment, when only speculative chuckles and whispers held silence at bay, Nesrin panicked again. Was she supposed to stay like this until someone told her not to?

"It is my pleasure to present Mistress Nesrin Bardakci, only child of Bardakci Pasha, heir to Mizraa and governor of the Southern valley," said the man in red.

There were too many things wrong with the introduction, the words simply fell away from her ears. She could not understand them. Her body was cold, her face hot, her hands shaking. She had only meant to prevent Sanem's heartbreak, and now she was standing before the Sultan? It was a fever dream. She curled her fingers into her caftan as the tiles below her swam in her vision.

Oh Wheel, was she going to faint? She'd never fainted in her life.

Nesrin swallowed, drawing a long breath through her nose, digging her nails into her legs. But the feeling was overtaking her, a fog swirling around her mind.

"What is the meaning of this, Grand Vizier?" someone barked from her left just as Nesrin lifted from her bow. Reyhan inhaled sharply but did not straighten from her own bow. Ending a bow early was better than sprawling on her face on the floor, wasn't it? Nesrin lifted her gaze to the men in front of her.

She had meant to look at the Grand Vizier, but her eyes landed on the other. That could not be the Sultan. He was too young.

They did not talk much of the Sehzade in the valley. Everyone knew his life was shaped by tragedy. It was one thing to listen to a story about a young prince, orphaned and disfigured, the grandmothers shaking their heads in pity as they told it. It was an entirely different thing to stand before him. To inadvertently meet his gaze.

The intensity of it sent winter's chill through her body, rescuing her from the lightheadedness. She would have stared, gawked like a girl, was in fact doing so. The prince's hazel eyes were made pale by glowing magic, an enthralling revelation. But the snarling voice to her left made her drop her gaze, mortified.

"You cannot mean for me to marry a void?" The way he said the word, more slur than proper label, made her wish to shrink into the floor. The Vizier stood and faced the Grand Vizier. "I will not."

Seven

Balik Pasha's declaration was like a stick to a hive. The Council buzzed. Enver Balik was on his feet, facing Kadir as though he meant to charge at him.

Meanwhile, his bride-to-be, her hands shaking, stared at Ihsan. That she did not belong in the palace, standing before the Council, was painfully obvious. But that was not a surprise considering she had been raised completely away from court. That was also an oddity. Most of the valley governors sent their children to the city to be educated, both in courtly politics and at the University. And despite a University education being unwarranted in the case of a void, she would still have benefited from time at court.

"You have already agreed to this marriage, Balik Pasha," the Grand Vizier chided. Ihsan tugged his gaze from the woman's, and she dropped her chin to stare at the floor.

"You kept this from me." Such an accusation was bold, and Ihsan half expected Kadir to retaliate with fire. But he preserved his calm. Even with space between them, the fitful lash of Kadir's magic snapped against Ihsan's senses. Kadir held it back, but barely.

"No," Kadir said, "I was unaware of it myself. But that does not change the fact that you asked for and agreed to a marriage before the Sehzade." It was unusual to hear that unsettled tone. Kadir was rarely caught off guard. Or never. Ihsan could not think of a single instance he had ever witnessed the man surprised.

Dark glee crackled through Ihsan as he watched the two men argue. But it only lasted a moment. He needed to seize this opportunity, as Naime would. He let out a sigh he knew could be heard throughout the hall.

"As there seems to be a misunderstanding"—Ihsan stood—"I call a recess of the Council. When I return, I expect this dilemma to have a resolution." He did not look at Kadir or wait for the Council to acknowledge him. He simply left. As he passed the woman from Mizraa, she fumbled a bow. A razor edge of ice sliced up Ihsan's spine. He would have blamed the fire mage maid who bowed a step behind her mistress. But the woman was an Aval, her magic not powerful enough to trigger his simply by existing. Ihsan shrugged off the oddness. His magic was never quite his own in proximity to Kadir.

He did not look back. He knew Samira would follow, and that she would make Kuhzey do the same, even if the boy had been mid-daydream, as he usually was when forced to attend any court events.

Ihsan turned down the hall and into the Sultan's sitting room—one of several scattered throughout the palace. They were places for the Sultan to escape when he did not wish to be bothered. This one contained benches and seats for entertaining guests. Ihsan crossed the room and collapsed onto a couch at the far end. He slung an arm over the back and stretched a leg out across the cushions.

Samira entered, Kuhzey on her heels, her expression disapproving of Ihsan's ease. There was more mother hen to her than Ihsan cared for, but he knew it soothed her, took her mind from her worry over Naime.

He was not Naime, however. Which was evident in a million ways throughout each and every day. That he could simply walk out of the

Council with a single announcement, for example. Or that he could use these sitting rooms, when Naime doing the same would be the source of much disapproving chatter. Hiding away, they would accuse her of. Or being overwhelmed.

Ihsan swiped a hand down his face. The room lacked the windows of the hall, and the early summer heat pressed into his skin. Wheel, he loathed summer.

"Will you intervene?" Samira asked. Kuhzey had attempted to sit on a couch, but she caught him by the collar and directed him to stand behind where Ihsan sat.

He dropped his leg, setting both feet on the floor, and leaned forward, elbows on his knees. The idea of that alliance still sat poorly in his mind. The implications of it spun out in his thoughts, tangling with the memories of the thin, tired soldiers in Saa'ra. What would he sentence them to by giving control of the fertile valley to an ally of Kadir's? And what of Narfour and its people? He rubbed his palm over the back of his hand, over the too-smooth, stretched scar that ran up his wrist.

Fire singed the edges of his thoughts. Heat crawling over him, but not summer heat. The usual feeling that overcame his senses at Kadir's arrival. But it was not Kadir's voice that spoke from the doorway.

"Aren't we cozy?"

Ihsan could picture Cemil's lazy stance in the doorway even before Samira whirled out of the way to reveal him. He leaned one shoulder against the frame, arms crossed. Every time Ihsan saw Cemil's face, regret needled him. Confusion. And anger, more than anything.

The friend who abandoned him when he had been most needed. Left Ihsan to suffer inside and out, alone. They had been inseparable, a rare friendship of fire and water. Until tested.

And how spectacularly Cemil failed that test.

The fire mage's gaze followed Samira as she moved as a shield between Ihsan and Cemil. "Dampen your fire in the presence of the

Sehzade." Her voice cracked through the room. Cemil pushed away from the door with a smile and a laugh.

"Such a fierce little Spark," he said, but he obeyed.

"Go," Ihsan murmured to her. Her hands shook, even when she clasped them in front of her and bowed to him. She retreated behind Ihsan, to stand with Kuhzey. Cemil moved forward to stand within arm's reach of Ihsan. He was alone, which was unusual. Almost as unusual as this meeting. Ihsan could not remember the last time he had been with Cemil without a council's worth of people to keep them company.

That taunting, tightlipped grin seemed permanently etched on his face. Ihsan wanted to punch it off of him.

"To what do I owe the pleasure?" Ihsan could not keep the sharpness from his words, or the accusation. He did not have Naime's composure.

Cemil glanced toward the mosaics on the ceiling of the circular room. "Perhaps I simply wanted to see you playing at Sultan." He dropped his gaze onto Ihsan's, pointed and hot. Ihsan glowered.

"You've seen it. If that is all?" Ihsan leaned back on the couch, attempting to mask his anger with boredom. Cemil seemed amused by his attempt.

"No, I have business."

"Unfortunate," Ihsan growled. He launched to his feet, despising how sitting made him feel vulnerable to Cemil; the emotions he evoked without effort. Cemil snorted at Ihsan's restless movements. "So, speak."

"Your decorum could use some polishing." Cemil gestured at him. "Even after all these Turns."

"I will take your critique under advisement. Now tell me your business and crawl back under your father's caftan."

Something flashed in Cemil's eyes. Not fire. Ihsan would have felt a flare of magic. Emotion. In fact, he could not feel Cemil's fire at all.

Was that on purpose? That would be too much courtesy to expect, to obey Samira's demand for Ihsan's comfort.

Cemil cut his gaze to the side. "The Grand Vizier sent me to ask if you will intervene to force the betrothal that Balik Pasha agreed to."

Ihsan raised his eyebrows. "I believe the Grand Vizier knows our stance on forced marriages." She was too valuable an asset to be given up lightly. Was this as close as Ihsan would get to watching Behram Kadir beg for favor?

"He thought you might understand the gravity, better than the Sultana," Cemil said, "given her…" He paused to smirk, though he was not looking at either Ihsan or Samira. "…proclivity to romantic notions."

Samira's sharply indrawn breath signaled she had taken Cemil's bait. Ihsan shook his head as Cemil grinned, still looking away.

Ihsan followed Cemil's line of sight as his gaze traced the curve of the ceiling upward and stayed at the pinnacle. "Balik Pasha is terribly insulted by being betrothed to a void, and will not see reason, despite the Grand Vizier's *valiant* attempts." Cemil dropped his gaze to Ihsan's and flashed a wan smile. Then he shrugged. "No one has ever accused the man of a surfeit of sense."

Ihsan controlled his own flash of smile. No. Balik Pasha was all temper and entitlement. Cemil watched the smile come and go, and appeared pleased. Irritation erased Ihsan's momentary good humor, and he tore his gaze from Cemil's. "Why should I intervene? If the Grand Vizier cannot reason with him, why should I force a woman into a marriage with someone who views her so poorly?"

Reason with him, or coerce him, more likely. Those two had been in political bed together for some time. Kadir could not afford to lose Enver Balik's loyalty, and Enver could not afford to lose Kadir's patronage. This marriage was as much about Kadir's control as it was gaining leverage for Enver.

Cemil sniffed, shifting his stance, and crossing his arms. "Perhaps your cousin is not the only one with romantic notions."

"I will not intervene."

"No matter," Cemil said boredly. "There are a number of Viziers who would happily take Balik Pasha's place." His gaze drifted behind Ihsan. Ihsan took a step sideways to block Cemil's view of Samira. "He will gift the betrothal to someone who appreciates its benefits."

Of course Kadir would use a valuable marriage to court more councilors to side against Naime. And secure one of the last supply lines away from her easy control.

Ihsan stilled the urge to rub his face in consternation, tucking his hand into the back of the fabric at his waist instead. If they had known Bardakci Pasha had a daughter, they might have been able to arrange her marriage to an ally before Kadir snatched the opportunity away. Though Naime was far less liberal with that particular power than her predecessors had been. She felt the sting of arranged marriage too keenly. Ihsan wished to respect that, as much as he could. Mistress Bardakci had already been overwhelmed in the Council Hall; he would like to avoid piling insult on top of that.

"If the union is so valuable, why not marry her to you?" Ihsan prodded. It was as unusual for Cemil to be a bachelor as it was Ihsan, but Kadir had given no hints at a match since his plans to marry his son to Naime had been undone. Cemil's gaze met Ihsan's. His irises glowed gold. But Ihsan could not feel his magic. His brow furrowed, and the muscles in Cemil's face tensed as he looked away.

"Perhaps he will, and then what will you do, little prince?"

"You will address the Sehzade with his title," Samira reminded him sharply, sparks cracking in her words. Cemil cast her a look that began with irritation and ended with resignation.

"Sehzade"—Cemil grinned, though for a moment it looked more like a grimace of pain—"you should be more concerned with who the Council will choose for you to marry, than who my father will choose for me." There was hurt in Cemil's voice. He'd always been stoic, even as a boy he had hidden his wounds. Samira twisted her hands together, and Ihsan did not need to look at her face to know he would see a matching expression.

When Cemil noticed Ihsan's scrutiny, he bowed. He turned as he rose and strode for the doors. "See you in Council." He lifted a hand in a casual wave.

Ihsan exhaled as he collapsed back onto the couch then bent forward and dropped his head into his hands. Samira stepped to his side, but said nothing. He turned his head to glance up at her. She offered the tiniest smile of reassurance, though her throat moved as she swallowed back her hurt. They understood each other. They had both lost him. Or rather, both been abandoned by him.

Ihsan looked at the floor again. At his boots, polished and gleaming, and thought of Makram, and the men he had seen in Saa'ra. Their dust-covered boots, stained and bloodied clothes. He would not sit and pity himself. "He's right. What will we do if Kadir marries Cemil to this woman?"

"Double down on Menei supply channels? Yavuz Pasha still has some stores in the North," Samira said, quietly in contemplation. She could not fully hide her sadness from Ihsan. Despite the ice in his power, he still had water's affinity for emotion. Cemil broke Samira's heart anew every time she saw him.

"I should marry her myself. If only to see the look on Kadir's face," Ihsan said. His brief moment of wicked amusement fizzled as he stared at the doors. He launched to his feet. That was exactly what he should do. While Kadir was preoccupied, Ihsan could snatch this victory from his fingers. Cemil had been right, in his own mocking way, that Ihsan should worry about his own marriage. He strode for the doors.

"Sehzade," Samira said in alarm, dashing after him, "you must consider all the ramifications of such a marriage. You do not have time to speak with the Sultana. Perhaps you can postpone the Council—"

He stopped, faced her, and she reeled in place, startled by his abrupt shift. Kuhzey was just behind her, appearing as alarmed as Samira. He signed his agreement with her in three sharp movements of his hands. One of them was the waver of his hand that meant *Unbalanced*.

Ihsan signed back for Kuhzey to meet him in the hall, choosing to ignore the insult. "If the only internal source of food for Tamar is controlled, even proximally, by Behram Kadir, what does that mean for Naime in the Council? With Sarkum's civil war stretching so much longer than we predicted?"

Her worried expression faltered briefly toward concession.

"There is an opportunity here to give Naime strength, rather than another blow. But what ally in the Council has a marriageable son? Yavuz Pasha already married his son to gain influence in the Northern valley. Esber Pasha's son is an absolute fool, and too greedy to be of any use."

"You do not know her, Sehzade. If Bardakci Pasha is an ally of the Grand Vizier's, then surely his daughter is as well. She could turn out to be a spy."

"Does that possibility outweigh the risk of Kadir gaining more influence over the governor of the Southern valley?"

Samira deflated a fraction, and cast her gaze away from Ihsan's. "No."

He gave a sharp nod as he turned and headed for the doors again.

"I still believe this decision to be rash and ill-advised," she called. "The Sultana will be displeased."

"I'll take your critique under advisement," he called back as he strode into the hall.

KADIR HAD NOT RETURNED TO the Council Hall when Ihsan did. Neither was Cemil present, or Mistress Bardakci. Despite his speech to Samira, Ihsan's thoughts spun, following threads to their possible ends, trying to foresee all the complications, the way Naime was able to. But his House was not air, it was water. He had always followed his gut more than his head. A great deal of good that had done him.

Cemil's face entered his thoughts. Not the taunting grin, but the expression at the end. The one that made him seem in pain. Had Ihsan interpreted that correctly?

Kadir strode through the doors at an uncharacteristically speedy pace, his staff tapping as he limped along toward the dais. The other councilors whispered. Cemil was not with him, nor was Balik Pasha. The Grand Vizier bowed at the base of the dais, then climbed to stand at Ihsan's right side.

"Forgive me for keeping you, and the Council, waiting, Sehzade."

"Where is Balik Pasha?" Ihsan ignored the apology, which Kadir did not mean, and looked at him. "Does he mean to make me wait as well?"

Kadir's lip twitched toward a sneer, but he controlled it, his gaze flashing to the doors. "As he has refused the betrothal, he has no reason to be at this Council."

"I see. Do I assume his request to annul the betrothal still stands?"

Kadir's jaw tensed, but relaxed as he forced a stiff smile and ducked his head. "My apologies for such an embarrassing waste of your, and the Council's, time, Efendim. I will return to you with a more agreeable match for Mistress Bardakci at a later date."

The whispers of the Council turned to murmurs and shifting. Urgency like frost spread through Ihsan, charging his whole body. He had a narrow chance to secure this betrothal before someone else tried to seize the same opportunity he saw.

Ihsan inhaled, an attempt to calm his racing heart and the cold of his power. This was rash, and foolish, just as Samira had said. His marriage was one of Naime's biggest concerns, outside of her father. Who he married mattered as much, if not more, as it had for her. Her control of the Council hung in the balance, and she was reluctant to force him to do what she had not had to do herself. Marry for power, instead of for love.

That thought, Naime jeopardizing all she had accomplished for his happiness, galvanized him.

"No need, Grand Vizier." The words sounded hollow and foreign coming from his own mouth. His heart was a hammer in his chest, its thumping the only sound in his ears. Ihsan met the eyes of the man he hated most in all the world, and for once, was able to smile. "As the Council has already demanded, I must take a wife of noble birth. Since Balik Pasha has insulted Bardakci Pasha with his refusal to marry his daughter, I can both accomplish the Council's demands, and lessen the insult, by marrying Mistress Bardakci myself."

Ihsan could not remember the last time he had felt the heady surge of triumph that filled him at the look of shock on Kadir's face. And was there also...panic?

"Absolutely not," the Grand Vizier blurted. Several gasps, then polite coughs of disbelief, cut the silence.

"I beg your pardon?" Ihsan scoffed. It was uncharacteristic of the man to openly defy.

"The match is wholly unsuitable for someone of your station. I cannot, in good conscious, condone such a union."

Ihsan's brows snapped together. The Council no longer bothered with polite murmurs; they chattered openly now. This was drama Ihsan had not anticipated.

"Why?" he demanded. It had to be a trick, one of his attempts to twist things to his advantage.

The Grand Vizier's fingers gripped his staff so hard they paled at the knuckles.

"You cannot mean to marry a void into the Sultan's line?" Kadir recovered from his surprise, his mien relaxing to an incredulous smile. "A void and an illegitimate son?"

Samira's fast inhale was loud enough for Ihsan to hear, and it made Kadir's smile harden.

"There was no requirement by the Council to produce an heir of magical talent." He could not respond to Kadir's baiting. "Only an heir of noble blood, and Mistress Bardakci is of noble blood, is she not?"

Kadir remained silent for a moment. The Council also quieted, their tension causing a mirrored stiffening in Ihsan's muscles. He was thinking, that much was obvious, and Ihsan needed to knock him completely off his feet.

"I do not require, nor was I asking for, your permission, Grand Vizier." Ihsan sat straighter, doing his best to mask his face and emotions. "We gave permission for Balik Pasha to marry Mistress Bardakci. He refused. No one else has asked to take his place. So I am."

"Surely you require time to speak with the Princess Sultana?" Kadir suggested with a smile tightening the corners of his eyes. "If you are so eager to fulfill the Council's marriage requirement, I am certain we can quickly produce a number of candidates more suitable than a woman with no magic."

Kadir was the most gifted liar Ihsan had ever encountered. It had always been a trial, even with Second House power, to discern lie from truth when the man spoke. But he was off-balance, perhaps as close to flustered as Ihsan had ever seen him, and though Ihsan could not identify *what* the lie was, there were lies. They clung to the man's words like hazy reflections, discordant emotions flashing in Ihsan's thoughts like mage orbs popping in and out of existence. But what was the lie, and what consequences threatened if he pushed forward with this decision?

If he could push Kadir to speak more, he might be able to tease out where the lie was, more specifically. But Kadir was too intelligent for that. He would know exactly what Ihsan was doing. He despised making a decision with this kind of uncertainty twisted up in it, but he had no other option. He had announced his intention before the Council. He had to finalize it, one way or another.

"Your only concern seems to be her lack of magic. Since that does not concern me, I see no reason not to move forward with a betrothal."

A rare silence took the hall, all eyes on Ihsan and Kadir. Kadir met his stare. Hot magic rolled off the man, igniting in his eyes. Sweat beaded on Ihsan's temples, every muscle in his body tensing.

"Efendim," Kadir said in a low growl that held no respect at all, "this woman is *not* for you."

The words were meant only for Ihsan. But it was Samira who answered, stepping between the Grand Vizier and Ihsan, bowing low to the man who had been instrumental in breaking her heart. Her answer was silence, doing nothing more than absorbing the flare of Kadir's power to allow Ihsan's head to clear.

Ihsan breathed deep and stood, pressing cold power through his body and skin to ward himself. Kadir would not bully him with his magic today, when Ihsan was winning, for once.

"If the Council cannot express a reason I find meaningful for me not to take this betrothal, then consider it done." He had an advantage Naime did not, and he knew it. They would never consider his decisions backed by nothing more than emotion. They would only make arguments against the facts or logic, never his feelings.

And they did not now. The whispers quieted, though men exchanged looks. Yavuz Pasha's expression reflected a similar set of emotions to Ihsan's. Concern, and calculation. There were so many benefits to the opportunity, it was difficult to weed through them to the repercussions.

Kadir's breath hissed between his teeth and his flare of magic died down. Samira bowed again and backed her way into place beside Kuhzey. Ihsan turned his head, meeting Kadir's gaze once more. Kadir produced a slow smile that chilled him even more than his own power.

Ihsan's feeling of triumph fizzled.

"As you wish, Sehzade."

Eight

Nesrin did not sleep.

They'd given her an actual bed. It was housed in a small room off the foyer. The room was meant to sleep four servants, but Nesrin had it to herself. The bed was small, but luxurious in comparison to the mat she shared with her sisters on the dirt floor of her home. The wooden frame creaked when she moved.

Nesrin tried to flatten the too-fluffy pillow but still it engulfed her whole head, pushing her hair into her face.

A few marks ago the steward had set out a plate of food for her to eat. Alone. Sometimes she had eaten by herself in the garden at the estate, shoving a bit of cold chicken and a flatbread round into her face on a break at work. But a full meal…no.

Here her own chewing was so loud in the empty dining room, the clatter of her movements grating on every nerve. She had barely been able to down more than a few bites. But now of course she was starving.

All those things combined to make sleep impossible. She flipped onto her back and stared up at the ceiling.

Or perhaps it was the silence. The house was unbearably quiet. She had never felt so lost, so anxious, never been alone with her thoughts and regrets in the dark. The silence in the absence of the movement, warmth, and breathing of others was suffocating. Her fears, closing in around her, the stench of fire everywhere, so she smelled it and breathed it and could not escape it.

No one had spoken to her after the Vizier rejected her. Reyhan had ushered her out of the hall, then the palace, and back to the red house. Would they send her home? As much as she wanted to return, that was fraught with problems. By taking Sanem's place, but being rejected because of her lack of magic, she had stolen the chance for them to receive money that might feed them through the Blight. And Bardakci Pasha might be furious at being embarrassed in such a way by one of his indentured.

But why had they tried to marry her to a noble? Not just a noble, a Vizier. And they had claimed her as Bardakci Pasha's daughter to do it.

Nesrin lay with those thoughts spinning around and around in her head like a vine climbing a tree, until she could bear it no more. She sat up, swinging her legs over the edge of the bed.

The house had quieted with the fall of night, but the sounds outside never did. The city carried on outside her window, which faced the main street. Carts rattled by and people shouted greetings to each other. What could they possibly be doing so late at night? She rose, her gaze skirting across the caftan, entari, and salvar that Reyhan had hung for her to wear the next day. They were brocade, which she had only ever seen, never worn until that day, stiff and heavy with the embroidery of blazing flames. The base fabric was so dark that in the wan moonlight the outfit appeared black, with slivers of blood red that shone brighter when a cloud moved away from the moon. Reyhan had chosen red for Nesrin to wear, since she was now representing the Grand Vizier's household, and not her own magic.

She tiptoed to the bedroom door and eased it open a crack. The first floor was dark but for a mage orb on its last breaths, and she saw no movement.

A lifetime of sneaking around a half dozen sleeping people served her well as she slunk from the room and toward the back of the house, and the kitchen, quiet as a mouse. Her stomach begged for food with cramps and rumbles, yet she did not know where to acquire food now.

Near the stairs, someone had left a smoking pipe and decanter for wine on the low table. The familiar scent of iron grass struck her like a slap. She'd never liked it; it was too sweet. The only teahouse in Mizraa was where most of the men spent their time after a day in the fields, smoking, laughing. Walking by it required walking through the haze of smoke and laughter. She sniffed.

Brightness flared in the moon-streaked dark.

Nesrin spun toward the couch, swallowing a shriek.

A man lounged there, one arm stretched across the backrest, one foot propped on the table, the mouthpiece of the pipe held loosely in his other hand. It was he that glowed, or rather, his eyes. Golden and fire-lit, the warmth of his magic outlining him as if the sun rose behind him. The smoke wafted in curls and ropes around him, and he exhaled a stream of it as she stood, breathless and quaking. The light faded, swathing him in darkness again, so that he was just a shape within shadows. Though now that her eyes were adjusted, she could see a dim outline of him from the moonlight.

"Little country mouse, out for a sneak. Where are you wandering, hmm?" There was fire in his voice, as there tended to be in Fifth House mages. But this was not threatening. It was hearth fire. Or she was so addled and terrified she had lost her mind and did not know a threat when she heard one.

"I..." Her voice sounded weak and afraid. Why was he lurking in the dark? She forced a smile. "I'm hungry."

He inhaled on the tube, and the smell of iron grass magnified when he exhaled again, rings of smoke drifting through a shaft of moonlight. Who was he? It was not Mahir, the steward, or the Grand Vizier.

"I am Nesrin, Master." She bowed.

He huffed. A laugh, or a snort. "I thought you said you were hungry."

She blinked, confounded. Then she understood it to be a jest and breathed her own disbelieving laugh. The man leaned forward, regarding her in the darkness. She wished she could see him better. It was difficult to speak with someone so obscured. Difficult to measure whether he was friend or tormentor.

"How do you like our city?" He hooked the tube onto the nargile.

"I have seen very little. It is…big." She could not have sounded less intelligent if she had put effort in.

"That it is," he said, dryly. "Try not to let it overwhelm your good sense, hungry mouse. Or you will find yourself in the jaws of wolves before you realize it." It was as if he were joking, but if he was, she did not understand. She thought there was a dark thread in the words. But that might just be the cloak of night, painting everything sinister. Or her jitters about the next day, and what would become of her.

"Wolves?" she echoed. "I am not afraid of wolves."

He shrugged, the movement slicing his shoulder through a blade of moonlight. She would have given all three of her stolen coins to see his face. "In Narfour, the wolves look like men."

"Like you?" Nesrin said, annoyed by his cryptic speech. He was playing with her, trying to scare her. She'd spent a lifetime with people like him. Bullies. They did not frighten her anymore.

He laughed. "Yes, just like me."

REYHAN DRESSED HER AGAIN IN the morning, in the clothes she had hung up the night before. She had questions, but Reyhan would not look at her, and did not offer any words. So Nesrin submitted to being dressed and having her hair braided and wrapped. Then she followed Reyhan from the small room, through the silent foyer, and up the stairs at the back of the home.

Nesrin tried to take in details when they emerged from the winding staircase onto the second floor but noticed only a few. A handful of cushioned benches and floor pillows. A nargile in the center of them. On the far end, glass-paneled balcony doors opened to a breeze that swept in from the ocean, briny and wet. Doors on either side of the long room, closed. A smell like hot stones.

All those things emptied from her thoughts when her gaze hit and snagged on the man standing to one side of the open balcony doors. He wore gold-embroidered red. It was the first time she had been this close to the Grand Vizier since the day her father had killed the horse that would have killed him. It brought back all the visceral memories of that day.

She had never seen that much blood on a person. And it had been everywhere. On Metin and his mangled arm, on her, on the horse, on her father. The room swam as she followed Reyhan toward him.

Her ears rang. She squeezed her hands together, to feel their solidness, to feel anything but the slippery illness writhing through her body as her memory overlayed her present. He burned. As he had the day she had first seen him. Broken on the ground, half buried beneath a horse. Red clothes, red blood, leg twisted, face flayed. Her heartbeat filled her body as she stopped, bowing mechanically as Reyhan did.

She would give anything to be away from the heat. It seared her, from his eyes, his skin, his magic, the colors of his clothes.

She remembered. Her small hands covered in red. Binding Metin's arm, bone protruding from gore. She could still feel the strain of her muscles, her fingers slipping through the mess. Her father's voice, inexplicably calm as he worked to free the man's legs from beneath the horse while giving her instructions.

It had been her grandmothers who taught her how to heal, but it had been her father that day, calm and controlled, saving lives, who made her want to. Both Metin and the Grand Vizier were changed from that day, but they were both alive. Thanks to Temel.

In her memory the Grand Vizier was limp and heavy. His face and head swollen, cut in a dozen places, dark hair matted with dirt and blood.

Now, only a crescent scar remained on his face. He was alive, standing. He could walk. He was healthy. He had aged, as she had. No longer a frightened little girl. She was grown and there was grey in his beard and hair.

Since that day she had worked on countless injuries, sewn closed wounds and washed blood from her hands. Helped to usher babies into the world, human and animal. Seen the last breaths of people she had known all her life. And now, buried half her village.

She was here to make certain her family was fed, clothed, and cared-for.

Nesrin bowed and spread her hands. Her pulse steadied more as she studied the carpet at her feet instead of the man who should be a whisper in the void. What would Sanem do in her place? Sanem had not been there that day. Had not been covered in the blood of their brother, a stranger, and a dying beast, trying to save a stranger's life while their brother screamed in panic and pain. Nesrin had survived that. She could survive this.

She straightened. She could not force a smile. Too much memory lingered, and the Grand Vizier's expression did not invite levity.

"Mistress Bardakci, Pasha," Reyhan introduced Nesrin. She left off the 'ih' that would indicate Nesrin's servitude. *Nesrin Irmak Bardakc-ih.*

A muscle twitched in the Grand Vizier's jaw as he looked at her, then his gaze lifted up and away. "Your father lied to me."

"No, Pasha," Nesrin blurted. When his gaze flicked back to hers, his dark irises were ringed in flame. Her pulse stuttered. A smile touched one corner of his mouth.

"Water mages and their ilk are such poor liars." The final *s* hissed. Nesrin inhaled through her nose.

"I wrote the letter to you, Pasha." She was a good liar. A lifetime of navigating a family of water mages forced one to be good at lying if ever they were to get away with anything. But these were terrible lies. And he knew it.

"I see. And if I compared your handwriting to the letter, they would match."

Her expression faltered, despite her attempt to hold it. He flashed his teeth in disgust as he turned his back to her to look out the glass doors. "I am being generous with my influence, and this is how your family repays me."

"The life debt…" Nesrin regretted her words immediately, even if they were true. It was not generous to repay a life debt, it was demanded by the Wheel.

"The life debt does not call for me to gamble my reputation by wedding a peasant to a noble. I have arranged things for you to marry leagues above your station. To provide your family with a means to live out their days, and for their children to live out their days, in comfort you cannot conceive of. And you"—his voice rose like sparks igniting rotten wood. But then he exhaled. And his next words were calmer—"since you have already accomplished one lie, another should not trouble you."

"My father did *not* lie." Nesrin hoped her voice tremored less than her nerves. "He asked for you to arrange a marriage to his daughter. I am his daughter." Intention, of course, mattered, and Temel had intended the marriage for Sanem. But Nesrin would not compound her problems by handing the Grand Vizier a rope to hang her with. But neither could she let any blame fall on her family for her decision, her deception.

His head canted toward her, just enough she could see his mouth flicker toward a smile despite that he faced away still. "I see you have a knack for details. That will be necessary, if you are to survive this."

"Survive what?" Nesrin glanced to Reyhan, but the woman stared at the floor. A droplet of sweat beaded against Reyhan's temple, and her expression pulled taut. Nesrin's brow furrowed.

"The Sehzade has announced his intention to wed the daughter of Osman Bardakci."

A beat of silence passed between them, where Nesrin tried to understand senseless words from a man who would not even look at her.

"Bardakci Pasha is childless."

The Grand Vizier made a sound, something like a joyless laugh, and turned to look at her.

"Bardakci Pasha has no daughters." He looked her over, as though evaluating an animal at auction, the look so piercing and disdainful that Nesrin could not think to question his odd phrasing. "Do you know who Balik Pasha is?"

"The man in the Council yesterday," she replied, as he circled her. The one who had refused her because she had no magic. They had lied about who she was then, too. This meeting was creating more questions than it answered.

Reyhan stepped out of the man's path, and what bit of safety she made Nesrin feel in the presence of the Grand Vizier shifted with her.

"He governs the land to the north of Narfour, to Golge. To the west of the mountains. Yavuz Pasha governs to the east." The Grand Vizier completed his circle and stood before her once again. The names meant nothing to her, but she understood the geography. If he was a governor, that meant he was a peer to Bardakci Pasha. Nesrin reeled anew.

The Grand Vizier's gaze bore into her, piercing, painful. His expression was fixed in concentration until suddenly it wasn't, softening, changing to a warm, welcoming smile. The change unsettled her, so she was not prepared for his next words.

"You are a smart woman, I can see it." His smile stayed fixed, lit with the warmth of the Fifth House. "I will explain to you. Balik Pasha is selfish, and greedy. For Turns he has been hounding me to arrange influence for him in the Southern valley. But he hoards what food supplies come from his holdings in the North, allowing his own people to suffer. I knew I could not let such a man have more control over what little food remains in Tamar." The Grand Vizier clicked his tongue, regret erasing his smile. "But the Council is a complicated web to navigate, and I had to appease him, lest he claim Unbalance in my dealings. So, I stretched the truth."

She waited for more. But he only watched her in a way that made her wish to squirm or run. Despite her unease, the tangle of emotions vining through her, the pieces began to align. Understanding settled with a wave of heat, then cold.

"You told him I was nobleborn. You told him I was Bardakci Pasha's daughter." The words tumbled, and she hoped, even as she said them, that she was wrong. He had tried to sentence her to an entire life of deadly lies.

This was not a repayment of a life debt. This was a trap.

His smile reanimated, this one delighted, as though she were a bright child who had solved an equation. "I did. But it was for the good of everyone, my dear."

That made no sense. Nesrin frowned. He would have found out she was not noble. Bardakci Pasha would surely not go along with such a falsehood? And what of when Balik Pasha tried to take claim in Mizraa based on her false lineage? She thought to voice her questions, but the Grand Vizier held up a hand, his smile transforming once more.

"But that is no longer the issue. Our problem is that he refused you, and the idea of your influence in Mizraa is too valuable. Another has extended a request for betrothal. Sabri Sehzade."

She could not think. She needed to sit, but he had her standing in the middle of the room, with the nearest seat several paces away. She could not simply turn and walk away from him mid-conversation.

They would have to reveal the truth to the prince. To that ice-eyed man in the Council room. And if she had learned anything of nobles in her life, it was that blame slid from them like water from a greased pole. It did not matter that this deception of her noble birth was not of her making. It would be she who paid for it. A dark runner of fear stretched, thin, spindly tendrils higher, toward her heart.

"Will I be executed?" Nesrin could barely form the words. Her anxiety burned in her eyes and her voice, made her breath quake and her skin cold.

The Grand Vizier shrugged. "Prison at the very least. The Sehzade can afford to be less harsh in your punishment than the Princess Sultana." Gravid silence punctuated the end of his declaration, heavy enough to bring her to her knees. Only the little, thorned vine of anger in her heart kept her rooted and standing.

This was not her lie. It was his. Why should she waste away in a prison for his deception?

The impassivity in his features warmed, and his smile returned. "There is a bit of fire's anger in you, some pride? That is good, I hoped there might be. You can go to prison or hang for the truth, if you wish." His smile turned conspiratory. "Or you can help me stop a tyrant. And ensure your family never wants for anything, ever again."

As with so much of what he had already said, it took long moments for her beleaguered thoughts to decipher the intent behind his words. She felt slow and dumb here, with these people, being shuffled about and bemused at every turn. Like a pastured cow suddenly thrust into a city street. But she was *not* dumb. And she could not allow them to make her feel so.

"You want me to lie to the Sehzade? To the Sultan and his family? To everyone I meet? To tell them that I"—she held up her scratched, callused hands—"am a noble daughter?" Even bathed and dressed up like a doll, no one would mistake her for nobleborn.

"Yes. Do not measure by the cost, but by the reward. The Sultana is bleeding Tamar dry of money, food, and men to fight a war that is not ours over a silly daydream she has. She has inflicted the Blight upon us by allowing Sarkum invaders to set foot on the Wheel's sacred ground."

"What does that have to do with me marrying the Sehzade?" No one spoke of the Sehzade. Everyone knew he existed, but all of the Sabris were little more than amorphous figures populating stories of the many ills of the world.

His hard eyes darkened, heat whispering beneath his skin. She remembered that too about him. A fire mage who did not hold his fire. She shuddered.

"The wife of a prince? Confidante of a man who holds the Sultana's ear, and trust?" He grinned at her as though he were surprised he had to explain. "Think of what you could do."

Do? She almost laughed. Do what? Win the Sehzade over with her tales of harvesting fruit and grain? Of shearing wool and shoveling manure? To what end? What secrets would he spill to her? It wasn't as if she would understand talk of politics and war. Or know what to do about any of it.

Perhaps he understood whatever of her thoughts showed on her face because he continued. "You underestimate the influence a woman can have over a man, whether he wishes it or not."

Did she imagine the twitch of his lips, or the bitter lining in his voice?

"You could save lives. You could be instrumental in helping me turn the tide of things in favor of Narfour. You could help stave off a revolution, merely by gaining the trust of one man. You can do that, can you not?" As if he were asking her to bake a loaf of bread.

Nesrin gripped handfuls of her caftan. "Not a man, a prince. I will reveal myself to be a fraud in every word I utter, every misstep I take. I was raised to plow fields and pick crops, not navigate court politics and palaces. And what is to happen to me when Bardakci Pasha finds out about this?"

"Bardakci will do as he is ordered. And as for your…" His pause stretched on as he surveyed her again. "…inexperience, Reyhan will continue at your side, to instruct you and guide you."

Reyhan's head snapped up. "That is not what we agreed—"

The Grand Vizier's stare flicked to her, and her words cut off in a strangled inhale. She lowered her head again, rubbing her left hand briskly over her wrist. Nesrin had thought Reyhan a servant only, but she had some kind of agreement with the Grand Vizier? Whatever that was, Nesrin could not add it to her growing stack of problems.

"I came to marry a peasant, a worker, a shopkeeper, anything. I just want to feed my family. You must know that what you are asking is impossible."

"You will feed your family. But you must learn to think bigger."

"Think bigger?" she scoffed. "I cannot be bigger. I am me. I am this." Nesrin gestured at herself, at the emaciated body beneath the borrowed finery, the girl who was accustomed to straw in her hair, not jewels. "The Wheel made me as I am, assigned me to this life. I cannot be more than what I was made to be."

"You can ensure that Narfour, and Tamar, are fed. That what remains of our own food stocks is not shipped off to foreign lands while our people starve."

It sounded noble, and it squeezed at her heart, still raw from burying so many in her village. The hungry, gaunt faces of her friends and family loomed in her mind's eye. She grit her teeth. She was the daughter of Temel Irmak, and he had gifted her with a strong back and a surfeit of common sense. This was a pretty picture the man before her was painting, but it was no truer than the clothes she wore.

"Do I have a choice?" Nesrin did not meet his gaze. There was something about it that made her squirm, and she needed all her wits. But she did watch his expression from her peripheral.

"There is always a choice, my dear. And always a consequence." He did not smile, and the look in his eyes was briefly distant.

A consequence. If she had not taken Sanem's place, Balik Pasha would not have refused the marriage. Sanem would be married to a noble, living a lie, taken from the man she loved and the family who adored her. Now, if Nesrin did not do as the Grand Vizier asked, the very best she could hope for was prison.

But would they stop with her? Would they blame her family, as if it were all conspiracy? All her father had done was ask for repayment of the life debt. All Nesrin had wanted to do was feed her family and spare her sister's heartache. She could still do that.

She closed her eyes and ducked her chin. She did not think it looked like the nod it was supposed to be, but a signal of defeat. The Grand Vizier understood.

"Excellent. Reyhan, prepare her for the ceremony."

Nine

IHSAN HOOKED A FINGER UNDER his collar and tried to force it looser. Since its tight grip on his throat was the imagined noose his looming betrothal was cinching around his neck, he was unsuccessful. The reality of it had been far away in the moment of his decision. That had been a political maneuver, pieces on a board. But now, one of those pieces was him, and the other a complete stranger, and both their lives were about to be irrevocably changed.

His father's marriage had been arranged. But Mazhar had known Lalam, even if they had not been friends before, and there had eventually been love between them, though nothing like the love between Omar and Dilay, or Naime and Makram. Ihsan thought he might be capable of the former, a friendship. But to love? That ability had burned in Wheel fire, along with his magic.

He could not bring himself to turn from the wall of latticed windows, from the balmy breeze that ghosted over his face. He had already seen her, though he could barely recall her face now. He remembered with perfect accuracy the offensive red of her clothes. And how obvious her discomfort and inexperience had been. But not her features. He was not in the habit of cataloging people's faces. They were all such fleeting presences in his life, there was little reason to note the details.

Ducking his head, Ihsan pressed fingers to the spot between his brows. This was the right political decision, but personally, it was a disaster. Which was why he'd refused to allow Naime to be present for this first meeting. She would see his distress and worry about him more, and already had far too much to concern herself with. He caused everyone he cared about nothing but worry.

"Efendim?" The quiet word came from an unfamiliar feminine voice. He bristled, ice crackling beneath his skin as he tensed and turned. But it was not her, not that woman he hardly remembered. This was her servant. She was bent forward, at just enough of an angle that he could see her tiraz with the single fire sigil embroidered in red. He clenched his fist. How long had she been there and he had not sensed her?

"Will you remain as her servant?" Ihsan hadn't meant to snap at her, but his voice projected the ice fissuring and spreading within him. She flinched, but straightened, her face still downturned. Was he also agreeing to a fire mage in his presence, every day, by agreeing to this marriage?

"I am the only one familiar to her in Narfour at this time," she said. "But of course, as it pleases you, Efendim." Her voice grated, with its unintentional hiss of fire. She grated. The color of her clothes, red and ocher, made him angry.

"What do you want?" Now he did snap on purpose.

"Forgive me." She bowed again, and this time her voice wobbled instead of hissed. "I was told you were waiting to meet my mistress. She is here." Without rising, she gestured toward the door. His gaze moved to it, but he saw no one.

"Is she?"

"She did not wish to enter without your permission."

"Just bring her in," Ihsan said. She turned and scurried for the doors.

Already a headache pulled across his skull, and he was not even betrothed yet. There was so much day left to torture him. And night. When he wasn't awake with his uncle, his sleep was plagued by nightmares. Summer's warmth always brought them back, and they were compounded by his mind racing around thoughts of the war, and the Blight, and the Sultan.

The maid returned, the Bardakci woman beside her. Watching her approach, his mind both hyper-focused on her and recoiled, refusing to allow him to make sense of anything.

She was a stranger.

The full weight of his decision crashed onto him, each realization of the ramifications a boulder slamming into his back. No longer would he have any privacy when he needed it. She would be in his home. No longer could he escape functions, unnoticed—she would be on his arm. Witness to all his weaknesses, all his failings. And she would have expectations of him, this person who knew nothing about him.

The crushing pressure of it shattered his hold on the ice, and it blossomed up his neck and the floor around his feet. His panted breath fogged the air in front of him.

She stopped. Her gaze darted. From the fractals of ice creeping away from his boots to his hands, where the fog of his power billowed like his breath. Then she focused on his face, and he waited for the inevitable moment where she registered his scars. He waited to see discomfort, or pity. Sometimes it amused him, to see people come undone with trying to decide how to interact with someone so scarred. Today, he knew it would enrage him.

Only, nothing about her changed. No twitch in her mien, no flinch, no flash of disgust or pity. Perhaps his angle had hidden the worst of it from her. She bowed, then rose, then she stood silent. She was close enough, perhaps ten steps away, that he could look at her as he had not during her introduction in the Council. Her perceptive silence allowed him a chance to control his temper, then the ice. His control gave him capacity to observe.

She wore makeup, and ill-fitting clothes. All of it meant to hide how fragile-looking she was. Spoke-thin. Her cheeks were sunken, her skin missing the color that the dull russet of her hair suggested she should have. Dark circles ringed her eyes, despite the makeup. His temper retreated.

She was starving. She was afraid. He had thought her silence a decision to please him, but now he recognized the truth of it. He frightened her. The anger resurfaced. He turned aside and strode past her and out the door.

WHEN HE WAS GONE, NESRIN released her held breath. She sucked in another that rattled with a controlled sob. She sank to the floor, curling her trembling hands into the stiff fabric of her entari.

"Get up," Reyhan ordered, hooking a hand beneath Nesrin's arm and tugging. "Princesses do not sit on the floor."

"Did you see the way he looked at me?" Nesrin said. "He hates me."

"He hates everyone," Reyhan grunted as she forced Nesrin to her feet. "It is the best we could hope for. Think of the alternative, if he were fascinated by you, and wanted to know everything about you." Reyhan examined Nesrin's backside as she spoke, brushing away dust from the floor. Nesrin spun away in indignation, repeating Reyhan's motion with her own hands.

"Don't *do* that." Nesrin glared.

Reyhan glared back. "Do you think this is a game?"

"No, I—"

"You will learn to walk, talk, and act correctly, whether by choice, or by fire." Reyhan spoke a word and a flame erupted over her hands, then died to encompass only her finger. "Now"—she pointed that flame-tipped finger—"follow him."

Nesrin balked. "I do not believe he wished to be followed."

"You are expected. Head up." Reyhan jabbed the candleflame of magic between Nesrin's shoulder blades. "Back straight." When Nesrin flinched away from the touch, she added, "Pretend you have some pride."

Nesrin turned a disbelieving, open-mouthed stare on the woman, who simply reached forward and flicked Nesrin's chin. She closed her mouth. Reyhan gave a critical visual sweep. She tugged at Nesrin's entari and readjusted the carnelian fabric that wrapped her waist. She picked at a bit of lint on the shoulder, then twisted Nesrin toward the doors.

They walked side by side, their silence charged. Reyhan guided her back down the hall and into another room. This one had tables set up against one wall, which was comprised entirely of arched windows that looked out over cliffs that dove into the sea. The Sehzade was there, and when Nesrin tried to whirl back around, Reyhan stopped her with another jabbed finger to her back.

They entered a room at the end of a sunlit hallway, through a set of doors that were only decorative, as they were openwork lattice, a masterpiece of vining flowers carved into wood of a reddish hue. Oak? Or cedar, perhaps. Distracted by the beauty of it, Nesrin almost tripped when Reyhan caught her by the sleeve.

"Bow," she whispered, dropping forward. Nesrin complied without seeing who she was bowing to. That, at least, came easy to her. She had spent her life bowing to everyone else.

"Efendim"—Nesrin recognized the Grand Vizier's voice—"it is my pleasure to introduce Mistress Nesrin Bardakci, void, daughter of Osman Bardakci Pasha, Governor of Mizraa, to you."

It took her a moment to hear her own name after she heard the honorific, amongst all the fancy titles. Amongst the lies. She tasted bile as she stared at the marble and her too-tight shoes. *Efendim*. There were only three people in the palace who would go by that honorific, and one of them had just walked away. That left the Sultan, or his daughter.

"It is a pleasure to meet you, Mistress Bardakci," a glacial, feminine voice said.

Denial left Nesrin lightheaded as she straightened and met the eyes of the speaker. She was clothed in ice white, with shining black hair braided and wrapped around her head, a sapphire nestled against the perfectly smooth skin of her brow, eyes like cinnamon. Nesrin reeled for a moment, thoughts whirling, as the Sultana stared impassively at her, beautiful, and cold.

Nesrin tried to speak, to acknowledge her. But words dammed at her lips. A sense of being buried beneath the lies she had to tell squeezed the air from her lungs. Her legs began to shake. The room seemed to spin a tipped circle.

It was already too much that she had to lie to a prince. To a Sival of the Second House. How had she not realized her lie would extend to the entire Sabri family? The Sultan and his daughter? Nesrin stiffened, panicked enough to run. She was a lie to all of Narfour.

The Grand Vizier's hand closed on her wrist. Pain lanced up her arm in heated warning, from his fingers to her throat and into her skull. Green light burst behind her eyes. The morass swirling at her feet yawned wide, spun up, and tried to swallow her. Her vision dimmed, and she swayed, her thoughts narrowing to a pinpoint of horror.

She took an unsteady step back, away from the Grand Vizier's fire-laced grip, trying to clear her head, and bumped into someone. A blast of wintry clarity banished the pain of the fire and the muddle of her own thoughts. Magic. Like water. Like the brisk, refreshing press of her mother's, but different. Chilled. Barren.

Lonely.

The Grand Vizier released his grip on her with a hissed curse, snapping a glare behind her.

Nesrin angled her head back, slowly, eyes lifting as well.

She had backed right into the Sehzade, who must have returned during her introduction to the Princess Sultana. Her head was now tipped against his chest. He did not look at her, and a muscle in his jaw ticked. This close, she could see the details of the scars that spread up his neck and right jaw. They reminded her of the burn scars she had seen on the smith's arms, as well as on Bardakci Pasha's hands. But fire could not burn a water mage.

His hands closed on her shoulders and pushed her away, but the net of glass beads Reyhan had arranged so carefully over her hair snagged in the button of his entari, and she gasped as it pulled, tugging painfully on her hair. Everyone stared at her, mutely, as surprised by her ineptitude as she was. She lifted her hands, covering first her mouth, then her entire face, and gave the tiniest of whimpers. The Sehzade made a noise that sounded suspiciously like a snort of amusement. Or impatience. Surely the latter. Nesrin hunched her shoulders as she turned and bent forward to prevent pulling it all into a mess.

"Shall I assist?" he asked, dryly.

"Wheel, no," she breathed, then cleared her throat. "No, thank you, Sehzade."

But when she reached for the button so did he, and their fingers tangled together. His hands were cold. Tears of humiliation stung along with a hysterical giggle, which hiccupped past her gritted teeth.

"Let me," he said, impatiently flicking her hands away. Reyhan appeared at her side with a murmured apology to the Sehzade and had Nesrin freed with a few expert twists. She made quick work of tidying Nesrin's hair, then stepped back with a bow, eyes trained on the floor. Nesrin's gaze skated across the Grand Vizier's face as she shuffled from between the Sultana and Sehzade, but it was relaxed and unreadable.

"Do you wish for this marriage?" the Sultana asked Nesrin, apparently willing to overlook her clumsiness. The truth welled. No. She did not wish to spend the rest of her life lying. No, she did not want to marry a stranger, this man who clearly did not want anything to do with her, and who was, apparently, part of the reason for this war. But there was no other way now.

"I want to do what is best for my family, Efendim." That was truth. *That* was how to lie in the presence of a water mage. Still, she could not look at the Sehzade, could not bear to see if he recognized her duplicity. Or the Sultana.

"Nesrin is a most filial daughter," the Grand Vizier said, in a jovial tone.

"Forgive my prying questions, but why is your father not here to present you?" the Sultana asked, as if the Grand Vizier had not spoken.

"Efendim, the valley is in dire straits," the Grand Vizier said, saving Nesrin from embarrassing herself further. "The northern half is decimated by Blight, half their working force is away with the Princess Sultana's betrothed, at war." He waved his hand as if to dismiss his weaponized comments. Nesrin took a surreptitious look at the Sultana's face, which revealed nothing of her thoughts. "And late spring is a critical time for farms and orchards. He could not leave the estate, and asked me to see to the care of his daughter in his stead. I have a letter with his seal here."

The Grand Vizier produced an envelope from the pocket of his entari and held it out.

The Sultana watched Nesrin as she took the envelope from the Grand Vizier. The woman's critical gaze turned Nesrin inside out, examining, weighing, judging. Nesrin's stomach, cued, perhaps, by the smell of charred meat that drifted from the tables, growled. The silent room amplified the sound. If the Wheel had given her the option to turn to ash and blow away at that moment, Nesrin would have happily accepted it. Heat shot up her neck and into her cheeks. She could not bear to look at the Sehzade, so her gaze landed instead on the Sultana's.

Something in the other woman's expression softened, her gaze flicking over Nesrin, critical still, but this time, observant. Surely she could not see Nesrin's bony frame, not beneath folds and frills and voluminous fabric. But perhaps she could see past whatever threat she saw in

Nesrin to the sunken cheeks, that the dark circles around her eyes were not for lack of sleep and her skin was not naturally so sallow.

"Samira, please invite the others to join us and celebrate. It is time to eat," the Sultana said. The woman beside her, a beautifully fiery counterpart to the Sultana's cold beauty, bowed and hurried from the room. "As our honored guest, please help yourself first," she added.

The last was a command, though it held no pity. Perhaps the woman saw nothing of what Nesrin had thought, and she simply did not want the crass sound of an empty belly in her palace.

Nesrin bobbed another bow and turned stiffly toward the table. The Sehzade's gaze followed her as she moved away, but she could not bring herself to look at him. Reyhan moved at her side as Nesrin left the nobles behind her.

In trepidation, she took stock of the tables of food. The smells made her mouth water, the artful arrangements of colors, shapes, and textures more overwhelming than beautiful to her. There were skewers of meat, and sculpted mounds of kibbeh. Platters of tabbouleh and mountains of falafel. Vegetables carved into shapes surrounded oil-drizzled puddles of labneh. Pitchers of jewel-toned fruit juices stood by a tray of blown-glass cups in a rainbow of colors.

More nobles had begun to trickle in, but still. Even if all the men she had seen in the Council attended, this was too much food. The arrangement could feed her entire village.

She could not eat these things. The fruit, polished and gleaming, some whole, some sliced and placed decoratively around the table, had likely come from Mizraa. She might have picked some of it with her own dirty, callused hands. The grain to make the kibbeh and the chickpeas to make the falafel belonged to the people who had grown it, harvested it, then had to watch it be taken away to feed these nobles while they themselves starved. While their children and elders wasted away. While mothers wept over whether their babies would survive.

Her heart beat against her ribs like the hard rhythm of a war drum.

She stifled an urge to pick up an apple and hurl it at the first noble she laid eyes on. "I am not hungry," Nesrin whispered, her throat closing with emotion.

"You are. I saw you almost faint." Reyhan's words were not kind, they were judgment. Nesrin reached for an apple, but Reyhan batted her hand away. "Those are decoration," she whispered, blocking everyone's view of Nesrin's blunder with her body. Hunger tangled with her anger. Decoration.

"What is done with this food after?" Nesrin asked in a matching whisper.

Reyhan's demeanor shifted, the passivity of her expression wavering as she looked at Nesrin, her gaze flicking to her feet and back. She shrugged, looking away. "Given to the servants, or tossed, perhaps. That is not your concern."

"Not my concer—" Nesrin's voice rose, and Reyhan snagged her by the wrist to silence her, casting a quick glance behind at the huddle of nobles. She shoved a plate into Nesrin's hand and used a spoon to dish a few choices onto it.

"You were told to eat. Do it. Temper tantrums win no battles in the palace."

Reyhan turned her back on the table, and Nesrin stared out the windows, trying to collect her emotions into something tidy and manageable. The sea crashed below them. She could hear it, now that she was listening, even with the windows closed. She had never heard that sound, something so elemental, so powerful. She might as well be a poppyseed in that seething froth below, she would be just as ineffectual there as she was here.

After she had forced down a perfectly crisp patty of falafel and taken a moment to be certain it was going to stay down, she turned to face the room.

"Thank her," Reyhan breathed, her head lowered demurely, as adept at whispering as an air mage casting her voice.

"Thank you for your generosity, Princess Sultana. I am..." Nesrin's gaze hung on the Sehzade's. "...overwhelmed." While impassive, his expression was not as devoid of emotion as the Sultana's. No water mage could do what an air mage could, and close themselves off completely. Though the ice in his expression was a good stand-in for his cousin's stoicism.

A glimmer of a polite smile darted across the Princess Sultana's mouth, and she ducked her chin. She took the Sehzade's arm and the two of them walked across the room to stand with three other men, presumably Viziers.

"Reyhan," the Grand Vizier half said, half growled, "your new mistress will not bumble like that again, will she?" He did not look at either of them. Reyhan threw herself forward in a deep bow.

"No, Pasha."

He strode away, his steward at his side, leaving only Nesrin and Reyhan by the tables. When he had joined the Sehzade and Sultana, Nesrin reached for a pitcher of water studded with slices of lemon. Her hands trembled as she drank from a cup of swirled blue and green glass.

"I cannot possibly do this," she breathed, mostly to herself.

"It is too late for that," Reyhan admonished. When Nesrin looked over her shoulder at the other woman, she accused, "Our fates are bound together now."

"Oh, not that—" Nesrin began in horror. She had come precisely to spare anyone else the fate of being bound up in something they didn't want. Not to ensnare strangers.

"*What*"—Reyhan's dark eyes narrowed—"do you think is the punishment for lying to the royal family?" The words were barely audible, but they had the intended effect. Nesrin's head swam again at the implications. "Learn, farmgirl, and learn fast."

Ten

She and the Sehzade walked around the sprawling room, he introducing her to a dizzying collection of men and women who only registered as blurry faces and a scourge of powerful mages. They did not look at each other or speak to each other. They did not touch, though she wondered if she was supposed to hook her arm through his, as she saw some of the others doing. But Reyhan did not prompt her to, and the Sehzade did not offer.

Reyhan did keep pressing small plates of food toward Nesrin, appearing every few introductions to force some new tidbit upon her. Nesrin could not even taste it anymore. She kept eating. To make the appearance of normalcy. Of courtesy. But the food was rich. She was full. Had been full at three bites. It was more food than she had seen in nearly a Great Turn. She'd cut back harder than the rest of her family, in secret. Because it took energy to fuel magic—extra energy that Nesrin did not need. But now her body rebelled. Her stomach felt stretched, and cramped around the weight of the food.

Nesrin excused herself from the Sehzade's side, though she doubted he noticed.

"I need water," she said to Reyhan, despairing at the saliva coating the inside of her mouth. Reyhan's first reaction was indignance, but it passed when she looked at Nesrin's face. She must be pale. Her skin was cold beneath a sheen of sweat. Reyhan pointed, and led her to a table set with pitchers of juice and water. Lemons and cucumbers floated in the water. If she had felt less nauseated it might have been one more thing to set her on edge. Food wasted to flavor perfectly good water. But her desperation quieted her righteousness, and she gulped at the glass Reyhan poured for her. She paced as she slowed her drinking, trying to walk away the feeling that she was going to be ill.

"Are you all right?" Reyhan whispered. She glanced around anxiously, likely trying to see who had noticed Nesrin's obvious distress. Nesrin swallowed, but it did nothing to stave off the tingles racing up her neck. No, there was no stopping it.

"I need outside. Now." She set her glass on the table and Reyhan, Wheel bless her, did not argue. She hooked her hand through Nesrin's elbow and guided her, as quickly and discreetly as possible, through a side door Nesrin had not noticed.

Her stomach swooped and she clapped a hand over her mouth as bile bubbled into it. Not on the floor...please not on the floor. She clenched her teeth. Reyhan pulled her faster once they were out of the crowd, and led her through a dark, windowless servants' hall. They burst through a door into the sunlight, and Nesrin surged out of Reyhan's grip. She made it three steps away from the tiled walkway and next to a bush. She retched before she'd fully bent forward, and some made it down her chin and onto her borrowed clothes.

It had been Turns since Nesrin vomited. She forgot how truly awful it was. Her whole body ached with the cramping, and she panted for breath when she was done, swallowing and coughing as her stomach continued to twist and contract.

Tears dribbled down her cheeks and her nose ran as a headache pounded through her face. Braced with her hands on her knees, all she could do was breathe and spit the vile taste from her mouth. She wiped her nose against her sleeve, then realized what she had done and tried to brush the foulness off the cloth as she straightened.

Someone giggled. Nesrin's immediate thought was Reyhan, but when she snapped a look at the mage, her eyes were round with horror. Nesrin glanced around. Reyhan had brought her to a pocket of garden within the palace, open on all sides to walkways that led to the palace interior. Two noblewomen stood in the corner farthest from Nesrin. That put them only twenty or so paces away, close enough to witness her humiliation. They whispered to each other, eyes locked on Nesrin, one with a sly grin, the other a pursed-lipped look of disdain.

Reyhan stepped into Nesrin's line of sight, blocking the women from view.

"Quickly, that way," she urged, pushing Nesrin toward the door they had emerged from. Nesrin went, silent with her shame. "If we are lucky," Reyhan added, "they don't know who you are and will not remember your face."

"I've never been particularly lucky," Nesrin muttered.

"Nor I," Reyhan said, her voice bitter as nettles. She did not speak again as she led Nesrin through a maze of halls. The sour smell emanating from her clothes made Nesrin nauseated enough to vomit again. Did she have to return to the gathering like this? Her eyes and cheeks burned. Her throat was raw. Her gut empty and aching. All she wanted was to find a quiet corner, away from prying eyes, and collapse.

Reyhan stopped abruptly in front of a set of double doors. She pushed them open. Nesrin hesitated in the doorway even though Reyhan strode right in. A lavish sitting room sprawled before Nesrin, larger than her home in Mizraa. Glass doors flanked by arched windows lined the far wall, thrown open to yet another garden. Daylight made the white and teal colors of the room seem to glow. This was a room for water.

"What is this?" Nesrin said it like an accusation. Reyhan had already crossed the space, footsteps silent on plush carpets of blue, turquoise, and silver. The fire mage pushed open a narrow set of doors at the far left of the room.

"The Sehzade's palace residence," Reyhan said. "You will be staying in these rooms for the duration of your betrothal. It is customary so that it can be assured the betrothal is a good match. Before committing to marriage."

She was going to be sick again. The tingling warning crawled over her scalp. Nesrin dashed for the doors to the garden and made it to the edge of the patio. Her stomach cramped and rolled, but little came up. Just more bile to coat her mouth. She spit it out, then grimaced.

Reyhan did not follow, and Nesrin was grateful for the privacy, at least for the moment. She squatted, rubbing the heel of her palm against her brow as she tried to settle herself. She drew three deep breaths, filling her lungs with the green, earthy scent of the garden air, touched with the brine of the ocean. What was she doing here? She had never even had nightmares as mad as this.

"Get up! Do not squat like a farmwife at the cows. And noblewomen do not spit." Reyhan grabbed her arm. She hauled her to her feet, dragging her inside before she had time to even collect herself to walk. Nesrin stumbled after the other woman.

"What am I supposed to do then?"

"Swallow it." Reyhan took her into a side room off the sitting area and released her grip.

"That's disgusting."

"Disgusting is relative." Reyhan moved efficiently, laying out a clean entari on the bed then going to work on the clasps of Nesrin's soiled one. Nesrin batted her hands away and undid the buttons herself. Reyhan set her jaw as she grabbed Nesrin's wrists and forced them away so she could complete the task. "Do you think the court cares about your comfort? No." Reyhan moved behind her and stripped the entari from Nesrin's arms. "They care about appearances, and decorum, and self-control. Of which you have very little." She held out a new entari, this one more muted, earthy carnelian that did not exactly match the salvar that Nesrin wore.

"Of which?" Nesrin demanded as Reyhan surveyed her clothes with irritation. She had always thought she had a great deal of self-control.

"All of them," Reyhan said dispassionately. She turned her back on Nesrin's nettled expression and went to a wardrobe in the corner of the room. She rummaged through it but came away with nothing. When she returned to Nesrin, she lifted up the edge of the clean entari and held it against her own leg, then clicked her tongue.

Reyhan unwound the cloth tied about her own waist and stepped out of her shoes. Then she shoved her hands under Nesrin's entari and her fingers worried at the knot that held the salvar around Nesrin's hips.

"Stop that!" Nesrin jerked backwards.

"Then take them off," Reyhan snapped, stripping out of her own salvar and laying them out on the bed.

"You want me to wear yours?" Nesrin frowned. How was that a solution?

"Noblewomen do not wear soiled or unmatched clothes. These are a better match." She held a hand out for Nesrin's salvar. "Hurry up. You have already been gone too long and they'll be talking."

Defeated, Nesrin did as told, shifting everything around to get out of the salver quickly and into Reyhan's. The waist sagged, slipping down over the protruding bones of Nesrin's hips. Reyhan was curvy, but not so much more than Nesrin had once been, until lack of food had stripped her of her own muscle and curves.

The fire mage's agitated expression faded as she finished setting her own clothes in order. Nesrin turned away from the woman's stare, tugging the pants around her hips again and yanking the ties as tight as they would go. The pants still fell awkwardly over Nesrin's ankles and slippers.

"Let me," Reyhan said, more gently than she had spoken since Nesrin met her. "Hold this." She lifted the caftan and entari up and

Nesrin held them out of the way, her face burning. Reyhan put everything in order, tugging the pants and rolling the waistline under so they fell more neatly around Nesrin's legs before tying them in place. "I thought things were bad in the city." Her voice was soft, and she continued working without meeting Nesrin's eyes.

"Everything we grow comes here or is taken by soldiers heading to Sarkum. Seeing what use it is put to here only makes me angry."

Reyhan paused in the middle of setting the caftan in order, her gaze lifting to Nesrin's face then back to her task. She tucked everything into place and rewrapped the vermilion cloth belt in a way that added volume to Nesrin's middle. "The food in the palace is grown in our sun houses or from stores already in the city. The Princess Sultana avoids using goods from Mizraa as much as possible."

Nesrin frowned, but Reyhan straightened with an exasperated sound. "How can you know so little?"

"Because I do not belong in a palace," Nesrin reminded her. "Ask me about plants. Ask me about seasons and stubborn horses. How to soothe a cough or birth a child. Politics do not matter to me and mine."

"They matter. You just do not realize it." Reyhan's voice returned to stone. "Go." She pointed toward the door and the sitting room. Nesrin plodded where Reyhan guided, like the livestock she had become. Reyhan cut in front of her and strode through the room. Nesrin followed, keeping her eyes on Reyhan's back. She could not look at the space, or ponder the implications of its decor or Reyhan's pronouncement that she would—live here. It was only more absurdity piled on to the fiasco that had begun when she left the valley.

Her. Living in a prince's palace quarters. Not as a maid, which would have been ludicrous in and of itself. She could never do what Reyhan did every day. Dressing perfectly competent adults, following them around sweeping up crumbs. Nesrin had never thought of the hard labor in her life as a kind of freedom. But at least it was free of those particular humiliations. Metin would be rolling in laughter to see her playacting at being a noble. Rather, *failing* at playacting a noble.

"Chew this," Reyhan said as she twisted a bit of parsley from a bouquet on a table by the door to the hall. Nesrin wrinkled her nose. "Your breath." Reyhan shook the sprig. "Are you going to question me on everything? This is only more excruciating for your intractable confusion."

Nesrin snatched the herb from Reyhan's fingers and shoved it in her mouth, chewed it, then blew a puff of air in Reyhan's face. The woman recoiled, her cheeks brightening.

"Better?"

They glared at each other for a beat before Reyhan's mouth twitched, perhaps toward a smile. Or a sneer.

The door flew open and they both wheeled toward it in guilty silence. The Sehzade stood there, his face reflecting first surprise, then confusion, then something Nesrin would have described as horror.

"What are you doing in here?" he demanded, his hand dropping from the door handle. Nesrin started to reply, but Reyhan moved in front of her and dropped into a bow.

"Mistress Bardakci wished to change before the ceremony, Sehzade."

His gaze flashed around the suite, as though he thought she might have ransacked his rooms. Then it flitted across her and her clothes. A judgmental frown that rivaled one of Beyza's best soured his expression. "If you insist on changing every candlemark, feel free to choose a less offensive color next time."

He moved aside, a signal for them to leave, and once they had shuffled into the hall, he entered the room and slammed the door.

Eleven

Ihsan had practically begged Naime to hold the ceremony in the relative privacy of the receiving hall, but they both knew that was impossible. A crowd had gathered at the Morning Gate. Not as large as the one that had assembled when Naime had been meant to choose a suitor, but enough to make him feel like a parade horse on display. His marriage belonged as much to the people of Tamar as it did to him, if he could even claim it belonged to him. The fact that he was about to be betrothed to a noblewoman no one had heard of would keep the city gossips busy until winter.

He doubted very much that a foreign general was going to arrive at the last moment to save him from marriage, but he was not above hoping.

He trudged down the steps from the palace entrance to cross the gravel courtyard. The exchanges of the crowd gathered beyond the line of palace guards rose in volume as he approached the ceremony.

The temporary dais was set up beneath a wood and gold frame draped with cloth in blue and silver to shade its occupants from the glare of the morning sun. The Sultan's absence was notable, but not unexpected. Even when he was well enough to leave his rooms, he was too unpredictable to be around anyone but a trusted inner circle of servants and family. Ihsan buried the twinge of emotion before he could acknowledge it, knowing that to feel it fully would send him spiraling into a swamp of anger and self-pity.

Naime sat upon a silk-upholstered bench in his place, Kadir standing beside her. Samira stood at the back of the dais, and the rest of Naime's attendants were arrayed in a fan behind it. To the right, benches were arranged for the Viziers to sit upon, the front row of them occupied by those with daughters who might have been candidates for marriage. Their fathers sat beside them. They were arranged in order by House, from air to Mistress Bardakci, at the end, wearing red as though she represented the Fifth. An involuntary shudder left gooseflesh on his skin as he took his own seat to Naime's left.

Nearly all the noble families of Narfour were represented, standing behind the benches of Viziers, conversing, though that quieted as Ihsan approached the dais. He bowed. When he rose, Naime nodded to him, her usual mask in place. But he had known her all her life, and he could see the turmoil in her eyes. Her worry made him doubt himself, his decision. But it was the best political decision that could be made under the circumstances, and as far as the romance angle, there was little that could be done for that. He turned away before he could sink too deeply into his worries.

The women sat across from him, only paces between them. He could feel their stares, the shimmer of their emotions as scratches across the ice of his magic. Nothing so clear that he could put name to it, but the discomfort that rose in him as ripple effect suggested a mix of resentment and relief.

Except her, Nesrin. She sat alone, with a space between her and the next candidate, her hands clasped in her lap, her face turned down enough that he could not see her eyes. Seeing Nesrin alone like that, with no father to present her, plucked at his emotions. His father was not there, nor his uncle. His mother should have been there to bind him, but neither his birth mother, nor Lalam, the one who loved him as if he were her own, were alive to do so. Not even Dilay, who had tried so hard to mend his broken soul.

Loneliness overtook him so swiftly he had to swallow a sound. No one seemed to notice him hitch forward a fraction.

Nesrin's head came up, her gaze fixing on his, and for the briefest moment his own pain reflected in her eyes. A flicker of a frown touched her mouth then her lips parted, recognition softening her features. He looked away. That had to be a poor omen, two people being betrothed without the balance of parents to link them.

Attendees who had still been conversing or standing sat abruptly when Kadir stepped forward and hammered the end of his jeweled staff against the dais. He bowed to the Sultana before announcing the beginning of the ceremony. He gestured to the Viziers and their daughters, then retreated a step on the dais. They stood, beginning with Yavuz Pasha and his daughter, Hazal. It was customary for the Viziers to name their assets and the reasons they would be a suitable match, as they had for Naime, but since Ihsan had blurted his decision in Council, Yavuz Pasha only offered his well wishes and sat back down. His daughter, Hazal, sat primly. Her gaze flitted to Ihsan's, then quickly away, and her cheeks colored.

Bahar Pasha and his daughter, Ekim, stood next, sitting again after bowing. Ekim fluffed at her caftan and entari in agitation, refusing to look toward the dais at all.

Ihsan itched to rub his hand over his face, to wipe away the feel of the stares. Instead he flexed it open and gripped his knee, as the next Vizier-and-daughter pair stood, bowed, and sat.

When it was Nesrin's turn, Kadir took a step forward.

"It is my honor to present Mistress Nesrin Bardakci ilr Mizraa, daughter of Osman Bardakci, in her father's stead. The Bardakci family governs Mizraa and the surrounding Southern valley." He paused, because she hadn't stood. Nesrin checked around, her neck reddening, then sprang from her seat. Some quiet chuckles and whispered disapproval stirred through the gathered nobles, and she dropped her gaze to her feet.

Either she was clumsy and dimwitted, or just unpracticed at ceremony and formality. The latter would not surprise Ihsan, considering where she came from. And he dearly hoped it was the latter. It was sentence enough that she was a stranger, but he could not abide a lifetime with someone lacking sense.

Kadir finished his introduction, and Nesrin sat back down, cheeks ruddy and expression miserable. Ihsan felt for her, he did. But court was brutal for everyone. Hopefully she would learn that lesson quickly.

When Kadir stepped back, Naime stood. Her hands were folded at the front of her entari, her smile stiff, gaze stony. She was braced for the backlash of announcing his betrothal to a void.

"It is an honor to have such respected families offer their most precious daughters in marriage to the Sehzade. The Sultan has given his blessing for the betrothal of Sabri Sehzade to Mistress Bardakci of Mizraa. May their union spin the Wheel for unity and acceptance in this time of turmoil and bring joy and prosperity to Tamar and her people."

Ihsan stood as stilted applause rose then faded, and Nesrin did too, watching him from the corners of her eyes. Perhaps he should have thought to ask her if she understood the ceremony. It seemed Kadir had not prepared her.

Samira strode from the back of the dais, with two younger maids in tow, each holding two cushions. She stopped between Naime and Kadir, offering a tray with a rope and a ribbon laid upon it. The two servant girls continued forward, placing the velvet pillows on a carpet laid over the gravel in front of the dais. The cushions formed a square, and Ihsan knelt on one.

Nesrin lowered to her knees on the pillow opposite him, her gaze flitting, to him, to the servants, to the cushions, reined panic widening her eyes. She tried to hide it with a downturned face, but he could see the rapid rise and fall of her ribs, feel the emotion ticking against his magic like a claw on ice. That feeling only aggravated his own sense of unease, the anxiety tightening a band around his chest.

Naime took the ribbon and rope from the tray and descended the dais, with Kadir limping behind. She knelt on the cushion to Ihsan's left, and Kadir circled them to the final one. No one spoke as he painstakingly lowered himself, having to manually bend his knee to kneel. Nesrin shifted as though she meant to offer him aid, but her servant gave the tiniest of hissed breaths, and Nesrin clenched her hands in her lap.

Ihsan extended his upturned hands into the space between them all. Nesrin stared for a moment, as she wound and unwound her fingers together, a little wrinkle settling across her brow when she lifted her hands and set them in his. It was a whisper of a touch, the tips of her fingers lighting on the heels of his palms, his longer fingers skimming the underside of her wrists. The touch struck him as unexpectedly intimate, and a tingle spread up his fingers. Her hands were unusually warm, their heat radiating down to his skin, something that normally sent him spiraling into a frenzy of tension. But this heat was…different.

He looked to her eyes. They were focused on him, and the corners of her mouth twitched shyly toward a smile. Her eyes were pretty. Wide, common hazel leaning more toward green than brown. They held a suggestion of genuine warmth, buried beneath the nervous tension of her expression and body. Ihsan looked down.

"The Wheel severs us and brings us together, circles broken and remade. In marriage we are a circle unbreakable, one for another"—Naime laid the ribbon over Nesrin's right wrist and held the jute rope to Kadir as she spoke—"and the other for one. Be betrothed and be bound, in glorious celebration of the Wheel."

Kadir dropped the rope over Nesrin's left wrist. Her hands twitched, her fingertips pressing to Ihsan's palms, and the tingle zinged harder, more like the sizzle of magic than the surprise of touch. Nesrin blinked, and a glint of sun flashed green in her irises.

"Silk, for the soft, and the gentle," Naime continued. "For the strength to hold each other up." Her voice faded in his awareness as he concentrated on Nesrin's hands in his. The touch was unsettling, unfamiliar yet also grounding. Naime knotted the ribbon loosely around their wrists. Nesrin's breath whistled out, and she blinked rapidly, staring blankly down.

"And hemp, for hardship," Kadir said. "For that which can be frayed by time and negligence unless it is cared-for." He knotted it. Ihsan's attention was drawn to the man's fingers, which he would have sworn were trembling. But before he could confirm it, Kadir and Naime stood.

When Naime returned to the dais, she announced the ceremony complete. The crowd applauded politely, if not enthusiastically.

Ihsan extracted his hands from the loops. Nesrin sat obediently still as he untied the hemp to retie it in a larger circle, which he hung over her bowed head. She followed suit with the ribbon, slipping it off his wrist and making a larger circle with quick, dexterous fingers. The skin of her hands bore a smattering of freckles. She held the ribbon necklace out and he bowed his head. Nesrin leaned forward and slipped it over his head. The briefest brush of her fingertips along his collar as she settled the ribbon caressed his skin with the same invigorating warmth he had felt from her hands. Not warmth like fire. Something else.

He must be more anxious than he'd thought, to have such an exaggerated reaction to the proximity of a woman he barely knew.

In a normal betrothal, the parents of those betrothed would mingle in the crowd, accepting congratulations, but since neither of their parents were present, the crowd swiftly dispersed. Fitting, his betrothal was as unnoticeable as the rest of his existence.

Nesrin touched the hemp rope around her neck, lightly, then drew away as if it burned her. She stood before he could offer a hand.

He should speak to her. But what to say? She bowed to him as he rose. Behind her, three of the Viziers stood with their daughters and wives. He could not hear their conversation, nor did he particularly care, but a few words drifted to him. One of them was "backbred," the descriptor used for people who showed lineage of trade-route ancestors, as she did, in her hair and eyes. This was delivered like a slur.

Nesrin straightened, eyes downcast, her hands falling to her sides in fists.

"What was that, Bahar Pasha?" Ihsan said. He did not have Naime's power to amplify his voice with magic, but he spoke loudly enough that everyone around him glanced his way. Bahar Pasha, whose back was to him, twitched in surprise, and his wife and daughter froze in guilty silence. The Vizier turned slowly, and smiled broadly as he bowed.

"I was expressing my pleasure to see you finally betrothed, Sabri Sehzade." His family bowed as well.

Ihsan did not reply, only stared at the Vizier until he jerked another bow then waved his family in the opposite direction. When Ihsan looked at Nesrin, her face was flushed, her breaths fast. She glanced aloft, then turned away. He did not know what to say to her still, and before he could try, she fled to her maid halfway across the courtyard and stood beside her. Wonderful.

Ihsan blew out a breath. While he had not spent a great deal of time envisioning what sort of woman he might marry, he had never imagined someone timid, who would run from him every chance she got.

Gravel shifted beneath the footfalls of someone approaching his back. "She will warm up to you, surely." Naime stopped beside him.

"Unlikely," Ihsan muttered. Time did not improve most of his relationships. His cousin sighed. He sensed the lecture she held behind the sound.

"Are you all right?" she asked instead. Naime watched Nesrin, though her gaze remained on Ihsan. The Grand Vizier had approached Nesrin and was speaking.

"They appear on good terms," Ihsan said conversationally. Naime noted his avoidance with a sniff. He did not know the answer to her question. Oh it was somewhere, deep, locked in ice. Fear, or anger. Disappointment. He did not want to feel those things. So he froze them along with everything else.

Naime murmured, "Appearances can be deceiving. Especially with him involved. Be careful, San."

"Do you think you need to tell me that?" He had not meant for resentment to chill his tone. She did not flinch or react. So he regretted his terseness even more. Her gaze swept him from head to toe, looking for something he could not guess at.

"I think I know what it feels like to believe you must bear everything alone," she said as she looked away. Naime touched her fingertips to his arm, then left him.

Ihsan tapped his fingers against his leg, glancing around what remained of the crowd. Kuhzey stood near the stairs to the palace, and when Ihsan caught his eye, the boy hurried over. He moved with the awkward gracelessness of a boy not yet grown into his body. It should have entertained Ihsan to watch him, but instead he blinked the sight away and turned his gaze up.

"Tell Deniz to come to the rooms," Ihsan said when Kuhzey stopped beside him. He would dream tonight. He could feel the threat of it ticking at the back of his mind, a claw against glass. He did not relish asking the woman to sit awake outside his rooms all night. But he could not be seen to abandon his newly betrothed on their first night, nor could he afford to send her running terrified for the valley. The thought of her bearing witness to his weakness brought his headache raging back.

He could feel the boy gawping at him, but did not meet his look, tracking the drifting clouds instead.

"*Now*, Kuhzey," Ihsan urged more firmly. Kuhzey gave a clumsy bow and took off at a run.

Twelve

The light crept away. Nesrin had never wanted so badly for the sun to set. But the Wheel made the day interminable. Now, with darkness settled deeply around the palace, she huddled on the floor, tucked into a corner between the bed and the double doors that opened to the garden. She would have preferred to be outside, but the thought of encountering anyone else made her want to vomit again.

Reyhan had demanded she bathe, but Nesrin had refused to be manhandled again. Rather, begged not to be. And whether she had taken pity on Nesrin or simply grown tired of arguing, Reyhan submitted. She had filled the tub while Nesrin cowered in her bedroom, then left to wherever she slept. There had been noises. Voices, the shuffle of people moving out in the main part of the suite. Her heart had pounded, waiting for someone to knock, to demand her presence, that she act like the wife she was going to be.

But no one had, and Nesrin's muscles relaxed in tandem with the fading light. Her hugged grip on her knees loosened, and she let her head sag to rest against them. Her heartbeat slowed, and with the relaxation came tears, silent and slow. Exhaustion weighed her down.

She wanted to collapse onto the rug beneath her and sleep. The bed was too large. The pillows and blankets too soft, too voluminous. She could not sleep there, like a tick buried in fur. The thought felt too close to the truth. She had become a secret bloodsucker. Taking what was not hers, hiding. The tears dribbled over her chin, onto the red fabric of her entari.

It was thirst that finally stirred her to move. She sniffed, wiped her palms over the dampness on her cheeks and nose, and unwilling to then transfer it to her clothes, she did so to the carpet. She could imagine the abject horror on Reyhan's face, were she to witness such crassness. Nesrin pushed to her feet.

Reyhan had left a pitcher of water and a glass. Slices of lemon floated in the water, and Nesrin frowned, but downed nearly half the pitcher. She was hungry too. So hungry her muscles screamed and her joints ached. But that was not new. That had begun when her body had used all its reserves, stealing away her shape and any buffer between her and hunger.

Hunger was no longer an ache in her belly, a warning, it was a creature that swarmed in her veins, stealing her energy, her breath, her joy. She cried more easily now. Lost her temper the way a fire mage might. Her fingernails tore at the slightest offense. Her hair was dry, brittle. Her skin felt parched and stretched too thin.

Nesrin fished the lemon slices out and ate them whole, wincing at the bitterness. They would probably do more harm than good in her tender stomach, but she could not bear the hollow ache a moment more. With something in her belly, she had enough motivation to strip herself free of the entari, then the red caftan beneath. Reyhan had hung a robe on the wardrobe door, but Nesrin left it. There was a door connecting her room to the bathing room. She did not have to set foot in the larger suite if she did not want to.

And she did not want to. She did not ever want to leave this room again. Unless it was to go home. But with the heavy entari removed, she could smell her own sweat. There'd been enough judgmental looks filling her day, she did not need to add *odorous* to her list of offenses. So she crossed the room and peeked through the doors into the bathroom.

"Stars," she breathed as she stepped inside. The room was tiled from floor to ceiling, in the Second House colors that dominated the rest of the rooms. A tub ruled the space, massive, like nothing she had ever seen before. Rose petals clung to the sides and oil had gathered in one end. The scent still lingered, though Nesrin suspected the presentation might have been better when Reyhan first created it, rather than marks later.

She thought briefly of eating the petals, as her stomach was already growling, but the scented oil put her off the idea. Her brother would laugh…eating lemons and petals for dinner. That seemed a properly highborn meal. Of course, he would imagine it as a glamorous choice, not one of desperation.

She dipped her fingers into the tub. The water still held some warmth. But she did not belong in there, slicked in oils that cost more than her family's home. With flower petals in her hair and fouling enough water to irrigate a garden.

Instead she skirted the tub to the far wall, and the vanity that stretched its length. There were two sinks, which made no sense, unless nobles simply could not abide using the same sink day in and day out. An ornate blue, white, and silver pitcher sat next to each, filled with water and a handful of dried herbs. A sniff gave the scent of lavender. A cloth was tucked through the handle of the pitcher.

Nesrin stripped the rest of her clothes off, pushing them into a pile with her foot, then wet the cloth with the pitcher. Except for the ostentatious surroundings, this ritual was familiar and calming. She had always bathed like this—but outside, over roughhewn pavers, huddled in a squat against the side of the house in full view of the path that passed by the front. It did not matter. Everyone bathed this way, if they bathed at all. Sometimes a summer swim in the lake was a bath. Sometimes her sisters tucked flowers or herbs into their braids, and hers.

It made her eyes and nose ache to think of them, of home. She scrubbed harder with the cloth to take her mind from it. When she had washed away the sweat and lingering scent of her stomach upset, she rinsed the cloth clean with the rest of the water from the pitcher.

The water swirled down the sink. Where did it end up? Judging from the pipe curved elegantly over the tub edge, there was a water room somewhere in the palace. It would house a stable of low-level water mages that took shifts moving water throughout the palace, cleaning water that was dumped down sinks and…other receptacles. Nesrin made a sour face. She was not squeamish, but that was a job that made her grateful to not have Second House power. If magic made one a glorified toilet scrubber, it did not seem like such a blessing.

There was a place tucked into the corner of the bathroom for that function, a drain and both a basin of water and a pipe to wash things down the drain. Better than the pot her family kept at home, though most of them just went outside to answer water's call. Nesrin relieved herself of all the water she had drunk, then fished her chemise out of the pile of clothes. Now that she was clean, however, its sweat-stiffened, pungent fabric made her recoil. She collected up the clothes and turned toward the bedroom.

The tub stood between her and the door. Fog lifted from its surface.

Nesrin blinked, then looked again. Ice had spread up one side of the tub, beautiful scrollwork that now unfurled across the water. As she watched, a rose petal froze solid. The oil turned opaque as it was overtaken by the creeping ice.

Cold singed her toes, and she looked down to see that same ice crawling over the floor tiles. Nesrin danced back in surprise, then dashed for her room. She dropped the pile of clothes between her and the bathroom door, as if that would protect her. But the ice was already frosting the carpet and base of the walls on the side of her room that led into the main suite.

She snagged the robe from where Reyhan had hung it and swung it around her body, jamming her arms through the sleeves and backstepping away from the ice. Her entire room would be covered soon.

Was this a joke? An attack? She'd never seen anything like it. Second House mages could cool water, certainly, though she had never seen one freeze anything. But she had also never met a Sival.

Frowning, she advanced. Gingerly, she set a foot down on the frosted part of the carpet. The ice retreated from the contact. From her body heat? She took another step, and it happened again. Nesrin forged forward, and gripped the frosted door handle. The ice retreated. She touched her hand to the door above the handle, and when it cleared of frost, she pressed her ear against the wood. She could not hear anything. She pulled the door open a crack and peered into the suite beyond. It was dark. No lamps or mage orbs lit the space, only the moonlight that filtered through the crack between curtains over the windows and garden doors.

She opened the door wider. Cold hit her as if she had stepped into a winter night. Moonlight shimmered off floors, walls, and furniture slicked in frost. Her breath fogged. The sitting area was recessed, and there was a hall, or walkway of tiled floor around that central area, which led past the bathroom, the door into the palace hall, and to the other side of the suite. Where *his* room was.

The moonlight did not reach there, but Nesrin could still see the dark huddle of a figure kneeling in front of the Sehzade's bedroom door. Alarm bolted through her and she ducked back inside her room, throwing the door shut. She took a moment to breathe away her distress. Had they seen her? What were they doing and was it ill intentioned? But how would someone get into these rooms, deep within the palace?

Nesrin darted away from the door, her skin crawling at the idea the figure might come after her. Frost covered the bed now, as well, the ice nearly reaching to the wall opposite the door. But as she moved forward, a damp path opened before her. She climbed onto the bed, sinking into it. When she reached the pillows she hugged her knees to her chest with her back against the headboard. The pillows were damp too. She tugged the coverlet up to her chin to ward against the cold, her stare locked on the door.

In the darkness her mind played tricks, convincing her she saw the door begin to open, or the handle move.

But no one came. The ice suddenly receded approximately a mark after it had begun. The room beyond was hushed, and Nesrin's eyelids began to dip. Exhaustion gnawed alongside hunger. But the moment she tried to lie down in the too-large bed, she was wide awake again.

She was so alone. It was too soft. Too cold. The embroidery on the pillows and coverlet was rough and strange on her skin. The moonlight through the windows and doors to the garden was too bright.

More than anything, the quiet was unbearable. She dozed, or perhaps she didn't, but when the moonlight faded and the sun spread gold through her room, she gratefully left the bed.

When she stood, a shimmering wave of dots passed through her vision, and she swayed. The dizziness, at least, was familiar. Though it was worse this morning than it had been in the past. At home she could ration bits of food throughout the day to stave off the worst of the spells. But she'd had almost nothing to eat the day before, at least not that stayed where it was supposed to. She needed food. Now.

But she was a mess. She returned to the bathroom, where the still-full tub lay quiet and unfrozen. The petals were wilted and dark from freezing, most had sunk to the bottom. Nesrin splashed water on her face from the pitcher and used a comb to brush the tangles from her hair. Reyhan had removed the net and pins. Nesrin tidied it and wound it into a quick braid, but cursed beneath her breath when she found no ribbons or string to hold it there. With a sigh, she left it.

Reyhan had put aside an outfit, as opulent as yesterday's, this one in shades of gold. It was expected that at court the nobles would wear clothes in the colors of their Houses. But Nesrin had no affiliation with color. She had never worn much color. People of her station had no access to dyes or expensive fabrics. They wore plain cotton and linen. There was no time for embroidery, unless it was a very special garment. And the threads for such endeavors were too expensive for most.

So she'd never thought about colors that she might want to wear, but she did have a particular affection for the green of growing things.

Nesrin dug through drawers and the wardrobe until she found the simplest style she could. A cotton caftan of washed-out turquoise, decorated at the hem and sleeves with blue embroidery of poppies. She also took down the closest matching entari and salvar she could find.

When it was all on and she had belted it with a blue sash, she felt a swell of pride. She did not need someone to dress her. This looked perfectly presentable. The only shoes she could find were the red ones that matched her outfit from the previous day, so she crept barefoot from her room and into the main room of the suite.

All was still and quiet in the grey, filtered light of new dawn. No dampness from the ice lingered in the carpets, or made puddles on the tiles. Had it been a dream? Hunger had made her dreams strange, but not more real-feeling. She cast a glance toward the Sehzade's bedroom door, and did not see the figure that had hunched there in the dark.

Dawn light made everything less sinister. Shapes that had threatened in the dark revealed themselves to be chairs and vases.

A tray of food sat on the low table in the center of the sitting area. Nesrin had not heard anyone enter. Either her room was well insulated against sound, or the palace servants were hired for their quiet feet. She knelt in front of the table, tucking her caftan and entari under her knees as she surveyed the offerings. She had not had a breakfast someone else had prepared for her since she was a child. Slices of fruits and vegetables were tiled around puddles of labneh. Boiled and peeled eggs glistened in a bowl. Another platter displayed slices of hard white cheese shingled with thin slices of meat. *Meat for breakfast*?

A basket with a towel served as a nest for a stack of still-warm flatbread. Nesrin plucked an egg away from its brethren and took a small bite. She did not trust her stomach, despite its insistence. A twin set of pitchers held water and some sort of pink juice. Nesrin took another bite of egg and poured herself a glass of water. It was a luxury to have water to drink whenever she wished it, without having to trek to the nearest bucket set out for the fieldworkers. A willing mage could call it out of the ground, clean and clear, if they wished. But, especially recently, Nesrin had never wished to ask for a favor she could not return.

She drank, then ate her egg, and waited for the cramping that always accompanied her meals. As though her ravenous body pounced on the food, so desperate it clutched at it savagely. When her stomach relaxed, she eyed a stack of pastries. But similar ones had been on offer the day before, and their smell brought the memory of becoming ill.

She ripped a piece of flatbread and folded it around a slivered duet of cheese and meat.

Someone out in the hall pounded on the door. Even as her body jerked in reaction, a foul curse bellowed from the Sehzade's room. Nesrin bolted to her feet. The latch on the Sehzade's door clicked, the door shifting open. There wasn't time to run for her room, so she fumbled the door to the patio open, flatbread still clasped in one hand. The curtains were half drawn over the glass, so Nesrin closed but did not latch the patio door. She didn't want him to hear the noise.

The garden was quiet but for the flit and titter of morning birds and the velvet shift of a brined breeze. Nesrin leaned back against the frame between the doors and the window, obscured from the inside by the drawn curtains.

She breathed away her silly, strange panic, then took another bite of her breakfast. Jumbled sounds from inside made it to her ears as the Sehzade, she presumed, left his room and answered the door. Then there were voices. A woman's. Nesrin chewed a bite of the flatbread, pausing when the voices lifted, to try to make out their conversation. Perhaps she should not eavesdrop.

She considered that, but unless he'd forgotten her existence, or was a simpleton, he would not be having any important conversations in that room. He had not struck her as a simpleton, at least in their few, brief interactions.

A male voice came. "I wonder what the balance paid for a moment of peace might be?"

The Sehzade? She'd noticed his voice's smooth, bracing cadence the day before during their trek around the hall, meeting nobles. Its contrast to the Grand Vizier's fire-sharp one had made it stick in her mind.

Just like a water mage, to have a voice that sent chills down one's back. In a good way. Nesrin smiled to herself as she tore another piece from her makeshift meal.

Now, she would have to figure out how to explain why she was hiding from her husband-to-be in the garden.

Thirteen

He'd been awake for some unblessed amount of time when the pounding started on his door, in time with the throb in his skull. It was a welcome and unwelcome distraction, as he had been fighting with his thoughts, trying to bury the memories of his tangled nightmares with an accounting of his waking one.

There was a stranger here. Too physically close. There was no sanctuary for him now, away from everyone. Somewhere he could breathe and be broken in peace.

He cursed in frustration as he levered himself from the bed and yanked on the same caftan he had worn the day before. It was only the plain cotton one, but he had an inkling who was banging on his door, and he did not feel the need to dress up for her.

Everything was dim and quiet when he stepped into the main suite. Kuhzey, likely under the direction of Samira, had laid out breakfast. His betrothed's—his mind spun at the label—door was still closed, thankfully. If he were lucky, she was a late riser.

With an exhale of impatience, he yanked open the door to the hall. As he had suspected, Aysel stood there, arms folded over her chest. The presence of the towering companion behind her surprised Ihsan.

"Commander," he grumbled, then dipped his head to Aysel. He *should* bow. But it was not even truly morning yet, and her assault of his door made him uncooperative. She raised an eyebrow and sidled her petite frame through the space between him and the door. Ihsan flicked a gaze to Bashir, whose lids fluttered down, the only sign of his exasperation. "Please, come in," Ihsan snarled as he turned away, leaving the door open for the hulk of a man.

Aysel had already planted herself on a seat and was picking through the breakfast offerings when Ihsan sat down opposite her. The narrow opening between the curtains framed a sliver of garden. And also that the door to the patio was open a crack. His brows knit. Had he forgotten to close it? It wasn't like Samira to leave a detail like that undone either, though it was absolutely something Kuhzey would do.

"Did you hear me, Sehzade?" Aysel said.

"No." Ihsan slouched against the back of the couch, turning his gaze to hers. She pursed her lips. Then she glanced up at Bashir.

"May I cast a dampening, Sehzade?"

Ihsan waved Bashir's question away and tipped his head back on the couch, closing his eyes against the throb behind his lids. Bashir's magic, fire adjacent on the Wheel, was like hair brushed the wrong way. Aggravating but not painful. The air muffled when the dampening was in place, and Ihsan lifted his head.

"What is so important that you arrive before dawn and require a dampening?"

Aysel wiggled a slice of cucumber as she punctuated, "Three wagons of supplies, near Golge, were attacked. Two stolen outright, one of them burned on sight."

"Golge?" Ihsan rubbed his fingers over his cheek. Golge was controlled by Enver Balik, who was struggling with keeping his holdings from revolting over the lack of food. If they were attacking supply wagons, that should not be a surprise, nor something that needed

Aysel's, or his, attention. Even if the movement of supplies and food was under careful control. "Where did the wagons come from?"

"Narfour," Aysel answered, "and Mizraa."

"There is an interesting coincidence." Ihsan's gaze went to Nesrin's closed door.

Kadir had been propping Enver Balik up recently by providing for him from his own considerable coffers. Was it just influence in the North Kadir was trying to maintain? Was brokering this marriage an in for Kadir in Mizraa as well? So he had access to food supplies he could use to bribe allies?

"Do we know what was in the wagons?"

"No, but I would like to send Kiya to investigate."

"That seems an intricate task for someone who has only been training for a season." Through the crack in the doors, Ihsan witnessed a handful of sparrows gathering on the stones. Intent on something.

"I'm not looking for finesse here, Sehzade," Aysel said impatiently. "I want her to frighten someone into telling her what was in the wagons. She's quite fierce when she cares to be. And underhanded. Just the type I need for this job. Unless you'd rather I go?"

"She's a child," Ihsan muttered, as the birds made a synchronous jolt and flutter backwards. Strange.

"Hardly. I will judge the capability of my people, thank you very much." Aysel crossed her arms and jutted one hip, which drew Ihsan's gaze to her again. The storms were in her eyes; he'd irritated her. Not a difficult thing to do.

"Aysel," Bashir rumbled. She blew out a breath that made her nostrils flare. "It could be as simple as another food shipment being waylaid by looters. The city is not safe for storage at the moment. Most merchants are either stashing their en-route goods on ships or at their holdings in the valley."

"Or," Aysel drew out with a sharp look at Bashir, "the timing and origins are as suspicious as they seem."

Movement drew Ihsan's attention back to the door. A spray of crumbs descended into the gathering sparrows, sending them into a frenzy of pecking.

"Drop your spell," Ihsan ordered Bashir. Aysel and Bashir looked at each other, but the guard commander obeyed.

"Show yourself," Ihsan said, glaring at the doorway. His face relaxed in surprise when Nesrin pushed the door open slowly, head down, then put her hands behind her back. "What are you doing?" He hadn't meant to bark at her, and she flinched.

"Uhm." She lifted her head, swallowed, and said, "Eating," around a mouthful of food.

"Eating," he intoned. She brought her hands around to the front like a child caught stealing sweets, to reveal a handful of flatbread. Aysel made a spluttering noise. "You were hiding."

She chewed, swallowed again, looking sidelong at Aysel and Bashir. "Yes," she admitted, and brushed at her clothes, dislodging crumbs. "You had guests and I did not especially want their first impression of me to be while I was chewing enough bread to choke an ox."

Aysel's splutter turned into a full-blown laugh. Ihsan grit his teeth, ruthlessly choking back his own laugh.

"Yes," Aysel said. "It is much better that our first impression was you hiding away like a chipmunk. Are you Mistress Bardakci?"

Nesrin nodded, her demeanor still reticent. She stared at Aysel's arm, at her tiraz. "Four," she whispered, her gaze lifting to Aysel's.

Aysel's eyebrows arched. "Well done. If you use your hands you can count to ten."

"You are a Charah," Nesrin said breathlessly, unfazed by Aysel's taunting, clasping her hands in front of her as if to control herself. "Of air?"

"She gets it in one." Aysel seemed intrigued. "I am also the lieutenant commander of the palace guard."

Nesrin's gaze slipped to Bashir, and up, then slowly back to Aysel. Her seemingly innocent wonder was…irritating. She only looked at Ihsan with hesitation and fear. Was he that much more frightening than Bashir? Ihsan scratched at the back of his hand and turned his attention to Bashir, who remained stone-faced.

"A guard? You are a woman."

"You are a sharp little knife. Yes indeed." Aysel smiled.

"Oh," Nesrin said, leaning closer. She stepped up to peer at the woman's eyes. "Lightning," she said wistfully. "You have baby storms in your eyes!"

Bashir broke, letting loose a gravelly laugh. Ihsan suppressed a grin. Aysel snapped the flat of her hand against Bashir's chest in rebuke. "If you ever repeat that I will gut you in your sleep," she said to him. To which he laughed harder. Nesrin's cheeks flushed.

"This is Bashir Ayan, Commander of the Palace Guard," Aysel offered. Bashir bowed to Nesrin, who took a step back, appearing surprised as she gripped her own arm, then smiled wanly. As Bashir straightened, Nesrin's gaze followed him, and Ihsan caught the brief furrowing of her brow.

"Are you from Narfour?"

He gave a nod. Her frown deepened. And she seemed to contemplate saying something more.

"Are you enjoying Narfour?" Aysel asked.

Ihsan cleared his throat. "Are you almost finished?" he asked when they looked at him. Invading his space and then making small talk while he was nursing a headache and going on no sleep was too much, even from Aysel.

Nesrin drew back as if he'd struck her. She executed a snap of a bow toward Aysel. "Forgive me"—she stepped away and bowed again—"I have never met a Charah."

"A pleasure to meet you, Mistress Bardakci."

Nesrin smiled. He had not seen her smile. Not like that. It was sunlight, open and true and guileless. Even Aysel seemed taken aback for a moment. Nesrin's gaunt face was transformed by the expression, offering a glimpse of who she might truly be in a place she was comfortable.

Ihsan looked down at his hands, and picked at a loose thread in his salvar.

"And you..."

"Aysel Attiyeh," Aysel supplied.

"Attiyeh Charah," Nesrin said. The shape of her hovered in his peripheral, near the edge of the table.

"You're staring at that food as if you haven't eaten in a fortnight," Aysel said dryly, and when Ihsan whipped a look at her, she frowned at him.

"I..." A slash of red along Nesrin's cheekbones gave her some much-needed color. She did not wear red today, but a watery shade of blue-green that Ihsan found much less irritating. It suited her better, as well.

"You didn't feed her?" Aysel blurted.

"Me?" Ihsan scoffed. "I am not a nursemaid. If she is hungry she should eat."

Nesrin shrank away at his raised voice. Aysel tsked. She snatched a plate from beside the tray, loading it with bits of fruit and bread and labneh. She pressed it into Nesrin's hands, who protested.

"Take it and go," Ihsan said. Nesrin obeyed, holding the edge of her plate pressed against her belly as she bobbed a bow. She dashed into her room, the door snapping closed.

He scrubbed his hands over his face. He hadn't meant to starve her, he just wasn't accustomed to having anyone to worry about but himself. Did she not know she could request food whenever she wished?

Aysel looked at him as if he were a rabid cur. "You're very bad at people, you have realized this, yes?"

"Aysel," Bashir warned. She shrugged when Ihsan glared at her over his fingertips.

"Finish telling me why you are here, then get out." He needed away from people. She was right, he was bad at them. His scars ached and itched and his temper was fraying.

"I simply mean you will have more success in relationships if people do not hate you right from the start."

"You mean I should apply the tactics you used on our commander?" Ihsan thought if he wounded her she would shut up.

"Yes exactly." Her eyes brightened, Bashir's face reddened, and pain throbbed across Ihsan's temples. The woman was impossible.

"We need permission to use guard assets to investigate." Bashir shoved Aysel behind him as she cackled. "The Sultana was busy with the Sultan and if we do not act quickly we will lose any chance of gaining evidence."

"Yes, go. For Wheel's sake. I'll inform the Sultana."

They bowed, and Aysel all but skipped from the room, Bashir behind her.

Ihsan collapsed against the back of the couch, his gaze fixed on the door to Nesrin's room. Her presence there felt like a wet cloak clinging to him, making him tense and irritable. He launched to his feet and went to the patio. The birds fled his arrival. He hadn't realized there were so many, and they trilled a pretty song to each other as they took to the sky. Well, at least she attracted good things.

Fourteen

"There is a Council meeting this morning," Reyhan said as she tugged and adjusted and redid all of Nesrin's work on dressing herself that morning. She traded out the contrasting dark blue sash for one that matched. Then combed and oiled and braided Nesrin's hair so part of it wound her head in a braid and the rest fell in curls around her shoulders. The pins holding the braid in place stabbed her scalp, but when she reached to adjust them, Reyhan slapped her hand away.

"Princesses do not pick and twitch," she said. Nesrin crinkled her nose, barely resisting the urge to mime Reyhan. "You will accompany the Sehzade in Council."

"What? Why?" A bolt of terror ran up Nesrin's spine.

Reyhan gazed upward, as if the Wheel would appear from the void and relieve her of burden. "Because you are betrothed, and the court must see you. You must prove you are up to the task."

"What task? And what if I am not up to it?" Nesrin sputtered as Reyhan latched a necklace around her throat. Nesrin plucked at it. It was a silver chain with twin pearls, stacked one on top of the other. Pearls belonged to the Second House.

"Princesses and Queens attend the Council. They always have. You must go." Reyhan dropped the necklace in place.

"We?" Nesrin rolled the pearls between her fingers, soothed by their perfect spheres. These were precious. Perfectly round pearls were rare, their connection to the Wheel and its circle coveted. How much food would these buy?

"You are not the only one with family obligations…Mistress," Reyhan sniped the last. Nesrin raised an eyebrow.

"You don't like me," she stated. Reyhan's expression strained then smoothed. She yanked at the fabric wrapping Nesrin's waist, tightening it. Nesrin grunted.

"I do not like your incompetence." Reyhan turned the fabric so the knot sat over Nesrin's hip instead of her belly. Bluntness was not usually a Fifth House trait, but Reyhan had it in cartfuls.

"I am perfectly competent when I am where I belong," Nesrin said. "I am trying." She was not accustomed to being hated. No, not everyone loved her, but in Mizraa the weight of her family name carried some sway with the others, and she was respected for her common sense and work ethic. That didn't matter here. Attiyeh Charah had been the kindest, and even that had been delivered with cutting sarcasm about Nesrin's intelligence.

"Trying? Do you still not understand what is at stake here?"

Nesrin rounded on her. Her temper was slow. She could count on one hand the number of times, as an adult, that she had raised her voice. But it was fraying. Fear. Hunger. Loneliness. Lies. And Reyhan's judgment. "I understand what is at stake. You have made sure to inform me every chance you get."

Someone knocked on the door. Nesrin stepped away from Reyhan, shifting the cloth belt back to where she had it, with the knot placed over her belly. Reyhan's eyes narrowed, but she spun and pulled the door open. Another woman stood there, stern and serene. Nesrin remembered her—she served the Princess Sultana. Reyhan bowed immediately, and Nesrin started to do the same, then stopped herself. She was a noble now. But it felt wrong and strange to stand before a Sival and not bow to her.

"Reyhan," the woman said, familiar but with distance.

"Mistress Azmeh," Reyhan said as she straightened.

"How is your family? And Kanat?"

"Well. Thank you." Reyhan's words were clipped and the muscles in her neck went taut. She fidgeted, spinning a bracelet she wore on her wrist. Samira did not seem to notice.

"You are late, Mistress," she said to Nesrin. "The Sehzade has departed for the Council Hall."

Already? When she had left him in the suite he had been dressed in nothing but salvar and the kind of cotton caftan one wore beneath their clothes. Nesrin had not been able to look straight at him. Silly, because she had seen men wearing far less. But there was something too intimate about seeing this man even close to undressed. A prince. A stranger. Her husband-to-be.

"I will take her now." Reyhan bowed again. Samira, placidly, ducked her head then left them.

"Hurry." Reyhan dashed to the wardrobe and retrieved shoes that matched Nesrin's outfit.

She had not thought to look in the wardrobe for shoes. Why would anyone store their shoes away like that, instead of by the door, where they would be of use? Reyhan bent beside her, grabbing Nesrin by one ankle then the other and tugging the shoes into place. Nesrin snorted a laugh. Reyhan frowned.

"I feel like a cart pony freshly shod," Nesrin said. Sanem would have erupted in laughter, but Reyhan only glowered harder, grabbing Nesrin by the shoulders and steering her into the suite. "I wish you would stop manhandling me."

"Wishes are worthless currency in the palace. I will stop when you move under your own power."

"I would if you would give me a chance."

"You are always at least two steps behind everything, you miss all your chances."

They continued snipping at each other, in near whispers, as Reyhan guided her through the maze of hallways and gardens. When they reached the now-familiar doors to the Council Hall, Reyhan paused to glance Nesrin over from the corners of her eyes. She nodded, then pushed the doors open and ducked her head.

With a hard inhale to steel herself, Nesrin lifted her chin and straightened her spine and shoulders. She strode forward, Reyhan one step behind and to the side, so Nesrin could just see her, red and brown in her peripheral. She felt successful, until the whispers, and the stares. She skipped her gaze from face to face. Some were curious, some openly hostile. None were women.

She shrank, her shoulders hunching, her gaze dropping. Her breaths became shallow and quick. What was she doing in here? Looking the part of a noble was one thing, and she was only barely accomplishing that. Would she be expected to speak? She lifted her head, ready to throw a panicked, questioning look at Reyhan, but instead her gaze was drawn to the Sehzade's. Just as it had that first time. He was handsome, bordering on beautiful, though the scars and demeanor lent too much ruggedness for that. His expression was as remote and icy as a glacier.

Reyhan bumped into her hip, guiding her to the right, to a bench that sat below the dais where the Sehzade was, on his left. She looked away from the Sehzade as she sat, and Reyhan took up a place behind her.

"Now that we are all here, perhaps we might begin?" the Grand Vizier said with a joyless smile. Chuckles ricocheted through the hall. Nesrin wished to disappear. Her pulse thumped in her ears, the flush that rose up her neck and cheeks like fire in her skin. She stared at the tiles, eyes tracing the designs as she counted them to calm herself.

Words flew back and forth, the emotions impacting her more than the meanings. They were angry, disturbed, speaking of fires and thieves in the city. Warehouses emptied overnight or set ablaze. Supply caravans robbed before they made it to their destinations. Villages rising in revolt, stealing grain and stores meant for Narfour. She raised her face at that accusation, to stare across the aisle at the man who sneered at such an idea.

It was Balik Pasha. Who had refused to marry her. He was on his feet, facing the Grand Vizier and the dais where the Sehzade sat. But he must have felt her stare, because he turned his face toward her suddenly, and their eyes met. Her throat closed.

"And what say you, Mistress Bardakci? We receive little word from Mizraa, but the supplies seem undiminished."

Every muscle in her body went taut. She did not know whether to stand, or speak, or neither.

"I..." Nesrin began, the sound more a panicked exhalation than the beginning of anything cogent.

Reyhan hissed under her breath, but Nesrin did not hear what word she said, because the Grand Vizier spoke. "Balik Pasha, this Council is for the Viziers to discuss issues, not for the conversations of women."

Balik Pasha's face shaded purple with rage. The Sehzade shifted in his seat, cutting off whatever the Vizier would have replied. "The Princess Sultana would be interested in that sentiment, Grand Vizier," he said, cold and low, his expression not wavering from frosted indifference. Someone near the doors to the hall outside coughed politely.

The Grand Vizier's smile hardened, and the Sehzade continued. "Please stand, when you address the Council and the dais, Mistress Bardakci." He did not look at her, though his voice was considerably softer. Still, she wished he would have driven a sword through her heart rather than put her on the spot once more.

Sick and shaking, she rose. She did not know where to look, and she had almost forgotten what had been asked of her. But Balik Pasha dropped to his seat as she stood, reminding her of his question. What did she know? What could she say?

"There is no Blight in Mizraa." Her voice was small and the hall swallowed it. A few men cleared their throats or chuckled. She was certain she heard whispers about women's voices not being made for council halls. "There is no Blight in Mizraa. But what we…" She gulped the 'we' and continued on, too quietly, timidly. This was not her, and she hated the way she sounded. "What is grown there is sent to Narfour, or with the soldiers marching east. The people are starving," she breathed, panic rising. "But they are not stealing, yet." They would take offense. Reyhan made a choked sound behind her at the words.

"Yet?" someone demanded. "It is inevitable that every lowborn becomes a thief? Is Narfour the only bastion of civility?"

"What is civil about them burning our stores and robbing our wagons?" scoffed someone else.

Her thoughts spun as the men began to snip and gripe at each other. Her panic turned to confusion, then lit the temper that was too near the surface. Her voice could reach across fields and orchards. It had the same strength and knowledge in it that her mother's had. That her grandmothers' had. It *was* made for council halls.

"What is civil about starving, you mean," she accused, her voice like a whip. They all fell silent to stare at her as if she had grown another arm. Her bravado shriveled under the scrutiny of so many eyes. "Are you…are we…" Her gaze flicked to them, then the floor, then her own hands, twisting together. "Are we not also stealing?"

Reyhan whispered desperately in her ear. *Be silent. Sit down.* Nesrin obeyed, dropping to her backside, tears and heat biting her skin and eyes.

"Stealing? From whom?" one of them guffawed. "It belongs to us, the grain, the food stores. They come from our lands, are funded with our money."

"And what—" Nesrin remembered herself and stood once more, tugging the caftan and entari away from where they had caught under her shoes. "What will you do when all your workers have starved to death? When there is no one left to harvest, process, store, load, and drive your shipments?"

"Leave it to a woman to speak about noble ideals while we are trying to deal with the here and now of governing during a war, and a Blight," someone snarled from behind Balik Pasha.

"Enough," the Sehzade commanded. "This discussion is accomplishing nothing."

When she looked at him he had the bridge of his nose between his fingers, eyes closed. She collapsed to the bench, hunching around her stomach, her stare locked on her feet. All she could think of was how she hoped to never return to this hall again. It was too dangerous, her alienness too obvious here. The Sehzade sighed, squaring his shoulders and dropping his hand to the arm of the seat.

"We came here to discuss the thefts within Narfour, and of the caravans leaving the ports. Instead you are bickering like children."

"I can report on what the City Watch has passed along." The Grand Vizier did not look at the Sehzade as he spoke. In fact, the two men seemed to do everything possible to look anywhere but at each other. The strangeness of it enticed Nesrin out of her self-pity. The Sehzade flicked a hand in permission. The Grand Vizier's mouth twitched in irritation, but he continued. "Captain Akkas has the main bulk of his guards patrolling the warehouse district. From what he tells me, these thieves are organized enough to work around the guards' movements and shift schedules."

"That suggests something more organized than desperate, starving citizens."

Nesrin glanced at the new speaker, because his voice was even and smooth, nonconfrontational. When she looked at him he inclined his head in acknowledgment, or apology. He wore the colors and tiraz of the Fourth House, golden tones. She had met him, briefly, during the gathering before the betrothal. She had met many of these men. Their wives, and children. But their names had come unrelenting, followed by titles and holdings and magic House and rank. It might as well have been hail pelting and falling around her. None of it stuck in her mind.

She did remember his daughter. Beautiful, and young, perhaps not even twenty Turns. She remembered the way the girl had stared at the Sehzade. She remembered because it reminded her of Sanem's lovesick gaze before she and Anil had begun courting. *Yavuz*. His surname surfaced in her memory. She repeated it mentally, plastering it across his face in her mind's eye.

"Yes," the Sehzade said. "We have assets investigating these incidents, beyond just the City Watch. As I informed you at the last Council." He swiped a hand down his face, and as he dropped it to his knee Nesrin caught the briefest flash of an exasperated expression. "When there is news, it will be shared. I expect the same from all of you." He drummed his fingers on the arm of his seat. "In the meantime, the City Watch has increased patrols, and assets from the palace have been assigned to key distribution points."

He stood, an unspoken signal that rippled through the room as the others followed suit. Nesrin didn't understand she was meant to move until Reyhan clicked her tongue, tapping her fingers between Nesrin's shoulder blades. The Sehzade had already descended the steps of the dais and was striding for the hall, his young steward jogging to keep up. He passed just as Nesrin stood, and she dropped into a hasty bow.

If he looked at her, she did not see it, and he was almost to the door when she straightened. She wrinkled her nose. Did he ever plan to speak to her? Beyond admonishments and irritated dismissals? Perhaps being ignored was for the best, as Reyhan had suggested.

Her gaze floated over the heads of the Viziers clustered in the aisle in front of her, talking. The Grand Vizier had not moved from his spot on the side of the dais, and he stared at her. Nesrin looked down quickly, startling at the simmering ire in his gaze.

In the tide of men exiting, Nesrin did not notice one approach until he stood before her. He bowed. It was Mahir, the Grand Vizier's steward.

"The Grand Vizier requests your presence in his office," Mahir said blandly. He did not have a cold demeanor, the way the Sehzade did. Simply an impenetrable one. Like a rock face. That seemed to be an odd requirement of the palace. The ability to hide one's entire self behind a blank face. Nesrin tried not to worry at the summons. What could he want with her? Of course she knew. She was bumbling everything. Wheel knew what he planned to do about it.

"Yes, Master Mahir," Reyhan murmured, bowing. The steward did not deign to look at the younger woman. He turned and crossed back to his master, who descended the dais as he did. They strode from the room together, and that was the signal for the rest of the men to filter out.

Nesrin took a breath in the thick silence left behind. The empty hall was huge. Swallowing her, and her anxiety. She collapsed onto the bench once more. Her sleepless night weighed on her, exaggerating all her fears.

"Get up." Reyhan rounded the bench to face her. Nesrin looked up at her. Would it kill the woman to be the least bit sympathetic? "You cannot keep the Grand Vizier waiting."

"Right." Nesrin followed Reyhan from the room, and as they navigated the halls, she said, brightly, "The good news is that I believe I'm beginning to remember some of these halls." It was more to cheer herself up than any expectation that Reyhan would care. Reyhan huffed a disdainful laugh, and when Nesrin peered sidelong at her, the other woman's brow was raised.

"You've only seen a quarter of the palace. At this rate you might have it memorized before you die."

Nesrin nearly threw her hands up in exasperation. If Reyhan wanted to hate her, she was not going to fight it.

They crossed through the foyer that opened to the gravel courtyard and the Morning Gate. Nesrin peered outside, to the sunlit city beyond, but they were across the foyer and into a dimly lit hall before the sun had a chance to warm her mood.

The hall was short and let out into a circular room with three doors at the end. Reyhan knocked on the rightmost one. The door swung open before Reyhan had dropped her hand to her side. Mahir stood inside, and stepped away to allow them into the room. Nesrin entered. The room was dark, the only window covered with a velvet or brocade curtain that blocked most of the natural light. A mage orb hovered above a desk, where the Grand Vizier sat, papers spread across the surface before him.

He was writing when they entered, and continued without looking up. Mahir closed the door behind them. He whispered the rocky, hard words for a dampening spell. *Twice in one day.* She didn't know if she had been witness to a dampening spell twice in her entire life. Was everything in the palace a secret?

His script flowed, the rhythm of him dipping the quill, the tap as he wiped the excess, the scratch and sweep against the paper mesmerized her. Her father had taught her to write, and it had been a utilitarian skill. Enough to communicate, but nothing like this. Nothing like art. She had not paid attention to that part of the letter he'd sent, sentencing Sanem to a loveless life. It had not looked like art then.

The Grand Vizier finished with the same elaborate, swirling signature that had ended the letter to her father, and set his quill aside. He stood, drawing her attention up and away from the letter before she could attempt to read the decorous script upside down. Beside her, Reyhan bowed, and so did Nesrin.

"How are you enjoying your new life at the palace so far?" the Grand Vizier asked, with an easy smile. He moved around the table, his limp not so pronounced in such a small space. It was a miracle he could walk at all. Beside her, Reyhan rocked as if she were going to shuffle back, but did not.

"I am..." She did not know how to encompass everything she had experienced in only these few short days. She doubted he cared, though his friendly tone was not what she had been expecting. "... adjusting."

"Are you?" He stopped in front of her. Reyhan's breath hissed between her teeth as she inhaled. Nesrin did not have a chance to glance at her, as the Grand Vizier had leaned forward so his nose nearly touched hers. The glimmer she had seen in his eyes was, in fact, fire. burning in the irises, its heat buffeting her now that he was close. "From what I have seen, you are intent on revealing yourself to anyone with half a wit to spare." The words came as though they amused him. But the fire made them lies.

Nesrin had a knack with animals. Had always had. And people were animals too, at their very core. This man reminded her of a village dog in Mizraa which gave none of the usual signs it was about to bite. One moment it would be happily wagging, the next it would attack. Viciously. It had killed a sheep and mauled a child before they put it down.

"I am trying, Pasha," Nesrin said.

His expression flattened. "You succeed or you fail. And I do not accept failure. You can have a good life here. I can help you, but not if you destroy the plan before we can accomplish anything. Do you understand?"

"Yes," Nesrin said.

"Yes?" he prompted.

"Yes, Pasha," she amended. Her insides were icy with fear, despite the heat of his magic. They were so many ways he could destroy her and her family. Reveal her lies. Claim no part in it. She had no allies here. Or anywhere, not that could help her against him. He turned his ire on Reyhan, who dropped to her knees.

"Please," she said, hoarsely. Nesrin blinked, surprised by Reyhan's deference. Kneeling was not commonplace. Or at least it was not in Mizraa. Did he have something on Reyhan as well?

"Get up, girl." He turned away from them and returned to his seat at the desk. Reyhan obeyed as he sat. Then he looked at Nesrin. "You will retrieve something for me from the palace library. Rather"—he rubbed his thumb along the curved scar on his cheek—"you will assist my son in retrieving something for me from the library."

"Yes, Pasha," Reyhan said, before Nesrin could even furrow her brow at the odd request. Nesrin wanted to protest, or ask for more detail, but Reyhan stuck on elbow in her ribs.

"Consider it a service to Tamar," the Grand Vizier continued. "He is hunting for evidence pertaining to a suspicion I have. Someone is being duplicitous, and I think it is important that her future subjects know that." He held Nesrin's gaze for a moment, as though waiting to see what she might say. But she said nothing, and he dismissed them by leaning forward and returning to work on the pages on his desk.

Mahir dropped the dampening spell, and even the usually muffled sounds within the hall seemed momentarily loud. Nesrin was still blinking as though she'd been blinded by bright light when Reyhan dragged her from the room. Mahir shut the door behind them with a hard snap.

"Why doesn't he just go to the library himself?" Nesrin whispered as they moved back down the hall. Reyhan shook her head, looking behind them, then around the corner of the wall as they reached the first turn.

"It is the Sultan's library. One needs permission to enter it," Reyhan grumbled, "or an excuse of ignorance. And no one fits that description better than you."

Nesrin held back a pointless rebuttal. Why would the Grand Vizier send an uneducated lowborn to retrieve something from the library? The same reason anyone would send someone else to do their dirty work. Either because they were disallowed from wherever they needed to go, or to keep suspicion from themselves. Lovely. Not only was she a fraud, she was also a pawn between some of the most powerful people in Tamar.

"Where is the library?" Nesrin asked.

Reyhan shook her head. "Master Kadir will find us when he is ready. Until then, you wait, and bask in your new life as the Sehzade's wife and the talk of all of Narfour."

Fifteen

The Sultan's room smelled of all the medicinal tea they were trying to fill him full of. Its herbal scents drifted even into the sitting rooms where Ihsan stood with Naime, looking over the garden.

"I think you should consider a break," Naime said, softly, to his back. "Some time in the city, away from the palace."

"And what of your break? You have no house in the city to escape to," Ihsan argued. The city was not the escape it had once been. Violence in the streets, the threat of more warehouse attacks, they made him lie awake at night, sweating and panting. The orange glow against an ink sky. The sour, devouring scent of smoke. Imagining it made his lungs seize and his eyes sting.

Naime's hand circled his wrist. "I am where I wish to be. But you are not."

"You need me here," he pleaded. If he had no task, if he was not necessary, if he had to be free to let his mind digest the impending death of Omar, he would go mad. "When else would you sleep? Who else do you trust to stand watch?"

She looked up at him, smiling sadly. "Do not make me order you, San." Her gaze left his to look out the glass doors and into her mother's garden. Night had cloaked it, though Samira had been through, her passing made evident by a flock of mage orbs of all different sizes hovering in the branches of the dead fig. It was an enchanting sight, one that had pleased the Sultan and made Naime smile and so Samira had done so every night since. But now, Naime's brows drew down, and Ihsan followed her gaze.

A shape stood just outside of the halo of light, a person. Ihsan frowned.

"What is she like?" Naime asked.

Ihsan squinted. "Who?"

Naime huffed, gesturing at the figure in the garden. "Mistress Bardakci. Your betrothed? Do you like her?"

Ihsan shrugged, registering belatedly that it was indeed Nesrin standing out in the garden. Her fire mage servant did not appear to be with her, or was disguised in shadow. Not usually something a fire mage could manage. Which made the fact that fire mages were somehow sneaking around Narfour at night even more baffling.

"San," Naime said, more sharply. He met her gaze, pulling his thoughts back into the moment. "You cannot hide from her forever."

"You underestimate me, Cousin." He smiled, but she frowned at him and he looked away, prickled with shame that she saw through him so easily. "Have you considered speaking with her?"

"Wheel, no. There is nothing to say."

Naime closed her eyes in exasperation. "And has she nothing to say about your nightmares?"

"She is unaware of them, as far as I know," he said. When Naime looked at him askance he waved her off. "I brought Deniz up from the city, she ensures my dreams stay mine." He did not wish to dwell on the subject.

"And you plan to have her do so all your days?" Naime murmured.

Ihsan grunted noncommittally and grasped for any change of subject. "Kadir called Mistress Bardakci to his office after the Council today."

"That is interesting." Her expression softened in thought. "I wonder how deeply she might be in his pocket. I know he has a relationship of some kind with Bardakci Pasha. I cannot recall ever meeting the man." She left his side to collapse into a chair, hugging her knees to her chest. Her hair was loose, tucked behind her ears, and she wore a simple caftan and salvar of pearl grey. Curled up as she was, she looked, for a moment, like the little girl who had always beat him soundly at chess but never at hide and seek. He closed his eyes against the memory, against the happiness that came with it.

"There was another hijacking in the North. Aysel requested permission to send a few guards to investigate. Three wagons of supplies, bound for Golge from Narfour and Mizraa."

A wrinkle appeared between her brows. She was too tired for this. For more. He cursed himself for his poor timing. He turned away and looked out the doors once more. Nesrin crept forward and stood on tiptoes, reaching for one of the mage orbs. The light of it cascaded gently over her, moon pale yet warm from the fire that birthed it. The memory of her smile from that morning assaulted him suddenly, and he shook it away like a dog freshly out of water.

"Is it related to the city lootings?" Naime wondered to herself. "I cannot decide if this is simply anger about the food shortage, or something more calculated. It feels calculated." She looked toward the ceiling. "But why?"

"It depends on what angle you view it from," he muttered. Nesrin had turned her attention from the orbs to the tree. She approached its trunk and pressed her palms to it as if greeting an old friend. "The attacks have only been on warehouses and supply caravans from supporters of Kadir. However, those are also the largest stores of food, so it may have nothing at all to do with him. There is some evidence that the food had been stolen and redistributed, though other evidence suggests the supplies are destroyed in the fires."

As he spoke, Nesrin leaned forward, pressing her forehead against the tree. It was too dark to see details of her face at this distance, but he was surprised by the curiosity that lit in his body. What was she doing?

"Nothing more from Captain Akkas and the City Watch?"

"I am not convinced Captain Akkas is not in Kadir's pocket as well," Ihsan said, absently. She was quiet so long that he turned his attention from Nesrin to her, only to see her watching him with one raised brow and a faint smile. He scowled.

Naime tucked the smile away. "No, I don't believe so. I've had Aysel investigate him once or twice. He is certainly crooked. But he seems to be equal opportunity in his willingness to be bribed."

"Should we replace him?"

"With whom?" She rubbed the furrow in her brow away. "There is no one left that is not necessary where they already are. At least I am aware of his resentment of the palace. Of me," she added. "The threat I know, for now, is better than one I do not."

Ihsan's jaw clenched. A petty man exacting petty revenge because she had given him punishment he deserved. She could have done much worse than she did, but that did not matter to the man. Ihsan had never envied Naime the burdens of the crown she pursued. But men like Akkas made him grateful to only play a support role. Tamar needed Naime, intelligent, honorable, and focused. Not someone like him, broken and bitter and selfish.

"It must be lonely, coming from somewhere small like Mizraa to somewhere like Narfour and the palace."

He focused again on Nesrin, leaning against the fig, the mage orbs washing light down on her undone hair. Guilt filled him up like a basin, overflowing the edges and boiling into resentment. It was not his fault she was here. He had tried to right a wrong done to her by Kadir and Balik Pasha. He should not also be responsible for her well-being. And he certainly could not be responsible for her happiness. He was nothing but the darkness of the Second House. Casting long shadows wherever he went, coating them in ice.

"I would certainly be grateful, were I in a similar situation, for a friendly face." Naime rose from the chair and moved to his side. Her shoulder brushed his.

"Then she should look anywhere but at me," he said, quietly.

Naime did not meet his gaze when he looked at her sidelong. "Do you think she had any say in the marriage that brought her here?" Naime pondered. Ihsan knew what she was doing, trying to appeal to a part of him he was certain had been excised with his burnt flesh. She thought it was still there. His empathy. The greatest of the Second House's gifts. But it was long gone. It was empathy that spurred his friendship with Cemil Kadir, and the end of that had taught Ihsan a lesson he would never forget.

"To a man nearly twice her age? No, I doubt it. Do I owe her more than I have given her? I will at least not abuse her. She will want for nothing."

Naime cast him her most scathing of silent stares. He bared his teeth. "Tell me, what sort of person did you see when you met her? You are better at assessing people than I am."

"That was not always true, was it?" she murmured. He shrugged. She knew as well as he did all that he had lost, beyond his family and his link to the Second House. "I have made no judgments of her, yet. I would like to see how closely she interacts with the Grand Vizier. But the few moments I have spent with her, she seems like someone trying her best to navigate something utterly foreign to her."

"You and I both know that *trying your best* is rarely enough."

Naime tipped her head to the side. "Do as you wish, San. But ignoring someone is also a kind of abuse. And I expect more of you."

She turned her back on him, then strode quietly across the room and into the Sultan's bedroom, pausing just before closing the door to say, "You will take at least a turn of rest in the city."

The door clicked softly into place.

Ihsan cursed under his breath, squeezing his eyes shut against the torrent of guilt that filled him up with its paralyzing itch. He knew what it was to be ignored. Even if it had not been malicious.

With a sigh, he opened his eyes. Nesrin still stood outside, leaning against the tree. "Void and stars," he growled under his breath, snatched an apple from the bowl on the table, and opened the door to the garden.

Sixteen

Nesrin could not remember ever seeing a dead fig tree. They were nearly indestructible, as trees went. Generally unbothered by pest or disease, happily carrying on, even as their leaves fell to rusts or insects. Perhaps the Blight had reached it. Though that was unlikely, considering the rest of the garden was hale. Looking at it had made her so sad.

She touched her forehead to the bark, eyes closing. She did not know if it was her sorrow that filled her, or something else. But it did not matter, it overflowed her in tears and a deep ache in her chest. Her mother said that plants, trees especially, had as many memories as people. More for their long Turns. But that no one could understand those memories. Not anymore. Nesrin liked to imagine she could touch trees and sense those memories, beneath the surface, like water beneath ice.

The fancies of a little girl who felt left behind by all the mages around her.

"They only speak to you that way in the Council because they cannot do so to the Princess Sultana," a crisp male voice said, more curious than accusing.

She swiped at her tears. She knew the Sehzade's voice by now, but he'd seemed to materialize out of the dark outside the light of the mage orbs.

"Why must water mages always skulk around?" she murmured, grumpily. There was no peace in this place. Nowhere to hide.

He huffed a laugh. "I was not skulking. If I had wanted to hide from you I wouldn't have spoken. You seemed busy."

She was too raw in whatever grief held her at the moment to bear any more from anyone. Certainly not his picking and rudeness. She'd never been anything but polite.

"I was," she threw at him. "Quite busy."

He looked as if he might smile. Just a twitch of his mouth. He moved suddenly, tossing something underhanded toward her. The dark shape arced through the air and Nesrin caught it. An apple. Her stomach tightened.

"Is this a peace offering?" She cupped it between her hands. He shrugged, glancing into the branches of the fig tree. The moon hung in the sky above the sea, appearing as if she could reach out and pluck it. The sight reminded her of the Sehzade. Standing right in front of her, but as distant as the stars. She took a bite of the apple.

"Is there not peace between us?"

"There is nothing between us," Nesrin replied. The apple was sweet, and just starting to soften from a long storage. In Mizraa they grew apples that kept over the winter and shipped well. She wondered if hands she knew had touched this one. She cupped it again, its rosy, polished skin against her palms, and tried to conjure her family to her, to banish her loneliness.

"You are better off that way," he said. Nesrin was not certain he had meant for her to hear it. He tipped his head back. One of the largest mage orbs pulsed and winked out. Nesrin frowned, watching in silence as he extinguished each one without a word or movement.

She took another bite of the apple. It was small, and her three bites had nearly finished it.

"You might have asked me if I wanted the light." Nesrin gestured at the tree with the apple. She nibbled the last bits away from the core and approached the base of the tree, where he stood.

"You will learn to abide the dark, if you intend to marry me." His voice was ice again. She recognized the bait of it. The test. Water mages tested—used their tone and their mastery of language to draw out confessions and outcomes. If he thought she would fall for such things, he was going to be disappointed. Whatever wounds he carried in those scars, in his clear aversion to the Fifth House, were too deep for her to dig out in their first days of knowing each other.

She kept her silence, kneeling on the ground beside him and scooping out a shallow hole, which she placed the apple core in. As she patted it into place, she sensed him turn his attention to her.

"What are you doing?"

"From void, to void," Nesrin murmured. "Dust to dust. "

"Are you giving an apple core a funeral?" he asked incredulously. Nesrin tipped her head back to glare at him. The moon framed him in pale light.

"If we take without returning, there is no circle. There is no Wheel." A truth she felt the palace had forgotten. Perhaps the entire city. "There can be no life without death. The Wheel honors both the same. The apple will feed the soil, which will feed the garden."

"That tree"—he crouched in front of her, just outside arm's reach—"has been dead for Turns. An apple core will not resurrect it."

"There is more in this garden than that tree," Nesrin retorted. "You are infuriating, has anyone ever told you that?"

"Everyone." He smiled lifelessly, gaze dropping to the grass. The moon and shadows were his friends, cutting angles across his face she hadn't noticed in the harsher light of day. Beautiful. He was beautiful.

She looked away. She did not want to notice him, the way he seemed intent on not noticing her. "Are you…barefoot?"

It was a strange question with an obvious answer, and she looked at him quizzically. He returned the look, and her face warmed. It was probably unheard of for a noblewoman to traipse about a garden in bare feet. She had needed that grounding.

After everything of the day, bearing the consequences of her lies and being brutally reminded that she was a weed among roses, she needed a reminder of who, and what, she was. Not soft carpet and hard tile beneath thin shoes. But cool, damp grass and the give of living soil beneath her. The symbiance of her life, simultaneous with the life teeming in the earth, bugs and worms and tiny creatures, birdsong around her, air and light. Plants that crept or reached for the sun. That was who she was. Not this…dress-up doll whose every decision broke some rule she had been unaware of. Was that how she was to discover them all? By embarrassing herself day after day?

"I like the way it feels." Well. Now she sounded unhinged. Nesrin closed her eyes against whatever expression he would make.

"Hmm."

When she cracked one eye to peer at him, he had his face downturned as he picked at a blade of grass. It was angled now so she could clearly see the scars that covered his right jaw, down his neck, and beneath his clothes. How extensive were the scars? The healer in her wanted to ask. Wanted to know if he was healed, truly.

She'd known one person who had been burned and had scars like that. Not a water mage though. An earth mage. A weak one. The girl had been young, perhaps ten Turns, when she had been trapped between fields being burned clean. Nesrin squeezed her eyes shut, exhaling hard as the memory of her cries made her entire body prickle in gooseflesh. The girl had not survived, despite the long candlemarks every capable healer in the village had held vigil. Fresh tears beaded between Nesrin's lashes.

"Are you all right?" he asked, voice soft, resonant in a way she had not heard him speak yet. The familiar warmth of a water mage's empathy. It washed her clean of the memory, and blanketed her in the comfort of the people she had spent her life with. The Second House. Nesrin opened her eyes and looked at him, with a small, thankful smile.

"Just a memory that surprised me," she murmured. He made a face of understanding, the edges of it tense with pain. "They can be brutal things, memories, can't they?" She said it in a tone that allowed him to take it as a statement, or a subtle invitation. But it was a mistake. His countenance turned glacial, and he stood.

"Good evening, Mistress Bardakci," he said curtly, and walked past her, toward his rooms. Nesrin tipped her head back in frustration. Then she looked after him. He had reached the stone patio outside his rooms, where she had left the door to the sitting room open.

"My name is Nesrin," she called. His shoulders hunched, a flinch against the unspoken rebuke, but he did not turn or respond. Nesrin wrinkled her nose. Well, at least now she knew there was a human beneath the prince's exterior. And perhaps even some gentleness.

She glanced at the spot where she had buried the apple core. With a groan, she rose, dusted off her knees, and returned to the suite. He had already disappeared, either into his bedroom or into the palace somewhere.

Nesrin hung her entari and switched to a simple linen caftan over her chemise. Reyhan had filled the tub again. Nesrin frowned at the waste of the water, but chose the pitcher and basin once more, using a cloth to clean herself. She unbraided her hair and combed it out with her fingers. When she finished, she returned to the bedroom and tugged the coverlet off the bed, wrapping it around her like a cloak, and settled onto the floor. Every time she tried to sleep on the bed she felt swallowed alive, and too aware of her solitude. The floor felt more familiar, a reminder of who she was. As long as she rose and set the blankets where they belonged before Reyhan returned and chided her for her foolishness, it was her little secret.

She was not aware of sleep taking her, only when it was ripped away by a pounding noise. Her eyes flew open, her heart thundering in her chest, its fast thrum making her breath come in gasps.

A thin layer of ice cracked and fell away from the outside of her blanket as she stood. Nesrin dropped it to the floor. Before thinking it through, frost burning the soles of her feet, she threw open her doors. It was someone knocking…but not on her door, perhaps the hall?

The sitting room was dark, but moonlight glinted off frost and ice. A woman stood on the far side of the room, outside the Sehzade's bedroom door. The Sehzade's steward stood beside her, both of them staring at the bedroom doors, with their backs to Nesrin. The woman pounded with her fist again.

The ice cracked apart, receding as Nesrin crept into the sitting room, then all melted away.

The door to the Sehzade's room swung open just as the woman reached to knock again. The woman gasped, slapping her hands over her heart. The Sehzade held the door open with one hand, the other cupped around his forehead. Nesrin stifled her own sound of surprise, only releasing a puff of air as she stared. His magic was in flux, the blue light of it manifesting in swift curls and gusts beneath his skin and lighting everything around him as though he were a lamp made of ice and snow.

Nesrin had never seen a Sival in flux. She had heard of it. The way magic could dance on the skin and in the eyes. A person made art, the Wheel manifesting in a body. Aval and Deval did not flux. So she had only ever imagined such a thing, as much a legend to her as tales of a time before the breaking of the Wheel.

One side of his body, which was naked from the waist up, was darker. The magic still moved there, but was not brilliant, ice blue, but muted, as though a screen obscured it from her view. It was the same up his neck and the right side of his face.

The scars. What had happened to him? Was it the thickened skin that obscured his magic, or the echo of the fire that had clearly caused his injuries, written forever in his flesh?

Sweat beaded on his skin then froze each time a blue swirl swept beneath it. Nesrin stood mesmerized, not just by the magic, but by him. Men in the valley were rarely beautiful. They were rugged. Hardened by a life of labor. Skin marked more harshly by sun and wind. He did not have the bulk of the men she was accustomed to. The heavy muscles and frame of workers who spent their days at hard labor. Neither did he appear weak, as she had imagined someone of his station would be, softened by Turns of doing nothing for himself. He was slim waisted and broad shouldered, a body shaped by some sort of physical endeavor, though she could not imagine what. Riding? Sword work?

His arm flexed as he held the door wide, and blue swirls of icy light outlined the muscles there. She curled her fingers into the caftan at her hips, surprised by her own curiosity.

She had touched, and been touched before. Had trysted. What would it feel like to touch someone in flux? Would the magic be a flutter beneath her fingers? Her heart raced, and sizzling energy twined within her. Or…

His magic brightened, the light of it as cold as snow. He grunted, his face scrunching in confusion. His effort to rein it in showed in the hard lines of his neck and a flex of muscles over his arms and stomach. Nesrin's voyeuristic imaginings died in a blaze of guilt. What was she thinking? The man was clearly suffering. He looked about to fall forward on his face, weaving in place. Where he gripped the door, ice radiated across the wood.

"You"—he glared at the woman standing before him, a mask of blue ice frosting over his eyes and temples, irises lit from within—"are late."

She did not quail beneath the frightening look, as Nesrin would have. She only took a step back and bowed.

"Forgive me, Efendim. There were protests that blocked my way. I am here now."

The light of the Sehzade's magic lit the woman's face and shape. She was older, soft and curved like Nesrin's mother. She did not speak to the Sehzade with a mother's gentleness, but with a servant's deference, and she was dressed as such. Her clothes plain and unembroidered, except for the tiraz on her arms. They were murky in the pale light, but Nesrin believed they bore the sigil of the Fourth House.

Nesrin involuntarily whispered *oh*. Of course. This was the figure she had seen knelt outside his room, casting a dampening. And with the Sehzade's sanction, it seemed. But why?

He must have heard Nesrin's exhale, because that icy stare shot to her. He might as well have cast her in magical ice, she felt cold enough under the look. Surprise froze to agitation in his mien. He twisted immediately, so his unscarred side was to her, took a step back, and slammed the door shut.

Nesrin blinked, and the woman and boy steward turned to look at her. She stepped back, uncertain. This was her home now, too, was it not? She could leave her room at will? So why did she feel like a busybody caught spying?

"What's this, lurking in the dark like a thief?" the woman accused as she moved toward Nesrin.

Nesrin retreated, until her feet hit the step that surrounded the recessed sitting area, and she dropped onto her bottom on the tile. Her exhaled *oof* made the older woman frown and the boy snorted a laugh.

"I heard—"

"What sort of noblewoman scurries about at night like that? They do not teach you manners in the valley," the woman continued as if Nesrin had not spoken. She approached, brusquely levering Nesrin to her feet with hands like iron manacles, and steered her toward her room. "Best back to your sleep. We wouldn't want you sallow and bag-eyed in the morning, hmm?" She shoved Nesrin into her room, and swung the door shut.

Nesrin stood where she'd been deposited, brow knitted, her slow anger bubbling from a simmer to a boil. She'd had all the pushing around that she could take.

Seventeen

Reyhan arrived in the morning, only moments after Nesrin had finished mussing the bed to make it look as though she had slept in it.

"You look terrible," Reyhan said with a frown as she closed the door behind her. Nesrin frowned back.

"Thank you, Reyhan. And you look as if you've eaten a lemon for breakfast." Nesrin sipped from a glass of water she had poured for herself.

Reyhan sniffed, but she did not respond beyond that, moving instead to the wardrobe and yanking open the doors. "We'll need to pack your things. I do not know how long he plans to stay."

Nesrin cocked her head, attempting to process the statement as she took another sip of water. The cool liquid soothed the burn of hunger in her stomach. Her body was growing accustomed to regularly available food again, and its demands were now less a constant ache in her muscles than an insistent demand in her belly.

"Is he leaving?"

Reyhan snorted, as if Nesrin had asked something silly. "You are both leaving." She pulled three entari from the wardrobe and laid them on the bed.

"Where?" Nesrin was only half listening, thinking instead of the food that was likely laid out in the sitting room. She was hungry, but she also did not want to face the Sehzade, or that pushy servant. Her thoughts drifted to the sight of him, radiant with magic, wearing nothing but salvar. She took a slow sip of her water, trying to ferret out details from her memory that she had not focused on in the moment.

Of course she had, briefly, considered that a noble marriage would require heirs. And heirs required intimacy. It was not so unpleasant an idea as it had been when she'd first thought of it.

Reyhan lifted her head from where she was mixing and matching clothing items, and stared at Nesrin. A quizzical expression signaled Nesrin that she had been standing with the water glass to her lips for too long. Nesrin hurriedly gulped the rest of her water and turned her back on the other woman. Heat crawled up her neck.

She set the glass down and patted her cheeks.

"I'll just…get some breakfast. Shall I get you a plate?" she affected a haughty tone as she offered. When she threw a glance over her shoulder, Reyhan's brows were drawn together, lips pursed. Nesrin grinned and pulled open her door. But she had forgotten her reluctance to encounter anyone from the night before. The young steward and the grumpy old woman both knelt at the table.

Her first instinct was to slam the door shut again. She was in her sleeping clothes. But they had already looked up, and focused on her immediately. Nesrin fought her body's urge to flee and stepped from her room, closing the door lightly behind her. She kept her chin up, but her gaze down and away from the horror of meeting theirs.

"Good morning," she murmured as she crossed toward them. As she had suspected, a tray of food was laid out on the low-set table. Fruit, vegetable slices cut into decorative shapes, nuts, and even flowers made the setting more art than breakfast.

"Ah, our mistress rises. They must start their mornings later in the valley." The woman's snipped words rubbed like cat's tongue on Nesrin's already-raw temper.

"My sleep was disturbed." Nesrin knelt at the table, her stomach clenching. She did not look up as she took a dried apricot from a plate stacked with them and nibbled at it. The other two rose, though the woman hesitated in what was clearly annoyance. "Please, stay. I did not mean to disturb you."

The boy knelt back abruptly, but the woman grabbed him by the collar and dragged him to his feet. Nesrin looked up at her and the woman gave her a tight smile. "I suggest you become accustomed to having your sleep disturbed."

Nesrin fought the urge to rise to that bait. "We have not met," she said instead. The woman's face registered surprise, then disapproval. Ah yes. It was likely improper for a noblewoman to introduce herself to a servant, which this woman clearly was, in some capacity. She had the soft curves of a woman who cared for others with food and nagging, as Nesrin had noted the night before. Her clothes were plain, brown, tan, and undyed fabric, but she did wear a Fourth House Deval tiraz on her arms, in marigold embroidery.

Nesrin knew women like her. The ones who took dogged ownership of whatever task they were assigned. Territorial and mean as cornered cobras. She seemed as though she might not reply to Nesrin's statement, from spite.

But Reyhan emerged from Nesrin's room, and though Nesrin could not see her, she could see the older woman's face flush with disgust.

"I am Deniz, caretaker of the Sehzade's home in the city, where you will be staying for the next small turn. And as I have been in the Sehzade's employ the longest of anyone, that means what I say is to be obeyed."

Reyhan dropped to her knees beside Nesrin. A furtive glance at the fire mage revealed an expression of annoyance. "You have been in the

Sehzade's employ the longest," Reyhan agreed as she dished labneh onto a plate for herself and arranged vegetables around it. "And I am Mistress Bardakci's longest-serving maid." She shrugged and dragged a carrot sliver through the yogurt. "I suppose that makes us equals." She took a bite.

Nesrin rose abruptly, taking her plate with her as she stepped out onto the patio and closed the door behind her. She took a deep breath and released it with a groan. A man's muffled laugh sounded in response and she whipped her head to the right. The Sehzade stood outside what must be the doors to his bedroom, leaning against the wall.

"I suppose you have met Deniz," he said, his normally water-smooth voice uneven. She desperately wanted to ask him what was happening in the night. The ice, Deniz's dampening spell. But no one had offered the information, and she did not want to risk damaging what little familiarity seemed to be between them.

"Have I offended her?" Nesrin asked, considering whether she should approach him. He was dressed in cobalt and silver. There was no shade of blue on the Wheel a water mage was not flattered by, but the darker shade made his pale eyes luminous. Even with the haggard, tired look on his face, he was a pleasure to look at. Though she ached in empathy for his lack of sleep.

"Most likely. Everything offends her." He tipped his head back against the wall and closed his eyes. A thought occurred to Nesrin and she grinned.

"You are hiding from her." She giggled. He opened one eye, turning his head just enough to level a look at her. But he turned away again without answering. Nesrin took a chance on approaching, and stood beside him, turning to lean against the wall at his side. He did not move away, which she took as a good sign. She held her plate out between them. "Hungry?"

He lifted his head to look at the food. "You need that more than I do," he said as he closed his eyes again.

"There is enough food on that one table to feed the village of Mizraa for a day. I will be all right. If this is not to your liking, I can retrieve you something else."

"So brave," he murmured as he ripped a bit of flatbread off the piece she had brought and dipped it into the yogurt. Nesrin breathed another laugh.

"I know her kind. All bark and no bite. I am simply too tired to be bothered with playing the game today."

"You are not sleeping," he said, continuing to pick at bits from her plate of food. The statement was guarded, Nesrin could hear the crinkle of ice in it.

"Is anyone in those rooms?" She chanced a look at him, and saw the wall go down in his expression. Her heart sank. "I am sleeping fine," she said, in an effort to salvage the ease that had been between them a moment before. "Last night Deniz's pounding on your door woke me."

"Ah." He took a piece of the bread in his fingers. He dropped his hands to his side and looked up at the cloudless sky. He did not offer any more, and Nesrin understood she should not ask.

"Reyhan told me I am to go into the city with you." She set her now-empty plate on a little table pushed up against the wall. "Would you rather I did not?"

He seemed taken aback by the question, eyebrows rising. He lifted the bit of bread he still held and looked at that instead of at her. Nesrin plucked it from his grip, too aware of her fingers brushing his. That was probably too familiar for him, for anyone in the palace.

His skin was cool. She crumbled the bread in her fingers, refusing to return the look he cast at her. He lowered his hand to his side, fingers flexing then closing into a fist.

Nesrin scattered the bits of bread across the patio in front of them. Birds that had been flitting through the bushes along the garden path and foraging in the grass descended upon the crumbs.

"Are you trying to avoid close proximity to Deniz?" He took a smidgeon of the remaining crumbs from her open palm, and flicked them onto the stones, watching as the birds fluttered in contest for them. "Or me?" he added, almost too quietly to hear. Metin used to do that. Assume people wished to avoid him before giving them a chance to make up their own minds.

"Deniz does not frighten me," Nesrin said gently, tossing the rest of the crumbs to the birds. She dusted her hands together. "And neither do you." She smiled conspiratorially. He glanced at her, and his gaze, frosted hazel, seemed to focus on her mouth. On the smile. Nesrin tried to hold it in place, but the intensity of the look made her falter and her breath whisper out.

Did she see a glimmer of pale blue in his irises? No. She flattered herself then. A skinny, half-starved, backbred peasant could not charm a prince with a smile. She knew that. But daydreams were nice. Especially since she had not felt safe enough for them since leaving her home. Not until this moment.

"I cannot decide if you are delusionally kind, or insufferably naive." All the gentleness disappeared from his voice, and he straightened away from the wall, putting distance between them. "Stay here or come to the city. It matters not to me." He was gone abruptly, his doors closing with a click as he retreated inside.

She tried to convince herself that the cruelty had nothing to do with her, and everything to do with him, but it was impossible. She was being naive. She should not be trying to make friends with the man, or solve any mysteries. She should absolutely be keeping distance between them. Guard her secrets as he was guarding his. She could never, never, forget this was all a lie and that the price of being found out was her freedom, at best, her life, and her family's, at worst.

Eighteen

Nesrin was transported to the Sehzade's home in a carriage. The Sehzade did not travel with her, and when she arrived at the house, she wondered if he had decided not to come. She did not ask Reyhan, but stood staring at the sprawling building as the driver and coachman unloaded her single trunk and carried it inside. Standing before the house now reminded her of arriving at the Grand Vizier's home, of the sickening uncertainty, and that same feeling welled back up as she took it in.

That home had been Fifth House in every aspect, and in contrast, this one was Second. Blue accents stood out against clean white plaster. Central doors were painted water blue and small fountains stood to either side of the door. There were no poisonous vines trailing across the door, though there was one sad, neglected rose bush in a pot at the base of the six steps leading up to the landing.

Reyhan followed the two men, and when they knocked on the door, Kuhzey opened it. Perhaps the Sehzade was already here. Nesrin could not decide which she hoped for, that he was, or that he was not. She followed Reyhan up the steps and inside the house.

Kuhzey led her and Reyhan through the house as the coachmen unloaded their things from the carriage. Inside was very much like the outside, with a fresh, airy feeling because of the pale colors chosen for everything. Her family had never had the luxury of coordinating their furnishings. Most of their things were purely functional, patched together as needed. Every fall she and her sisters restuffed all their cushions with straw and coarse wool. Wool, linen, and cotton were the fabrics she had known. Her fingers trailed over the embroidered edge of a turquoise silk pillow. It was cool and smooth to the touch.

In the Grand Vizier's estate, the lower floor had been dominated by long couches and a large, low table. Clearly a man who liked to entertain. The Sehzade had two benches and two chairs, all of them with the unrumpled appearance of furniture never used. At the back of the entry level was a curving stair, very much like the one in the Grand Vizier's home, but at the base of this one was a brazier.

It should have been lit. But, just as the fountain in the Grand Vizier's home had been dry, no fire burned in the decorative metal bowl. Reyhan gave the empty brazier wide berth as she followed Kuhzey toward the stairs. She seemed more on edge than usual, her gaze dancing from spot to spot. Perhaps the Second House energy resonated strangely with her own magic. Or like Nesrin, she distrusted the unbalance suggested by an empty brazier in a Second House home.

They climbed the stairs in silence. Kuhzey offered no word of welcome or explanation. In fact, Nesrin did not think she had ever heard Kuhzey utter a word. Was he shy?

Upstairs was not much different than down. Though, there had been no carpets covering the tiled floor below, on this floor lay one large, elaborate carpet of blue, white, and silver, large enough to span the upstairs. The Sabri crest dominated, but there were patterns of chrysanthemums around the edges. Comfortable chairs were scattered in pairs, for a total of six. Reyhan and Kuhzey followed the two men carrying Nesrin's trunk through a door at the far end of the common room. There were six doors total, three on each side. Bedrooms, likely an office or library, she guessed.

There was a thunk as the men dropped her trunk on the floor in the room that was presumably to be hers, then they left, ducking their heads to her as they made their way back to the stairs. Reyhan did not reemerge, but Kuhzey did, and stopped just outside of the door, staring toward her, his gaze darting awkwardly.

"I do not bite," Nesrin said, trying to control her amused smile and failing. She'd never heard of a steward so young, and he certainly did not inspire confidence, awkward as he was. "Am I allowed a tour of the home? Or am I to stay to that room?" She pointed at the bedroom. Surprise crossed his features as he glanced behind him, then was replaced by uncertainty. "I promise not to touch anything," she offered. He considered, then shrugged. Nesrin's brows knit. "Can you not speak?" She'd never met anyone who couldn't, but she supposed it was possible.

He tapped his lips and shook his head, then made a series of fluid gestures with his hands. Her curiosity ignited. "You speak with your hands?" she breathed in wonder. He nodded. "Will you teach me?"

His face lit with surprise, then he grinned as he nodded.

"Good," she said. Her attention slipped to his tiraz. He wore embroidered blue air sigils, one on each arm.

An Aval? But they could only speak their magic. Was it trapped within him then?

She pulled her gaze up to his face. "Now, about that tour?"

He pointed toward the glass balcony doors. The layout of the home could have been an exact copy of the Grand Vizier's estate. Perhaps they were designed by the same architect. Or the Grand Vizier had modeled his home after the prince's.

She clasped her hands behind her back and crossed the room as he pushed the doors open for her. The balcony was small, only large enough for two people who were *very* cozy to stand side by side. But the view was worth it. The home hugged the slope, which continued down, so it was high enough above the houses in front of it to command a perfect view of the glittering ocean, cast in fire and ash from the setting sun.

"Never mind the house." She clutched the iron railing of the balcony. "I'll stay here."

Kuhzey nodded when she looked over her shoulder at him.

"All right, let's see the rest." She pushed away from the railing and stepped inside once more. He went to the door on the wall to the right of the balcony and cast a glance toward the stairs before he dropped the latch and opened it. Her guess had been correct. This room was an office. Kuhzey put a finger to his lips as he moved aside for her to step past. Nesrin slipped sideways between him and the door.

As he followed, he made a motion with both hands like doors closing. "Is that an office?" Nesrin asked as she mimicked him. He grinned and repeated it.

There was nothing notable about the room, except the floor-to-ceiling windows at the back, behind the desk and overlooking the city. Bookshelves covered the other two walls, packed to the brim with books. Previously, she would have been thrilled to see so many books in one place. Her reading in the valley was confined to the five tattered volumes her father had collected over the Turns. Her favorite was a collection of fables and she would be thrilled to discover new stories. Nesrin moved toward one of the shelves, but stopped when she remembered the Grand Vizier's request, and that Cemil would be coming for her. To help him *retrieve* something from the palace library.

She was in deeply now. Surrounded by factions whose aim she did not comprehend. Between powerful men at odds. At the mercy of anyone who discovered her. She crossed the room to the windows and looked out over the city.

Learn. And learn fast, farmgirl, Reyhan had warned.

Grow where you are planted, tatlım. Her babaanne's words. The more philosophical of her grandmothers. The poetic one. A plant must take nourishment from the earth and sun where it was, or it would not survive.

The city sprawled, vast and incomprehensible. Like the palace. Like the people around her. But she could choose to wither, to hide in her room, to avoid them all. Or she could choose to adapt, to stretch her roots to ground herself and turn her face toward the sun and grow into something else.

"Teach me some more words," Nesrin said as she turned back to Kuhzey.

He scrunched his face in thought. Then he made a sweeping gesture toward their surroundings and made a steeple with his fingers, then a circle.

"Hmm…" Nesrin considered.

Commotion, outside and below her, drew her gaze back to the window, to the main street that ran in front of the Sehzade's home. An open wagon stood stalled in the road, its load of burlap bags and crates of vegetables being tossed into the street by two men, to the crowd that surged to steal it. A family cowered in the wagon, but several within the mob were trying to haul them from their seats and into the crowd. The woman's scream, and her children's panicked cries, made it all the way to Nesrin and Kuhzey.

Nesrin spun and bolted for the door. Kuhzey lunged out of her way as she careened around the doorframe and darted for the stairs.

"Mistress!" Reyhan gasped as Nesrin scurried down the stairs. Nesrin ignored her and Deniz, who appeared from a side door on the bottom floor as Nesrin darted through the downstairs and burst out the front doors and onto the steps. She snatched up her caftan and entari to free her feet and took the stairs in a leap, then raced down the street.

Nesrin did not bother shouting or trying to coax anyone to sense, they were far past that point, merely starving, frenzied beasts now. She elbowed her way through the crowd. When bodies pushed too tightly for her to get to the wagon, she resorted to shoving.

"Move," she barked, and that order earned her venomous looks from those nearest her. They parted anyway, and she grabbed the bridle of the horse, whose head was thrown back, his eyes rolling, ready to bolt. "Easy, easy," she said to him, holding his bridle in one hand and stroking his neck. He calmed beneath her touch. She kept one hand on him as she sidled her way to the wagon.

A man was trying to drag a bag of lentils over the wagon, seemingly unaware or uncaring that it would drop from the edge of the wagon onto the two small children huddled on the seat. Nesrin grabbed handfuls of the cloth at his waist and pulled. Her body was diminished, but the ghosts of the strength she once had remained—created over a lifetime of labor.

He spun toward her when his feet hit the ground, face scrunched in rage, but she was already climbing onto the wagon, blocking the small bodies of the children from the frenzy. Their panicked mother was crying, clutching a baby against her chest. The man with them had crawled into the back of the wagon, trying to wrestle what was left of his supplies away from the thieves. He resorted to using his whip to lash at people, but someone caught the end of it and ripped it from his hands.

"These do not belong to you, you Sarkum filth. Give us back what is ours!" someone shouted. Nesrin had not had time to ponder *why* people were attacking a wagon in broad daylight. "We won't suffer for the Blight *you* brought to us."

Refugees. That explained the vitriol. She could not save the wagon, but the people…

She urged the children closer to their mother, pointing to the far side of the wagon bench. There was a temporary gap in the crowd there, as looters moved to the back of the wagon to clamber for the remaining food. The woman nodded, reaching an arm around the young girl closest to her, and Nesrin guided the little boy as his mother scooted toward the edge of the seat.

Whoever had stolen the whip cracked it through the air, and the man fell onto his belly in the wagon to avoid it.

"Get them out of the wagon," the same angry voice ordered again, somewhere behind Nesrin. Her skin prickled, and chaos broke out again. She gasped in horror as hands reached for the mother, to pull her out of the wagon, even as she still clutched the baby. Nesrin lunged, grabbing the hand the woman stretched toward her. The two young children—smashed between their mother and Nesrin where she knelt on the wagon bench—shrieked.

Nesrin pulled, hiking one foot onto the bench to balance herself, and gripped the woman's arm in both hands.

"Let her go," she demanded.

The whip cracked again as the woman's husband tried to scramble to her aid, but two people from the crowd were attempting to haul him sideways out of the wagon. Nesrin saw from her peripheral when the man who had taken the whip turned from the husband in the wagon, to her. He lifted his arm, flicking the whip back, and the crowd cleared to give him space. Fire ignited along the length of the whip.

Nesrin threw herself flat, across the children and their mother, wrapping her arms above her head and the woman's. The crack of the whip echoed above her head as it missed.

She stood, helping the children to do the same, urging them toward the far end of the bench to escape the trap of the wagon. The heat of the fire-laced whip registered before the pain of the strike. It burned through her clothes and her skin as it spiraled around her torso, the tip flicking around her neck and jaw. The woman stared in mute terror.

Then the pain hit Nesrin, fire and lightning a streak along her back, her neck, and her cheek. She swallowed back a scream, squeezing her eyes shut as tears leapt into her eyes and throat.

Was no one going to come to their aid? In the entire crowd? That realization was nearly as painful as the whip track burning around her body. It uncoiled from around her, leaving a singed trail as the fire mage withdrew it.

Wheel, at least the people in her village could be reasoned with somewhat. But this crowd was feral. She had to get these people away from here, damn the food.

"Kuhzey!" She lifted her head to cry out. Had he followed her out of the house? Had anyone? "Reyhan!" she shouted again, levering herself over the back of the bench and turning so she could kick at the man trying to drag the mother from the wagon. Her foot caught him in the face and he wheeled away, spitting blood. Nesrin jumped out after him, reaching up to the woman, who shoved the baby into Nesrin's outstretched arms.

"You noble bitch!" The man recovered, spinning around at Nesrin's back and snaking an arm around her waist. She clutched the screaming baby to her chest. Her breath huffed out of her as the man's arm tightened and he turned again, slinging Nesrin toward the crowd behind him. All she saw were blurred faces and outstretched hands. All she could care about was the bundle in her arms, wailing and squirming, fighting her hold even as she tightened it, terrified he would be wrenched from her grasp.

Someone caught her. She did not see them, only felt her body collide with theirs. She braced for tearing hands, strikes, anything, hunching her body around the child to protect him.

Instead big hands settled on her shoulders, steadying her. Nesrin twisted and looked up…and up. He was the biggest man she had ever seen in her life outside the guard who had been with Attiyeh Charah.

She had also never seen a Meneian. His expression was kind, his hold supportive.

He jerked his chin, a command not meant for her, and someone shot out of the crowd, leaping onto the wagon like a cat, circling it once and kicking away hands and makeshift weapons. Another Meneian, though this one was smaller, and younger, than the man who held her. Once he had cleared a path, he helped the mother and children out of the wagon, into a circle created by three city guards, then the father, who was curled into a fetal position on the road, clothes torn and bloodied.

"I'm all right," Nesrin said to the man holding her. He dipped his chin to look at her. He was missing an eye, the place where it should have been a starburst of scar. He nodded agreement, and released her.

The appearance of the Meneians had immediately changed the mood of the crowd. Many dropped what they were holding and ran. Those who stayed seemed to have the fire of frenzy snuffed out, but their hunger kept them here. And the shouting began to die down.

A woman's voice rang clear and musical over what was left of the chaos.

"Go home," she said, like a mother chiding children. Nesrin searched the faces for her, and found her at the south end, downhill. Another Meneian, seated on a horse as placid and unbothered by the crowd as a plow horse. When the crowd milled instead of dispersing, she spoke again, and Nesrin not only heard, but felt the power of water in her voice. A familiar ache bloomed in her body. "Leave now, under your own power, or do so under mine. But you *will* leave."

They obeyed, reluctantly, some with anger on their faces and curses on their tongues.

"Not you," the big man at Nesrin's back rumbled. His voice, directed over her head, was accented with the song of his mother tongue, but the threat was unmistakable. A man on the far side of the wagon tensed.

"That one to the Cliffs," the Meneian continued, pointing. The city guards obeyed him as if he were their commander, breaking away from the woman and her children and sprinting after the man as he tried to bolt. He dropped the whip he held as he darted up the street. But they quickly caught up, grabbing him, and the whip.

The mother ran to Nesrin, arms outstretched for her baby, her sobs stifled but tears still streaming down her cheeks. Nesrin handed the child back into her care and wrapped her arms around the woman, who fell apart in wracking sobs. She pressed her head to Nesrin's shoulder, so heavy in her fear that she dragged them both to their knees on the stone.

Nesrin had no words, so she simply held the woman as she cried, and as her own fear drained, slowly, from her body. It left a brilliant, throbbing fire from Nesrin's cheek to her thigh by way of her back.

The whip. She hadn't forgotten she'd been struck; the bedlam had kept her mind from it.

The two older children had taken up at their mother's back, also crying, though they clung to her and did not wail. A much smaller crowd milled, those who had hidden during the fray, who had been brave enough to watch, but not to assist. They crept from inside their homes, stood in doorways and peered over high garden fences. And for a moment Nesrin hated them all. These were expensive, rich homes. Those people keeping themselves safe had means to help. Had chosen not to.

"Here now, here," Nesrin murmured to the woman. She held her sleeve over her palm and gently blotted away the woman's tears. "I know you are frightened. Are you hurt?"

The woman shook her head. Then she took a deep breath that swelled her chest and straightened her spine, and let it out slowly, closing her eyes.

"Thank you," she said to Nesrin, turning her attention to the hiccupping infant, who clung to her neck. She shushed him, patting his back as she met Nesrin's gaze. "We'd heard it was bad…but the camp needed supplies, and no one else would go for them."

Nesrin looked past her, to where her husband had been lying on the stones. He was sitting up now, and a guard and the young man who had jumped on the wagon were loading him onto a guard's horse. He looked battered, but coherent, and seemed able to sit the horse without aid.

"They are taking your husband to the healer," the towering Meneian said to the woman, returning to stand over them. "Do you need a horse?"

"The wagon," she said, standing. She dropped a hand down and her two older children clung to it. "Is there anything left?"

"Some," he said, with little emotion. "Mutar Charah is arranging for a guard escort to take it to the camp. Why were you not escorted?"

"They could not spare the men until the nighttime. But, it is much more dangerous at night." The woman shifted the baby to her hip. The man grunted acknowledgment, his gaze traveling to the woman he was with. She was speaking with one of the guards who arrived, and as far as Nesrin could tell, it was not an enjoyable experience for the guard.

"It is our fault," the woman murmured.

"It is not your fault," Nesrin said. The woman smiled weakly in placation.

"Go with your man to the healer," the Meneian said gently. He had enough gravel and bass in his voice that she would have guessed him a Fourth House mage. But he wore no tiraz to mark him such. What little spirit had been in the woman for a moment dissipated, and she nodded, giving Nesrin one last thankful glance. Nesrin nodded.

"Mistress!" Reyhan called from behind. The sound of Reyhan's voice, now, when all the danger had passed, made Nesrin ready to laugh or scream.

"Your people," the Meneian began, then a furrow bisected his brow and he frowned.

"They are not my people." Nesrin pressed a hand to the cobbles to lever herself up. She made it halfway, still bent, when pain zipped down her back and a dizzy wave buckled her knees. His big hand caught her beneath the arm, hauling her up.

"You need a healer too," he said sharply.

"No. I think I'm just bruised and dizzy," she mumbled, head swimming. "I'll just take a rest inside."

"You are bleeding all over your clothes. Did someone cut you?"

"The whip," Nesrin said. Was it that bad? Reyhan reached them then, Kuhzey at her side. Reyhan gasped, pressing her fingertips to her mouth. Nesrin looked down at the stones. Dribbles of blood oozed into the cracks. "That's mine?" She looked up at the Meneian, who regarded her with a raised brow. "I think I should…" She should sit, but the world spun from beneath her, rushed around her. She cursed, and as her thoughts slipped free of awareness, she heard a rumbling chuckle.

Nineteen

Ihsan studied the map that Bashir had laid out on the table and pinned in place. The destroyed warehouses were marked with red ink. Their reconstruction was underway, but it would be turns, at best, before they could hold stores again. If there were even stores to be held. Supplies dwindled, the shipments from the valley slowed anyway until summer's crops came in, now cut in half by the Blight.

"Would Mistress Bardakci be able to give us an idea of the status of crops and shipments in the Southern valley?" Bashir suggested. "No one else seems to know, even the Grand Vizier."

"Or he is keeping it to himself," Ihsan muttered. The mention of Nesrin made him irritable. She was sweet. With her sunny smiles and her shy attempts at connecting with him. How could he explain to her that it was in her best interest to keep distance between them? For her emotional, and physical health. For his.

"There is an interesting rumor circulating the palace," Bashir said, uncharacteristically reticent. Ihsan glanced up at him, but Bashir was studying the map. Intently.

"You do not strike me as a man prone to rumor mongering, Commander." Ihsan placed the flat of his hand on the table and leaned on it.

"I am not. Generally." Bashir rolled one shoulder, then the other. "But I cannot help being suspicious of Mistress Bardakci, and her ties to the Grand Vizier, and so Attiyeh Charah passes along anything she hears."

"Ah," Ihsan grunted. Bashir cleared his throat. Was he flushing? Ihsan recoiled.

"It seems that"—Bashir's gaze flicked from the table to the walls of his office—"some believe your betrothed to be with child, from you, and that is why you chose to go through with a ceremony with a woman not from court."

Ihsan's brows dropped, as did his stomach. What in the Void?

"She is nothing but skin and bones, where did a rumor like that come from?"

Bashir grimaced. "The other theory is the reverse," he added reluctantly.

Ihsan scowled. That she was with child from someone else and rushed into a betrothal to hide it? Wouldn't that be the Wheel's sinister spin. A bastard child before he'd even been married. He wouldn't put it past Kadir to engineer such a thing, to make certain Ihsan's marriage, which was supposed to cement his place in line for the crown, was tarnished from the start.

He didn't like it. He wanted to believe her smiles, the real ones. They felt like the only sunshine he'd been able to bear in Turns. No one at court smiled like that. Genuinely. It was all games and deflections.

But it would make sense. A noblewoman appearing out of nowhere, from a father who had been silent at court for decades. To foist off their shame on him. Cold temper sent ice skimming across the table from where his fingers touched it.

"It is only a rumor, Efendim," Bashir said, careful, as he eyed the frost crawling across the map. Ihsan swept the thoughts away. He did not have time for this kind of entanglement. He lifted his hand from the map. The frost melted, and he brushed at the residual water droplets, smearing the paint.

"What is the current disposition of the City Watch around these?" He tapped the warehouses in the process of being rebuilt. They were in random places around the pier district, no pattern to suggest the aim of the vandals besides theft and chaos.

Bashir watched him for a moment too long, before he perceived Ihsan was finished with pregnancy rumors. "They have to rotate patrols. My men are covering supply movement from the districts to elsewhere, and the Watch moves patrols, at random as much as possible, between areas that have yet to be vandalized and those that have."

Ihsan nodded. Bashir's voice reflected his contemplation. There were not enough bodies to protect all the places that needed protecting. They knew it, and whoever was masterminding the attacks knew it as well, if anyone was masterminding them. That was the question that gnawed at Ihsan in the quiet moments, threading his nightmares with some unknown evil setting fire to the world.

When the nightmares came, in the past, they had always featured Kadir, or his son, or whatever random fire mage had sent Ihsan into a spiral that day. But for turns now, they had been vague, incomprehensible. Just fear and fire and amorphous figures slipping away before he could see them.

The nightmares had never lingered so long. Always they had come for a day, or two. But this endless misery whittled his temper to an edge and addled his thoughts. He barely slept, and when he did it did nothing for him.

Someone pounded on the door to Bashir's office then threw it open. Bashir looked up and Ihsan half turned around to see. A guard addressed Bashir from the doorway.

"A wagon of supplies headed for the northern camp was looted in the Water District," the man said. "A family was attacked, and most of the supplies looted off the wagon."

"Anyone hurt?" Bashir asked as he came around the desk.

"The report was unclear. No one is dead, Mutar Charah and her men intervened, and a bystander who tried to help the family was injured."

"Where?" Bashir gestured at the map. The guard edged into the office, bowing to Ihsan then giving him as wide a berth as the space allowed. He studied the map, then touched a finger to the main road running through the Water District.

"What is a family doing transporting supplies to the camp? Why weren't they escorted?" Ihsan did not like how close it appeared the riot had been to his home.

"We have to take volunteers from the camps, and provide them guards. Neither I nor Captain Akkas can spare men to run the supplies frequently enough if we're also playing wagon driver."

"But a family?" Ihsan said again.

Bashir shook his head. "I'll speak with my men. It should not have been. But they are getting desperate. So many of their shares have been stolen or burned."

Ihsan held back an explosion of curses. If people would stop panicking. If they did not resort to violence at the first opportunity…

Footsteps raced down the hall outside the office, and Kuhzey appeared in the doorway. Ihsan frowned. The boy was panting and sweating, his gaze manic. He did not bother bowing as he moved his hands at lightning pace. Ihsan had been speaking with Kuhzey like this for Turns, but still, even he could not keep up. He saw only panicked fragments.

Mistress. Wagon.

"Slow down," Ihsan said, and signed.

Hurt, Kuhzey emphasized.

"She's hurt? How?" Ihsan barked. Kuhzey jabbed a finger at the map, near the same spot the guard had, and hit his fist into his opposite palm. "Did she get caught in the mob? The looting?"

Kuhzey grimaced, shook his head, then changed his mind and nodded.

"Where is she?"

At the city estate, he signed at a more readable pace.

"Is anyone with her? Did they send for a healer? How badly is she hurt?"

Kuhzey nodded, touching four fingers to his upper arm. A Charah? Ihsan groaned. Bashir made a sound, like a suppressed laugh, and Ihsan cast him a sharp look. Aysel was in the arena, running soldiers through exercises. That only left one Charah. Who was now apparently in his home. "Wonderful," he breathed.

Kuhzey tapped his shoulder to get his attention, then pointed toward the door.

Ihsan threw a look at Bashir, who ducked his head in understanding.

"I will meet with Captain Akkas and see if there is anything to be done about the looting."

Ihsan nodded but held no optimism for the discussion. For one, Captain Akkas still maintained his anger at Naime for relieving him of his, admittedly, untaxing, position in the Cliffs. That manifested in several ways, one of which was his unwillingness to work well with Bashir and his men. For another, there were simply not enough food stores to feed the city and the refugees. And many, many of the citizens of Narfour blamed the Sarkum transplants for the Blight, for every ill that beset them. They took every opportunity to display their displeasure. Looting supply wagons meant for the camps, attacking any stands the refugees attempted to set up in the markets. They'd already attacked the camp several times with fire.

"I'll return shortly," Ihsan told Bashir.

"No, Efendim. The Sultana has ordered me to refuse to meet with you for at least a small turn after today." He smiled apologetically.

"Curse her." She really meant to take away anything that would distract him from his nightmares and his grief.

He followed Kuhzey out of the barracks. Kuhzey had brought the carriage Reyhan had arranged to take Nesrin into the city. When they were seated, the driver started the carriage with a lurch.

Ihsan stared at Kuhzey, trying to separate his thoughts into distinct threads. But everything jumbled together. "Is she all right?"

Kuhzey winced in answer. He touched his jaw, then drew a spiral around himself. Then he jerked his chin toward Ihsan and patted his own neck before drawing the sigil for the Fifth House. A burn of some kind. A shiver raced down Ihsan's arms and he wrenched his gaze from Kuhzey's to look out the small window of the carriage.

"How did she even get caught up in a mob like that?" She should have been in the house. He wasn't looking at Kuhzey, so the boy tapped him on the knee to get his attention.

She went to help.

Ihsan closed his eyes and shook his head. What kind of utter fool… She did not even have magic. The carriage ride seemed to take triple the time it usually did, Ihsan growing more tense with each passing moment.

When the carriage did finally pull around to the front of his home, he strode out of it before the driver even had time to put the brake on and dismount to open the door. Evidence of the looting remained, shredded burlap, scattered grains and root vegetables. A few children milled, searching the scraps.

Kuhzey jogged behind him, Ihsan's long stride nearly double the boy's.

The downstairs was silent, but voices drifted from above, which only increased his agitation. People. In his house. Amara, who he could not look at without shame drowning him. His pace slowed and he took the stairs reluctantly. Deniz and Reyhan sat on opposite ends of the one couch in the common area, Deniz looking resentful, Reyhan worried.

Djar and Bek stood shoulder to shoulder, in mirrored poses with legs shoulder-width apart and arms folded over their chests, with their backs to the wall. They were a few paces forward from the open door of the bedroom Nesrin was using. That is where the voices issued from. When Deniz saw Ihsan, she rose from the couch and bowed to him, her expression sour as she approached.

"She doesn't have a mote of sense in that thick head," Deniz began. Reyhan threw a glare at her and jumped up like she meant to charge at Deniz. Ihsan held up a hand to Deniz to halt what would surely continue to be a stream of insults. That seemed to mollify Reyhan, who bowed to him as he passed. His initial reaction was to agree with Deniz, but he should at least give Nesrin a chance to explain.

His steps remained reluctant as he approached the open door.

"It still burns." Nesrin's voice. Gentle, as if her proclamation were a burden.

"It will for some time, I'm afraid," came Amara's reply.

"These poultices will help. Are you ready for the bandages?"

That sounded like Havva, and some of his tension eased.

Ihsan stepped into the doorway when Nesrin gave a whimper of agreement. The three women stood huddled with their backs to the door, Nesrin in the middle. Havva held a roll of white cloth in her hands. A basin of water rested on the floor at Nesrin's feet, the water murky and a crimson-stained rag draped on the edge. She was naked from the waist up, her clothes cut so they hung low over her hips.

A raw, red, oozing mark circled her body, beginning at her left hip, across her back, presumably over her stomach, and spiraling twice more. It wrapped her neck. He could not see if it reached to her face, because her hair was falling out of its braids, obscuring his view. Amara was doing her best to hold the hair up.

The smell. The burn ointment. All the light in the room rushed to a pinpoint, until black crushed him in from all sides. His stomach roiled, and he took a panicked step backwards as hot hands wrapped around his throat. Someone, Kuhzey, yelped as he backed into them. The women turned as one, Nesrin only twisting her head. She immediately whipped her head back around with a sound of shame.

He forced a breath through his teeth, as Amara regarded him with a measured expression. He could handle this. He breathed through his mouth, trying to ignore what traces of the stench tried to trigger him. Questions rushed to his lips, but he stifled those. Phantom pain sizzled over his scars. He grit his teeth and stepped closer.

Wheel, she was so thin. Eaten away by hunger. He could count her ribs from three paces away.

"Sehzade," Havva said matter-of-factly. She was busy passing a bandage around Nesrin's body. The first layer bloomed with the ooze from Nesrin's wound, turning Ihsan's gut.

Wet, raw skin. Pain that burned into his bones. Seared him to his soul, so he wanted to die all over again. The agony every time a heal cracked open and wept more into cloth. His breath rushed away.

"Peace," Amara murmured, her stare catching on his. Silver shimmered in her irises. Her power hummed around his. She could control his, if she wished to, though he doubted Amara would ever do that to him without permission. The song of her magic soothed his panic.

Havva finished the first layer of bandages, and applied a second, tighter.

Nesrin whimpered.

He could help. He could. Ihsan lifted a hand. It tremored. He balled it into a fist in a futile effort to control it, then flexed it open, hovering just behind Nesrin.

"May I touch you?" he asked, hoarse with the effort to hold on to his sense, instead of falling into memory.

Nesrin tilted her head to look up at him. Her eyes were dappled olive by the light, and glossy with tears. The trail of the whip wrapped her neck and ended on her left jaw and cheek, just at the end of her eyebrow.

"I can help," he added. She blinked, holding his gaze as she tipped her chin down a fraction.

Havva put her hands on her hips, some reprimand held back as Ihsan cupped his hand over the back of Nesrin's neck. Nesrin tensed under his touch, shoulders hunching as she hugged her arms around herself. Amara's calm settled on Ihsan, and he whispered cold over Nesrin's skin. He touched his thumb to the uninjured skin just beside the wound on her cheek, funneling magic along the furrow in her skin.

He closed his eyes. He did not need to see to follow the track left behind by fire. Its signature was still in her skin, magical residue like breadcrumbs his magic could trace in a helix around her.

Her skin was warm in his palm, her slender neck fit easily in the curve of his hand. Tendrils of her mussed hair brushed the back of his hand, tickling. Distracting. He squeezed his eyes shut as he concentrated.

"No you don't," Havva said, her admonishment aimed toward the door. "Out you get, boy."

Kuhzey must have succumbed to curiosity. Ihsan couldn't blame the boy, he hadn't given thought to the fact she might be uncomfortable with him in the room with her, exposed as she was. Beneath his hand her skin prickled, and a violent shiver shook her body.

Ihsan released his hold on her, but kept his magic on her skin as he flicked the buttons open on his entari and shrugged out of it. He dropped it over her. "Forgive me," he said, hands resting on her shoulders. "It was thoughtless of me to come in here."

She hugged the entari closed, turning just enough to meet his eyes. "I will consider it." Tears streaked her face, her expression vulnerable, but a smile teased at the corners of her mouth.

He did not belong anywhere near her—should not have offered kindness he did not have the capacity to repeat.

"What does she need?" he asked Havva. He retracted his power as he let go of her shoulders and backed away. Nesrin's lashes fluttered, her expression wilting as she turned her head away again.

"Salves and bandage changes for at least a turn," Havva said brusquely, the tone something she had clearly passed along to her son, Bashir. She packed away her scissors, bandage scraps, pots of salve, and a little packet of herbs. "I'll write it out for her maid, and I'll check on her for the first few days."

Ihsan looked to Amara, tipping his head toward the common room. She followed him, closing Nesrin's doors behind her. Reyhan jumped to her feet and rushed for the door, knocking before slipping inside. Ihsan led Amara into his office, directly across the space.

"What happened?" he demanded, more harshly than he had meant to. He continued through the room to his desk. He turned then, leaning back against it, arms folded. Amara stood just inside the doorway, taking in the office with a raised eyebrow and judgmental silence. She was good at that. Shrinking him with just a look.

"I think that is the kindest thing I have ever seen you do, Sehzade." She looked at him curiously, as though reassessing him.

He chaffed under her measure. "Answer my question."

She sniffed dismissal of his prickliness. "Another mob, trying to loot a supply wagon for the northern camp. It's the third time in just as many turns. This one was the biggest crowd I've seen yet. And the most unreasonable. There was a mother with children, one still a babe in arms," Amara said.

"Is the family all right?"

"The father was beaten, and has injuries as you would expect. The mother and children were spared injury because she"—Amara swept a gesture to indicate Nesrin in the other room—"used her body as a shield. The man who did that to her is on his way to the Cliffs."

Ihsan pressed his thumb between his brows, his eyes going to the floor. "Why would she do that?"

"Because she is decent and brave?" Amara suggested.

Was she? Was she gentle and selfless and brave? Or was she something else—something that belonged to Kadir and his schemes? What was worse? That she was an actress and a spy…or humane, and kind?

Ihsan pushed the musings aside. "Thank you for seeing to her." He looked sideways, unwilling to endure whatever expression Amara wore.

"Send her to my shop when she is feeling better. I would like to get to know her." Amara's tone was placid, but when he glanced at her, her look was pointed. He tipped his head to one side in acknowledgment. Perhaps Amara could drag things from her Ihsan would never be able to. Even if he dared allow her close. Which he did not. He pushed away from the desk and bowed to Amara.

She gave a pleased sound and turned, pausing to look back at him. "Forgive me for saying so, Sehzade, but your vine seems limp."

His gaze shot to hers, and she gave him a vulpine smile as she pointed to something beside him. He glanced and saw the potted plant he kept there. A failed experiment. He glowered at her and she laughed in glee as she shut the door behind her.

Twenty

Nesrin opened her eyes to a starless, moonless night. She was curled around herself like a babe, knees and elbows tucked in, lying on her side. For a moment she did not move, disoriented by a complete absence of any sensation. She blinked slowly. She could not see.

She could not move.

Her body did not obey her command to unfurl. The blackness pressed from all sides, holding her, binding her as she was. She strained and bucked against it, but she might as well have been wrapped tightly in cloth, like a moth cocooned. Nesrin tried to draw a breath to scream, but she could not breathe either. That sent her into a spiral of panic. Until she realized she could not breathe, but neither did her body seem to need it.

A dream. Nesrin settled. *Wake up*, she told herself. She had never had a dream this vivid, or this terrifying.

Something shifted at the edge of her vision. Shadow on black. A fuzzy apparition that loomed just outside her ability to see it.

Pain raced over her body. A skein of lightning wrapping around her, and it felt as if her skin were peeling away. Nesrin gave another soundless scream.

And woke.

She bolted up, sucking in great breaths. The pain from the dream remained with her, burning a corset around her body and a chokehold on her neck. Reality hit her in a disorienting jumble of memory, too chaotic in the wake of the strange, empty blackness.

Then the cold hit. The moonlight streaming in from her windows made the sheet of ice crawling up her door glint. She glared at it. The fear of her dream morphing swiftly to anger. Enough. That was enough.

Nesrin got up from the floor, where she remembered huddling once everyone had left her. Reyhan was asleep downstairs in the servants' quarters, along with Kuhzey and Deniz. Reyhan had yet to experience the nightly frost storm. Did she know about it? Surely not. She would have mentioned it.

Nesrin moved in halting steps, each shift an assault on her tortured skin. She grabbed for the robe Reyhan had hung on the outside of the wardrobe then shrugged gingerly into it. Her door opened silently when she lowered the latch, and she stuck her head out to survey the common room. It was empty, but just as Nesrin stepped from her room, Reyhan appeared on the stairs.

She darted to Nesrin's side.

"What is that?" Reyhan clutched at Nesrin's sleeve. Blue light flashed in the crack beneath the middle set of doors on the far side of the common room. "There is ice covering the downstairs, but Kuhzey and Deniz are sleeping!"

"I believe they are used to it," Nesrin murmured. "It has happened nearly every night." But why was Deniz not working a dampening as she had at the palace? Nesrin hugged her robe around herself and crept forward. The ice crunched then melted under her feet.

"No!" Reyhan gasped, grabbing for her, but she missed, and appeared unwilling to move any closer. Nesrin was not afraid. This ice, this magic, had the same feeling as that he had soothed her burns with. It was his.

But she did move cautiously and set her hand reluctantly on the latch when she reached the room. The blue light spilled and undulated, like sun reflecting off clear water. Nesrin held her breath and lowered the latch, pushing the door open. Behind her, across the room, Reyhan gave a whimper of fear.

Nesrin peeked around the edge of the door as soon as she could fit her head. It was indeed his bedroom. It looked exactly like hers, though a bit bigger. He lay face down on the bed, still as a corpse, magic dancing across him and out from him. She pushed the door wider and stepped inside. Her heart had never beat so hard or so fast.

She knew the folly of what she was doing. But she had to know what was happening. On quiet feet she crept across the thick carpet and to the side of his bed. He was rigid from head to toe, his hands clawed into fistfuls of the sheet, his face turned away from her and pulled into an expression of agony or terror or both. He wore only salvar, as he had the night she'd seen him come to his bedroom door in the palace. But tonight she was close enough to see his scars.

Furrowed flesh and twisted skin covered the entirety of his right side, from his jaw to the waist of the salvar he wore, and likely beneath. His arm as well. It must have been excruciating. Even her small wound had been unbearable when she woke from her unconsciousness.

His mouth moved. The only part of his body that did. She could not read what he was saying. She wanted to wake him. He was tortured, that was plain. She reached, but her hand hovered above him. The whip mark around her body flared with pain, just as he woke with a gasp, launching up from his belly to his elbows, head hanging as he drew a jagged breath.

Nesrin snatched her hand back and stumbled away. The movement and her gasp of surprise caught his attention and his head whipped around to look at her. Blue-white light flared in his eyes.

"Out!" he barked, launching up as if he meant to attack her. Nesrin scrambled back, then darted for the door, slamming it behind her.

Reyhan came to her side. "Are you all right?"

"I'm fine," Nesrin panted. "It's fine. I… I think he's having nightmares."

Reyhan stayed silent until they were in Nesrin's room again, with the door shut. "It would make sense," she mused. Her attention fell to the blanket on the floor. She cast a mage orb.

"What happened to him?" Nesrin asked.

Reyhan gathered up the blanket and put it back on the bed. "I only know that when he was younger, he was trapped in a burning building. It burned down around him."

"But…his magic did not protect him?"

"I think it did." Her face twisted in sympathy. "I think it kept him alive."

"What sort of fire could burn a water mage with that much power?" Nesrin sat on the edge of the bed. She was dizzy again.

Reyhan hesitated, her face going slack, then tense. "Something, or someone, with more power."

That thought left Nesrin colder than the ice had. And the look on her maid's face, reluctant, suggested she knew more detail than that.

"You should not pry." Reyhan glanced behind her, toward the door, then back. "Keep distance between you. It is safer."

Nesrin nodded. Sadness wound tightly with all the other confusing emotions. Reyhan was right. This was all a lie, and the more she tried to connect with the man, the more likely he was to realize it.

"You look pale. Are you in pain?" Reyhan asked, grudgingly.

Nesrin shook her head. She did not want to keep Reyhan awake any longer than she already had.

Reyhan lifted her chin with a sniff. "I'll bring you some tea, for the pain." She left, leaving Nesrin's door open a crack. Nesrin slipped off the bed and looked through the slit toward the Sehzade's room. No more light came from inside. *Let it be.* Nesrin sat awkwardly on the bed, trying to avoid the place on her hip that ached with the pain of the whip.

It was going to scar, Havva had told her. She could not tell how badly, but the mark would remain. Nesrin closed her eyes. Scars did not matter in the valley. In fact, smooth, unmarred skin was the mark of someone who did not work. Who enjoyed their ease at the expense of others. She touched her fingers to her jaw, below the place that ached with raw intensity. Now, she was marked by the city. By hate. Scars earned through work were prideful things. This was something else. A crack in who she was. The hairline fracture in a pot before the slightest jarring made it shatter to pieces.

Nesrin rose, resigned to a confrontation with the Sehzade. Dreading it. How could she defend that she had entered his private room without permission? Curiosity? Did she have a right to know secrets he seemed intent on keeping, simply because they were betrothed? They were still strangers.

The Nesrin from the valley would have easily defended her action. It was unreasonable to expect someone to live in a house where they were exposed to magic nearly nightly without some kind of explanation. But she did not know who she was here.

The man was clearly traumatized by the fire that burned him, or something else. If he did not want to share…

She needn't have worried. He was not there, when she left her room and hobbled down to breakfast. The dining room, which connected to a small kitchen, and past it, to a yard, was empty but for her and Reyhan. They ate in silence. The breakfast was humble, much closer to one she might have had at her home. Scrambled eggs with tomatoes and a sprinkling of za'atar. Tea.

Nesrin sipped at the blindingly strong brew, wincing. Reyhan set down the piece of flatbread she only picked at. Nesrin looked at the other woman. She was familiar enough with her expressions now to brace for a lecture.

"Princesses do not run into danger. They will not see you as brave, they will see you as foolhardy."

"Yes I know." Nesrin set the teacup down harshly. "Princesses don't do this, princesses don't do that." She waved a hand vaguely. "What do princesses *do*?"

"They do not falter. They do not stumble, stutter, or hesitate. They do not allow weakness to show. Weakness invites discredit. It invites them to believe you are incapable. They are wolves, and sharks, ravenous to pick off the weak."

"And how is helping people a weakness?"

"Expose your heart, Mistress, and they will pluck it from your body. Do not let them see you care." Reyhan dropped her gaze, poking at her half-eaten eggs. "If you wish to survive this, you have no alternative."

She heard everything Reyhan did not say. Remembered how she had fallen to her knees before the Grand Vizier. For the second time, Nesrin had a sense of being trapped in a web. But she did not yet know whose. The Grand Vizier's? The Sehzade's? The two men disliked each other, at the very least. But what kind of pawn was she in that game? A wife-to-be in name alone—a princess crowned by lies.

She finished her food. When she stood and reached to collect the dishes, Reyhan slapped her hands away with a glare. Nesrin did not bother to glare back. She left the dishes to Reyhan and walked through the kitchen and out the back door. It led to a patio where an oven very much like the one her family used sat hunched with a wild, overgrown garden as backdrop. It made her heart ache, and her fingers itch. How many days had it been since she had cooked? Fed anyone? Created anything?

Princesses likely *did not do that.* She limped her way out from under the overhang of the second floor and into the sunshine. She passed beneath a tangled rose vine growing up one of the supports. A few sad, shabby blossoms hung sadly. Nesrin trailed her fingers over one she could reach, a silent greeting.

There had been a path that led from the back doors of the main downstairs. Weeds and grass grew amongst gravel. She followed its ghost, noting the high wall that surrounded the area. Another house rose tall on the other side of the stone wall. The yard was small. Not much larger than a goat pen. Manageable.

She wondered if princesses were allowed to dig in gardens and care for flowers. Doubtful. Everything was crowded and overgrown. She spotted some hardy survivors, a few more roses. Vines trailing up the back of the wall.

Honestly...what is the point of a garden you do not maintain? Perhaps he did not have any servants for it. He did not strike her as a man who dabbled with flowers, but she knew next to nothing of him. And people could be surprising with their secrets, and their hobbies.

At the northern wall, farthest from the house, Nesrin was delighted to find a Tamar cedar growing up, twisted and leaning over the fence toward the street on the other side in a bid for more light.

A few paces away along the same wall, an old apricot tree in desperate need of pruning had set a meager load of fruit that was not quite ripe. Nesrin reached up and snapped a gnarled, dead branch off. She circled the tree, doing the same with any she could reach without stretching too far. Too much movement sent a rending pain spiraling along the length of the wound that wound her body.

It did not take her long to tire, weak from seasons of hunger and the toll of the chaos of the day before. She sat in the shade of the tree, leaning awkwardly against its trunk. Idly, she snapped a long twig into bits. Perhaps tidying up the garden could occupy some of her time.

At least she was competent at that, and might feel useful. But first she would need permission, and that required her husband-to-be to show his face.

They would have to discuss the nightmares at some point, though she did not know what to say to him. They shared a house now, not a grand palace. He could not avoid her forever.

Twenty-One

"Mutar Charah has requested you join her for tea, when you are feeling up to it," Reyhan said, with a critical stare.

Coming up with what to say to the Sehzade turned out not to be a problem, because she had underestimated the man. He had successfully avoided her for a whole turn.

"You disapprove?" Nesrin murmured as she used the rusty shears she had found to trim the climbing rose on the patio. The idea of company besides Reyhan and an occasional glimpse of Deniz's surly face or Kuhzey's apologetic one sounded like sunshine after rain.

"What do you think?" Reyhan asked acidly, standing with arms folded as she watched Nesrin snipping at the rose. "The most powerful water mage in Narfour. It is a good thing you have no secrets to keep."

Nesrin hesitated, shears held open over a fading bloom. Reyhan made a mocking face. Nesrin snapped the shears closed. Before she could respond, Kuhzey appeared on the patio, saw them, and wheeled around to reenter the house.

"Wait, Kuhzey. Could you help me?" Nesrin said. He stopped, turning once again toward her, face flushed. "I want to take some flowers to Mutar Charah. Will you please find me a basket to carry them?"

Kuhzey returned to the house.

He'd been giving her lessons at night on his language of hand signals. It would take her Turns to master, but she enjoyed it. Sometimes she tried to ask him questions about the Sehzade, but he brushed them off. Their relationship did not seem to be purely prince and servant. But closer to brothers. Or at least Kuhzey got away with a great deal more morosity and ineptitude than the servants at the estate in Mizraa, or the few she had interacted with at the palace.

Nesrin frowned, pondering as she searched the vine for the best flowers. By the time Kuhzey returned, she had an armful that she deposited in the basket as he held it out to her.

"Thank you." Nesrin beamed at him and he returned the look like a rabbit caught in a burst of light. "Will you take them into the kitchen for me?"

He nodded, but did not go immediately.

Reyhan clicked her tongue at him in threat and he jolted, scurrying past her to the kitchen's back door. Nesrin stifled a giggle, and even Reyhan appeared amused. They followed him, Nesrin kicking off an older pair of slippers she kept on the patio for her forays into the garden. The sun lingered above the mountains in the east, so its light would be in the garden for another few marks. It would be hot soon. If they were going to travel, best to get it done before the heat set in. The sun made Nesrin's wounds blaze with pain.

She ducked into the kitchen. It was a small space, lit by lamps. Reyhan eyed them grouchily. But she did not dare cast an orb for its clearer light. The one time she had done so, Deniz had come charging out of nowhere, screeching like an angry gull about Fifth House magic in the Sehzade's home. No mage orbs meant the house was dim most of the day, except when the angle of the sun was right, and so Nesrin much preferred to be outside in the garden.

Kuhzey had left the basket of white roses on the long oak table that took up the majority of the kitchen's space. There were also narrow counters on three of the four walls, and herbs hung from the ceiling along the rafters.

"Wet some of that burlap for me," Nesrin said to Reyhan. The fire mage obeyed, turning her back on Nesrin to soak the cloth in the basin of water on one of the counters. Nesrin pushed her caftan sleeves up to her elbows and took a knife to the stems, stripping the lower leaves and cutting their ends fresh, so they were all similar in length.

Reyhan approached her side, holding out the burlap. She made a disgruntled sound and tugged Nesrin's caftan sleeves back down. Nesrin plucked the burlap from her and wrapped it around the rose stems, then tied them with twine. Just as she deposited the bundle back into its basket, Deniz came in from the dining room, with a lamb leg hanging from a hemp string in her meaty left fist. She reeled in the doorway, looking from one to the other of them, eyes widening then slitting.

"What are you doing in my kitchen?" She swung the raw shank onto the table as though it were a club, splattering bits of the fat. Nesrin suspected she was trying to unnerve her. She spun the knife she'd been using on the roses and stabbed it into the meat.

"I'm finished. You'll probably be wanting that," she said sweetly, then scooped up the flower basket and strode past Deniz and her gaping-fish expression.

When they were out of the kitchen and through the dining room, Reyhan burst into a laugh, bending forward and bracing her hands on her thighs.

"Do I hear a donkey out there?" Deniz snapped from the kitchen, and Nesrin and Reyhan exchanged a humored glance. They made their way upstairs. Reyhan selected an outfit she deemed appropriate to meet with a Charah, and a Master Merchant. Everything in shades of sea green.

They changed Nesrin's bandages first, applying more of the pungent salve. Reyhan was careful, apologetic even, and was especially careful around the neck and face, gingerly combing her loose hair away. Nesrin could not help but think of the Sehzade, of his broad hand on her neck, the chill rush of his power, the gentleness in the words he spoke to her. That he thought to cover her when she was cold. The Grand Vizier would have her believe Ihsan was a monster. But she struggled to. It was not the Sehzade who had threatened her into this charade.

Reyhan dressed her, and for once, Nesrin needed the help, struggling to get things over her head and around her waist without gasping in pain. Reyhan belted the cloth loosely.

"Is it all right?" she asked, as kindly as Nesrin had ever heard Reyhan ask anything, and she nodded.

"Is it very far?" Nesrin picked up her basket of flowers. She could not accept tea without a gift, at least. In Mizraa, no one would take without giving. There seemed to be a great deal of taking in Narfour.

"Not terribly, but it might feel so. Would you rather I ask for a carriage?" Reyhan peered out the bedroom window to see if there was one parked below.

"Wheel, no. All that bouncing." Nesrin shook her head. Reyhan nodded understanding. They headed back downstairs. If she did not try to walk too quickly, nor with too long a stride, it would be all right. She hoped. She'd really only been wandering around the small garden. Like a dog circling. Yes. This would be good. A bit of freedom. It would be good to learn her way around the city. If it was to be her home.

Reyhan reached the first floor a few steps before Nesrin and turned to watch her slow progress. Some of her prickliness had disappeared after the melee in the street. Occasionally, she was outright kind. If only Nesrin had thought to wound herself in the name of justice sooner.

At the bottom step she stopped, leaning on the railing to catch her breath. The stairs were the most challenging, stretching and pulling. She hadn't needed stitches, but that was almost worse, as the shallow wound easily cracked open, bleeding and weeping, if Nesrin was not conservative with her movements. Something she was not accustomed to.

"..*in my kitchen*!" Deniz's voice, from the kitchen, rose on the last of a complaint. A male voice hummed in response, too low-pitched to make out words. Nesrin's gaze whipped to Reyhan's, whose brown eyes widened as they both looked toward the kitchen. "I'll not have it!" Something banged in punctuation, and Reyhan startled. Then she tossed Nesrin a wicked grin.

Nesrin was too panicked at the sound of the Sehzade's voice to feel humor.

"Go!" Nesrin whispered, flapping her hands toward the door as she moved in that direction. Reyhan rushed to the front doors and pushed one open, circling her hand in the air to encourage Nesrin to speed. But Nesrin was moving as fast as she could, which was not fast enough. She reached the front door as the Sehzade emerged from the archway that led into the kitchen and dining room. Reyhan bowed, which made it necessary that Nesrin stop and turn to face him.

She bent into a bow immediately to spare herself the mortifying experience of meeting his gaze. But he had not turned away when she rose.

"Good morning!" she chirped then spun away.

"Are those my roses?" he called at her back as Reyhan swung the door closed behind them.

The city bustled with noise, activity, and smells, just as it had the day she first arrived. It was an entirely different experience on foot. The Water District was dominated by a public bath. Once Nesrin was on the street and walking, she could see its domed facade cresting above the homes that surrounded them.

"I will take you, when you're healed. It's almost as old as the palace," Reyhan said.

They passed small markets, stalls in groups of three or six. Most selling meager selections of produce, textiles, or housewares. Nothing especially interesting that made Nesrin wish to pause and examine.

By the time they reached their destination, which was tucked into a narrow street full to the brim with shops, Nesrin was sweating and exhausted. She said nothing, and neither did Reyhan.

There were shops with great glass windows, larger than Nesrin, displaying baked goods, bread, or meat. Nesrin had never seen a shop selling nothing but sweets, and she did linger at that window for a moment. They seemed more like works of art than anything someone might eat. Sweets were a rare indulgence in the valley. Time-consuming and requiring precious sugar or honey to make. Not to mention the literal fortune in nuts. Her mouth watered.

"You know," Reyhan said thoughtfully, "the Sehzade should be providing you a stipend. To spend as you wish. I can ask about it, if you'd like."

"Oh." Nesrin flushed and shook her head. "No that's all right. What could I possibly want that is not provided?"

Reyhan frowned. "Autonomy?"

Nesrin smiled sidelong at her. "Yes. But how will a stipend give me that? It might as well be the leash."

Reyhan waggled her head back and forth in regretful agreement. "Come. The shop is just there." She pointed down the street. Nesrin wilted with relief. The slope in this part of the city was less than the Fire District, with its genuine hills, but even that small amount was taxing on her still-healing skin.

The shop Reyhan led her to also had a glass front. Two great windows faced the street, with swaths of stunning silk and brocade hung to showcase their colors and clothing fit for sultans and sultanas displayed on dress-forms. Reyhan paused to look at the clothing as Nesrin had looked at the candies in the last shop.

Nesrin's brow furrowed. "Is the Grand Vizier paying you?"

In a flash, all the ground she had gained with Reyhan disappeared. The woman tensed, her expression going hard and sharp. "After a fashion. Shall we?" She pointed at the door, her voice brusque, distant. Nesrin held her other questions, barely.

They climbed the three tiled steps and entered through a glass-paned wooden door that struck a bell as they opened it.

A head popped up above a stack of silks at the very back of the long, narrow space. Nesrin recognized the young man immediately. One of her saviors from the looting incident. He did not smile, but ducked down again, calling in a language Nesrin assumed to be Meneian. Noise came from above them, footsteps. A moment later the Charah descended.

She was so beautiful. Nesrin stared, swallowing back her nervousness. There were beautiful women in the valley, certainly. But none who carried themselves the way Mutar Charah did. She flowed like water, red-brown skin aglow against caftan and entari of shimmering teal.

"I am so pleased you accepted my invitation." She reached her hands forward as Nesrin approached. Reyhan took the basket of flowers from Nesrin and bowed, and Nesrin set her hands in the Charah's outstretched ones. Her fingers were long and cool, a relief after their sweaty trek across the district. Nesrin bowed over their joined hands and Mutar Charah waved a hand in dismissal.

"These are for you." Nesrin felt shy as she took the basket from Reyhan and held it out. The woman's dark eyes lit with pleasure, and Nesrin smiled.

"Lovely. Thank you." She glanced over her shoulder. "Bek. Put these in some water for me?" She slid them out of their basket cradle and handed them to the young man when he approached. He was energetic, bouncing on the balls of his feet when he stopped in front of her and took the armful of flowers. He flashed Nesrin a bright grin before he loped upstairs. "And bring tea!" Mutar Charah called after him. "Come," she said to Nesrin and Reyhan, leading them through a paradise of fabric bolts, half-finished clothing on forms, baskets of sewing necessities, bobbins and ribbon spools. Nesrin had never seen anything like it.

"It is wonderful in here," she said reverently as she touched what appeared to be a pristine bolt of silk the color of spring leaf buds. The Charah noted the touch with a smile.

"I am glad you think so. It is a place of sanctuary, for me, and others." She gestured them to a circle of well-worn chairs and couches. Unlike the furniture in the Grand Vizier and Sehzade's home, these were clearly a gathering place oft used. When Nesrin sat in a velvet-covered chair, its soft cushion seemed to envelop her and she moaned in relief.

"Yes, I am certain you have been much deprived of comfortable seating. The palace, and certainly the Sehzade's home, suffer from an affliction of looks over function," Mutar Charah said in amusement.

"Yes." Nesrin rested her head on the back of the chair and closed her eyes. Reyhan protested weakly, to which the Charah chuckled.

"You needn't keep the facade up here. In here, we are ourselves, yes? And you may call me Amara…and you?"

"Nesrin." She sat up straighter despite the offer to relax.

"Do you think the Sehzade has ever sat in any of the seats of his home?" Amara mused to them as Bek reappeared with a tray laden with a pot and small glasses for tea. He set it on the table between them, then slunk back to whatever task he had ensconced in a fort of bolts.

"No," Nesrin said. She automatically moved to pour the tea for everyone, but Reyhan beat her to it with a quick look of rebuke. Nesrin tried to turn her motion into folding her hands in her lap, but it was awkward. Amara noted the exchange but did not comment, her gaze following Reyhan's movements as she poured.

"How is Kanat?" Amara asked Reyhan. The fire mage stiffened, though the teapot in her hands was unsteady, and she splashed a bit onto the tray. Regaining her composure, Reyhan dabbed at the spill with a linen cloth that Bek had brought with the tea. "I was saddened that he withdrew from the guild." Amara took her cup. "His glass-work is unequaled."

Nesrin sipped at her tea politely, instead of ogling Reyhan in curiosity.

Reyhan took overlong refolding the linen cloth and setting it just so on the side of the tray, her gaze on her task.

"The guild was too demanding. Kanat could not keep up with it, by himself. This fulfills our needs and he does not have to work from dawn to dusk." The answer was monotone, unusual for Reyhan. Or any fire mage.

"He is always welcome back," Amara said with a smile, her dark eyes glittering as she stared at Reyhan. "You will tell him that? If he needs…assistance, the guild can offer him that, certainly." The smile was too tame. Nesrin sipped at her tea again. She was missing something. The subtext.

Reyhan gave a short, soundless nod, and retreated to a chair with her own cup of tea.

They sat in awkward silence for a few moments. Then Amara leaned forward and set her glass back on the tray.

When she sat back she focused on Nesrin. "It is a rare noble, and rarer still for a woman, to act as you did. For the good of lowborns. For the good of refugees," Amara said, kindly. It seemed an innocuous enough statement, but Nesrin knew a water mage's probe when she heard one. The lilt to Amara's water-song voice, even disguised with the flavor of Menei in her words, was the same Nesrin's mother used when she wanted one of her children to admit to misbehaving.

Reyhan's admonishments lingered in Nesrin's thoughts, niggling at her daily. Show them your heart—and they will pluck it from your chest.

"I meant only to help them out of the wagon," Nesrin said, mining the event for broad truths.

"I see," Amara said. "I had hoped you might be interested in assisting me in my work with the refugee camps. It would do them, and the city, much good to see someone of high rank in the palace working toward a mutual good."

"Oh! Yes I would love to." Nesrin barreled through the response without thinking, and before Reyhan's flared gaze could stop her.

"Wonderful!" Amara said, with what appeared to be genuine enthusiasm. "I visit once a small turn. I will send Bek for you when I go in a few days." She poured them more tea, and lifted a cup and saucer toward Reyhan. "And you, Reyhan?"

"I go where my mistress goes," Reyhan said, bitterness biting in her tone. She twisted the bracelet on her wrist, a thin gold band set with red stones, before reaching for the offered tea. Nesrin frowned into her cup.

Amara quickly guided them away from the topic. If she noticed Reyhan's odd behavior, Nesrin could not tell. But they talked of Nesrin adjusting to the city, and the palace. Of Mizraa, which made Nesrin sad to speak of in half-truths and avoided topics. But then they moved on to the Sehzade. She did not reveal his nightmares. They were not hers to speak of. Though she longed for advice on what to do.

When Djar, the towering Meneian who had assisted during the looting, joined them, he and Amara spun tales of their travel to the Republic. Of the Suloi, and the men who hunted mages with poison and guns.

The afternoon drifted away, and Reyhan suggested they should leave before the streets became unsafe.

"Let me measure you before you leave." Amara rose from her chair as they did. She collected a few strips of blank paper from a basket on a dresser. The dresser was pushed against a wall, tucked in amongst bare dress-forms and leaning bolts of cloth, with empty baskets in precarious towers on top. Its turquoise paint was cracked and chipping. Like everything else about the shop, it was a glorious mess, used and loved, and Nesrin wished she never had to leave to return to the sterile, tension-filled home of the Sehzade.

She stood, obeying Amara's orders for positioning her arms and body as she laid strips of paper against her in various places and marked them with a pencil. "Hmm. When your color returns"—she circled Nesrin thoughtfully, pausing to examine her hair—"green I think. I so rarely get to work with green."

"But I don't have money to pay you," Nesrin murmured. Reyhan sighed. Amara gave a secretive smile.

"We will put it on the Sehzade's account, yes?" She chuckled warmly to herself as she turned away to place the paper measures into a basket, which she labeled with another piece of paper with Nesrin's name.

"I can walk you back," Djar said in his rumbling voice, rising from his seat when Amara faced them once more. Nesrin hesitated. That was so much trouble for him, all the way to the house and back. She glanced at Reyhan, who only shrugged a shoulder.

"No, I do not wish to burden you with that. We will be all right. Reyhan can be quite fierce when she puts her mind to it," Nesrin teased. Djar frowned.

"It is less trouble than explaining to the Sehzade why his new bride-to-be was robbed or mugged on the way back from my shop," Amara said. Somehow she made the entire sentence into a command, and no one said anything to argue. Djar took a sword belt from a hook on the back wall near the stairs and fastened it around his hip. The sword was a wicked half-smile, deeply curved and without sheath. Nesrin suspected the mere sight of it stopped most trouble before it even started.

Their walk back was conducted in amicable silence. Nesrin was aware of a tension in Reyhan that had not been there earlier in the day. She wanted to ask about it, to ask about the things Amara had brought up. About Kanat. The mere mention of him had closed Reyhan like a door.

"Do you know," Djar said as they turned onto the main road that would take them to the Sehzade's home, "that Amara was supposed to wed the Sehzade?"

"Noooo," Nesrin breathed, looking up at him wide-eyed.

He grinned at her. "She eventually canceled the arrangement."

"Were they in love?" Nesrin asked. Perhaps he was brusque and rude because he loved another?

Djar cast a look at her. "No. Broken men cannot love. Nor broken women, for that matter."

Nesrin had already surmised that whatever traumas lay in the Sehzade's past lingered with him still. "Is Amara broken?" She seemed the most confident, capable woman.

"Not anymore. We all carry ghosts within us. One must face them, or be ruled by them."

"That is very poetic." Nesrin smiled.

"Yes. You did not expect such beautiful words from someone with no hair, hmm?" He smoothed a hand over his bare head.

Reyhan snorted, then covered her mouth, glancing at them both as her cheeks colored.

"It was the sword, actually. Is hair required for poetry?" Nesrin teased. Djar grinned again.

"It is a burden to be so handsome and so gifted with word and sword," he said, "so I tried to be fair by cutting away my hair but, alas." He shrugged. Nesrin liked the music in his accent and Amara's. She liked this moment of feeling ordinary again, her words just words. Inconsequential. She missed the comfort of that. Of being unextraordinary.

They did not speak anymore as they drew close to the Sehzade's home. The setting sun still blazed, and though Nesrin was sweating what felt like buckets by the time they had climbed the sloping cobblestone to the house, Djar seemed to be untouched by the heat. There were fewer people on the trek back than there had been when they left for Amara's shop. Most had gone home to their dinners and their families. Warm light glowed from windows; the smells of cooking filled the air. Roasted meat and toasty spices. Wouldn't it be lovely to be returning home to one of those, with her own boisterous family, instead of a cold house with people who barely tolerated her?

Djar delivered them to the steps of the house.

"Will you be all right alone?" Nesrin asked as she stepped onto the first of the three stairs. Djar drew back as though insulted. He looked at Reyhan, his joviality hardening.

"Remember Amara's offer. The guild takes care of its own."

Reyhan nodded stiffly.

Nesrin thanked him and waved exuberantly as he turned and walked back down the road. Reyhan grabbed Nesrin's arm and pressed it to her side with a glare.

The crossroads near the bottom of the hill still teemed with cart traffic, bound for the warehouses near the piers. Wasn't that where Harun had said his mother's inn was? Reyhan had sketched a rough map of the city for Nesrin, and forced her to copy it daily, so she could memorize it. Strange to map a place she barely knew, had only seen a fraction of. But today's jaunt would help.

"And now," Reyhan bemoaned, "to whatever dull and dusty meal our dearest Deniz has prepared."

Nesrin wrinkled her nose. It was true. She had been spoiled by the food in the palace. That and her grandmothers' cooking. And her own, for that matter. She had not known it was possible to turn flatbread into a weapon. Deniz made food as if it had offended her and she was returning the slight with brutal treatment.

Reyhan passed Nesrin on the stairs and reached for the door.

"Who is Kanat?" Nesrin asked, softly. The tension came back to Reyhan, she flinched, and that glassy-eyed look of shutting down fell over her face. Her fingers tightened on the door handle, a muscle feathering in her jaw. Her opposite hand closed over her wrist, and the bangle there. Perhaps that was a gift? From Kanat?

"My promised," Reyhan said, curtly, then shoved the door open and went inside.

Twenty-Two

Ihsan sat on the worn velvet couch, staring at a wall of square shelves filled to bursting with fabrics. Restless, his right leg bounced. He'd noticed and stopped it several times already, but then his attention would wander and it would start again. In a corner, Bek sat cross-legged on the floor with Kuhzey, attempting to teach him to play dice.

She was making him wait on purpose. One of the many small things she did to remind him of how he had slighted her. He deserved it, he knew. But he wondered when it would end.

"Your betrothed is sweet." Amara's voice preceded her. She appeared on the stairs, carrying a tray set with coffee. She placed it on the low table between the seats, a nicked, scratched oak affair in desperate need of some attention. Though she seemed to like her surroundings with signs of use. She poured the coffee from its metal ibrik into the cups, and its bitter scent filled his nostrils and his memories. It was a comforting smell, evoking Turns of quiet moments with people he cared about. But also reminded him of tense interactions with people bent on twisting things to their own ends. She gestured to cream and sugar but he waved her away.

"What did you speak about?" Ihsan sat back, sipping at the harsh brew. He'd had coffee with Amara only a few times, and Mathei had typically been present. Or Cassian. Both men brought levity and ease to the interaction that Ihsan sorely missed at this particular moment. His leg began to twitch again. Amara noted the movement with a flick of her gaze, her mouth quirking, as she settled into her own seat.

"Nothing," she said as she dipped her nose toward the steam of her cup and inhaled with closed eyes. "Nothing of import." Her tone held curiosity. "Have you noticed that she is both innocently open and… cagy?" She opened her eyes to meet his gaze.

"No," Ihsan grunted, finishing his cup and setting it down. What did that mean? "We have hardly spoken."

Amara gave one slow blink, which held enough critique in it to make heat tickle up Ihsan's neck. "Is she not staying in your home? In your rooms in the palace? How have you managed to avoid conversation?"

"We all have our talents." He tugged at his sleeves to pull them down over the scars.

"And is avoidance her talent or yours?"

"You said she was cagy, not I," Ihsan said in a lame attempt to turn her focus from him. Amara set her cup on the table.

"What brings you here, Sehzade? To ferret out secrets about your betrothed? Secrets you could easily have by now if you spoke with the woman?"

"I do not have your talent for people, Mutar Charah," he echoed her hard tone, sharp enough that Bek lifted his head from their dice game in curiosity. Her brows dropped, and she clicked her tongue in admonishment.

"Yes you do, son of the Second House. You have built too many walls in your own mind with that ice of yours." She relaxed back into her chair, regarding him with a neutral expression. He bristled, but did not reply immediately, instead channeling that energy into refilling his coffee.

"I cannot help the ice," he mumbled into his cup as he lifted it to cover his scowl. Amara tipped her head sideways in concession.

"But the walls," she said, gently, pushing.

"She said *nothing* of interest?" He'd come to find out more about Nesrin, not have his own mind picked apart.

Amara exhaled in defeat. "We spoke of mundane things. I wished to know why she would put herself in danger for refugees. I can think of few other nobles who would do so. I simply noticed that she spoke very little of her life in the valley. Of her father. Or even her mother. Do you know anything of her parents?"

"Bardakci Pasha has never been to court. He casts his votes through the Grand Vizier. I know he is capable. The chiflik at Mizraa was plagued with issues when the previous Sultan reigned and the Altimur family controlled it through a subsidiary. Bardakci Pasha made it productive within a few Turns of taking over control."

"And her mother?"

"A water mage from the valley. I only know from the records. She was marked as deceased."

"I see." Amara examined him, and Ihsan averted his gaze, scanning the shelves of fabric on the wall opposite him. "I would like to make clothes for her. May I put them on your account?"

Ihsan scowled. "How many did she ask for?" He had known that whoever he married might see him as little more than a purse to draw from.

"So jaded," Amara purred. "I am ashamed on your behalf that you have put no effort into coming to know the woman who will share your home and life, presumably until one of you steps into the void."

He tried not to think about it. Endless days of it. No escape. Already he was on display for her. Already she was forcing her way into his secrets. The memory of waking to her looming over him sent a jolt of hot ire down his spine. Amara noticed, of course, and remained silent for the long moment it took him to wrestle it under control.

"You cannot do it this way," she murmured when he relaxed. "You cannot ignore her into a comfortable place." That the woman seemed to understand so much about him with so very little interaction was like burrs in his clothing. Scratching and enraging. But she was water. More powerful and more in tune with the Second House than he would ever be again. He could not hope to hide from her.

"Do not presume to meddle in my private affairs, Mutar Charah. I will conduct myself in this however I see fit."

She remained silent for a period that stretched and stretched.

"You owe me a favor, I think, for the trouble I went through for a betrothal that was not given."

"A betrothal *you* chose to refuse," he corrected. It had been the only decision. He could not be whatever Amara needed, nor could he bear the reminder of all that he had lost in the fire. Of what his power had been. Cassian brought her joy. She deserved that.

She shrugged one shoulder, and one brow lifted. He waved his hand for her to continue.

"Speak with her," she said. "And I do not mean a single sentence as you pass each other in the hall. Share a meal. Sit with her. If you will not do it for her, or yourself, then do it because of what you and the Princess Sultana asked of me."

His leg twitched. Face her? After she entered his bedroom without permission? After she had seen him at his weakest? Nothing more than a broken, helpless child?

"We all bear scars, Sehzade. Just because you cannot see them, does not mean they are not there. Do not think you own a monopoly on wounded pasts," Amara said into her cup of coffee.

He flicked his gaze to hers and she half smiled, rising from her chair. She gave a twitch of her fingers and Bek rose from the floor in the corner and approached. "See the Sehzade and his steward out, please."

Ihsan almost laughed at her abrupt dismissal, but was grateful for it. He stood, and Kuhzey got up and made his way toward the front of the shop. He seemed to be in search of something, though he was trying hard to appear as if he wasn't.

"She is not here," Amara said with a knowing smile.

Kuhzey's shoulders bunched, and he swept his fingers in the question, "*Who*?"

Ihsan and Amara shared a conspiratory look. "Thank you for the coffee."

Amara ducked her head. "You are welcome anytime, of course. And do let me know when you are ready for new clothes for yourself. It will be so tragic when she outshines you at court because I've been commissioned for her but not you." With a wink she turned and headed back upstairs.

THE MOON HUNG BRIGHT AND porcelain overhead, nearly full. Ihsan stood with hands clasped behind his back, his face tipped back toward it, eyes closed. The nights still clung to a bit of spring's crispness, but it would be gone soon. The endless heat of summer would fall upon Narfour shortly, more profound and consuming for the Blight and all it had wrought.

Voices interrupted the quiet of the garden, and his eyes opened. Women's voices. Most likely Nesrin and her maid. It was unlike Deniz to spend time in the garden at night. He cursed under his breath and strode into the shadow of the garden wall, away from the moon's spotlight and the requirement of pleasantries.

The gravel of the path shifted under their feet, marking their movement from the house toward the end of the path, where it circled beneath the trees on the side opposite him. He could see them through the screen of an overgrown, shaggy tangle of grass and bush. Nesrin held a knife in one hand, a basket tucked beneath the other.

Reyhan tried twice to take one of the items from her, but Nesrin only shook her head. Whatever they were talking of was in hushed tones, and only the rhythm of it reached him, not the words.

Drawn forward despite his reluctance to face her, Ihsan moved after them, clinging close to the wall where he could. Aysel was not the only one who disappeared when she wanted to. All Ihsan needed was shadows. He did not go ephemeral, as Aysel seemed to, but let the dark claim him. Fire and the Fifth House were light and warmth. The Second House dark and cold. The depths of the ocean, the cloak of night's blanket. He leaned against the wall a safe distance from them, taking slow, steady breaths.

After a moment, Reyhan threw her hands up in exasperation and stalked back down the path, to the house. Nesrin watched her go. She was too far and angled away for Ihsan to see her expression, but the set of her shoulders spoke of frustration. She turned and crouched, setting the basket beside her.

She hummed to herself, her movements falling into a practiced rhythm. She grabbed a handful of something, swiped at it with the knife, then tossed it away. The pattern repeated until she had revealed a crown of green shoots, curled and pale from lack of light. Nesrin paused, resting her arms on bent knees, and turned slightly toward him, still crouching on the gravel path.

"You can come out, you know, or shall I continue pretending I do not know you're there?"

He hesitated a moment as he considered whether to call her bluff or not.

"Suit yourself, *Sehzade*." She went back to her work. With a low snarl, Ihsan left the safety of the wall and moved to her side on the path.

"Do you plan to denude my entire garden? Or just the roses?"

"Oh, are there more roses?" She stood, wiping a bit of fallen hair from her forehead with the back of her wrist. "I thought you were in the practice of cultivating weeds." She still held the knife.

"Is that Deniz's kitchen knife?"

Nesrin's gaze flicked up to her hand and she lowered it from her forehead, turning the knife one way then the next. She made a sound of affirmation. The moonlight suited her, softening some of the angles that were a result of the lack of food she had clearly endured. But the moonlight was kinder to nearly everyone than the sun. He looked up to the sky. Stars shone, brightening as the tail end of the sunset faded from the horizon.

"The Wheel is bright tonight," Nesrin said, pointing. The bright circle of stars ringed the moon. Six stars, with a moon as their hub. Not an impossibly rare event, but occasional enough that it was worth noting.

As they stood, the unspoken things between them coalesced into something physical. Afraid she would bring it up, he blurted, "Have dinner with me."

Nesrin lowered her chin slowly, and he could see her staring at him, though he did not lower his head to meet her gaze. Instead he concentrated on tracking a handful of bats that swooped above them, night-dark streaks that blotted the stars.

"Do you..." She hummed her hesitation. "Do you enjoy Deniz's cooking?"

A surprised laugh burst out, more cough than anything. "Are you picky?" He finally dropped his gaze to her, skipping her face to glance from her shoulders to her feet, which were bare. "Wheel and stars, woman, do you ever wear shoes?"

When he finally did look at her face, even the quiet moonlight could not hide the warming of her features, her curled shoulders. "I will change into appropriate clothes," she said, her tone suggesting he'd offended her. He grimaced, but she was already past him, basket and knife in hand.

"Don't bother," he called after her. Her steps faltered. She stopped, spun toward him, and gave a stiff, short bow, then disappeared around the corner of the path, hidden from view by a dwarf tree overgrown with some vining atrocity. He spat a curse. He would never get her to open up to him if he offended her with every word from his lips.

Amara's mention of Nesrin being limited with details had piqued his interest. He was still not convinced she was not a spy put in place by Kadir. If Naime insisted on banning him from the palace, he could turn his energy to that.

No one was *that* innocent. Or sweet natured. Or selfless. No one. She could not hide herself from him forever.

No one hid from the Second House.

Deniz slapped a plate of kofta onto the low table. They were crisped to blackness. She flounced back into the kitchen and returned with another plate, this of tabbouleh arranged on a circle of wilted lettuce leaves, which took its place beside the kofta. Next came a pitcher of water that sloshed her unspoken resentment all over the table. When she bowed to Ihsan, Nesrin placidly mopped at the spill, irritation showing through her attempt at a placid expression. Deniz glanced at her, then skulked back into her kitchen.

Nesrin cleared her throat as she scooted herself and the cushion she sat on closer to the table. She used the serving spoon to place a single kofta on her plate and a modest scoop of the tabbouleh. She did the same for him without a word. She broke the kofta apart with her fingers, and it resisted her, cooked beyond recognition. Her movements were slow, unenthusiastic.

"Aren't you hungry?" He picked up the one she'd placed on his plate and took a bite of it. He set it back down, trying to suppress his cough at the acrid taste of burnt meat.

"Mmhmm." She wrapped a bit of tabbouleh in a sad lettuce leaf and took a bite. Her gaze remained downcast. They ate without speaking, each bite an act of will. That Deniz was not a master cook capable of competing with the food prepared in the palace had never troubled Ihsan. He did not keep her around for her kitchen skills. She kept them fed, and that was all he had ever required. But perhaps he should care more, since it was not just his tastes that mattered anymore.

Nesrin worked through her serving of food, tucking bits of the kofta into the bites of lettuce and tabbouleh.

"Djar mentioned you were to be betrothed to Mutar Charah," she said as she wiped her hands on a napkin. Ihsan choked on his bite, turning sideways and coughing. Nesrin poured a glass of water and pushed it toward him. As he drank, she poured another and sipped at the glass. "Are you all right?"

"I'm fine," he said. "You also conversed with Djar?" Despite that Ihsan and Amara had made peace, Djar still seemed far too willing to cleave Ihsan in two given the tiniest of reasons.

"Yes." Nesrin's stiff smile appeared and disappeared.

"Mutar Charah said you spoke of Mizraa," he prodded. He saw no reason to talk about his doomed arrangement. It had worked out to everyone's benefit in the end.

Nesrin took another sip of water, then a slow breath. Collecting her thoughts. *Cagy*, Amara had called her. "Only the state of the valley. They are affected by the Blight in other parts of the valley, though the crops haven't succumbed in Mizraa, so we've not been hit as hard. Yet."

As hard. But here she sat in front of him, a noble starved. What must the state of the people in Mizraa be? The subject troubled him greatly, but her steering of the subject did not go unnoticed. "And what is your father doing about it?"

Her lashes fluttered, her gaze flicking. Tension settled in Ihsan's muscles. "What can he do? Ration. Quarantine affected fields."

"Is the rationing effective?" He tried to keep his voice neutral. She was not lying. But she was omitting. She had shredded a piece of lettuce into ribbons on her plate, her fingers quick and restless.

"It would be"—her voice became hard, though it shook with emotion—"if what was left was not so frequently taken by the soldiers traveling through."

Her accusation was sour, and it drove Ihsan's thinking offtrack. She nabbed another kofta from the plate and tore it to pieces, eating one as if to silence herself. Her gaze fixed on her plate.

"Why had your father not mentioned this to the palace? Requested aid?"

Her hands stilled on the meat and her gaze flashed to his. He swore he saw green glinting in the plain hazel, but it must have been a trick of the flickering lamps. "I do not know."

"You do not know your own father's mind?"

For barely a breath she went as still as a startled rabbit, then looked down again, flicking the bite of food she held onto her plate. "Bardakci Pasha does not inform me of his plans."

Wheel and spokes, they were there. The lies, on the edges of things, flitting just outside of his grasp. But everyone lied. Everyone held back. The important thing was why. Was she guarding a strained relationship with her father? Or protecting a connection with Behram Kadir?

She tapped a nail on the edge of her plate. "I did not realize when you invited me to eat with you that you meant to interrogate me. Are we going to address at all that your nightly terrors cause your surroundings to freeze? Am I expected to endure that with no explanation whatsoever? Ignore it?"

The sudden switch of topic sent all his defenses up. "It is none of your business." The response was automatic, sharp like the cold spike of his power in the back of his skull.

Their gazes locked across the table. He saw the held temper in hers. It ruddied her cheeks, put an edge to her expression. Almost like magic. But he felt no magic, saw none; she was a void. He did see the held tears, the tiniest quiver of her lip.

For a moment shame and regret warred for a spot in his thoughts. She did deserve better. And more, than he could give her. Amara was right, she was sweet. There was kindness in her he did not deserve, nor could he bear it.

But then his rational mind won over. She might be all those things, but she could also still be a spy. A convenient trap laid by Kadir.

"I think we're done here." Dropping his napkin onto the table, he rose.

"Thank you for dinner," she called as he strode away.

He almost turned back to respond, but no. It was better that she was angry. That she did not know his weaknesses. That she did not care for him. People who cared for him were in danger.

And people who knew his weaknesses…could destroy him.

TWENTY-THREE

NESRIN STEWED.

Wrapped in a blanket, huddled on the floor like a moss-covered log in front of her window, glaring at the silver city. Dawn was coming too slowly, and she could stay idle in her prison not one moment more. She stood, the fluffy coverlet still looped over her head and shoulders like an absurd cloak. No. This morning she was not going to wander pointlessly, bored and dull.

She gathered the coverlet off herself and threw it onto the bed, then turned to her wardrobe. After a moment of shoving things back and forth, she pulled out the plainest caftan she could find. She suspected it was a servant's, as it was undyed linen, with embroidery at the cuffs, the neckline, and the hem. The stitches were blue, though whether it was meant to invoke the First or the Second House, she could not tell. It leaned neither silver nor turquoise.

After arranging her underthings, she pulled it on and belted it with the cloth that hung on the hanger. A paler blue sash with the same darker blue scrollwork. She knotted it and set it askew, as Reyhan had instructed her was in fashion. Not that it mattered. She did not intend to go out in public. Not this morning. Today she would be digging out a place for herself within the walls.

Nesrin cast a glare at the Sehzade's closed doors and made her way downstairs. They had been long enough in the home that Nesrin knew its rhythm, knew when Deniz would rise and begin cooking. The household was not an early rising one, and Nesrin estimated she had at least a mark before anyone else stirred.

Once she was in the kitchen she lit the lamps. The familiar smell of the burning oil, and the dried herbs, coupled with the peaceful solitude of a kitchen to herself, brought her into herself, and her memories. It was both painful, a searing down the back of her throat, and freeing. This was who she was. Where she belonged. She was not a noble. Not a wife. Not a princess. She was this. Someone who gave. Whether it was food, or comfort, or a smile.

It took a few moments to make herself familiar with the contents of drawers and cabinets. She went around the room collecting the tools and ingredients she would need. There was not time to use the mother yeast bubbling away in a bowl in a corner. She would do that another day. Today she would make an unleavened bread. While not as tasty, certainly better than what she had sampled thus far from this kitchen.

Outside the kitchen, Nesrin rolled her sleeves to her elbows, eyeing the oven and the untidy pile of wood beside it. Stacking that would be on her list for the day. Once she had the fire stoked in the oven then banked down to coals, she left it to heat and returned inside.

On the table that was centered in the kitchen, Nesrin scooped handfuls of flour onto the work surface. Turns of cooking had taught her to do things by feel and sense memory. Which is what she did now, falling into the comfortable, mindless routine of making flatbread. She kneaded in more flour. The wetter air of spring still clung, making the dough sticky.

Once the dough was smooth and beautifully rounded, she set it aside and tossed a towel over it. Into a large stone mortar she dumped sesame seeds from a jar she'd found tucked into the back of a cabinet. Next went leaves she stripped from dried za'atar she'd had to rustle the dust from. Then salt. And dried sumac, another jar she found languishing in the back of a cabinet she suspected was rarely opened. When it was mixed to her liking, she scooped the seasoning into a small wooden bowl and took it out to the oven. She set a flat iron pan on the edge of the oven and dumped the mixture into it, giving it a little time in the heat to toast.

When that was done she returned to the kitchen to chop up what remained of the lamb leg Deniz had brought home, until it was well mixed. She added it and a generous glug of golden-green oil from a small pitcher onto the pan and returned it to the heat of the oven. There was a firepit, but Nesrin was nervous about starting two fires in proximity to the Sehzade. She did not want to bring attention to herself until she was too far into her project to be forced from it.

After a few stirs the lamb was cooked. For a brief, unexpected moment her heart tipped, as she thought of Buse and the scraps of the meat fat he would have been keen to sample as she cooked. The thought plucked at her loneliness.

Nesrin dropped in a handful of cumin seeds, coriander, and crushed garlic to cook from the heat of the meat as she pulled the pan from the oven. A gangly, crawling mint plant made a bid to take over one side of the bed on the east side of the kitchen area. She tore a handful of leaves off and ripped them into bits, tossing them into the lamb mixture as well.

She returned to the kitchen to find Reyhan standing on the far side of the table, arms folded over her chest, her face a storm.

Nesrin averted her gaze, her pulse ratcheting. She set the hot pan on one end of the table and withdrew her dough from beneath the towel. With a wooden hand blade shaped like the wedged edge of an ax, she divided the dough into sixths, working silently beneath Reyhan's furious stare.

"What," she grunted, "are you doing?"

Nesrin dusted the table surface with flour. "Is it not obvious?"

"Have you lost your few senses?" Reyhan snarled. "There is not a noblewoman in Narfour who would be caught dead with flour on her hands and…" she spluttered as she pointed, "in her hair!"

Nesrin swept up a bit of excess flour and met Reyhan's stare with a blank expression. When Reyhan opened her mouth to speak again, Nesrin flicked the flour in the woman's face.

Reyhan gasped, then coughed when she inhaled the flour, brushing at the white that dusted her clothes. Nesrin raised an eyebrow when Reyhan slapped her hands on the table and glared. "If I have to drag you screaming from this room, I will do it. By your hair if I must."

Another puff of flour in her face made her cough anew. She cursed, whirling back from her coughing fit to snatch at the pile of flour on one end of the table and hurl a handful at Nesrin. Nesrin ducked with a laugh of disbelief, crouching below the edge of the table. When Reyhan reached to reload, Nesrin popped up and splattered flour across Reyhan's caftan.

"Ugh!" Reyhan stamped her foot, slapping at the flour, only to take another hit to the cheek. She bent across the table, trying to grab for Nesrin, who burst into giggles and darted away from her grabbing hands. Reyhan came around and chased Nesrin for two laps, grabbing a handful of flour and throwing it in an arc so it struck Nesrin across the jaw and neck. Nesrin halted, astonished, and Reyhan's eyes went wide as she covered her mouth with one flour-stained hand.

Reyhan hiccupped. Or laughed. Then they were both laughing, and coughing, as flour dust snowed down around them, like ash lit by streaks of dawn coming in through the panes of window glass. Nesrin wiped the flour from her face, swiping her eyes with her sleeve to try for the powder sticking in her lashes.

Every time Nesrin tried to speak, she started giggling again, so hard her belly ached with it, and Reyhan was nearly doubled over.

Movement in the door to the dining room preceded a scandalized gasp that silenced their laughter. Both shot straight, shoulder to shoulder, and Nesrin clasped her hands behind her back as she had when she was a child and her mother had caught her at mischief. Reyhan's nose wrinkled and her mouth quivered as she held back more giggles and tried to look serious.

"This is a fine mess." Deniz jammed her hands against her ample hips, revulsion written in every tense line of her face. "How am I to prepare a breakfast now, hmm?"

Nesrin let out a soft cough that made flour billow from her lips and Reyhan fell apart, laughing as she sank to her backside onto the flour-coated floor. That sent Nesrin into another fit and she collapsed forward over the table, giggling until she couldn't breathe, resting her head and arms on the edge as she slowly crouched. In the back of her mind she knew she was half hysterical, but she could not bring the laughter under control.

"I'll have you in front of the Sehzade, you—" Deniz snatched up a broom and came around the table as if she meant to bat at them like they were mice. Nesrin shrieked in laughter and concern as she stumbled away from the portly woman. She scooped a handful of flour as she spun to her feet, narrowly avoiding a swipe of the broom meant for her backside. She tossed the flour at Deniz.

Deniz reeled as if someone had socked her in the jaw, the broom frozen halfway to a stab at Reyhan. She blinked, flour cascading from her eyelashes and over her pouchy cheeks. Reyhan rose, eyes wide.

"We will set your kitchen to rights," Nesrin said primly, tugging the broom from Deniz's hand. Then she patted at Deniz's hair, trying to dislodge the flour, though she did not feel an ounce of remorse, about any of it. Deniz brushed her hands away then spun around and marched out of the kitchen.

"Well," Reyhan said breathlessly, "I will clean, and you finish whatever this is." She gestured at the abandoned balls of dough. "I'm hungry."

Nesrin grinned, handing the broom to Reyhan.

They worked well in tandem, swinging around each other as if they had been doing it all their lives. Reyhan wiped flour from the many places it had settled while Nesrin shaped the dough into ovals. She rubbed oil into the middle of the pide, then added a generous palmful of the za'atar, then the chopped lamb. Reyhan peeked over her shoulder as she cracked an egg into the center of each. She made a soft noise of approval that made Nesrin smile. The oven was big enough to hold three of the pide at a time, so Nesrin shoveled them in with a wooden peel.

By the time the first batch was done, Reyhan was finishing up tidying up the flour. She swept a great cloud of it out onto the kitchen patio, and stood in the doorway watching the dust of it drift away. Then she swept the bulk of it off the stones and into the overgrown dirt bed that ran along the edge of the circular patio. Nesrin intended to weed it and plant more herbs, but that was a project for another day.

Reyhan helped her get the pide onto the peel and into the oven, then dug up plates for the three that were done.

"I can take them," she said, as Nesrin dusted her hands off on the apron she'd tied around her waist.

"No. I do not want to give Deniz a chance to blame you to the Sehzade. Besides, he likely isn't even up. I've never seen him rise this early." She scooped up two of the plates as Reyhan stammered a protest, and strode into the dining room.

Nesrin lurched to a halt when she saw that the Sehzade was standing on the far side of the table, with Kuhzey at his side. Reyhan nearly ran into the back of her. Nesrin squared her shoulders, her gaze fixed on the center of the Sehzade's chest, and circled the table to deposit the plates of pide. When she finished, she bowed to him, then met his gaze. Her cheeks burned.

"What..." His gaze ricocheted between her and Reyhan, flicking to her flour-covered clothes, then her hair, and finally her face. Nesrin clasped her hands in front of her apron, waiting for him to speak. Hoping, or dreading. She did not know which. "Should I...ask?" His brows dropped low, and his mouth twitched.

Nesrin tried to think of something witty to say, but Deniz called from the foyer. "They've ransacked my kitchen. *Stolen* ingredients to make Wheel knows what atrocities." Something crashed. A broom handle on tile, Nesrin suspected. Ihsan directed his gaze back to Nesrin's.

"A thief, are you?" he said. His thumb was on her cheek all of a sudden. Everything inside her went still. He brushed his thumb over her skin. He was only wiping away flour. The little thrill that had gone through her fizzled.

Breathless, the touch still on her skin as if he had branded her, Nesrin swallowed. "First the flour, then the silver."

His mouth quirked, and Nesrin had to tear her eyes away and turn on shaky legs. Reyhan took her by the elbow, dragging her back into the kitchen. When they were well out of sight, Reyhan spun her around so they were face to face, hers as full of excitement as Nesrin had ever seen it. She gripped Nesrin's elbows, and Nesrin gripped hers in return.

They stared at each other, Nesrin's thoughts spinning. Until she truly took in Reyhan's mussed and flour-stained hair, the smudges that remained on her face and neck. She must look the same.

"Wheel and spokes," Nesrin groaned. "I look awful."

"He did not think so," Reyhan said, as if she were proud. Nesrin pulled a face, incredulous.

"He has ignored me when I looked better than I have ever looked in my life, but you think, now, this..." She swept her hands up and down to indicate her body. "...has suddenly caught his attention."

"Not suddenly." Reyhan shrugged enigmatically.

Nesrin puffed a breath and pawed at the hair falling loose into her own face. She turned away and rescued the remaining two pide from the oven, sliding them onto plates that Reyhan provided.

"We should eat in here," Nesrin said, tugging a stool from beneath the table. Reyhan shoved it back, then pointed toward the dining room.

"Who are you? What have you done with Reyhan? You'll allow me to present myself to the Sehzade like this? Like a scullery maid who fell into a flour barrel."

"He seemed to like it. Take the wins you can, Nesrin."

Nesrin's eyes rounded. She hesitated, then picked up her plate. "Nessa."

"What?"

"My friends call me Nessa."

"Hm." Reyhan approached to examine her critically. She picked and combed at Nesrin's hair with her fingers. Then she took the linen towel to Nesrin's face and neck. Nesrin submitted to it with an eyeroll, holding the plate out of the way as Reyhan dusted her clothes with her hands. Then she stood back to survey her handiwork.

"The Grand Vizier"—she glanced over her shoulder toward the kitchen door as she murmured—"would be very pleased to know you made inroads where no one else has been able to." She seemed giddy. Did she agree with the Grand Vizier? That the Sehzade and the Sultana were bleeding Tamar dry? Was she meant to be a spy?

Nesrin's bubbling feeling of triumph settled, heavy in her stomach. "You said it was safer to keep distance."

"If he was suspicious of you, yes. If he finds you charming"—Reyhan prodded, gently—"then he will be distracted."

Was that what she was doing? Nesrin's throat tightened. She had been following her natural urge to make friends. But…she was here by the grace of the Grand Vizier, and if he asked of her, surely she should provide? He held her life in his hands, her family's. She shuffled toward the dining room when Reyhan nodded approval.

The Sehzade and Kuhzey sat at the table, though Deniz was still absent. Neither of the men had started on their food, and it was clear they were waiting for Nesrin, though Kuhzey looked like an animal half crazed with starvation, hunched over his plate. Nesrin smiled a little to herself, then lifted her face to offer the smile to the Sehzade in thanks as she sat on the cushion across from him. Reyhan settled beside her.

They all attacked the food enthusiastically. Except Nesrin. She ripped a corner off one end of the pide and pressed it into the center of the egg, dabbing up some of the yolk. This was the closest she had been to all of them. Yet she was lonely. The isolation closing around her like iron bars. It was a different loneliness than what had plagued her at the start. She sat with it, its vine like tendrils wrapping around her as she took nips of her food.

Still her body struggled with food. Her stomach was not right. It cramped, sometimes turning her insides to water. Sometimes her body bloated and her joints ached. She should have expected it. Her grandmothers had nursed a starved family from the North back to health during the winter. Coming back to health was nearly as harrowing as starving. The body rejecting and rebelling.

"You are not hungry?" The Sehzade's voice rolled across her. A water mage's voice, filled with song and seduction. They could not help it. It was their nature. But at the moment, it was thorns, pricking her skin and her heart. Making her bleed truth and lies.

"I sampled too much while I was cooking," she lied outright. She did not dare look at his face, he would know she was lying, but perhaps he would be polite enough not to inquire further.

He was silent, and the sounds of everyone eating were abruptly overwhelming. Each movement. The chewing. Her gut rolled, her skin crawled as though insects raced beneath it.

"You are a gifted cook, Mistress Bardakci," the Sehzade offered. The lie of a name was too much. Nesrin stood, inexplicably enraged.

"My name is Nesrin, Sehzade. Do you intend to refer to me by title for the rest of my days?" She did not allow him time to answer, ignoring his stricken expression and grabbing up her plate to return to the kitchen. She set the plate on the table, racing through the kitchen to the garden. Nesrin crouched, bunching up the hem of her caftan and yanking it out of the way as she was sick.

Tears streamed down her face, her breathing rapid and uneven, and her body heaved even after there was nothing left. She wiped her mouth on the apron and sat down, pressing her face into her knees and trying to breathe away the emotion and the urge to be sick again.

The sun warmed her back, and she unwound the cloth from her hair, letting it fall loose down her back as she laid her head sideways on her knees. She did not know how much time had passed before Reyhan sat down beside her and offered her a cup of tea. Its steam wafted into Nesrin's face, the scent of anise soothing her.

"Yansoon," Reyhan said, taking Nesrin's hands and wrapping them around the cup. "It will help your stomach."

"Being anywhere but here would help my stomach." Tears burned her eyes again. She blinked them back. "Thank you for the tea." Anise seed tea was a staple of her grandmothers' apothecary as well. And its sweet scent put Nesrin back on the worn cushions inside her family's home, one grandmother fussing at her hair, the other plying her with tea. Their warm, gentle hands crooked with arthritis. Their hummed songs to soothe the ill.

She closed her eyes. "I miss—"

"Shh," Reyhan hissed. Nesrin opened her eyes, looking toward the kitchen door, then into the golden tea in her cup. She drank it, crunching the anise seeds swirling in the bottom. When she finished she handed the cup to Reyhan and stood, brushing the grass off her caftan.

"Thank you," she said, her words dull. Then she left Reyhan sitting in the garden.

She could not face any of them again that day, even though she ached with loneliness.

That night, Nesrin dreamed of tumbling through endless black, curled around herself while her skin fractured like eggshell. She was dragged from the dream by a man's hollow, desperate scream.

Twenty-Four

His dreams were not coherent things. They were fear and fire, fingers that dragged him toward oblivion. They were pain that was gone when he woke, smells that did not linger when his eyes were open. Nothing but hopeless, consuming terror.

He could not remember their details. He could only lie suffocating in his body's memory, his breath ragged, his heart pounding, his eyes filled with tears and his throat with screams.

This time, in the flames, someone spoke. Or something. With a voice of whispers and joy. There was no joy in this place. For the first time, he opened his eyes to the inferno of his nightmare, and saw green. A figure coalesced in the fire, and the flames fell away, so then he was tumbling through void.

Ihsan woke with a gasp, green fading from the edges of his vision. Warm, whisper-soft fingers rested on his shoulder. He jerked his head to the side. A face peered at him, level with his own, big, lambent eyes and a mouth moving with words he could not hear. The light of his nightmare faded from his memory. Nesrin knelt at the side of his bed, looking equal parts afraid and concerned. It was her fingers on his shoulder, her voice, coaxing.

"Shh," she murmured, petting his shoulder, "you are safe."

He should have been angry, was angry, but it warred with his gratitude. Not even Naime could wake him from his nightmares. They were as gripping as sucking mire. Void he was sick of nightmares. Of dreading his nights. Nearly two Cycles of suffering that would not end. He put a hand to his face and tried to form words past his swollen throat.

"No one is to disturb the Sehzade," Deniz barked from the door. Tension seized his chest and he bolted up. Nesrin fell backward with a squawk of surprise. Meanwhile Deniz advanced, Kuhzey on her heels, and Reyhan hanging back in the doorway. "Get out this instant," Deniz ordered, reaching for Nesrin. Nesrin bolted to her feet, stumbling away from Deniz. Ihsan's head swam and he squinted at the melee. All of them. All of them were in his room, with him sweating and all his terror and scars in full view.

"No," Nesrin said, firmly. Deniz stopped, hand outstretched, eyes bugging and mouth pinched in disbelief, then anger. "Enough. Am I Mistress of this household, or not?" She did not direct the question at anyone. In fact, it did not sound very much like a question at all. "If I am expected to sit through night after night of someone being tortured in their nightmares and do *nothing*, then I wish to live apart from you."

The edges of the nightmare lingered, but Nesrin's words cut it away like razors. He could not think with so many people in his space.

Deniz drew breath as a rooster might before crowing.

"Out," Ihsan commanded. "Everyone, out." The rest was not shouted, but just as firm and angry as Nesrin's. They obeyed, Nesrin moving as if to follow. "Not you," Ihsan said. Nesrin stopped. Reyhan hesitated, standing on tiptoe to see past Kuhzey and Deniz, but Deniz pulled the doors shut behind her.

"If you mean to shout at me again, I will not be staying." She folded her arms across her chest, drawing his attention to the fact she wore a sleeping shift and nothing else. He looked down and threw the covers off his legs so he could get out of the bed. He crossed the room away from her and yanked his robe from where he'd tossed it over a chair, slinging it around his body to hide his scars.

"I'm not shouting, am I?" He shoved his fingers through his hair to get it off his face. It was plastered there by sweat. When he chanced a look at her she glared at him. All her gentleness buried beneath this new version he had not seen. This was the person, perhaps, who had leapt into a carriage that was being looted to save a family. Was she trying to save him? Throwing herself in front of another whip? Why?

"You were screaming, actually," Nesrin accused, and looked away when his eyes narrowed.

"Are you mocking me?" he asked, low, anger prowling just below his exasperation. She dropped her arms and turned a scathing look on him.

"Of course not. I am not a monster. Do you truly think no one is capable of bearing this alongside you? That anyone with even a mote of mercy would not understand you are suffering?"

"I do not want your understanding, I want to be left alone."

"No." She set her chin. He advanced on her, but she did not flinch or back away, only tipping her head enough to meet his gaze. "Does this work with other people? This…" She unfolded her arms to gesture at him. "…ice monster act you do? That constant angry face?" She jabbed a finger at his chin, indicating his clenched jaw. Then she screwed her face up in a mimic of his expression. Which looked silly and charming on her.

"If it does not, I bite," he said, baring his teeth in threat. But Nesrin's eyes crinkled at the edges, a radiant, laughing smile spreading wide. She touched his chin with her outstretched finger.

"No you don't."

He jerked away from the touch and grabbed her wrist, scowling. She startled, her smile fading. He had angry warnings to use as axes on this closeness she was trying to build between them. But she twisted her hand in his grip. She closed her fingers over his wrist. Her touch was warm. Not like fire and sun. It evoked the warmth and love of his aunt, Dilay. Of Lalam, and the way she would lift him and spin him in dizzying circles as a boy. Of Omar's proud pat on his shoulder when he accomplished something of worth. Just care. Stringless, chainless. Kindness.

"You are safe with me," she murmured, "Sehzade." Her voice held so many promises, for a heartbeat he cracked open, exhaustion pouring out of the shell of him. It was warm, and quiet, no threat, no requirements. For a heartbeat, he believed her words, the warmth and strength in the grip of her hand on his wrist. The only warmth he had been able to bear in a decade.

But he did not know her. And she could not know him. Could not shoulder all the jagged pieces of his pain and his loss, of his consuming fury. If she was gentle, as she seemed to be, then she was not strong enough for that.

"You are *not* safe with me." He pulled his hand from her grip, and she pressed her lips together.

"No? What are you going to do to me? Rip me from my home? Take me from all I've known? Force me into roles I have no idea how to fulfill? Parade me before people who mock me, and whisper lies about me? Lock me away with someone whose nightmares cover me in ice every night and will not even speak to me as if I am a human?" She took a step back. "How terrifying."

"What do you want from me? Whatever it is, I do not have it to give." He sank onto the edge of his bed.

"I do not want anything from you," she said. "I want to find a peace between us. And make a home for myself, and you, if you'll allow it."

"You have a home. Two. Here, and the palace. Do what you will."

"Will you honor my wish? I will not be half frozen every night, and woken by screams, for the rest of my days." She sat beside him on the edge of the bed without so much as a look for permission, but with enough distance they did not touch. She was so light the bed barely registered her weight. He wanted to stuff her full of food until her ribs disappeared and the hollow ache in her eyes abated. But instead, she was feeding him. The pieces of her did not fit together, and it exasperated him every time he tried.

"Deniz is not accustomed to casting her dampening here. I will remind her. And I do not always have nightmares. They come and go…they …" His words died away. They came when he was angry. When he spent too much time near Kadir, or any fire mage, for that matter. When emotion made its way into his walls. It was because of Omar. Because he was more father to Ihsan than Mazhar had ever been. The pain welled in his throat.

"My b—" She swallowed, and pulled her knees to her chest, hiding her face in them. "My babaanne knew a man who lost an arm when he was a child. His nightmares came when he was troubled. By interactions gone wrong, problems he could not solve. When he was rejected or teased." Her voice was muffled into her sleeping clothes, but he heard the sadness. "Until he had come to terms with his accident, and accepted that it would never be undone, and that was all right, the nightmares came. The fits of rage. The belief that he was alone, and the only one who could bear his torment."

Sympathy was not the only thing in her voice. Admiration. And love.

"You know a great deal about this man. Was he a worker for the Pasha?" Did she love him? A twinge of feeling made his neck tense, his hands curl into fists. He remembered the rumors of pregnancy that Bashir had mentioned. How she had run out to be sick at breakfast. "Is there something I should be made aware of?"

"Such as?" she asked, warily.

"Such as the rumors in the palace that you are with child. Mine, or someone else's. Obviously it isn't mine."

"With child?" she choked. Then made a breathy sound of understanding. "I could not have imagined a more ruthless and busy rumor mill than that which existed in Mizraa." She adjusted the hem of her caftan over her legs to avoid looking at him. "Before our betrothal, I ate too much. My body..." She shook her head. "...it isn't used to it. There were some women who observed me get sick. I can only imagine they jumped to a conclusion that you now have as well. I am not, if my word means anything.

"As for the man—" She made a little sound, and he was certain he heard a discordant note of sadness in the tone. "He was a worker in Mizraa. Is it unusual that I would know their injuries?"

She turned her head, resting her temple against her knees as she looked up at him. Her undone hair cascaded in russet waves over her legs. It had been some time since he'd sat with anyone like this, exposed in heart and skin. Let alone a woman. The awareness came with a flush in his body. Her face was filling out in increments. Her skin gaining color over the days since he had met her. A bit of ruddiness, and permanent flush to her cheeks and nose. A hint of the freckles that came with hair the shade of hers. She had a little Northern in her face, a smaller nose, squarer jaw than most women of more pure Tamar lineage.

Until this moment, he had not been able to stomach the idea of thinking she was lovely. Beautiful, even. Because that thought opened a crack in him. And because she had clearly suffered, and he could not bring himself to diminish that by admiring something so trivial.

Her eyes mirrored the movement of his, aware of his examination.

"It is unusual," he said, lamely. He pulled his gaze away from her face.

She turned her head again, setting her chin on her knees. One slim shoulder lifted. "Here, I suppose it is. Mizraa is…"

"Different? Who taught you to cook?" He dropped onto his back, suddenly restless and overwhelmed by her nearness. He did the math in his head of how long it had been since he had been even this close with a woman. He grimaced. She was still silent. He lifted his head, and saw she had buried her head in her knees again. She was crying. He bolted up.

She was trying to hide it, holding perfectly still, regulating her breath. But you could not hide tears from a water mage. He reached to touch her, then hesitated. What right did he have to comfort her? He could not even hope to. There was no friendship between them, nothing between them. But his heart beat in time with her breaths, and his power rippled with each tear.

Ihsan slipped his hand to the back of her neck, beneath her hair. He had only a moment to revel in the revitalizing warmth of her skin and the softness of her hair before she unfolded and slung her arms around his neck as though she were clinging to keep from being swept away by a tide. Ihsan froze in panic. His breath hitched and his heart raced, his mind going still.

Her sorrow suffocated him like a living thing coiling in his throat, and his arms cinched around her on instinct.

"It's all right," he murmured, turning his face against her hair as if it were the most natural thing in the world. She smelled like his garden. Flowers and sunshine and wind and rain. Life. He drank in the scent. He did not deserve this vulnerability, had not earned the trust for her to fall apart like this. But he realized, with clarity that sank like a blade, that she was alone. He stroked her back, carefully, remembering where his power had traced the still-healing wound. He had missed this, being needed, trusted to comfort, had not understood he was starving for it.

She sniffled, tucking her face into the crook of his neck, her tears sliding over his throat and collarbone, tracing a path down his chest. He felt one, then two, a third, each like the searing, hot stroke of a finger. And her breath like a caress.

Suddenly she jerked back, ripping out of his arms. "I'm so sorry." She swiped at her tears with her fingers. "I…I am sorry," she said again, and bowed quickly, then raced away. The door banged shut behind her. He stared at it, so tangled inside he could not put words to it.

He fell onto his back again, rolled onto his belly and reached for a pillow, which he buried his face in.

"Shit," he snarled.

Twenty-Five

Now it was her turn to avoid him.

Reyhan had the look of someone who desperately wanted answers to questions she was afraid to ask. Nesrin did not volunteer information. What could she possibly say? When Reyhan had met her outside the Sehzade's room with a wide-eyed look, Nesrin only shook her head and ensconced herself in her room.

Nesrin had never in her life hidden from a confrontation with someone over an awkward interaction. But Wheel and spokes, she'd thrown herself at him. The next morning she stared out her window, her hands pressed to her cheeks, hoping it might make the flaming heat in them die back. She wanted to hide away in her room all day, just to avoid accidentally meeting his eyes. He had not seemed particularly interested in being around her before the incident, perhaps he still felt that way? She could not be so lucky. He had probably interpreted her heartache-induced lapse in judgment as some kind of assault. Or invitation. She could not decide which was worse.

A soft knock nearly separated her from her skin. He would not knock like that, she told herself. Would he knock at all? Nesrin opened the door a crack to see Reyhan on the other side. Nesrin glanced past her. It was early. On a normal day the Sehzade would not be awake yet. His door was closed, so that gave her hope she might be able to sneak out and find some task to occupy herself. Elsewhere. Anywhere else.

Nesrin captured Reyhan by the wrist and pulled her into the room, shutting the door behind her.

"Is something wrong?" Reyhan asked. "You are jumpy."

"I am not jumpy."

Reyhan made a face. "Very well. Then would you care to accompany Mutar Charah to the refugee camp today? Bek is downstairs."

"Yes please."

Reyhan gave her an incredulous look as she went to work selecting clothing and helping Nesrin into it. She changed her bandages first. The wound was healing well, but a few of the spots that had been burned more severely still required bandages.

"Hmm." Reyhan poked around the edge of the wound closest to Nesrin's low spine. Nesrin hissed. "We should poultice this tonight. It is swelling again, and a day sweating in the camp will not help it."

Nesrin nodded. They dressed her and Reyhan braided her hair and wound it around her head, pinning it in place. It was beginning to feel less like an assault and more a ritual, calming in its way. It helped that Reyhan had found a softer touch worked just as well as her previous yanking.

"Do you think it's all right if we take something with us? To give to them? I know it is a camp, but it is still their home and…"

"Your presence there, as the future wife of the Sehzade, is gift enough," Reyhan said haughtily as she pushed the last pin into place. Nesrin squinted.

"Not if they are hungry."

Reyhan sighed. "There is not enough food in this house to feed them all."

"But I could fill one belly," Nesrin argued as they slipped out of the room and tiptoed downstairs. Bek lounged on the couch in the entryway. He sprang to his feet and bowed when they appeared. Nesrin held a finger to her lips and made a sign for him to wait where he was. When she turned toward the kitchen and dining room, Reyhan gave another martyred sigh and followed her.

A basket of apples sat on the dining table, and Nesrin swept it into her arms.

"No!" Reyhan hissed, glancing in a panic toward the door to the servant rooms. "Deniz just brought those from the market yesterday."

"I will deal with that when I must," Nesrin said. She returned to Bek, and he held out his arms in offer to take the apples. When they were outside, Nesrin eased the front door closed, glancing up at the balcony. She half feared she would see him standing up there, glaring down at them. But the doors to the balcony remained closed, and no one came after them as they walked down the hill.

A tight little knot in her chest made her look back once as they walked down the hill, and she frowned when she still did not see him. Perhaps the moment between them had meant nothing at all. The knot in her chest tightened, and she fought an emotion she could not put name to. Anger or disappointment. Or it might have been every emotion.

There was a carriage stationed outside Amara's shop. Djar leaned against the side, near the front, watching their approach with folded arms. Nesrin approached him and offered an apple, which he took with a broad smile that, were she in a sunnier mood, would have made her heart flutter.

"You could cut this." She held out another apple and waggled a finger at his sword.

He raised an eyebrow and leaned down so his face was level with hers. "It is not a kitchen knife, Poppy."

Nesrin blinked at the nickname. Bek laughed, plucking the apple from her hand as he drew a knife from his belt. "What else are you going to use that sword for, old man?" he taunted.

Djar rapped his knuckles against Bek's brow and the boy flinched, handing the split apple to Nesrin. Their antics brought about a reluctant smile, which broadened when she offered each of the two carriage horses one half of the fruit. She stroked the black cheek of one, murmuring a soothing tangle of nonsense. The horse stamped and flicked one ear back, listening to her, then tried to shove his nose into the basket of apples she had propped on her hip.

"Pfft." She turned at an angle so he could not try again. Their smell, dust and hay and horse sweat, was achingly familiar. Nesrin denied the urge to bury her head against his mane and live in the scent for a moment.

Bek called something in Meneian as Amara emerged from the shop, and Bek's voice made her look at Nesrin. Amara's eyebrows rose, but she said nothing. She greeted Reyhan as she climbed into the carriage, and Nesrin skirted the horses to join the other two. Bek and Djar climbed into the driver seat.

"I am pleased you decided to join us," Amara said as Nesrin settled in next to Reyhan. It was only the second carriage ride of her entire life, but this one was significantly less terrifying. They shared laughter over the incident with the flour, and Amara demanded she be invited to sample Nesrin's cooking.

The carriage climbed a winding, steep hill. Nesrin noted the switch from the cobbles to packed dirt. She had to brace her feet to keep from sliding forward out of the bench as the carriage slanted. They paused once the hill flattened out, and Djar's voice carried from where he spoke with someone. Amara leaned forward and opened the door, and a guard circled around to peer in at them. He greeted Amara, eyed Nesrin, then swung the door shut. Nesrin glanced at Amara, but she seemed unperturbed.

"They are accustomed to me, though my visits seem to vex them," she said.

Djar coaxed the horses forward with his voice, though they did not go much farther. When the wagon stopped again, the door opened to reveal Bek, and the three women exited.

The camp was initially hidden from view by the wagon, and when Nesrin came around, she stopped to take it in. Her heart ached, her throat tightening around her sorrow. As far as she could see, dwellings constructed of detritus, discarded boards, cloth, and crates. The ground was dirt trod into a hard clay, the kind that turned into a nightmare of slippery mud when it rained.

Amara walked into the camp, with Nesrin and Reyhan to either side. Behind them, Bek and Djar carried two crates each.

The ground was uneven, creating pockets where water would stand. Many of the lean-tos and structures sat in the depressions. The spring rains would have flooded them constantly. Some had procured pallets to sleep on, lifting them out of the water, for the most part.

The smell of so many humans packed too tightly together, without places to bathe, and few places to deal with their waste, turned Nesrin's stomach. She blinked through watery eyes as Amara guided them toward the center of the camp. They collected a following of curious children and adults, though most stayed at a distance.

Nesrin held an apple out to one child that followed, who wove expertly between fabric walls and leaning support poles. He darted in, snatched the apple, and met her eyes for an instant. He seemed to hesitate, deciding whether to speak a thank-you, but Nesrin smiled and nodded her chin for him to go. He did. In his place more children appeared, clamoring, surrounding her, so she had to stop to hand out her apples.

She did not have enough, her basket empty while small, dirty hands still reached, bright eyes still pleaded. Wheel, she could not bear it. Nesrin crouched, opening her arms to gather the children she had been unable to give anything to. They crowded near, some with tear-filled eyes, gaunt faces that were all too familiar.

"I will come back," she promised. "I will bring enough."

Behind her, a woman's voice echoed hers, but in a different language. Nesrin turned and rose, her hands automatically closing around smaller ones that reached. A woman well into her final Turns, with wiry grey hair in twin braids and dark eyes like ink stains in her sockets, smiled at Nesrin. Some of the children broke from around Nesrin to cling to the woman's threadbare caftan and entari.

"They do not all speak Trade," she said in a voice that creaked with age. She brought to mind the oldest oaks in Mizraa, whose spreading branches were home and shelter to everyone and everything. Nesrin knew a matron when she saw one. She bowed, and the woman laughed, looking past her to Amara.

"What have you brought us today?"

"A princess," Amara said as she came to Nesrin's side. Nesrin flinched, glancing at Amara, then back to the elderly woman.

"I am not," she said, with a spear of guilt twisting in her belly. She was no more than any of these people, belonged more truly here, with them, than in the manicured life she was lost in, in the city below.

"Mmm." The woman surveyed Nesrin's clothes, hair, and face. Then she moved forward, using a gnarled stick to keep her balance, as she hunched forward a bit. The rounded back so many women adopted over Turns of caring for men and children and the never-ending work of a home. "I see." The children followed her in a small, clinging tide, like chicks to a clucking hen. They spoke rapidly, and the woman answered, though Nesrin understood none of it.

"Who is that?" Nesrin murmured to Amara once the woman was past them. Reyhan brushed at dirt clinging to Nesrin's clothes.

"That is Emine, the elected spokeswoman of the camp."

They followed her, Nesrin's mind circling how she could get more food to the children. Reyhan had been right, there was not enough food in the Sehzade's home. She thought of the wagon of supplies, looted and scattered over the street, and her anger swirled. She knew there were hungry people in the city, but had yet to see a face as thin and fragile as the children she saw here. No homes, barely any shelter, or food enough to survive.

"Do they have clean water?" Nesrin asked as they arrived suddenly in a central open space which the shelters encircled. Crates had been placed as seats around a large firepit. A wagon was parked there, with a contingent of brawny men, several of whom appeared to be guards of the same ilk as those who had seen them into the camp.

Nesrin was relieved to see bags of rice and lentils, and an orderly line of people with whatever they had scavenged as a container to receive their rations.

"There is a source." Amara pointed toward the hill that sloped away from the east side of the camp, which sat on a plateau and cliff edge that overlooked the city below. "And over there"—she swung her arm to point north—"is a small field for growing crops. But we've been struggling to find seeds, and that which we find has failed to grow or thrive. Some of these are farmers, but not many. Most of them fled Al-Nimas at the start of the conflict."

"I see," Nesrin murmured. Fields and seeds that were not producing sounded like something she could assist with. "Might I see the fields before we leave?"

"If Emine agrees." Amara nodded to the woman as she stopped to oversee the supply rationing.

"I thought it would be more…"

"Hopeful?" Amara suggested, her expression pensive. Nesrin did not respond. It seemed foolish, now that she was confronted with the reality. That something wrought of war could bring hope. She should know that. Perhaps spending these turns in the palace and the homes of the wealthy had dazzled her eyes, so the truth was warped to her. If it could warp her, then what would it do to those who never left their gilded lives?

Emine returned to them, having shooed her chicks off, and Amara offered her an arm. "Mistress Bardakci would like to see your field and crops. Can someone show her the way, while you and I discuss supplies?"

Emine sniffed, glancing from Nesrin's hair to her shoes, which she could admit were not appropriate for this place. Too finely made, the soles too thin and the goatkid leather too delicate and expensive to be tromping about in dirt and scrub grass.

"I grew up surrounded by fields and orchards," Nesrin said, defending the prickle of pride the woman's dismissive look caused.

"Mmm," the old woman hummed, then she tipped her head. She brought her hand up and touched a finger against Nesrin's jaw, turning her head. "What is this…" She jutted her chin toward the angry red line that snaked from Nesrin's temple, down her neck and into her entari collar. "A whip?"

Nesrin nodded, taking a step back so the woman's hand fell away.

"I know who you are," she said, some of her dismissiveness giving way. Nesrin went cold for a breath, and Reyhan pressed close to her side, expression tight. "You helped Ilayda and her little ones in the wagon when they were attacked."

The tension eased. Reyhan relaxed. Nesrin ducked her chin.

"You are welcome here, princess or not," the woman said with a grin. Then she looked over her shoulder and shouted with surprising volume, "Ozan, fetch Ilayda here!"

"Oh no, I do not wish to bother anyone." Nesrin put her hand on Emine's. The elder woman closed her other hand over Nesrin's and gave it a shake.

"A debt is owed. They would not dare bring more poor turns of the Wheel upon us by neglecting it. You quite likely saved a life that day. The least they can do is show you whatever you wish to see of the camp."

She turned to discussing shortages in the camp with Amara, and Nesrin glanced to Reyhan. The woman's face was uncharacteristically placid, her gaze trained on the horizon.

"Are you all right?" Nesrin touched her elbow. Reyhan drew a quick breath and dropped her gaze to Nesrin's with a wan smile.

"As one can be, I suppose. I had not visited any of the camps before today. It is—"

"Heartbreaking," Nesrin finished for her. Reyhan only nodded. "Why is the palace not doing more?"

"It is more complicated than simply doing more," Reyhan began, but could not elaborate, as a man and woman emerged from amidst the tents and strode toward them. Nesrin recognized them as the couple who had been attacked. The woman, Ilayda, wore her baby wrapped against her by a long strip of woven cloth. Her two other children lagged shyly behind her. When the woman saw Nesrin, she hurried forward and dropped to her knees, cradling the baby's head as she bent forward at her feet. The man did the same.

The people around them, those lined up to receive rations, the men handing them out, a scattering of people talking at the edges of the circle, stopped to look at the spectacle.

"Oh no," Nesrin mumbled, crouching to take the woman's hands and urge her up. "Please don't." She gestured at the man as well. "That is unnecessary."

"I never had a chance to thank you, Mistress." Tears welled in her eyes, as she reached as if she would touch the healing mark on Nesrin's face, but drew her fingers back quickly, and the tears spilled from her eyes, streaking her cheeks. She reached down, cradling the head of each of her older children against each hip. "If you had not…" She looked from one to the other, her exhale ragged as she raised her gaze to Nesrin again.

"I am grateful I could," Nesrin said.

"What can we do to repay you?" Ilayda's husband asked. The bruises on his face were still fading, a multicolor reminder of the violence that could grow from seeds of fear.

"She wants to see the crops," Emine interjected. His face registered surprise, then he nodded.

"Return here when you finish," Amara said.

Nesrin and Reyhan followed the man out of the center clearing, past staring eyes and whispers. Nesrin did not relish the feeling of being a spectacle. It seemed she had been nothing else since arriving in Narfour, in one manner or another.

He led them along a well-worn path through the shelters. Cookfires were banked, thin trails of smoke rising to choke the air, settling thick over the camp, held in place by the damp morning air. Nesrin saw all manner of salvaged pots and utensils. Some did not even have spoons to stir, just whittled sticks. Several fires warmed pots that were clearly shared by more than one family or person, too small to cook for the number of people depending on them.

Her heart grew heavier with each sight, each drawn, ravaged face. Every set of eyes that looked through her, hopeless, choked her with desperation, anger, and shame. While her family, led by the open hearts of her mother and grandmothers, had been more open to the idea of refugees entering Tamar, Nesrin had not truly paused to consider the effects beyond Mizraa's own dwindling supplies of food.

Tamar was not the only place suffering. How quickly the mind pushed away everything but the inner circle, when threatened. How quick it was to strip the woes and trials of others to prioritize itself. Sometimes it was necessary, of course. One could not worry about others when they were literally on death's door. But…she could. She had more ability to give than she had ever had, and perhaps she could balance the cost of the lies she was telling to gain that ability.

Ilayda's husband stopped at the northern end of the camp, on a gradually sloping clifftop that overlooked the sprawl of the palace. A rough rectangle had been dug up, by hand, if Nesrin were to guess. She cringed at the thought of the back-breaking labor involved in that. When she strode forward, Reyhan and Ilayda followed. Sad, stunted plants peppered the rows in irregular patches.

Reyhan groaned in protest when Nesrin crouched down and dug her hand into the dirt.

"Mistress, please." Reyhan lowered beside her as she hissed the request. "Fooling the Sehzade is one thing"—she glanced around—"since he barely pays attention. But Mutar Charah is more worldly. She will notice."

"She might," Nesrin mused, barely listening. The dirt was packed hard, crumbling to dust only when she applied all the strength in her hand to it. Clay. Not surprising on the top of a windswept cliff where all the water would run away down its slope. She straightened, letting the dust sift away through her fingers. Seedling roots would struggle.

"Where is your seed from?" she asked over her shoulder. Ilayda's husband replied with a shake of his head. "It was brought to us by the guards."

Unless someone had picked it out with care from a seller who wasn't shilling castoffs for a bit of side profit, there was no telling how old or viable the seed had been. Wild edibles would grow well in such packed earth. Mallow, chicory, and sea holly.

Nesrin looked up the slope of the hill that rose to the east of the camp. It continued on, growing steeper and steeper until it joined the spine of mountains that dropped away from the Kalspire. Even with an army to forage out enough to plant the field, it would take a Turn or more to establish enough to feed this many people. They needed fast-growing foods. Nesrin wrinkled her nose.

Someone called her name. When she turned toward the voice, Amara stood at the edge of the field, with Djar, Bek, and Reyhan.

Amara watched her return to them with a contemplative look on her face that made Nesrin realize how odd it must have looked. She'd been standing alone in the field staring at the dirt and the hillside for at least a mark, according to the sun. Everything else in her life felt too big for her, at the moment. This was within her abilities.

She stopped in front of them. "I think I can help."

Twenty-Six

Ihsan stared at the little plant on his desk. He turned its pot one way, then the other. His lack of sleep was making his faculties fail him. He knew that only a small turn ago it had been near death, if not dead. Amara had even commented on it. But today it had new leaf buds, emerging from the juncture of its shriveled stem. Another shoot had poked out of the too-dry soil. He regarded it in suspicion.

Something was happening to him. He collapsed into the chair at his desk, tipping his head back to stare at the ceiling. His power was erratic, with unusual, hard-to-control flareups that had nothing to do with his emotions. Or rather, were more powerful than they would usually be. Kuhzey and Deniz told him that his ice had spread farther and thicker during his nightmares than it had in more than a Cycle.

Was this because of the Sultan? Because Ihsan could not cope with his emotions? Because he was not sleeping and so lacked control? Because of *her*? Being in his space, upending the habits that helped him manage himself?

The door to his office swung open. He startled, whipping his head forward.

She stood there, eyes rounded in surprise, hands together, skin pink in embarrassment, breath fast. *Wheel save him.* She was the last thing he could deal with. He let his head fall back again. He did not know how to look at her. They had not spoken since she'd cried on him, then ran from him. What was there to say?

"Sorry," she said breathlessly, then, "I am owed a stipend." She paused. "And I would like to collect it."

Ihsan stopped a bitter laugh by adjusting his jaw so it popped. Then he raised his head to look at her. "Of course you would."

Her brow twitched, but her chin was set in determination. It must be her temper that made her eyes seem to shift from muddy hazel to a greener hue, a trick of the heat that also colored her cheeks and made her freckles stand out. He straightened so he could fold his arms on his desk. All his frustration, all his uncertainty and confusion roared up, and slipped from him before he could rein it in. Ice shot across the surface of his desk, and the pot containing the resurrected vine shattered, spilling dirt and pot shards everywhere.

She jumped like a startled rabbit, eyes flaring wider with fear. His flux disappeared as quickly as it had reared up, and shame left him colder than his ice. He stood without a word.

"I will arrange it," he said in a dull voice. "If that is all?"

She was owed a stipend, of course. He'd already arranged for the money due her father to be sent regularly. She was within her rights to ask for hers. But it rankled, being seen as a purse for someone. It especially rankled because there were moments between them where he could feel earnest, easy truth.

She knelt beside his desk, though he had not noticed her cross the room, and began picking up shards of pottery. She tugged up the edge of her entari to collect them in. Ihsan crouched, shaking the broken pieces out of the corner of fabric she held.

"Don't," he said, his resentment in his voice, though he had not meant for it to be. He had never been so conscious of how he spoke. How he sounded. She retreated, her hands going to her lap.

"You do not wish to let me into your life. Any part of it. Even as a friend," she said, so quietly he had to concentrate to hear her. "You will not even let me help you with the smallest thing." She gestured to the mess of pottery, dirt, and the beleaguered plant. With careful fingers, she rescued the vine, laying it across her knees.

"I am not worth helping, Mistress. Some broken things cannot be fixed." He nudged one of the shards.

"No"—she picked it up—"some broken things were never meant to be as they were. That does not mean they are unsalvageable, or not worth the effort." She swept at the dirt, then hissed, drawing her hand back. Blood welled along the pads of her fingers and dripped onto the tangle of vine in her lap.

He closed his hand over her bleeding fingers, pressing them into his palm as he willed his power over them. The cold slowed the bleeding until the body could stop it, a useful trick he had learned at Dilay's urging. Always trying to find the positive in his circumstances.

"See?" Ihsan teased quietly, though he fought back a wave of sadness, "some things will only hurt you."

"But you are helping me." She nodded to his fingers around hers. "Just as you helped me with this." She gestured to the mark on her jaw and neck with her free hand. "Only you can do so."

"Do you think you are the first person to try that line of thought on me? It did not work for them. Why should it work for you?"

"I will wear you down," she said, with a soft smile that was apologetic. "I have been told I could make friends with a pile of dung if given enough time." She stiffened as soon as the words were out, her breath indrawing.

Ihsan gave an incredulous laugh. "Did you just call me a pile of dung?"

Something like relief relaxed her face, which was unexpected. He was still trying to make sense of the series of reactions when she shook her head. When the silence had lingered for a moment too long, she tipped her head back a bit so he could not meet her eyes.

"I hope you can forgive me for crying on you." Her shoulders rose and fell in resignation. "I did not mean to be a burden."

He could not tell her that her lack of inhibition was refreshing. It had felt good to be useful. And every time he thought of it, of her vulnerability gifted to him, he grew more enamored of the feeling. No one else had trusted him with vulnerability in so long, because they thought he could not shoulder it alongside his own suffering. But Nesrin thought he was strong enough. And she did not feel like a burden, when she clung to him.

That desire warred with every other thought in his head. There was nothing of Kadir's, not person, nor plan, that could be taken at face value. Ihsan knew that better than anyone. But her gentleness was addicting. And frightening. Lulling him into complacency he had not felt with someone outside his family since the fire.

She lowered her chin to hesitantly lock her gaze to his, looking for a response. Shyness or concern drew a furrow in her brow, and she caught her lower lip in her teeth, waiting. He was trying his hardest not to allow the seed of attraction to grow. But she made it difficult, in moments like these, when she was both guileless and clearly comfortable with herself. It more effectively chipped at his walls than anything overt ever could. And she was so close to him now; the way her teeth sank into the softness of her lower lip was hard to ignore.

A strange welling of heat, like he was holding a sun-warmed stone, made his power flare again, ice lacing Nesrin's skin. She squealed in surprise, tugging her hand from his.

"Forgive me, I…" He balled his hand into a fist as she cradled hers against her chest. "My magic has been erratic."

"There is nothing to forgive, I was not expecting it, is all. May I see?" She held her palm open between them.

She was, oddly he thought, peaceful. Settled as if this were the most comfortable place she could be. Comfortable in his presence and with his twisted magic. So few people were, he felt lulled despite himself. He should know more about her. What had made her this way? If she was truly what she seemed to be.

He held his hand out to her, and she took it in both of hers. The bleeding of her fingers had stopped, though the red line remained. It must not have been as deep as he thought, to be so quickly closed. She ran her thumb across the arc of his palm below his fingers. His hand twitched closed as a sizzle of surprising intensity jolted over his hand and up his wrist. He would not have suspected that to be a spot sensitive to touch. She stared at his hand, waiting. He could not help a muted chuckle.

"First a dung heap and now a puppet show," he said. "Your disrespect knows no bounds, does it?"

She glanced up in distress, but saw his teasing smile. Her gaze lingered, a moment more than necessary, then dropped. "Mmhmm."

A tangle of feeling pulsed in his belly. Had she been looking at him, as he had at her?

He brought his power to the surface, and its gusts and spirals trailed pale turquoise and ice white over his palm and wrist. Her delighted gasp was worth putting himself on display like a circus performer.

"I have never met a Second House mage that could make ice," she mused. Her thumb tapped against his palm, trying to catch a wisp of magic. He watched his own magic on his skin, their heads both bowed over their clasped hands, brows nearly touching. He remembered, now, why he kept away. That desire, need, to be touched, and comforted, suffocated him when he put his guard down. But it hurt. It hurt to be touched, to be looked at, to explain his body to someone when he barely knew it anymore.

His skin and his magic, even after all these Turns, were strangers to him, and trying to speak of his scars made him angry. Made him sick. Made him weak.

"Has your power always been this?" She slid one hand up, innocently, her fingers wrapping his wrist, her thumb claiming his pulse point, and a spiral of blue-white magic. It whisked away, not corporeal enough to be affected by her touch. Not the way he was affected by her question. He had sunk into a kind of languorous stupor, mesmerized by the warmth and impossibly soft grip of her hands, his mind numb and blissfully empty. But the question was burning pitch, lighting fire in his mind and over his skin.

Ihsan pulled from her grip. "No," he said, curtly, and got to his feet. "I should go. I will send Kuhzey to clean this up." He gestured at the mess. She looked up at him. What he needed to see on her face was disappointment, or insult at his abruptness. But what was there was understanding, a quiet patience in her eyes that threatened to crack him open. "Don't look at me like that," he snarled.

She dropped her gaze and got to her feet. She still gripped the homeless vine in her hand. "May I put this in a new pot?"

"Do as you wish," he said, gripping his fists hard enough that his knuckles cracked. An ice storm of emotion was threatening in him, confusion and resentment and grief.

"Anything I wish?"

He did not understand her at first, but when he did, he met her gaze again. This time she had challenge in the dusty hazel of her eyes, in the set of her mouth and chin. And his muddled thoughts tumbled into insanity as he stifled a desire to kiss her. Not the gentle kind, but a challenge to match hers.

Ihsan swallowed. "I care not, Mistress Bardakci," he said instead, putting distance between them with the title.

Her expression turned to exasperation. "My name is *Nesrin*. Is it so hard to say?"

Yes. She spun before he could answer. His door closed behind her, leaving him standing in a mess of broken pottery and scattered dirt. Somehow, that felt appropriate.

Twenty-Seven

She was growing accustomed to waking up in a vast emptiness. It was not that which was frightening, but her inability to move. She could see, and hear, but there was nothing to see, or listen to. There was nothing to feel but her own body curled around itself.

At least, that had been the case. Now there was something. Just outside her peripheral. Light. Or the suggestion of it. She had to stare away from it to register the color. Blue. Turquoise. And something that was not light, yet showed up in the nothingness all the same. Shadow within shadow.

There was a sense that she was surrounded by it, by the lights. That they were waiting…for something from her. But what could it want? She was trapped. Could not move, or speak.

Then the sense of that faded away, as did the black nothing. Instead there was cold. Ice that made her breath fog. She woke.

Nesrin gasped for breaths she could not take in her dream. It was not a terrifying dream, but she woke from it discomfited every time. Her room was cold but not icy. She got up from the floor, shedding the blankets, and grabbed her robe from the corner of the bed. This time, when she left her room, it was not because of curiosity, or to offer assistance. She sought…comfort. From her strange dreams. She was so desperately tired of being alone.

She opened his door. There was no light, curtains were drawn over his windows, which faced south anyway and would not catch the moonlight. But the swirl of his power was light enough. The ice had only just begun to spread away from him, over the blankets, creeping down the supports of the bed toward the floor.

She hugged the robe around her and closed his door softly. Then she padded to his bed and sat on the edge. He slept on top of his blankets, his arms crossed over his face, muscles rigid, breathing too fast. This was the first time she had seen him sleep in both caftan and salvar. His magic shifted and flitted beneath the fabric, a beautiful show of light, though she hated that it was because of his terror. Nesrin pressed a hand over his heart.

"Ihsan?" she murmured, reaching her other hand to slide over the back of his left. He sucked in a deep breath, his hand spreading wide beneath her touch, then his fingers twisting enough to catch over hers. He bolted halfway up. But she resisted, her hand on his chest, and he relaxed backward. He dropped his right arm to his side, blinking in the dark, and slid his left arm, fingers still gripping hers, to circle his head. It pulled her awkwardly, so she had to lean over him.

He peered up at her with sleepy eyes. "You aren't going to stop doing this, are you?" he muttered tiredly.

She shook her head. He groaned, closing his eyes. Sweat beaded, froze, and thawed on his brow as his power flickered and his breathing slowed. His fingers on hers were frigid. She wanted to stroke his hair, the way she would have comforted anyone else. Any person she or her grandmothers had been treating. Especially someone suffering from so much lingering trauma. But she feared if she pushed, he would shut down even more.

What was she to do about her fierce attraction to him? She could not look at him without wanting to draw closer, could not talk to him without wanting to tease, could not help but admire when she should only be listening. But that felt like a betrayal of the trust she was trying to earn. And trying to earn his trust reminded her she had no right to it, because she was a liar.

"Is this normal in Mizraa? Inviting yourself into bedrooms whenever you wish?" His voice was sleep-rough, a delicious departure from its usual smooth cadence.

"Not usually, no." She was uncomfortable, stretched as she was, but he had not let go of her fingers, and she did not want to pull away. She could not help wondering what he would do if she simply collapsed on his chest. "But this is an unusual circumstance, is it not?"

His eyes opened, light swirling in their depths—like flickers of snowflakes through a window. Her breath fogged. She had leaned in too close to look.

"You do not have many boundaries, do you, Nesrin?" His lids lowered, directing his gaze down, to her mouth, or lower. That he had said her name made her gleeful. A battle won.

"You have enough for us both." Nesrin pushed up, though it took a strength of will she resented having at the moment. He lifted his arm from around his head and dropped it into her lap, keeping their fingers interlaced.

"Hmm," he sighed. His eyes slid closed again, and she realized he was only half awake. Some of her elation fizzled. He might not even remember this in the morning.

He seemed settled at least, the ice was gone, and the magic fading away. Nesrin stood, keeping her fingers around his for a moment more as she looked down at him. Then she gently pulled them free and laid his arm across his belly, and quietly slipped out of his room.

Ihsan was gone when she rose in the morning. His bedroom door was open, the room empty. He was not in his office, or in the dining room. Nesrin, grumpily, searched for him everywhere. But he was not in the house. Had he run away because of her? No, that was silly. Self-absorbed, even. He was probably attending to something important.

She sought peace from her warring thoughts in the kitchen. The morning sun was just warming the back of the house, though it had not risen high enough for its light to reach into the patio area. Nesrin started a fire in the pit and put a pot of water on the hook to boil. Back inside, she tied an apron on, and wrapped her hair in cloth. Humming, she lifted the trap door in the floor by the wall and descended three steps into the storage beneath the house. She retrieved the labneh she'd been draining overnight and returned to the table. Nesrin crushed and minced a head's worth of garlic and stirred it into the yogurt.

A healthy ladleful went onto four plates. She cracked eggs into four small wooden bowls, then lined a basket with a linen towel. She carried all of it out to the patio, where the water was not yet boiling. While she waited, she arranged the burning wood and coals to separate sides of the little firepit, and set a heavy iron pan on top of the coals to heat.

Birds flitted through the garden beyond the kitchen area, singing their dawn songs. She whistled some of their songs and was rewarded by a few answers. One or two brave souls flew over to investigate, and seemed puzzled to find no potential mates. Nesrin scattered a handful of crumbs from a leftover flatbread for them.

Other creatures skittered and prowled, causing leaves to rustle or branches to bounce. When the water boiled, Nesrin dropped the eggs, one at a time, into a swirl of the water, waiting for each to poach and removing it to the towel-lined basket before adding the next. When they were done she wound her apron around the pan and carried it inside along with her eggs. She set it all on the table, and poured a healthy glug of oil into the pan, where it sizzled. A palmful of chili flakes dyed the oil a savory orange. She set an egg into each mound of labneh, then dribbled spoonfuls of the toasty chili oil over each.

The others were stirring as she carried the plates into the dining room and set them on the table. Kuhzey was the first to sit, drowsy, hair mussed and lopsided. It warmed her to see him. He reminded her of Metin, though they shared little in personality. Metin was gangly and clumsy, perpetually hungry and his hair and clothes always a mess.

Good morning, she greeted him.

He motioned back with a phrase she didn't know. So he tapped his nose then pointed at the food.

"Smells good?" she suggested and he nodded. She pushed a plate to him and he dug into it immediately with the bread she brought in next.

Reyhan arrived, collapsing onto a cushion beside Nesrin. She made a little sound of excitement at the sight of the eggs. "My mother used to make these. I make them for Kanat when I can." Her tone went pensive at the last, but she did not appear ready for conversation.

Kuhzey inhaled his portion, then leapt up from his floor cushion and disappeared into the kitchen.

Reyhan shrugged, breaking open her egg with a corner of bread, then swiping up a mouthful. She made a pleased sound as she chewed, and Nesrin grinned. Deniz finally skulked in, making a fuss of setting her cushion just so before sitting as far from Nesrin and Reyhan as she could. Reyhan rose, picked up the final plate, and set it in front of Deniz.

"Thank you," she mumbled. Nesrin watched her surreptitiously, her face turned to her own breakfast. Deniz took the smallest sample possible, chewing slowly. Nesrin could imagine her thoughts churning, searching for anything to criticize. Deniz swallowed, then drew a breath in as she blinked, ready to expunge whatever she had come up with.

"I can see why you are so protective of the Sehzade," Nesrin said first. Deniz's mouth pressed closed. "How lucky he is to have someone so loyal and caring in his employ."

Kindness in the face of enmity was a kind of strength Nesrin had watched her mother and grandmothers wield with precision all her life. Trading insult for insult, slight for slight…waging a war of personalities, that was easy. Anger was easy. But kindness was work, and weapon, in a way. Though Nesrin could not always summon the self-control to use it as such.

Deniz poked at her egg, mollified, as she bobbed her head in acknowledgment. "I have been with him since…" She inhaled the next words, shaking her head. Deniz blinked rapidly and stared at her food. The fire? Did they share more than just time? Trauma as well? That would explain a great deal.

"I would never try to supplant you," Nesrin said, softly. "I am merely looking for a place, my own role in this—"

Reyhan dug an elbow into Nesrin's ribs, eliciting a squeak of pain.

"Ow!" Nesrin clutched at her side. Reyhan kept her face forward, eyes wide, as she stabbed at the dregs of food on her plate with her remaining bit of bread. Her head gave the slightest twitch, indicating up and behind, and Nesrin twisted around. Since she was on the floor, her gaze landed on the vicinity of Ihsan's hips, then traveled up to his face, hers flushing. He leaned in the archway to the kitchen, shoulder propped against the frame, arms folded over his chest, one eyebrow raised.

"Efendim." Deniz moved to get to her feet. He waved her off, revealing he held a bit of paper in his hand, sealed with wax.

"You seem to have forgotten a plate for me," he said, gaze fixed on Nesrin's, "the master of the house." He wore his usual shuttered expression. But the irritability usually etched in a furrow on his brow was missing, though she could not name what had taken its place. Nesrin's frustration at him abandoned her. He was not hiding from her.

Dropping her napkin onto the table, she rose. "You were not here. I assumed you would be fed wherever you were."

As she straightened, Kuhzey emerged from the kitchen with a tray of tea, which he set on the table before bowing to Ihsan. He gave Ihsan a bright greeting before he returned to his place. Ihsan watched Kuhzey like he was a stranger who had appeared in his house. He poured tea for everyone, and with each cup Ihsan's expression grew more disbelieving.

Kuhzey pointed at his empty plate and held his open hands toward Nesrin. She suppressed a grin as she nodded. When she turned, Ihsan was still exactly as he had been, leaning in the doorway, tall enough and broad enough to take up the majority of the space. She raised her eyebrows in request, and he straightened enough that she could squeeze past. Nesrin did everything she could not to bump or brush him, casting him a little glare as she did, which seemed to amuse him. "Have a seat, and I will make you something to eat."

He twisted, coming away from the wall to follow her. She turned on him when they were in the kitchen, perplexed. "Go sit," she demanded. He frowned back.

"I'll stand where I like, thank you."

"Loom, you mean," Nesrin grumbled as she circled the table to the opposite side from him.

"You've done something to Kuhzey. That was positively cozy," Ihsan accused.

"The table is the family," Nesrin quoted her father's mother. It was a silly thing to say under these circumstances. This was hardly a family. He did not answer, and she did not look at him as she cracked two more eggs. "Kuhzey—bring me your plate," she called. The boy practically skipped into the kitchen, putting his plate on the table with such force that it nearly spun off the opposite side.

Ihsan caught it, watching Kuhzey dart back out again, then looked to Nesrin as he slid it closer to her. Nesrin nodded her thanks, but did not speak. There were too many feelings to sort. Irritation at him, for his hot-and-coldness, though she understood why he did it. Embarrassment, for the moments of closeness the day before that had felt like something to her, but she suspected had gone unnoticed by him.

"Are you cross?" he asked, hitching up to half sit on the far edge of the table. Nesrin snapped a towel at him. He hopped off, staring at her in astonishment.

"I will be if you sit on my table again," she said.

"Your table?" he echoed, approaching a bit closer with caution, though he did not join her on her side.

"While I am using it, it is mine." She ladled labneh into Kuhzey's bowl. "And backsides do not belong where food is prepared."

"I believe I've made a mistake," he said. She quirked an eyebrow and stopped her work to look at him. "I thought you meek and shy when I first met you."

Nesrin spluttered a laugh, then waved in the vague direction of one of the cabinets. "Get me another bowl?" she asked. His face went blank, his gaze darting around. Nesrin laughed outright. "You don't know where they are?"

He grimaced, and she grinned, hiding it by pretending to scratch an itch on her nose. Then she picked up her basket, eggs, and the pan she had used to warm the oil. She left him to hunt for a bowl. She added water to the pot and put it back over the fire, sliding her pan onto the coals to heat. In the kitchen, cabinet doors creaked open and snapped shut as he searched.

"You know," he called from the doorway of the kitchen, "it is unusual for a noblewoman to cook her own food." He emerged, triumphant, a bowl in one hand. He did not move beyond the doorway, and Nesrin wondered if he could not even stand the heat of a cookfire. She dropped an egg into the boiling water and glanced up at him from her crouch.

"In Narfour, it is. In Mizraa…we are not so stuffy." That was close enough to a lie that she turned her face away so he could not see it in her expression.

"Stuffy?" he scoffed.

Scooping the egg out, Nesrin threw him an incredulous glance.

"If I was stuffy, I would be angry that someone insists on sneaking into my room every night." His voice lowered. "Or claiming my home and furniture as hers."

"I do not sneak, and it is not *every night*." She set the egg in the basket and swirled the water before dropping the next egg in. Did he remember? Did he remember that he had not let go of her hand? That she had been so close his magic had made her breath turn to fog? "I only came to wake you from a nightmare. You were the one who would not let me go." Her skin prickled at the memory, her thoughts whirling like leaves in a breeze. His hand in hers as she watched his magic in his office.

He made a sound, a rumbling noise that reminded her of the gravel in his voice the night before.

"And is this not my home now as well?" It was not. She could feel that, feel that she was unwelcome and unwanted in a myriad of ways. But a seed must grow where it was planted. Even if the soil was poor or the weather unwelcoming, its roots could break open a place for itself, its leaves spreading to what sunlight it could find.

She snuck a glance at him from her peripheral. He was rolling the bowl between his palms, eyes fixed to the patio stones.

Ihsan was nothing like the men she had grown up with. They were…earthier. No nonsense, no games. Most of them hard and harsh from a life of back-breaking work. She had thought that was what she wanted. A farmboy. A man with work-rough hands. Not someone like this, someone who could just as easily be described as beautiful as he could handsome.

He had fine hands, no calluses. He had scars on his heart. Scars she suspected would never be fully healed. And…this …whatever she felt…was all part of the lie. She would be a liar for the rest of her days. What right did she have to work for his trust, to ask him to bear his scars to her, when she was…this?

Nesrin dipped her spoon and retrieved the second egg. Perhaps staying in the palace was better. It reminded her she did not belong. Reminded her to keep her guard up. This, in his home—it would be too easy to fall into this lie.

She wrapped the apron around the pan handle and lifted it from the fire.

"Shoo," she said as she approached the door, which he was still blocking. He moved out of the way, but followed close behind as she set the pan on the table and the basket beside it. He stayed at her side while she poured in oil and pepper flakes, then added the labneh to his bowl, followed by egg and a drizzle of oil.

He turned the bowl one way then the other. "I suppose I could grow accustomed to unusual." He took the spoon she held out to him.

"Unusual does not mean dangerous," she teased as she reached for a flatbread and handed that to him as well. But was she dangerous? What would it mean for him, to be irrevocably bound to a woman with no noble bloodlines? A void? Someone essentially in the employ of a man he clearly hated?

"For you, perhaps." He poked at the egg with a bit of bread, then handed her the piece. "Prove it isn't poison." His lips twitched as he suppressed a smile. She could not resist that. She plucked the bite from his hand.

"Three people and myself have already eaten it and that is not enough proof for you?" She took a nibble. He gave a minute shrug.

"Perhaps I just want to make certain you are eating enough."

Her chewing slowed, her gaze lifting to his face, which was turned toward his food. Her throat tightened.

"You were gone when I rose this morning," she said, trying to ease the awkwardness. "I was beginning to think you abhorred mornings."

"I do," he admitted. Nesrin could not help a breath of a laugh. He patted at his entari, then pulled out the paper he'd been holding earlier, handing it to her. "You asked for this."

She took it, confused, and ran her nail underneath the seal to break it. "I did?" She unfolded it, half engaged in watching him devour the food. Few things made her feel happier than someone enjoying food she had made them. Especially someone who seemed to treat food as necessity more than connection.

"What do you wish to buy?" His voice took on an edge. She realized she was holding a writ and ledger, signed with an official-looking signature that was not his. She almost laughed. She'd been expecting a bag of coins for her stipend. But of course a prince would not hand out coins. Whatever she bought would be notated here and subtracted from the total listed at the top. Then paid for by the palace. She looked at the total, notated at the top of the ledger.

Nesrin nearly gagged.

"This is a mistake." She shoved it toward him. He wiped his hands on his entari. She gasped, batting his hands away from the beautiful blue and silver brocade, and dabbing at the crumbs with the towel she'd used to carry the pan. "Are you a street urchin? Don't put your greasy hands on that! Use a napkin for Wheel's turn," she scolded. Ihsan snared her by the wrist and tugged the towel from her fingers. His grip was not hard. His expression was playful. Her heart lurched.

"I'll put my hands on whatever I want," he said. They both stiffened. She stared up at him. He let go of her. "Not…" he started and faltered, expression twisting in regret. "Of course not…people." The knot in his throat bobbed, then the muscle in his jaw feathered. He shoved the paper back into her hand. "There is no mistake." He wheeled around, and left.

Nesrin swallowed a shriek of frustration. Why must he *always* leave like that? She stomped her foot, so filled with chaotic energy that she had to move or lose her mind. She propped her elbows on the table and dropped into a crouch behind it, closing her eyes against frustrated tears.

"What are you doing?" Reyhan murmured.

Nesrin looked up and shook her head. "Running in circles." Why was she even trying? Because she could not help it. It was her mother who had joked she could make friends with a dung heap if given enough time, not that she could have told Ihsan that. Nesrin had been making friends her entire life. She was as drawn to that as her siblings were to playing with water. Friends, care—love. It was her nature, kindness and compassion her only magic.

That nature did not belong here. She was a fish attempting to soar.

"The Sehzade said to prepare you to return to the palace tomorrow," Reyhan said. That was good. That would remind her to keep her distance.

That meant she would need to dispense with what she wished to do in the city today. This would be a long day. But the idea of being away from the house, away from any more encounters with him, appealed greatly.

She held the paper out to Reyhan. "This cannot be right? It is a ransom." Enough to purchase the village of Mizraa.

"It seems correct." Reyhan handed it back, searching Nesrin's face. "You expected more?"

Nesrin burst into laughter. All she had wanted was enough to buy more apples.

Twenty-Eight

She did buy apples.

A cartload of them. It cleaned the merchant out of what they had left. Nesrin had inspected most. She did not want to give anyone a mushy apple. She also bought seeds. Seeds for fast-growing, hardy greens. There was no point in giving them grains. They took too long to grow and the processing into something useful was another mountain to climb. Root vegetables, it was still cool enough for most to grow.

The stalls she visited seemed to be, to a man, swindlers. Nesrin inspected every batch she purchased and turned many away. At one point her argument with the vendor was so loud and contentious that Reyhan had shielded her face with her hands before stepping in to remind the man he was speaking to the future princess consort, and not a cart-wife.

The most precious, expensive purchase were two figs, potted, and old enough to produce fruit. The pair of wiry, dour men whose cart she had hired loaded the trees and their cumbersome pots into the wagon without so much as a raised eyebrow.

"You cannot ride in the back of an apple wagon," Reyhan argued in a furious whisper. "You are a princess. It is absurd."

"I am not a princess yet." Nesrin gripped the back rail of the wagon, prepared to hitch herself inside. But Reyhan had an iron grip on her arm.

"You are. You were the *moment* you put that hemp around your neck. Being eccentric in the Sehzade's home is one thing. Doing so in public is entirely different. You must not." Reyhan looked around desperately to see how many people were watching.

"What do you propose?" Nesrin released her grip on the wagon with a resigned sigh. Reyhan relaxed, but still clutched Nesrin's arm.

"Have them meet us at the guard station. We can hire a carriage."

Nesrin nodded. Reyhan relayed her orders to the cart men, who started off immediately. "Do you think they'll be attacked?" Nesrin asked. The market bustled around them, busier now than it had been when they arrived earlier in the morning. One part of Nesrin desperately wanted to explore. There were things here she had never seen, and she hadn't had a chance before. Herbs and roots and spices, jewelry, fabrics hung to blow seductively in the breezes that wafted through the stalls. The smells of cooking food threaded through everything.

"There has yet to be an attack this early in the day," Reyhan said, but her fingers knitted together and apart as she watched the cart make its way.

"Do we have time for you to take me to your promised's glassworks?" Nesrin grinned. Reyhan went still. Her expression shifted, too quickly for Nesrin to catch a glimpse of emotion. In the pit of her stomach, a hard, hot lump formed. What was Reyhan hiding? Did it matter? Reyhan's hands flexed open, then closed, her lashes fluttering in a way that suggested she was weighing options. "What if I make it a command, as a princess?"

Her shoulder twitched, her gaze snapping to Nesrin's, and a weak, sad smile thinned the fire mage's mouth. "You're learning." Her fingers clasped her opposite wrist, worrying the bracelet there. "But I cannot, today," she said, then added, "he is away."

Nesrin was no water mage, but even she could recognize Reyhan's evasion. Reyhan ignored Nesrin's frown and crossed the street to a carriage parked by a food stall. The driver sat in his seat, eating a pile of shredded meat stuffed into a rolled-up flatbread. It dripped sauce all over the bench seat. Nesrin's stomach rumbled. Would the food stall vendors give her food for their name on a ledger? If she were one, she doubted she would trust paper instead of coin.

Reyhan returned, and caught Nesrin's longing stare. She groaned and led Nesrin to the stall. Then she ordered for them both. The man running the stall barked orders, and a younger man who looked like a stamped copy rushed to obey him. He had been busy turning a spit of roasted lamb, but he paused to shave off bits into a flatbread he held. He slapped on a scattering of pickled vegetables, a ladle of sauce, and wrapped it into a roll before handing it to the man, who passed it along to Reyhan. Reyhan gave the first to Nesrin, and took the second, then paid the man from her own money.

"I'll pay you back," Nesrin said, around a mouthful. Reyhan shot her a stern look. Nesrin did not know if it was in reference to the offer of money, or to talking with her mouth full. They finished the food in amicable silence, though Reyhan remained pensive. Nesrin finished first, and waited for Reyhan before they climbed into the carriage.

Despite her worry that the two cart men might be robbed or make off with her purchases themselves, they had not, and were waiting at the guard station as instructed. Emine was also there, along with several men Nesrin recognized from her first visit to the camp. Despite her unease and questions about Reyhan and her possible secrets, Nesrin smiled to see the elder woman. She almost bowed to her, but thankfully Emine bowed first, reminding Nesrin not to.

"You have been generous," Emine said.

Nesrin shook her head. "It is not enough, but it is a start. Can these handle distributing the apples, and is there anywhere dry to store seeds?"

"We have a few barrels set aside that might do, come." Emine gestured. The two men drove the cart into the open space in the center of camp, with Emine's men trotting behind. They made quick work of unloading the fig trees and burlap bags filled with paper packages of seeds.

Reyhan finished up with the cart men, noting their charges against Nesrin's ledger. They turned their cart and guided it back to the main path and back to the city. Emine recruited a few sturdy-looking children to haul the trees and seeds to the edge of camp. The sunlight was fading swiftly, painting the city below them russet and gold. The palace shown paler colors, gilt in the sunlight. Nesrin and Reyhan followed Emine to the field. A leaning structure made of poles dug into the ground and canvas stretched at an angle sheltered three barrels beneath.

"I'll return soon to help with these, if you can hold off on planting." Nesrin dropped the bags of seeds into the barrels Emine indicated. The lids were secured in place and oiled canvas draped over the tops, held tight with rope. Emine nodded, then turned her attention to the trees.

"Are we to plant these?"

"Yes, they will grow fast here, but they'll need water this first Turn." Nesrin shaded her eyes with her hand, planting her other against her hip as she looked over the furrows. There was a place where the clifftop met the rising hill where the grass was long and lushly green. More water there. Nesrin pointed. "There, I think. Give them room between."

"Figs do not like the Sarkum winters," Emine commented as the two of them oversaw the placement of the trees. "I've never had fresh."

Nesrin grinned. "You are in for a treat then. But you'll have to beat the wasps and ants to them."

"And the children," Emine added with a chuckle. Nesrin agreed. Reyhan stood like a ghost at her side, morose. Though she did put on a mask of helpfulness when spoken to directly.

When they returned to camp, there was laughter. A game of chase among a herd of children. They surrounded Nesrin, begging for her to play, and when she agreed, they cheered. Reyhan did not even protest, only watched wordlessly as Nesrin removed her shoes and raced after them.

She only spoke up when darkness crept down the mountain to swallow the camp. "It is time to leave, Mistress," Reyhan called, like a mother summoning a child to dinner. Nesrin crouched to give hugs and kisses on cheeks, making promises of more games of chase, and of course they asked for more apples.

One little girl, with dark hair captured in two tight braids and eyes like a doe's, held Nesrin's hand as far as she was allowed, nearly to the edge of camp. Nesrin stopped and picked her up when Reyhan continued to the carriage.

"Will you come back?" the little girl, Leyla, asked, her small hands fluffing at Nesrin's hair. She was much younger than Nesrin's sisters, but reminded her of when they were smaller. It was comforting to hold her, but also a knife to the heart. Did they miss her as much as she missed them? She missed things she never would have thought she'd long for. Their incessant squabbling. Their whining demands for her time and attention. The feel of their hands in hers. The quiet moments of passing along knowledge which their mother, and Sanem, had already taught her.

"I will come back," Nesrin promised.

"Leyla," her mother called gently, "it's her bedtime too."

The girl's eyes widened and Nesrin nodded gravely in agreement. "Goodnight," Leyla said. She kissed Nesrin's cheek before wriggling down out of her arms and racing back to her mother.

Reyhan climbed into the carriage after Nesrin. They sat in silence until the carriage began back down the hill.

"You are too kind," Reyhan said, so softly Nesrin barely heard her.

It was a warning.

THEY STOPPED AT AMARA'S SHOP just as darkness descended on the city. Nesrin motioned for Reyhan to wait in the carriage. "I just wanted to tell Amara what I've done, and see if this is enough to buy a set of clothes in that green fabric." Nesrin waved the ledger at Reyhan. "I'll only be a moment."

"I cannot sit in a carriage while my mistress goes into a shop. I despair of you ever learning," she grumbled as she followed Nesrin from the carriage. Nesrin had hoped to go in alone, but could not argue with Reyhan without raising the fire mage's suspicion.

Amara was at the back of the shop when they entered, pinning fabric in place around a dress-form. Djar sat in one of the cushioned chairs, nursing a cup of tea. He saw the two of them first, and a grin split his face.

"Our Poppy has returned," he said. Nesrin returned his smile, then Amara's when her head bobbed up from behind the dress-form.

"I heard you had gone to the camp," Amara said around pins clenched to one side between her teeth. She selected a pin and wove it quickly into place, pinning a fold in the fabric.

Nesrin nodded. "I received my stipend from the Sehzade."

Amara plucked the pins from her mouth. "You spent your living stipend from the palace on the refugee camp?" Her gaze slid to Djar's, then back to Nesrin.

Nesrin struggled against the upwelling of embarrassment that threatened. "I—was it not mine to spend as I wished?"

"I would think so." Amara's edged smile made her doubt herself. "But we shall see what the palace says, hmm? What can I do for you?"

"I wished to purchase a set of clothes."

"Oh? You do not wish to put it on the Sehzade's account?" Amara came around the dress-form, revealing that she had pieces of fabric draped over one shoulder. Nesrin shrugged, glancing at Reyhan. The fire mage was preoccupied, staring at a collection of red brocade with yellow embroidery.

"It seems silly to do that, when I have been given my own money." She took the opportunity to cross the distance between them and press the ledger and writ into Amara's hands. Then she leaned close and whispered her request in the Charah's ear. Amara drew back, surprised, gaze flicking, once again, to Djar.

"As you wish," she said, and took the ledger. She went to the dresser on one wall, where baskets of bits and bobs covered most of the top, except one clear edge, where a bottle of ink and a quill sat. Amara made some notations, pausing to think, then made a few more. "It will take some time. I have a number of orders ahead of yours," she said as she waved her hand above the paper to dry the ink.

"No hurry."

"You must stay, and eat with us. Bek is cooking now if you would care to sample dishes of Menei?"

Nesrin's body lit with excitement. She had only ever sampled a few simple things from some of the traders that passed through Mizraa. Nothing so involved as a meal. When she glanced at Reyhan, the fire mage dipped her head.

Nesrin smiled brightly. "I would love that."

Twenty-Nine

Nesrin had not returned from whatever had occupied her out of the house that day when Ihsan went to bed. Probably spending his money. Her money. He grit his teeth, glaring at the plaster ceiling.

He lay, hot and uncomfortable in caftan and salvar, fighting a simmering vexation he could not explain. He threw an arm over his eyes, considering whether or not to strip down. He despised sleeping in so many clothes, but it had become necessary when she kept insisting on invading his room.

When the door to the front of the house opened below, feminine laughter filtered up to him. The muscles in his jaw relaxed, and he sat up. She was just emerging at the top of the stairs when he opened his door and stepped into the dark common room. Nesrin stopped. He could see her fine, in the dark. A gift of the Second House. Not the way a fox could see in the dark, he simply had a better sense of things even without light.

She could not make him out, he could tell by the way she tilted her head.

"It is late," he said.

"Oh," she said. "Did we wake you?"

"I was awake." His hand squeezed the edge of the door. What was he doing? "You should not be out at night."

"Djar and Bek were with us. Were you worried?" The lilt in her voice carried both apology and teasing.

"No."

She picked her way over to him, moving carefully around furniture in the dark. She stood in front of him, her hands behind her back. Too close. He could feel the warmth of her pushing against the ice of his power. "Did you want something? Or are you just ill-tempered and need someone to scold?"

What did he want? He knew. But he couldn't say that. He wanted to see her. See how she acted now that she had received money. See if all her playfulness was gone, now that she had what she wanted. If she seemed happier after spending a day away from him.

Why did looking at her settle him and disrupt him in equal measure?

When he only stared mutely at her, tangled in his thoughts, she prompted, "Are you having trouble sleeping? I could sit with you until you fall asleep."

"I do not need a nanny," Ihsan said. "I am not a weanling."

"No. But I think you could use a friend," she coaxed in a low murmur. "I won't force you, though. Goodnight." She turned.

The voice gnashing in his mind about keeping his distance lost, and he reached, catching his fingers in the back of the cloth around her waist.

"I have friends." He pulled. He was only acting, not thinking. But Nesrin came easily, spinning as she did. She stopped just short of him, tipping her head to look at him. He unhooked his fingers from the cloth and spread them over her waist. He tried not to think anything of the touch. Her eyes were wide and dark and earnest.

"Name one," she said, her expression a playful taunt. He resented the relief that replaced his earlier petulance. Did she know what she was doing? She could not possibly be innocent to how her teasing and her light touches muddled him.

"One what?" He had lost the trail of thought.

She laughed. "One friend." Her hands closed in fistfuls of his caftan and she twisted, pulling him into his own room as she walked backwards. His mouth went dry as he followed.

"The Princess Sultana." His voice was too rough. The urge to escape held him, making his steps unsteady. But it was no stronger than his curiosity, his want, to cross the boundary between play and...something else. His fingers curved, pressing through the fabric to feel the soft give of flesh beneath.

"Family does not count." She released her grip on his clothes. His hand fell from her waist. Had she sensed his twin desire to stay and flee? Felt his discomfort? Or had he done something to drive her back? The touch?

"Samira Azmeh." His voice betrayed him with its hitch.

"Neither do servants." She wheeled her hands to encourage him to continue trying. Oblivious to him. He bared his teeth.

"You are making up rules as we go along." He took a step toward her. A familiar thrum began in his low belly. With that came a heaviness in his limbs. His body was as confused as his mind.

"No, that is common sense. That you do not know they wouldn't count only serves to prove my point." She moved around him, little more than a darker shape in the room. Was that a rejection? He wished for light, as he had not, in Turns. So he could see her, see the smile he could hear, watch her eyes to track where they looked. At him? She was so unreserved, it made it difficult to read her intentions. And he did not wish to misread her, to misunderstand or push her.

"What is your point?" He thought, briefly, of naming Cemil. But could not. The silhouette of her moved around his bed and settled on the side opposite him. Sitting, she drew her knees up to her chest.

There was some little moonlight, though his window faced the wrong way to get the full power of it.

"You do not know that friends help each other, without expectation."

He stood beside the bed. The distance to where she sat was vast, and charged. If he lay down, they would not be touching. She sat as far to the edge of the bed as possible. But he knew if he lay down, it would reshape things. For him, at least. He was not certain he should.

He hesitated so long that she asked, "Do you want me to go?"

"I thought I said you could do whatever you like." He sat, with his back to her, then lay back, hands folded over his belly. The bed was large enough that if he stretched his arm toward her it would barely reach. Yet he could hear her breaths. If he held still enough, each little movement she made caused the bed and blankets to shift.

He tipped his head back and closed his eyes, jaw jumping as he clenched his teeth. He massaged the bridge of his nose as a headache began behind his eyes.

"You are very bossy," she said.

"Telling you to do whatever you like is not being bossy," he mumbled into the palm of his hand. "It is exactly the opposite."

"Yes, Sehzade," she said, a giggle suppressed in her voice.

"Are we not using names now, instead of titles?" He wanted her to say his again.

"I was using names, but you were not. Do you know mine?"

"Nesrin," he said. For a moment she was quiet, and he thought he'd somehow offended her, but then she spoke.

"Nessa," she said. "You may call me Nessa, if you'd like."

"Nessa." It was a nickname as soft as its owner, too sweet to bear.

"Ihsan," she responded, and he heard that there was more. He braced. He knew what was coming. That she had gone this long without asking was impressive.

"What are your nightmares?" Her voice was so warm, and soft, his eyes closed to hold on to the sound rather than the upwelling of panic that made his heart beat a hard, sharp rhythm on his ribs.

"Fire." He swallowed the bitter burn in his throat. It threatened to engulf him up, the black terror that gathered at the edges of his mind.

"Oh?" she said, the lilt of teasing in her voice a lifeline he clung to. "I thought they might be about hugs, soft blankets, and conversation."

The black fell away. He drew in a breath and turned his head to stare at her in disbelief. She had tipped her head toward him. The moonlight lit her smile, both gentle and mischievous. It took everything in him to lie still. Her playfulness was a weakness he had not known he had.

Whatever made her come to him, like this, as though he were not a wounded beast that would bite and claw and leave her ruined, he needed it. He wanted to play back. But his play was rough, too demanding. It was twisted up with lust. If he kissed her with all the savagery his fury demanded, she would understand. She was too tender and kind to withstand him.

"You do not have to tell me anything you do not wish to," Nessa said.

"There is little to tell, because I remember very little." He surprised himself by saying anything at all. But he could not lie there next to her, mute, and unmoving. His temples throbbed. His heart thumped in warning. "A house burned around me." He gulped as a shudder of nausea rolled through him. "I was trapped." There was much more to it, but he had so few words to explain. He could barely think as panic blanketed him, his vision tunneled. "I remember fire." He could not breathe. He did not remember the pain, exactly. Only the way he became an animal, consumed by it, by fear, the searing, tearing, melting heat.

Her fingers slid between his. "Breathe." She squeezed. "In," she ordered, "out. Deeper." Her other hand spread on his chest. He obeyed, once. Then again. It hurt, the air coming in a thin stream. "Another." She rubbed a circle on his chest, distracting him from the panic, though the touch was not gentle. Green laced the ebony swirling around his vision.

The color spread, tendrils unraveling the winnowing black. And in the shapeless, featureless terror of his memory, came voices. Shouts. Someone called his name. He could almost grasp the memory, grabbed for it with desperate mental fingers. But his power surged as it had not since he was a child.

Nesrin drew a sharp breath as his skin lit with blue-white and he jolted up, trying to pull back the magic. Ice covered his body, frosting the blanket and her clothes, then spreading from their intertwined fingers up her arm and neck. The heat of her skin melted it instantly. Her hands bracketed his face, her quick breaths white between them.

"Ihsan," she said, turning his head so his eyes met hers. "You are here. You are safe. Breathe." His magic crawled up her arms, thick ice. He seized her wrists.

"You cannot help me," he rasped. But he did not want her to let go. Her touch was the only thing keeping him from spiraling.

"I am here, Ihsan. Can you feel me?"

"You should not touch me." He wanted to spare her the cold. The ice, somehow, avoided the scar that wound her neck, melting before it encompassed it.

Her voice deepened to a tease. "I put my hands on whatever I want." Then she smiled. *That* smile. The one that held joy and sunshine and everything he thought he would never feel again. His mind emptied. His lungs filled. The black ebbed, and he coughed a laugh.

"You are the only person I have ever met who would mock me while half frozen by my magic," he said in a gravel-rough voice. His throat felt like he'd been screaming. Had he?

"You can unfreeze me whenever you wish," she said, her teeth clenching against the cold. He called it back to him, and the frost receded. He fought the shame that banded his chest, for hurting her. She had put her hands on him. She should not be surprised she got hurt. But he could not bring up his anger, his normal shield against the shame. Perhaps she was thawing more than his magic.

She rubbed her hands together and blew on her fingers. "How do you conjure ice from nothing?"

"I don't. There is water in the air. On your skin. On mine." He pressed his hands around hers. She blinked at him, but he could not meet her gaze. Her fingers were so, so cold. "Are you all right?"

"I've been colder," she said in an attempt at bravery, but her chill-slurred words gave her away.

He scoffed. "I'm insulted."

She laughed weakly. "Really, I'm all right." She pulled her fingers free but immediately hugged her arms around herself.

"Are you lying to a water mage?"

He awaited an answer for so long, he peered hard at her in the dark. "Some lies are necessary," she said.

"Why is it necessary to tell me you are fine when you are clearly half frozen?" He did not like the way her silence resonated in his magic. The way it felt wrong, ill-fitting, somehow.

"So that I can escape to my room and wrap myself in a blanket to warm up."

He did not want her to leave. He stood and tugged at the top blanket, then swung it around her shoulders. He knelt in front of her, tugging the thick blanket tightly around her, tucking it in beneath her legs and feet. He pulled it so tight that she laughed, and squirmed to free a hand so she could push him away.

He grinned. "Better?"

"Do I take this to mean you wish me to stay?" she murmured, her face half hidden behind the blanket.

"Do whatever you wish, Nessa. I care not," he lied.

"I should push you off the bed and claim it for myself." She wriggled herself onto her side, rewrapping the blanket like a cocoon. Slowly, he stretched out. Propping himself on one elbow, he looked at her a moment. She stared back. He rolled to his back.

"Can I ask you something?" Nesrin asked.

"Are you giving me a choice?"

She clicked her tongue in reprimand, which made a smile tug at his mouth. "Kuhzey is an Aval? But he cannot speak?"

"He speaks, just not with his voice." Ihsan had answered this question countless times. It lanced at his heart, but Kuhzey had accepted it, so he must as well.

"So he cannot cast?" Her thoughtful statement did not hold the same sadness most did when they reached that conclusion. But she was uniquely capable of understanding it was difficult to miss something you had never been able to do.

"No," Ihsan said, curious where she would go with it.

"You fit well together, then. An Aval with no voice, and a water mage with no water." Her voice was dreamy, so he could not be mad at her for her needling. He made a sound of agreement.

This was the first time he had shared a bed with a woman like this. Simply as company. It calmed him as much as it unsettled him. He lay with it for a few moments. When he checked on her again, she was asleep. He snorted a laugh, and closed his eyes.

Normally the dark pressed at him, mocking him with taunts of what might haunt his sleep. Normally the quiet was a noose, keeping his eyes wide and his thoughts spinning freely with nothing to interrupt him. But there was no silence now.

Her breath came in a steady rhythm. Somehow it chased it away, that threat at the edge of his awareness. She would be here, if they came again. She would not let it consume him, over...and over.

His muscles unwound.

When he woke, she was gone.

Ihsan stared at his coffee, and Naime considered him. Her wordless appraisal weighed like bricks hung from his neck. Her rooms were bathed in midmorning light, and he found it offensive to his pounding head. There were an assortment of plates laid out on the table, left by Samira and a gaggle of other servant women. Ihsan kept scanning the offerings as if they might change. He was hungry. But all he could think of was the breakfast Nessa had made him.

"Explain," Naime said.

"My nightmares are disturbing her. I'll sleep in the city and she can sleep here." He took a handful of pistachios, trying to ignore the insistent memory of standing in the kitchen with Nesrin, eating. That had felt good. It was hard to separate himself from all the moments he was collecting with her. Which was why he had to detach from her. She was winding herself around his life like a choking ivy and he struggled to keep his thoughts where they should be. Reactive. Ready. Kadir had been quiet these few days Ihsan had been gone from the palace. But he never stayed that way for long.

"I see." Naime took a sip of her coffee. Ihsan curled his lip but hid the expression, ducking his head. "She complained to you?"

He turned his face to the windows and the garden. Not complained. Demanded. He grunted noncommittally.

"You are pushing her away?" Naime suggested, her eyes wide and innocent as she took another sip. Curse her and her unerring observation skills.

"She's playing a game whose rules she does not understand. I am protecting her."

"Ah." She set her cup down. Ihsan rolled his eyes and collapsed against the couch. "Have you been able to discover anything about her ties to the Grand Vizier?"

"No." Ihsan had thought about it that morning, when he woke and she was gone. Everything about her was gone. He'd felt something he could only describe as a frantic anger. But Deniz reminded him it was by his own order.

"I am reluctant to bring you back to the palace. You still look..." She shrugged and he grimaced. Plagued. He was. He did not know what to do about the dreams. He just wanted sleep. He had slept the night through, with Nessa beside him. "But I am afraid I must."

"I am happy to do whatever you need me to, Naime. I wish you would stop trying to shield me."

She cocked an eyebrow. A knock from the hallway interrupted. "Come," Naime called.

Samira entered, with a palace clerk in tow. The young woman was new to the position, one of Naime's attempts to staff more male-dominated areas with women. Ihsan liked this one, Hatice. She was an unerring accounts keeper. It was quite possible there was nothing but numbers in her head. She was petite, almost as short as Aysel, but curvier. She put Ihsan in mind of a quail, bobbing about nervously.

"Good morning, Hatice," Naime said as the clerk bowed. She clutched a rolled paper in her hands. As she straightened she offered Naime a quick smile, then looked at Ihsan. His brows drew down, because she had the look of someone about to give a lecture.

"I requested an audience to check this ledger, Efendim."

"An audience with me?" he asked.

She blinked owlishly at him. They regarded each other for a beat then she huffed impatiently and thrust the paper toward him. Levering himself off the couch, he plucked the ledger from her fingers. He turned it over and spun it so it was right side up, uncomprehending for a moment. Then it struck him. This was the stipend he'd given Nesrin the day before.

"She spent it *all*?" he blurted. Hatice made a noise of agreement. "In one day," he breathed in disbelief. It was an absurd list. Seeds. Far more than would ever fit in his garden. A literal cartload of apples. Where had she even put a cartload of apples? He dragged his thumb and forefingers together over his eyes, blinked, then looked again. "Trees?" he mumbled, dropping backward onto the couch. And clothing from Amara. Maybe she wasn't sweet and simple at all. Maybe she was Unbalanced. That would be his luck. And would explain her reckless insistence to try to stop his nightmares.

He held the paper toward Hatice. "Verify it." If it had been affection growing in him for her, it was something else now. Good that she was going to be easier to avoid now that she was gone from his home. He would need time to deal with his surge of...disappointment.

"Yes, Sehzade." She bowed again then retreated. Naime watched Ihsan shrewdly as Samira escorted Hatice from the room and closed the door. Samira remained behind, returning to sit with them. She refilled each of their cups with coffee, then poured her own. Ihsan could see her trying to maintain a straight face.

"Go ahead."

Samira shook her head, covering her mouth with her hand, her gaze askance. Naime gave a small, soft laugh. A rare sound lately.

"It could be worse." Samira stirred a dash of sugar into her dainty cup.

"Yes? How? *How* could it be worse?" He snatched a spear of carrot and snapped a bite off before he pointed it at her. "You do realize those could be completely false? To cover up something else. Whatever she truly bought." It was hard to believe that of her. A woman who buried apple cores for balance and came to comfort him no matter how rude he was. He had believed the best of people before, and been disastrously wrong.

"We will know soon if something is amiss," Naime suggested. "Try not to let it run rampant in your thoughts, San."

He disregarded them both with a wave and slumped into the seat.

Another knock sounded, and Samira set her cup down before rising to answer. It was Ruslan, the Sultan's steward. The look on his face had both Naime and Ihsan on their feet instantly.

"Forgive me, Princess Sultana. I cannot find the Sultan."

Thirty

Nesrin set a small, round side table in the sunlight of her window. Then she placed the vine she had rescued from Ihsan's office in the light. With fresh water and a new pot it was well recovered from its abuse of the previous day, healthier even, for the change in location. But caring for it was a quick task, leaving Nesrin little else to occupy her.

Reyhan had forbidden her from helping. She was all business, overseeing the loading of her things into the carriage to carry them back to the palace. Nesrin had tried to be of assistance, but between Reyhan tutting at her with every attempt and Nesrin being distracted and clumsy, it was pointless.

Her thoughts were ricocheting too quickly between nervous elation at the events of the night, and burrowing shame and fear.

Are you lying to a water mage?

She returned downstairs and planted herself on the too-stiff, blue velvet couch. The two coachmen carried a trunk of her things out to the carriage.

"Are you ready?" Reyhan appeared before her. Nesrin stood to follow her outside. They were only a few moments into the ride when

Reyhan leaned forward, eyes sharp. They sat across from each other, making it impossible for Nesrin to hide her face from her.

"You were not in your room this morning."

She did her best to meet Reyhan's look with a challenging stare, but fell apart immediately. She desperately wished for Sanem to unburden her heart to. Her mother. Even Metin. Metin would know better than any of them what she should do. What she was doing. He had some inkling of the loss Ihsan had suffered. But all she had was Reyhan, who was neither friend nor enemy, right now.

"The company seems to keep his nightmares at bay."

Nesrin tried to keep her voice neutral. But Reyhan sat straight again, saying, "The potential of this situation is lost on you." The words were harsh; her tone, dull.

"What? You told me it was better to keep my distance. Safer."

"But you cannot, can you?" Reyhan's expression wavered from exasperation to pity. "And it seems, he cannot either."

That warmed Nesrin's cheeks. She did not have a great deal of experience with such things. Certainly some. There was not a young person in Mizraa who had not, at the very least, snuck behind a building during a season's Turn festival and engaged in necking. Nesrin had done more, but had found it…unremarkable. Sweaty and messy and lacking in any sort of emotion.

At least not the depth of emotion she had witnessed between Sanem and Anil. Or her parents. The fondness. The love. The laughter and play. Perhaps it was magic, more than love, that created that. Nesrin did not know, and had accepted she might not ever.

Thinking that a prince might want more from her than the simplest of physical intimacies was…difficult. Especially this prince, who was so wounded, and conflicted, and whom she was meant to spy on. It felt improper to wish for anything at all from him.

"I want to help him, is that wrong?" It was the touching. The touching that muddled her, made her thoughts grind to a halt. Made her body wake whenever she stood near. His hands were bigger than hers, had swallowed her frozen fingers. Gently. His voice, sometimes water-smooth and melodic, sometimes rough and irresistible, made her want to kiss him, to make it part of her.

"It is not wrong, it is *kind*." The last word sounded like an insult. Wheel, what a backwards place, where kindness was a failing.

"I cannot help what I am."

"Then use it," Reyhan told her, sternly. "Tame a prince so he protects you, or spy on him and sell his secrets to the Grand Vizier for your freedom. Use them, before they use you."

"Is that what a princess would do?" Nesrin tested. Reyhan looked away.

"That is what someone smart would do. Manipulate instead of be manipulated."

"What has happened to make you so bitter?" Nesrin forced temperance into her voice, despite her rising temper. Reyhan cast her a dead smile.

"The same that will happen to you, if you do not listen to me."

Nesrin trudged after Reyhan as she strode through the palace halls. This was good—she reminded herself. She needed to clear her head of the little fantasy she had existed in during her stay at Ihsan's home. That she and Reyhan might be friends. That she could find a place in Ihsan's life and heart.

She was alone. The palace would remind her. Help her decide if she should listen to Reyhan. If she *could*.

She nearly collided with the back of the fire mage when she stopped abruptly with an audible inhale. Nesrin lifted her head to peer around Reyhan. Cemil stood in the hallway before them, blocking their way. A smile curved his lips. Nesrin's stomach dropped at the look in his eyes. She had forgotten. How could she have forgotten the Grand Vizier's order to help his son?

"I heard a rumor," he said, "that you were returning today. And that is excellent timing. Because I am here today too." Bright teeth flashed.

"She is expected in the Sehzade's rooms," Reyhan said, benignly. Cemil's grin became a threat.

"I will deliver her there when I am finished with her." He moved forward, and Reyhan stepped sideways to block Nesrin more completely. Cemil stopped in front of Reyhan, and there was nothing of the joking, easy manner Nesrin had associated with him after her first encounter. Danger emanated from every bit of him. "Do not test me," he growled, fire in his eyes and his voice. Reyhan made a sound, her hands spasming open.

Nesrin touched Reyhan's back and stepped around her, slipping in between the two fire mages. Reyhan grabbed for her sleeve, but Nesrin touched her fingers. "It's all right." It did not feel all right. She was afraid. Afraid of the intensity in Cemil's expression, the fear that made Reyhan stiff and wide-eyed.

"I do not know the way," Nesrin told him. He dragged his gaze away from Reyhan to focus on her. Their eyes locked for an instant. A razor of pain raced along Nesrin's whip scar and she gasped, her knees buckling. Cemil caught her arm, but dropped his gaze from hers, and the heat disappeared from the space between them.

"Are you in pain?" Reyhan cupped Nesrin's elbow, then accused Cemil, "What did you do to her?"

"Nothing."

"I should go with you," Reyhan said.

"No." Cemil turned, hauling Nesrin after him. She glanced back at Reyhan, but had to turn her attention quickly to her steps or lose her footing.

"You do not have to tow me," she said.

"How have you managed to turn Reyhan into a snippy little guard dog, I wonder?" Cemil said as he released his grip. "She has not been so reckless in some time."

"Reyhan is the least reckless person I have met here," Nesrin said. Cemil slowed his pace, which had been fast enough that Nesrin had to trot to keep up.

"A lesson hard learned, for her," he said under his breath. He paused at the intersection of the next hall to look both ways before turning left.

Nesrin's next question was cut off when he grabbed her by the wrist and pulled her through an archway and onto a garden path. "Are we sneaking?"

"Not yet."

Nesrin groaned. "Do you know that half the problems of this place would be solved if people spoke in complete thoughts rather than half-truths and riddles?"

Cemil stopped, turning to look at her with incredulity. "You exist in an absurd little world, don't you, country mouse?"

He had all the gifts of the Fifth House in excess. Sharp angles to his jaw and cheekbones, handsome the way fire was beautiful, in a dangerous kind of way. But most noticeable were that his eyes were, in fact, gold. She had thought it a trick of his magic, shining through brown irises. Perhaps amber was a better description than gold. They were striking.

He also, true to his House, had a love for jewelry. This close, she could see three piercings in each ear, all of them with matching gold studs set with red stones. Rubies, maybe. A necklace of gold and garnet hung against his ocher caftan, and bracelets that looked remarkably similar to the one Reyhan wore circled both wrists. Fire mages and their baubles.

"When I am married you will have to address me as Princess instead of mouse," Nesrin said. He looked surprised, then grinned boyishly, an expression she thought suited him much more than the more sinister ones she had seen.

"Princess Mouse," Cemil said. "I bet he likes you."

"Not that I can tell, no," Nesrin bit back. That was not a total truth. He did seem to be warming to her. But that felt like a vulnerability she did not want to give this man.

Cemil's gaze whipped over her face, then he looked away. "Good girl," he murmured, then started off again. Nesrin followed of her own accord. Neither spoke again. Cemil stopped where the hallway let out into a large, circular kind of gathering space. Across from them a set of doors massive enough to be a palace gate loomed. Carved intricately of some dark, ominous-looking wood, they drew Nesrin's attention away from even the stunning frescoes above them on the domed ceiling.

"Ready?" he asked. Nesrin threw him a look.

"I cannot answer that, because I do not know what we are doing."

"I am going to look for something, and you are going to make certain no one sees me doing so."

"Perfectly clear, thank you," she mumbled as he snared her wrist and pulled her across the space. "How do you know no one is in there?"

"Banu," Cemil said. He released her and pushed the door open, taking a cautious peek inside before entering. Nesrin followed, but stopped just inside the door, her breath stuttering as she took in the room before her. Cemil closed the door quietly behind her. A library of such a vast size Nesrin thought she had fallen into a dream. She had not known this many books existed in the entire world.

Cemil strode in confidently, and she followed a few steps before spinning. There were two floors, though the second was only a walkway, reached by stairs to either side of the circular room. A railing enclosed the walkway above. Ladders were pushed against the shelves on both the first and second level. There were several standing-height tables, and two set low so one sat on cushions on the floor instead of on chairs. Benches were built against the walls in between shelves, with cushions and reading stands.

"You really are a country mouse," Cemil taunted as she gawked. "Watch the door, and if anyone comes in, distract them. Worst case, tell them you didn't know the library was off-limits. Yes?"

Nesrin nodded. Cemil moved quickly, as if he knew exactly where he wished to look.

A trio of books sat in a neat stack on one of the tables, and he pulled one from the bottom. Its cover was leather dyed blue. Opening it, he flipped quickly to the back. His face twisted.

"Naime," he whispered, followed by a curse, "where is it?" He slammed the book closed and pressed his fists to the table, hanging his head. After a moment he rallied from whatever disappointment had occurred, then started another search. He checked every book that was already out, reading the spines or fronts for titles, she guessed, and replacing each exactly as he found it.

"I could help look," she suggested, when he had finished with all the books that she could see on tables and stands.

"Unlikely," he said, distracted as he combed a shelf. "Just do as I asked." He exclaimed to himself, tugging a book off the shelf and laying it open in his hands.

At that moment, one of the great double doors moved as if someone on the other side had tried to open them and failed. Nesrin swallowed the desire to flee, or hide. Cemil spun and sprinted for the windows on the far side of the room. They were not windows at all, but doors to a balcony. He slipped outside just as the doors to the hall opened, jamming the book into the back of the fabric at his waist.

Nesrin wheeled around to face the doors, clasping her hands together and trying desperately to look innocent and lost.

An older man entered. He was dressed in simple white caftan and salvar, without entari, and no belt. His hair was mostly grey, cut short, with enough black to tell what it had once been. He was tall, and thin, and walked haltingly. His brows were knit together, his mouth turned down, his hands linked behind his back as though he were not certain how he had arrived where he meant to. Nesrin recognized the look immediately. Her mother's father, for the Turn before he passed, had born the same confused, distant expression.

"Hello," she said, softly enough not to startle him.

"Oh. Have you seen my wife?" The man squinted at her. A fit of coughing unbalanced him, and she feared he might topple. Nesrin crossed to him.

"No. I am new here. Who is your wife?" She kept her voice easy, tone curious. She wanted to steady him, but did not want to alarm him.

"Usually she is here. But I…" He looked at her, eyes of a deep reddish brown taking her in from head to toe. "Who are you?"

"I am Nesrin." She could not tell by his clothes how to address him. They looked like what he might sleep in. He could be anything from an elderly servant to a retired Vizier. "Does your wife enjoy the library?"

"Yes…yes." He wheezed, glancing around, up at the ceiling as though she might be up there. He did not look well, his breathing seemed too much effort, his skin grey-cast. When he unclasped his hands they tremored, and he swayed a bit on his feet. If he fell, she was not certain she could help him back up. Would Cemil bother to assist?

"Would you care to sit?" If she could keep him comfortable, it would also help prevent him becoming upset about his wife. Her grandfather had been unable to handle too many upsets, toward the end, without disintegrating into anger. "You could tell me about her favorite books while we wait for her."

Someone would come looking for him, soon, surely. Perhaps she should lead him out of the library, so she and Cemil were not revealed when someone did come for him.

"Do you like books? Are you a student of the University?" he asked as she took a step toward the doors, hoping he would follow.

"I am not a student, but I do like books. I have not read very many. Have you?"

"A few." He smiled and offered the crook of his elbow. Nesrin gripped it in both her hands, relieved to be able to steady him. "What subjects are you interested in?"

"Plants, and healing," Nesrin said, shuffling beside him as he wandered toward a table despite her urging toward the doors. "And stories. I have a book of stories at home." The book she'd read so many times to her sisters that it was falling to pieces.

"Yes? I read stories to my daughter..." His smile disappeared and he stopped and looked around. Nesrin took his hand in hers to ground him. He stared at her hands. "She likes books too."

Could he have been a librarian? If he had spent time in the library before his decline he might remember something helpful to whatever Cemil sought. Her grandfather could remember details of his childhood, but not his grandchildren. But...a knot of guilt writhed in her belly, disgust at herself.

"Do you know all the books in the library?"

"Most"—he gazed around—"most."

Nesrin swallowed. She took her hands from his so he could not feel how clammy they were. She despised this. Lying to someone already suffering. To what end? To protect herself. To protect Cemil, and whatever plot he and his father had.

His gaze suddenly fixed on something behind her, his mouth working. Nesrin peered over her shoulder. Cemil stood there. For just a moment, too brief to be sure, she thought his face was scrunched in misery.

"Who are you?" the man demanded. Cemil came forward, his steps lacking the surety they had before. "Oh," the old man said, "Osman. Where have you been?"

Nesrin's brows drew down as she looked at Cemil. He shook his head at her.

"It is me," Cemil said, his voice hoarse, "Sultanim. Cemil."

Sultanim. Nesrin choked. Wheel and spokes. He was the Sultan.

"No, no, Cemil is...small. Just a boy. We play chess sometimes. I teach him. He's bright though, so bright. A little fire." The Sultan's brow furrowed, and Nesrin saw the fog take his eyes as he tumbled through broken memories and confusion at what was before him. Cemil's jaw clenched, his eyes taking on a hammered gold color as his magic rose.

"Stop," she hissed at Cemil, putting herself between them. She touched the Sultan's shoulder. "Efendim. Tell me your daughter's favorite books." She steered him gently to a bench but he resisted sitting. Still he glanced between her and Cemil. Then suddenly he gripped her arm.

"Are you a void?" He was looking at her lack of a tiraz to mark her House and power.

She grasped at the distraction by nodding. He smiled warmly, and Nesrin could not help but return it. He would have been a handsome man in his youth, though whatever ravaged his mind had clearly stolen his health as well, making him appear older than he likely was.

"Seeds of potential. That is what my wife called you." He glanced behind him for the bench, but was unsteady trying to sit. Cemil caught his arms and helped lower him down. The Sultan nodded his thanks. "That's her, there." He pointed. "They did not do her justice."

Nesrin turned. In an alcove between shelves, a collection of portraits hung in tidy lines. Nesrin recognized the Princess Sultana's immediately, and to either side of it had to be her mother, the Queen Sultana, and then, of course, her father. And others. A grandmother perhaps, and the Sultan before this one. Ihsan's was there as well, turned in the depiction so his scars were not displayed. Another of a man who was clearly Ihsan's father. The Sultan's brother, and a woman who was likely his mother.

She stared. Generations of royalty displayed before her. And she could not imagine her portrait among them. A princess. She barely suppressed a scoff. A portrait of a tree would be more regal than her.

The doors opened again as Nesrin was turning back to the Sultan. The Sultana entered, and Nesrin's heart scuttled into her throat. The woman's expression somehow went from surprise, to relief, to cold ire in the space of a breath. Nesrin tried to find coherence to explain, but she was upon them in a matter of a few steps.

"Remove your hands," she said to Cemil in a voice so chilling it put Ihsan's magic to shame.

Cemil lifted his hands from the Sultan's shoulders, holding his hands up and open as he took a step back, a mocking smile on his mouth.

The Sultana motioned behind her and two guards hurried to her side. "Are you looking for the Queen Sultana again?" she said to her father. He nodded, but he was barely paying attention. Fading, beginning to lean to one side. "Sultanim, please go with these men." She offered her hands to him, and he took them, peering up at her without recognition. It pricked at Nesrin's heart. What would she do if her own father looked at her as a stranger?

The Sultan complied, surprisingly placid, for all the chaos, as she helped him to his feet. "Have Ceylik see to him," the Sultana ordered the guards as they politely steered her father toward the door.

Nesrin was as cold as when Ihsan's ice had overtaken her when the Sultana turned her focus back to Cemil and her. The Sultana inhaled deeply, and when she exhaled, the emotion disappeared from her face. That couldn't be good.

"Explain to me why you are in the library, why you dared to touch the Sultan." All her wrath was directed at Cemil. He lowered his hands, crossing them at his back. To hide the book.

"She asked for an escort because she could not find her way. Her maid was seeing to having her things delivered back to the palace. Such a pity our dear prince has kicked her out already." Cemil smirked. "I assumed she would not have asked if she was not allowed to go."

Nesrin hunched, her throat closing. Was that what Ihsan was doing? Getting rid of her?

"Out," the Sultana said, pale light ringing her irises.

"As you wish." Cemil held his mocking smile in place. "Follow me, Mistress," he said to Nesrin. He caught her by the arm, maneuvering her behind him as he passed the Sultana. Nesrin bowed in passing to the other woman, whose shrewd gaze fixed on her in a way that made her stomach plummet. Now she had caught her attention in the worst of ways. Could whatever was in that book be worth that?

For the Grand Vizier, perhaps. Nesrin doubted the same was true for her. At least it had been the Sultana, and not Ihsan. She did not know if the burgeoning connection between them would survive him witnessing her sneaking around with a man he hated.

Outside the library, Cemil nodded to the guards, who returned the gesture. When they were in the hall they had come from, out of sight of everyone, Cemil paused and reached behind him to adjust the book more securely in the cloth.

"You did well," he said, distractedly. Nesrin faced him, observing him carefully as he adjusted his clothes. When he noticed, he pulled a face. "What?"

"Who did he think you were? Who is Osman?" Osman was a very common name. It did not make any sense, but inside her, something tugged. Something was unsettled. It spun out away from her like a web, and the sense of being inextricably tangled made it hard to breathe.

He stepped closer, nearly touching, his face above hers so she had to tip her head to meet his eyes. "Country mice should not sniff around questions that will bring them to the attention of things that might eat them." Fire flickered in the gold of his irises, and that something in her, that sense of…wrongness …zinged like a nerve struck.

And as she opened her mouth to reply, Ihsan came striding around the corner with Kuhzey at his heels.

His mien transformed from worry to suspicion in an instant. "Hello, San," Cemil said, smiling like a cat at milk. Ihsan's attention hit Nesrin, briefly revealed distrust, and then the mask of ice hid the emotions as he walked past them without a word.

Thirty-One

Nesrin tried to find Ihsan, to talk to him, but he stayed away, in the city. Days passed in which she was left alone, except for Reyhan. She might have returned to the library to find something to read, if her first venture there had not put her under suspicion.

The isolation left her nothing to do but chase her thoughts in circles. Her guilt wrapping around her, a bramble of thorns and whispered crimes. Lying to him. Whatever the Grand Vizier thought of Ihsan, Nesrin could not bring herself to believe it. Yes, she tended to assume the best of people until they proved otherwise. Imagining Ihsan plotting wars and conquests at the expense of starving people was too much to believe. But Sanem had always chided her on her naivety about people and their motives.

Eating dinner, alone, for the third day in a row brought her to tears. The rooms were silent and too still. Reyhan took her dinners with the other servants, and when darkness descended, Nesrin's thoughts became even more burdensome. Even a walk in the garden did not silence the voice telling her all the things that were going wrong.

Neither did sleep offer her a respite. Her dream…or nightmare… had been growing stranger. More real. More insistent. Nesrin did not understand it.

Always it began the same. In a place where nothing existed. It was not that it was dark, just emptiness. Voices whispered, hundreds, if not thousands—words in languages she did not understand. They tumbled under and over each other, in chorus and dissonance, so that every now and then a word would echo alone that she did understand.

Wake.

Every time the word came, her body ached. At the edges of her vision, green glowed. But she could not find its source. She could not move to obey the command. She wanted to. Was afraid to. Each time she tried, the scar that wound her body blazed with ice and fire, as though she were ripping apart.

But tonight was different. There was something with her in the darkness. Something she could not see or feel. A presence nonetheless. Nesrin knew, without looking, without seeing, something was wrong. She craned her neck, straining against whatever cocoon held her curled around herself. She managed just enough, a fraction, the tiniest turn of her head. All she saw was a shift on the peripheral of her vision. Something trapped.

The awareness of it was a connection, and for a moment, enough to send her heart racing. Nesrin felt panic. Not her own, but someone else's. Panic—and wrath. Something reached for her, a tendril of ending that terrified her.

IHSAN CURSED HIS RACING THOUGHTS. Cursed the anger that turned the edges of his mind to ice that threatened, promised, to consume him when he slept. It had been the same every night since the one he'd spent with her next to him, and he could not bear another. He got up and dressed, trying not to dwell on the decision he was making. He told himself he was not deciding, he was simply moving instead of lying, pointlessly, in his bed.

There was no moon when he left the house. He considered walking, but it would be morning before he made it to the palace. All he wanted was sleep. So he took the carriage parked up the street, feeling only moderately guilty for waking the sleeping driver.

His palace rooms were so silent he wondered if she was even there. Her bedroom door was open a crack, so he pushed it wider. She was not on the bed, and a surge of suspicion held him in place, until a whimper of sound drew his gaze to the floor and a bundle of blanket between the bed and the doors.

"What…" He stepped toward it, crouched then released a huff of disbelief. A not insignificant relief settled away his temper. "Nesrin." He pulled a handful of the blanket away from her face. She twitched and gave another whimper. "Nessa."

She jerked awake with a scream, staring at him as if he were standing over her with a dagger. Ihsan fell backwards onto his haunches.

"Spokes, woman," he breathed as his heart thumped hard from the surprise of it. She threw herself at him, wrapping her arms around his body, her chest heaving. His instinct was to lean away, to try to escape, but instead he relaxed into the way it felt to be wanted, for comfort.

"I did not mean to frighten you," he said into her braided hair. She smelled like fresh air. She'd probably been outside half the night. He wrapped his arms around her as she knelt between his bent knees.

"It was a nightmare," she said, her voice muffled in his shoulder.

"I am wearing off on you. Why are you on the floor?" He resisted the urge to nuzzle his face into the curve of her neck. This felt good. Holding and being held. Too good, considering how many questions he had, and how much effort it was taking to maintain some level of anger.

“I must have moved in my sleep. Why are you here?” She lifted her head so she could look at his face.

“To sleep,” he said. It shouldn’t make him so happy, to sit with her like this. He was angry at her. At the way she’d been looking at Cemil. The way they had been standing so close. In a place they should not have been. Together. All the questions.

“You came all the way from the city to sleep?” She was petting his shoulder. He almost laughed. Instead he stood, catching her by the elbows and pulling her to her feet. He drew her in close and lifted her against him. Nesrin’s exhale puffed out. Her hands went to his neck.

“To sleep,” he told himself, out loud, as he dropped her on the bed. Too aware of her body. The way it was filling back out from having food, the soft press of her breasts and hollow of her waist. As he put a knee on the bed it occurred to him this was not his room, but hers, and he should at least ask permission. “If that’s all right.”

She scooted back, kneeling in the middle of the bed, to give him room. “Yes,” she said, quietly. He pressed one fist into the mattress as he leaned forward and put his face level with hers.

“You spent all the money I gave you.”

There was just enough light to see her gaze drop, her teeth pinch her lower lip. No. He told himself. He did not trust her. No. He could not confuse himself further by acting on desire. But he did not want to question her. He wanted to kiss her. Touch her. Find out if she was as guileless in lovemaking as she was in everything else.

He did not think he could bear it if she was.

“I bought apples,” she admitted in a whisper. “For the children in the camp.”

“Of course you did.” That is what Hatice had said after her sleuthing, but he wanted to hear Nesrin say it. “Seeds? And trees?”

“They are hungry.” Folding her hands, she set them on her thighs. She picked at her nails to avoid looking at him.

They were. But many people in the city were. He did not have it in him tonight to explain to her the gravity of her kindness in this. *Why* her mercy was going to cause him more headaches and aggravations. Why it was dangerous.

"You are angry about the money?" She peeked up at him. Void. She was going to kill him like that. His questions dropped away and he lost the battle with his body. He advanced on her, and she fell back with a soft exhale.

"Yes," he burred, trapping her on her back, on all fours above her like an animal. The thought sobered him and he moved off of her, lying on his belly instead, and turning his head away from her. Yet another terrible idea. At least if he had stayed alone in the city he could have dealt with this…longing. Here it would be compounded by her being within arm's reach all night.

"Ihsan…" She leaned over him to scrutinize his face. It could not be possible that she had no idea what she did to him.

"Go to sleep," he groused.

"Fine." She flicked his ear. He jerked his head up to glare at her, but she lay down with her back to him. Rolling to his side, he wrapped his hand around her messy braid. He tugged it in retaliation, and she gave a bubbly, heartwarming giggle.

SHE DID NOT REMEMBER SNUGGLING into Ihsan in the middle of the night. But she must have, because that was how she woke, facing him, her arms tucked in between their bodies, her head beneath his chin tipped against his chest. Their legs were a tangle. It was not an unusual position for her to wake up in, but she had only ever done so with her sisters. This was much different.

She was afraid to breathe or move. One of his arms draped over her, his left leg snug between her thighs. *All the way up.* Her breath caught. Carefully, she tipped her head back just enough to look at his face.

His eyes were open, and as she lifted her gaze, his lowered to hers. She stared, hopeful, and confused. Did he…want her like this? He wasn't moving away from her. Should she move? What were the unspoken rules a noblewoman would know about that she did not?

"Hello," she whispered. He did not answer. His eyes slitted. "Are you still cross with me?"

"Mmm," he rumbled a gravelly sound that started a heat in her belly. She crept the fingers of her right hand up to hook in the collar of his shirt. His throat moved against her knuckles.

"BECAUSE YOU SAW ME WITH Cemil?" Her thumb drew miniscule circles on his chest, over the caftan. It was all he could feel, every place she touched. He made another noise of affirmation, not trusting himself with words.

"Why do you hate them so much?"

The question was as effective as iced water, clearing his mind and cooling his body. Her thumb stopped, her expression strained at his reaction. He flattened his hand on her back when she moved as if she would give him space. He did not want space. He wanted to hold her tighter, like a buoy preventing him from drowning.

"Behram Kadir murdered my father. Poisoned him." The words came, but he did not remember thinking them, or forming them. That black panic was swirling. He was too close to the fire. It was going to devour him all over again. "And when I went to his estate, to look for evidence to prove it, he tried to do the same to me." He could not breathe.

"Ihsan."

He could not answer. Her hand slid from his caftan to his neck, her thumb stroking over his jaw. She slid her fingers up the back of his neck and into his hair, and he shuddered, some of the panic bleeding back. "It will be all right."

"It has not been all right. Not for Turns. Not for nearly two Cycles."

"Wounds heal when they heal. You cannot force it faster, or pretend it is not there."

"Some never heal," he argued, closing his eyes. His lungs squeezing for a breath. "They fester."

Nesrin issued a thoughtful hum, then she wrapped her arm around him and pulled herself closer, her body molding to his, tucking her head and face into the slope of his neck.

"They kill you, or they do not," she said, her breath warm on his skin. She squeezed him tight. "And you are not dead. You are not broken. Scars are not defects, they are proof of the strength it took to endure the wounding. Whether they are on your body, or in your mind. You were burned, and you survived."

"I was burned," he repeated, trying to let the words settle without being seized by breathless panic. Her embrace helped, held his mind in the physical instead of the memory. It was like wrestling a two-headed serpent. One head intent on burying the threat of the memory by overrunning it with something visceral and present, kissing her. Feeling her. The other, the memory, weaving and trying to strike, to poison him with black fear.

"Why did you come last night? After you had sent me away?" she said, casting every one of his thoughts in disarray.

"To sleep," he said. That was never going to work again. Not after all this. The more time he spent with her, the more he wanted, the more he thought of her in her absence. The more he craved all the things she made him feel. Safe, and light.

Her eyes met his. The wan morning light that fought its way through her closed curtains did its trick with them again, catching some fraction of lustrous green in the hazel. Some unnameable thread of emotion cracked him open like pick and hammer.

"Because you dream of fire," she whispered, "because your mind is trying to heal."

He had never heard anyone say it like that. Few dared talk about it, or fire at all, in his presence. As though he would transform into smoke and drift away. And so he was not allowed, by that same reasoning, to speak of it. To purge himself of it.

The pitying looks came and shut him off. They could not bear to hear his pain. And so it was his, only. His, twisted into nightmares, paralyzing fear at even the most benign heat. Only Dilay had ever listened. But no one, if they did say it, ever said it so simply. Just a fact. An open invitation. *Tell me. I am strong enough.*

"It must have been a powerful fire," she offered, that same open expression on her face.

"An entire house burned around me." He could say that and not feel anything. Though it stirred, below the ice, in the dark. "The fire was so big they could see it from the palace, all the way in the Fire District." The ice around his emotions cracked, and his voice hitched. "Deniz says I saved her. That she was trapped in the kitchen and I broke down a door to free her, but that wall collapsed over me. I do not remember any of that." He remembered fear, and pain.

Horror flashed in her eyes, her expression going taut, then smoothing, her smile tighter. He braced for the words. *I'm so sorry. How terrible. That is awful.* But they did not come.

"You were trapped," she said. "That much fire would have evaporated all the water."

"Obviously." He grimaced at his tone, the closest he could come to an apology. Nesrin cupped his face again, her thumb tapping the corner of his mouth.

She gave him a quick smile of forgiveness, then said, "But you got out?"

"Someone got me out. I do not know who." He could recall, vaguely. Something about having her there rooted the memory enough to take hold of. A shape, a voice. Hands. A command, *don't die*. Agony. *San, please.* Then nothing but cold.

"Someone got you out, but you lived because of your magic," she said. He started to protest but she continued, "It transformed. It saved you." Her words were reverent.

But that wasn't right. It was not benevolent; it had failed him. It was warped. He was. His scars pinched and ached, itching like they were on fire again. The pain shot into his flesh, his bones. He scratched at his clothes, where the damaged skin spread down his chest.

"They hurt you still?" She gave him the escape with gentleness, unprovoked by his anger, and he took it, grateful.

"Sometimes."

"There are salves that might help."

"No," he rasped, that cracking sound of jagged ice crunching his voice. He wanted to tell her. It wasn't her. He hated, and longed, for his scars to be touched. He could not separate the want from the fear of shame. Of judgment. It was too exhausting to cope with. Better if he just avoided it all… but he wanted her. He wanted to believe her words and her kindness.

"Is that why your power is ice?" The question hit him like an arrow, stopping his breath. Perhaps they did not talk about such things in the valley. How a prince was destroyed.

He ground his teeth, wanting to pull her closer and push her away. He curled his fingers into the thin material of her chemise, at the small of her back, and hooked his other arm beneath his head. He tried. "That is what we assume. There are no records of ice mages specifically. But there are vague records of mages whose magic was changed or suppressed by traumatic events. No names. Most records are so old, if there were details they are lost."

Her hand closed into a fist at his back. Her lashes fluttered as though she would shut her eyes. "If all of this is true, why was the Grand Vizier not jailed? Or executed?" Her voice was weak, as though she were speaking around a knot of emotion.

"Because the only evidence was the word of a boy who could barely speak in complete sentences. Who would fall to pieces at the slightest test of his story, a story he could not fully remember, who could not control his magic or himself. Whose power was warped and twisted. And too many voices against him." He could not read her face, and did not want to. He wanted to escape. "And now? Too many Turns have passed. He has too many allies for anyone to take such a claim seriously. I never found evidence of the poison he used. It burned with the estate."

This was too much. That she could break him open and see all his fractures. And he cared—he *cared* what she thought. Curse her. It hurt. Burned in his throat.

How could he care for someone when he was barely whole? Or worse, if she cared for him, needed him. She'd become someone else he could lose, or fail.

Nesrin's breath shuddered. "I believe you." Her eyes glistened, pink tinging her cheeks, her lips parted. "Does that matter?"

He exhaled, long and deep, the tension of waiting for her to reject him or the story lifting away. He had not realized how much he needed her to say it.

"It matters," Ihsan said. Her gaze flitted over him, and her hand relaxed against his back. He felt each of her fingertips. Then she was all he could feel. She was malleable. Soft, her thighs on his, her fingers pressing barely to his spine. She watched him, tranquil.

His fingers curled, obeying his desire to pull her tighter, absorb the gift of her peace.

His. She was his, wasn't she? *His* betrothed. His.

HER HEART WAS BREAKING. EACH sentence he uttered. Each revelation hammer to chisel, shattering her. Her father…she…had helped to save the life of a man who would go on to commit atrocities. It had been like a dream to wake up with Ihsan there. The best sleep she'd had since arriving in Narfour. Now it had deformed into a nightmare as terrifying and paralyzing as those that plagued her sleep.

A tear slid loose, puddling between her nose and eye. She lifted her hand to brush it away, but he got there first, his fingers feather-soft on her skin.

"Are you sad for me?" he asked.

"Yes. And furious."

"For me?" He stroked his fingers over her cheekbone and into her hair, resting his palm along her jaw. She gave the barest nod. She wanted to tell him. Had to tell him. But the words tangled in her throat.

"Ihsan," she tried.

"San," he said, "my friends call me San." The way he was looking at her, intense and restrained, made her pulse jump. She could hardly bear it.

"You have no friends, remember?" she teased, gently. Her finger pressed into the muscles of his back. She willed them to relax. It did not matter if he wanted to kiss her. Or if she wanted to be kissed. This…them…was impossible.

"I used to," he said, but she could tell he was hardly listening, his gaze searching her face. Her heart squeezed, then broke at the words, and she took his head in her hands and touched her forehead to his. They stayed like that.

Until he moved, tilting his head, his nose trailing up hers, then his lips, the revelation of their softness making her own part. He pressed them to her brow, then dipped his chin again, to press another soft suggestion on the bridge of her nose. Then he held still, and she knew, this was for her. He was asking permission.

"Do I have you?" he said, low and rough. He pressed the smallest, barest of kisses to the corner of her mouth.

There were no words. No possible way to defend her lies. To justify anything of what she was. To say yes was to lie to him again, to say no was to lie to herself.

So she kissed him. It was the only way she could think of to be gentle, to tell him goodbye. She could not do this, lie to him anymore.

Ihsan wriggled his right hand between them and beneath the curve of her waist, mirroring it with his left, and pressed her into him. For a moment she lost herself, knew nothing but the desperate softness of his kiss. He stroked her waist, her arm, her back, everything he could reach with them lying on their sides as they were. She dug her fingers into his hair, gripping lightly as she tried to match his pace. No one had ever kissed her like this. Like he knew every move she would make, matched every breath and push and pull.

She was breathless and senseless when he pulled back. The heat in her belly curled into a spiral of want that made her legs squeeze around his. His pupils expanded, and in them and around them, a flicker of light sparkled then disappeared.

"Again," he insisted, his hand flattened on her back, angling her pelvis against his so his thoughts on the matter were *very* clear. His fingers curled to grip as he stroked his hand over her thigh to hook beneath her leg and hitch it up high on his hip.

She could not. Even one more kiss would be a wound that would never heal, for either of them.

"I am meeting Mutar Charah," she murmured, unconvincingly.

"She can wait." Blue ice crept through his irises. The cold of his power skimmed her skin, making her shiver.

"It's important." Nesrin searched his face. Would she ever get to look at him again, like this? Close? No, he would never trust her now. And after he revealed so much to her.

With her arms, she cradled his head, pressing her forehead to his. "I cannot stay. Not today."

"Are you running now? Because I've kissed you?" His hold on her was unrelenting.

"No, San."

He sat up abruptly, his magic snapping away as he stood. "Whatever you wish." The surge of magic was a crack of his voice. "It doesn't matter to me."

"Liar," she sighed.

"That makes two of us." He tugged at his clothes in an attempt to smooth some of the wrinkles from sleeping in them. Then he stopped, shut his eyes, and inhaled deeply. "I did not mean that…I…"

"I know." Nesrin stood. "I did not mean to hurt you."

"No," he said, drawing her into the haven of his arms. "I don't think you did." He dipped his head. "No more apples," he whispered in her ear, making her laugh despite her sorrow. Then he released her, fetched his entari, and left.

Nesrin sank to the floor, and swallowed a sob as her eyes filled with tears.

Thirty-Two

Nesrin swiped the tears off her cheeks and stood. Resolve took the place of sorrow.

She had been powerless and afraid when she arrived. Easy to manipulate. But she did not have to be those things, was not truly those things. The Grand Vizier was not the only one with leverage. She knew everything about this lie of his, how he was deceiving everyone. How he had a life debt decades unfulfilled.

When Reyhan arrived, Nesrin had nearly completed dressing. Reyhan was quiet and watchful as she helped to arrange Nesrin's clothes and braid her hair.

"Do you wish to talk?" she asked with an air of suspicion, as Nesrin slipped into shoes.

"Please find out where the Grand Vizier is this morning. I need to speak with him." Nesrin kept her tone firm. She had no doubts Reyhan would protest violently if she knew what Nesrin intended to do.

"Oh?" Reyhan said, brows raised. "About what?"

"Find out, please." Nesrin did her best to sound imperious. Reyhan frowned, but ducked her head and left the room.

Nesrin swallowed back the bitter rush of nausea and followed. She would need some food in her belly for this.

IT WOULD HAVE BEEN BETTER if he were in the palace. Staring up at the Grand Vizier's home, with its poisonous vines hanging like curtains around the door, the entire facade fiery and offensive, Nesrin felt transported back to her very first day in Narfour. Some of her bravery shrank.

The people on the street around her and Reyhan continued on, a current that parted around them as Nesrin tried to dig into the resolve, the fury, that had driven her here.

She would not save herself at the expense of someone else. She would not be more torture for a man who had been tortured enough.

"I do not expect you to stay, if you do not wish to," Nesrin said to Reyhan, who gave her a bemused look. Nesrin's heart ached and raced, her fingers trembling. She tried to remain calm by running through her mental list of things to say, bargaining chips she had. If he threatened her, her last resort was to turn herself in, and ask for leniency for her family. He could not win. Even if she lost, so would he.

That thought gave her resolve. When she moved forward it was fast—long strides and clenched fists. She did not stop to knock, knew that if she stopped, if she allowed even a moment of obsequence, her resolve would fail. So she pulled the latch and shoved the front door open.

"Stop!" Reyhan grabbed for Nesrin's sleeve. Nesrin twisted out of the way. Mahir looked up from where he was wiping down the table in the center of the sitting area, and his brows shot up as he bolted upright.

"I want to see the Grand Vizier," Nesrin said as she continued forward.

"How dare you enter here without permission," Mahir boomed.

Do not think, just do. That was her father's mother. When Nesrin doubted a decision about caring for someone. *Trust your instincts. Only think of the thing just in front of you.*

She needed to get upstairs. She turned, stepping to put the couch between her and Mahir, and strode for the stairs. Reyhan wore a look of fear.

"Stop!" Mahir came for her. Nesrin broke into a run, taking the steps two and three at a time. Mentally, she held on to that momentum, concentrating on her feet instead of the fear that burned hot in her belly. Her heartbeat was a war drum, thrumming through her limbs, but she could not concentrate on that, she had to keep ahead of Mahir, who could not navigate the stairs as quickly as she could, youth and a life of hard labor working in her favor.

Nesrin propelled herself up by pulling against the railing and flinging herself faster, until she emerged on the second floor, into the common area.

The moment she stepped onto the second floor, she was overwhelmed with the heat of fire. Both magical and mundane. The dry, hot air seared the breath out of her lungs. Nesrin reeled in place as she tried to catch her breath and wits.

The Grand Vizier stood at the far end of the room, in front of a broad, open brazier lit with glowing coals. The curtains were drawn over the glass doors behind him, so the only light was from the brazier and several mage orbs that floated above him. The flames flickered on the walls around them, making the entire room seem to be ablaze.

Cemil stood on the opposite side of the brazier from his father. Both whirled to look at her.

Mahir barreled into her from behind, almost knocking her to the floor. It did not matter that she kept her feet, because he continued his forward motion, snagging her by the arm and marching her across the red and orange carpets to fling her at the Grand Vizier's feet. Her knees slammed onto the stone tiles between carpets, and she landed forward on her elbows with a grunt.

When Reyhan made a sound of protest, Mahir forced her to her knees beside Nesrin.

"My deepest apologies, Pasha." Mahir bowed, his hand on the back of Nesrin's head to keep her in place. "She ran from me." His fingers snagged in her hair, pulling it taut while simultaneously forcing her to stare at the floor. The wheezing sound she heard was her own frightened breaths.

"Did you do the things he said?" Nesrin strained against the force of Mahir's hand, trying to lift her head. "Did you murder his father? Burn him?"

Something clanked against the side of the brazier as the Grand Vizier set it down, and he moved to a chair to sit. "Let her go," he said.

Mahir released her. Nesrin lifted her head. The Grand Vizier drummed the fingers of one hand on the arm of the chair, his other elbow propped on the arm and his head tipped into his fingers.

"What are you hoping to accomplish by barging into my home this way?"

"I am finished with this. I will not be a part of this deception any longer," she said. It felt like the time Metin had convinced her to jump off a rock outcropping into the river. A moment of exhilarating freedom, then a rush of crushing fear.

Fire lit in his eyes. "What makes you think I will let you?"

"I will tell them all of it. How you meant to use me against a Vizier, then a prince. To trap them in an illegitimate marriage. How you threatened my family to keep me quiet."

"You believe they would take your word over mine?" he deadpanned. "You lied to me. You are a grasping, devious shrew of a woman, who pretended to be the daughter of a noble, who meant to use me and the Sehzade for her own gain." He sat in the armchair as if it were a throne and he a sultan and she his evening's entertainment.

Nesrin's surety began to wilt, shriveling beneath the heat of his stare and his magic.

"You have an unfulfilled life debt," she forced out, though even she could hear the uncertainty in her voice.

"Oh, little girl"—he smirked—"you do not have the intelligence to play these games with me."

Resentment speared down her spine. They all thought that, didn't they? Little country mouse who could not possibly stand among them. Too simple. Too *kind.* Nesrin shot to her feet. Pain and anger and energy twisted oddly through the scar around her body, into her face, over her skin. Something that was hers, as pain was, and something that was not. A weak green corona of light ringed her vision as if she were viewing everything through a haze, and her mouth filled with a taste like wild summer wheat.

Cemil let out a soft grunt, grabbing for the edge of the brazier as his knees nearly buckled and the coals roared to life. Fire sprang up in a halo around the Grand Vizier, flames pouring from his scalp down his arms and body. For a moment, his face went slack in confusion.

Reyhan cried out as fire erupted around her in a circle and she struggled to pull it under control. The mage orbs blazed with light. The house rumbled, and Mahir cursed under his breath behind her.

Nesrin could not draw a full breath, and gasped for air. It felt like her life was being sucked from her, like her knees were going to give beneath her. "What are you doing?"

The Grand Vizier looked at his hands, at the flames skittering over his skin, and gave a wondering chuckle. His gaze landed on her as he rose from his chair, closing his hands into fists and extinguishing the flames. He waved a hand carelessly at the brazier and it died to coals once more.

The orbs dimmed. His expression was wild and hungry as he took the one stride between them and caught her by the jaw. His fingers clawed into muscle and bone and she let out a pained cry.

Reyhan went to her feet, protesting. But Cemil put a hand on her shoulder and shoved her back to her knees.

"Well," the Grand Vizier hissed, flames cracking in his voice and eyes, "what a very fortuitous turn of the Wheel."

"Let *go* of me." Nesrin's words garbled because of his grip on her. She clawed for his face, but he was too strong.

"You have no idea, do you?" he said, curious. He turned her face one way, then the other. "Poor, simple child. You do not even know what you are. What you can do. What you can help me to do."

She clawed his head, digging at his eyes with her nails, and brought a knee up into his groin with all the force she could manage. He doubled forward with a grunt, releasing her. Nesrin tumbled to the floor and jumped up to bolt, but remembered Reyhan. In her moment of hesitation, the Grand Vizier recovered and caught her by her hair, wrestling her to the floor on her belly.

"I cannot abide a fool who does not even know themselves." He pinned her to the tile with a knee in her back and a hand on her shoulder, the other in her hair, smashing her face against the floor. Pain like a knife slicing her open went through her newly healed skin, as if someone were trying to peel her like a lemon. She cried out.

Black swept over her, dragging her into the emptiness of her dreams.

Reach for me.

"Rings," the Grand Vizier said, like an order, and the room flickered back into existence. Cemil crouched in front of her and held his open palm out to his father. Nesrin gulped a breath, and when she squeezed her eyes shut, she was back in the dream.

Reach.

The voice was hollow. Yet, everywhere. Male, but millions. It was echoed, into darkness, into ages, beyond existence. Old, and new. Demanded.

Break.

"No!" Reyhan's voice rent Nesrin's dream. The blackness intertwined with reality, fissures of the scene before her. Cemil met Nesrin's eyes when she opened them. He was pale, and stank of alcohol, unsteady as he crouched next to her, his pupils wide and fire-filled.

"Coward," she spat. One side of his mouth kicked up. Then he reached down and shackled her wrist, holding her hand up for his father.

Wake up!

"Please! I'll keep her silent, I will," Reyhan croaked, but there was a crack, like someone hit her, then a whimper. Something hot circled her mind, burning like firebrand, and she screamed. The Grand Vizier had just slipped a ring onto the middle finger of her right hand. He still held her head pinned to the tiles. And the black dream, the sense of an *other*, slipped completely away, replaced by a feeling like fire blazing up her arm.

Nesrin tried to buck the Grand Vizier off, but he only pressed harder on her head, until it felt like it might split open like a melon. Her senses dripped back to her, grounding her in reality. Was she losing her mind? Mahir came up behind Cemil and held out a small, wicked-looking knife. Panic made her flail again, as the Grand Vizier reached for it.

"Hold her," he said, calmly, as his magic heated the blade red hot. Cemil pinned her arms to the floor. Mahir held her legs. The Grand Vizier grabbed the neck of her caftan and yanked it downward, cutting off her air and voice, and exposing the back of her neck. "If you move, it will only worsen and prolong your pain."

She tried to yell as her vision clouded and her lungs seized, sensing the approach of the knife to her skin. But the sound was little more than a squawk.

"If you mark her, the Sehzade will see it," Cemil said in apathy. "Perhaps even read the sigil." Mark her? A person? With sigils? She'd never heard such a thing.

"You are right, of course." The Grand Vizier released her caftan, and when the pressure eased off her throat she gulped air. Tears dribbled down her cheeks. She was nothing. Reduced only to what she felt. Pain, and fear. Fury. He stood, but neither Cemil nor Mahir released their grip on her. "A sigil bracelet will do well enough. For now."

The two men held her until the Grand Vizier returned. Then Mahir took over from Cemil. But when Cemil let go, Nesrin managed to catch one of Mahir's hands as he grabbed for her, and bit him. Hard enough that he felt it, through caftan and entari sleeve. He shoved his knee into her back, yanking his arm from her grip and pulling backwards on her hair so she was flexed at the waist like a drawn bow. Behram leaned forward and took her hand.

"Don't be feral," he said in disgust. "The trick"—he held her gaze, flames crackling in his, as he slipped the bracelet onto her wrist—"is not to control what someone can do, but what they cannot." A quick, mocking smile flicked across his expression as his fingers tightened over hers and the ring and her wrist with the bracelet, until she thought he might crack her bones. "Deny them a direction, thereby forcing them where one wants them to go. Something I learned from our late Queen Sultana."

The ring and bracelet heated, and the flames in the Grand Vizier's eyes brightened until they consumed the pupil, the iris, and the white, until bits of flames bled from his scalp and cascaded over his shoulders. The sleeve of Nesrin's entari where it touched him began to smoke, shrinking back from him, and a smell like burnt meat filled the air. Her voice and her breath burned away with the heat, leaving her nothing but mute fear, writhing and twisting through her. Void she might be, but she could feel the magic he poured into the jewelry, the barbed chains it wrapped around her mind and body.

His voice hissed with magic. "Nesrin Irmak and her family do not exist," he said, and the bracelet heated. There was more. Each intention burning into it, into her mind. The only daughter of Osman Bardakci. Grateful to the Grand Vizier.

The men released her. The pain of his fire trickled away, leaving her sweating and weak, her muscles twitching and her mouth full of cotton and copper.

She grabbed for the ring, trying to yank it from her finger. It heated, hot as a kettle fresh off the fire, burning the finger it resided on and those she grabbed at it with. Nesrin let out a wail of desperation. Furious, she launched to her feet, thinking only in shades of rage, intent on enacting some kind of revenge for yoking her like a beast.

A flick of his fingers brought her to her knees as fire sped through her veins and a scream cut off as if hands held it down. She nearly vomited, crawling across the stones toward him, trying to breathe and think and barely able to do either. She grasped at the only idea she could.

"Bardakci Pasha will—" Arrows of searing fire shot up her arms and her words became a gag of pain. Her vision went black and she smelled nothing but ash.

The Grand Vizier leaned forward, leering. "He is my creature just as much as you are. With just as much to lose."

Nesrin hugged her arms around herself, hands trembling, though the pain receded quickly. "I am *not* your creature. I am Nesrin Irm—" Again it blazed through her. This time hotter. A poker straight from the fire into her spine. She sobbed a breath. What had he done? He was not casting a spell on her. She looked down at her hands, flexing her fingers open then curling them together. There were no burns on her skin, despite that she had felt the jewelry heat. Both ring and bracelet bore gold filigree and red stones. Garnets, or rubies. Flares of red winked out in their centers just when she looked. *Sigils.*

"You—" *enchanted these.* She could not voice the words, though the thought continued as fire whipped her breath from her lungs. She let out a growl of fury and frustration, glaring up at him through her tears. "I will run." Nesrin swayed on her hands and knees, her voice ravaged. She tried to summon the strength to get to her feet. Behind him, Reyhan knelt, hands to her face, her shoulders shaking in silent sobs. Behram gave Nesrin a piteous look.

"And the first place I look for you will be with your family, and if I do not find you there, I am afraid I will be very cross." He smiled as he said it. "I am so unpredictable when I am angry, my dear."

Her body chilled. Her family flashed in her mind, and the biting pain of his magic. The chill disappeared, replaced by scorching horror.

His expression changed, wiping clean of anything but the glow of flames in his pupils. "You wish to be noble?" Behram jeered. "Then you should think of these lies as your gift to him. He needs a highborn wife to keep his place in the succession. He's a bastard, did he tell you? The kindest thing you can do for him, and yourself, is to marry him. Consider it my gift to you. Marry him. Enjoy your promotion from beast of burden."

Nesrin spit on his feet. Mahir dove for her hair again and she dodged. The Grand Vizier held up a hand, and his steward stilled. Nesrin sat back on her heels, every emotion but loathing burned away. But her body was too leaden to move now, crushed by the weight of his threats.

"If you attempt to defy me again, then my only other option is to kill him, anyone who helps you"—he lifted one shoulder with an unconcerned frown—"and you." He caught her gaze the way a snake caught its prey's. "Then everyone you love."

Thirty-Three

"I am not your personal errand girl," Aysel said, as she dropped from the roof of the palace and landed a few paces from Ihsan on the garden path.

"And apparently incapable of using halls and pathways like a normal person," he said under his breath as she strode toward him.

"I am not a normal person, I am the Charah of Air." She grinned broadly. "Try to contain your jealousy."

"I will do my utmost," Ihsan said tartly. "Did you find her?" He had to shove the guilt and shame behind a wall of ice, especially when Aysel raised an eyebrow at him in what was absolutely a judgment.

"I did. A city watchman saw her enter the Grand Vizier's home this morning. But he could not tell me when she left. If she left."

A cold weight slowed his thoughts, his heart, and smothered what joy the morning had given him. He had not liked the gnawing feeling of vulnerability that had accompanied his euphoric start to the day. She was closer than anyone had been in Turns, thawing out walls of ice that had kept him safe for just as long.

"You don't know where she is now?" Ihsan glowered. Aysel huffed, jamming her fists against her hips.

"That's a great deal closer than you were before I helped you."

He made a sound of dismissal and turned from her in frustration.

"This does not definitely mean she belongs to Kadir, Sehzade," Aysel said, apologetic. "There are any number of reasons she might have gone there."

"And how many of those include her telling me she was going somewhere else this morning?" he replied. Her silence was answer enough.

San. Naime's voice whispered in his ear. He knew her nearly as well as he knew himself, and her voice, even distorted by the cast, was broken. Ihsan whirled and ran into the gallery that framed the garden and beyond it into the palace. He tried to think only of moving, not of what had caused that tone in Naime's voice. Tried only to hold himself together. He could not be weak now, not if she needed him.

Aysel kept pace with him. It did not matter that her legs were so much shorter, her magic made her as fast as she cared to be.

When he reached the Sultan's door, the guard appeared bewildered by Ihsan's wild-eyed look and winded breaths. Whatever had upset Naime was not known yet. He took a moment to compose himself. Naime didn't need him causing rumors. He scrubbed his hands over his face. He'd forgotten to shave. He'd forgotten, because he was thinking of Nesrin. Of how there were lies in her voice when they parted. He scowled, running a finger around his collar to make sure it was standing as it should, then gave a tug to his entari. When he shoved his fingers through his hair to straighten it, he remembered hers, more demanding.

He knocked on the door, too harshly. After a moment, Samira opened. She took in his face, and clothes, and hair, and Wheel knew what she was able to discern from them. Samira had not always been so quiet and stoic. She had been the bright, sparkling flame to Naime's cool air. But she had been through everything with them. The slow, painful death of Naime's mother, the murder of Ihsan's father, Ihsan's accident, and of course her plans to marry Cemil stolen from her. Her fire was banked.

"Sehzade," she said, more accusatory than welcoming. What had he done now? He edged past her, and she kept out of the way. Naime sat in the central room, with tea. Coffee had begun to make her too jittery. She did not greet him, but stared out the window at her mother's fig tree. Ihsan approached and touched her hair in passing, sitting across from her. She returned from wherever her mind had been and looked at him. The hollows beneath her eyes appeared bruised, her skin leeched of life.

"May I?" Aysel said, gently, and Naime nodded, gesturing to a seat near Ihsan.

"You have not been sleeping," he said. Her lashes fluttered and she focused out the window again. For a moment, he was looking at Dilay, just before she passed. Gaunt and sleepless. His throat closed.

"The Blight has reached the Southern valley. The farms north of Mizraa have succumbed." Her voice lacked any of its usual strength. The news was dire. That meant their last internal supply of food would be gone within turns. There was trade, of course, but supplies for such were limited, as most of Tamar's resources were now turned toward feeding, clothing, and outfitting an army. Ihsan glanced at Samira, who moved to sit beside Naime and took her friend's hand between both of hers.

"Elder Attiyeh has sent a missive," Samira said, reaching to fuss at a bit of Naime's hair. "The Agassi is missing."

Ihsan exhaled, capturing his dread in ice. He kept his face as neutral as Naime's usually was. Aysel stiffened, her lips pressing tightly together to hold back whatever questions she had. The color leached out of her golden skin, and a tickle of magic stirred the air.

Samira continued, "A contingent of riders has been missing since they went north to Dar Afir to scout supposed Republic activity in the area." Ihsan remembered Makram mentioning them. "The Agassi took a section of his men to search for them. Master Attiyeh says only two of the Agassi's men returned, claiming an ambush conducted by both Sarkum soldiers and Republic centurions. The section was slaughtered, and the survivors could not find the Agassi...or his body."

"They are..." He could not say the words.

"It appears that Al-Nimas and the Republic have some kind of accord, yes," Naime said, her voice as dull as fresh-hewn granite.

Ihsan sat with the crush of the news, composing his voice and his manner. Naime was strong, but he did not know if anyone was as strong as all this.

"What do you need?" he said. If she could not answer, he would pick something and act.

Naime drew a shuddering breath. He could see, in the set of her jaw, the shimmer in her eyes, she was blaming herself. For all of it. Doubting herself as she rarely did. Then it whisked away, hardness coming into her eyes. "This will be enough to sway the majority. Behram Kadir will use this to take the throne from me."

THIRTY-FOUR

"STOP!" REYHAN IMPLORED WHEN NESRIN fell to her knees in the grass and vomited, nearly blacking out, again. They were in the garden at Ihsan's home. It was the only place she could think of to go. The only place she had wanted to go.

Nesrin's head pounded. Something tickled her lip and she swiped at it, only to discover a streak of red on her hand when she looked. Nesrin closed her eyes. She had tried everything she could think of. Writing the truth. Plunging her hands into water to counteract the fire magic. Speaking in absurd lies.

She could not remove the jewelry. Reyhan could not remove them. Talking about herself, her real name, her real past, what had happened, any of it. And every time she tried, the pain became worse, until it felt like her bones were melting, until finally it had knocked her unconscious. It was only for a few moments, according to Reyhan. And now this, bleeding. Could this kill her then?

Reyhan was right. She had to stop.

The fire mage sat on the edge of the pavers that marked the kitchen area, her face drawn, eyes hollow. The Grand Vizier had cast a spell on her bracelet as well, after finishing with Nesrin, then cut a sigil into

Reyhan's skin. He did it with a knife heated to glowing red, while Mahir and Cemil held her and Reyhan screamed into Mahir's hand cupped over her mouth.

Because he was a Sival, he had not had to speak the spell, only think it, and Nesrin had no idea what constraints he had put on Reyhan. But she had seen the other sigils, carved and scarred over, permanently embedded in Reyhan's flesh.

What secrets had Reyhan already been keeping, and for how long? What did the old sigils protect? Nesrin had not even been able to treat Reyhan, because every time she tried to move Reyhan's clothes it caused Reyhan's jewelry to attack her. Guilt pecked at her, that Reyhan's new pain was her fault. For choosing to confront Behram.

Nesrin lay on her back in the grass, giving her body time to recover from the pain of her efforts. Perhaps the worst part, it left no mark. No evidence of the magic that seared her blood and bones, that made screams well in her throat. She had never felt pain like this. Like she was being burned alive from the inside, her mind and body and blood.

The control of the spell was thorough. She knew nothing about enchantments, except that they were a long-forgotten, illegal art. She did understand sigils, though. Her family all used them, the hub and spoke of Deval magic. Each stroke was a direction in a spell, a command, a thought. They were flexible creations, built off a common base form. First, the sigil of the House, then strokes that controlled the magic, then strokes to develop the intent of the spell. There were books of sigils, related to professions and art. Developed sigils were often passed down through families, guilds, and tradesmen. Her father had told her that some guarded their sigils if they were unique, or had a particularly powerful effect.

But their magic was short-lived, and sucked power from a mage at an intense, dangerous rate, if they were not careful. Because a sigil was essentially a tap to the magic of a mage, and without proper balance, intention, and control measures in place within the sigil, that tap simply siphoned magic until there was no power left.

It was why Sival did not use them often, even though they could. It was easier, more economical, to create a spell through intention in the mind—at least, that's what Nesrin's family had told her.

Something like this would have to be intricate. He would have had to practice with it. Develop it. Test it.

The implications made Nesrin's stomach and head spin. She opened her eyes to stare at the sky, clear and blue. Too beautifully bright to make sense to her in the moment.

He might have cast the spell, but how was he powering it? Presumably she and Reyhan were not the only ones under such control, he could not provide magical power to multiple enchantments… could he? Could he design the sigil to draw on the victim's power? But that would not work on Nesrin, because she was not a mage. If such a thing were even possible with a sigil.

She pressed the heels of her palms against her eyes. Advanced sigil work was the realm of scholars, not irrigation mages and their void siblings. Still, if she could examine one, she *might* be able to recognize some of the strokes. She suspected that was why he put the sigils on Reyhan's back. Not only did it make them less likely to be seen by other people, it made it very difficult for Reyhan to study them and find a way to unravel them. For anyone to do so, if they triggered pain for her simply for being looked at.

Nesrin stood. She needed something productive to do. She was only going in circles now.

"Stay here," she said to Reyhan. The fire mage was in no shape to move around. Nesrin had wanted to treat the pain of the newly burned sigils for Reyhan, but could not without causing more pain to her. So Nesrin's first destination was the Grand Market. She went to her room and scavenged the coins she had taken when she left

Mizraa. She'd hidden them beneath the vine she'd rescued from Ihsan's office. It was happy in its new location, nearly triple the size from when she saved it.

She solicited a carriage parked at the top of the street. Initially she had meant to walk, but it would take her what was left of the day. She paid him with one of the coins, and he gave her a scattering of smaller ones in change.

The market hummed and buzzed like a hive, crowded with workers looking for a midday meal, women paused in their chores to shop for necessities. Nesrin wove in and out of rows of goods. Food stalls filled the air with the scent of spices and meat roasting. Smoke and steam curled between stalls, sometimes temporarily blinding her.

Her stomach ached. Lightheadedness came and went. She was accustomed to that.

She did not have enough money to buy food and the herbs she had come in search of. So she ignored the stalls, searching out the section of the market dedicated to spices, herbs, and medicines. But it felt good to have a purpose, something useful to take her mind away from how powerless she was.

After asking directions several times she finally emerged from a row of booths selling bits and bobs of cheap jewelry to a street with a clear view of the Sun Sea. In every direction booths were arranged beneath tarps to keep their wares dry. Slouched burlap bags were filled to the brim with seeds, chilis, herbs, nuts, and dried fruits. The smell was a wondrous assault, alluring and repulsive, too many threads to put name to. She bypassed the spice sellers calling out to her about the freshness of their grinds or the far-flung origins of their spices.

The herbs and medicinals were farther down, and were not in open containers to be easily snatched. Samples were laid out on tables, or hung on frames that held up the tarps, well out of reach of passersby. These were hand harvested, she knew, because she had often been the one sent to gather such things for her grandmothers. She knew what she wanted. Comfrey, for pain and swelling, calendula, and mallow. None of them should be particularly dear, they were easy enough to find. But it took her time to find some that looked fresh, and whose proprietor gave her confidence in their honesty.

The woman appeared to be of a similar age to Nesrin's mother. Nesrin greeted her with a smile, pointing to what she wanted. As she watched the woman wrap her purchase in paper, she noted a stack of willow bark shards behind her.

"A handful of those as well," she said. The woman hummed her answer, looking at Nesrin critically as she added that to the order. Her gaze flicked over Nesrin's clothes, hair, and hands, her mouth twitching as if to repress words. Nesrin did not prompt her to ask whatever questions caused the examination. Questions had become even more dangerous to her, now.

"You're the Sehzade's wife," the woman said nonchalantly, as she slid the wrapped herbs toward Nesrin over the table.

"Betrothed," Nesrin corrected. The woman made a small sound, a smile playing at her lips.

"I saw you. I was at the palace for your betrothal."

"Oh?" Nesrin said politely when it was clear the woman expected her to inquire.

"Sometimes I supply the doctors up there with medicinals they don't want to hunt for themselves." She shrugged. "And they've been asking for a lot lately, trying to get that Republic man back on his feet." Her look was surreptitious and sly. She wanted something, but Nesrin wasn't certain what.

"Republic man?" She tidied her stack of herbs into a pile, trying to decide how to leave without being rude.

But the woman planted her forearms on the table and leaned forward. "They say he's dangerous."

"How so?" Nesrin's brows stitched. She had no idea what the woman was talking about. Republic man? Was he a prisoner?

"They say Mutar Charah brought him to the city, near dead with poppy in his blood. They say he's a Charah too. They've got him up there in the palace with all those doctors watching him. That's four then. Some are sayin' the Princess Sultana is trying to stand a Circle."

"Four what?" A Circle? She'd only heard of a Circle of mages in the stories her grandmothers told them about the Sundering War and the Old Sultanate.

"Chara'a," the woman said with eyes rounding. "Four Chara'a in one place. I thought you would know, if you're to marry the Sehzade." She straightened and swiped at bits of dirt on the table, clearly disappointed. She was hunting for gossip then.

"I am from Mizraa," Nesrin said lamely. "The palace and its plans are as unknown to me as they are to you."

"Doesn't seem smart," the woman said, avoiding Nesrin's arched look, "to be ignorant of what's going on in the palace if you live there."

Well. Nesrin could not argue with that. It wasn't smart. Ignoring things, wishing for things to be as they were, for herself to be as she was, had only gotten her enmeshed in danger. She did not respond, only collected her packages of herbs and turned away. But a basket with a tangle of familiar plants caught her notice.

"Is that skullcap?" She paused. The woman followed her gaze and nodded. Nesrin did a bit of calculating, then set her bundles down. "I'll take some of that, turmeric, nutmeg"—she pointed as she ordered, already thinking about what sort of balm she would make—"and more comfrey." The herbalist nodded thoughtfully, packaging them up and accepting the last of Nesrin's coins.

"Here," she said as Nesrin tried to gather everything into her arms. She reached beneath the table and withdrew an empty burlap sack, then helped Nesrin carefully put everything inside.

"Thank you," Nesrin said in farewell, and the woman waved her off. Initially Nesrin headed in the direction of the Water District but did not get far before the woman's words needled her.

Ignorant. There was no going back to who she had been. No pulling the curtain closed on these new things. This new awareness. Even if everything else disappeared, even if there was no enchantment on her, no threats to her family. She knew things she could not forget. Narfour, and the palace, were not imaginary to her anymore. Her family would be ashamed of her not taking advantage of a chance to help someone with less than her. And she had so much now.

Maybe she could not talk about her enchantments, her lies. But perhaps she could unravel Reyhan's. Or help someone else unravel it. Before she had decided, her feet were moving, back down the hill, from the market and toward the Fire District. When she had been with Reyhan, she noted the entire neighborhood dedicated to blacksmiths and the like. And Amara had mentioned that Reyhan's promised, Kanat, was a glassmaker.

She lost track of how much time passed, how many people she asked vague questions of. But she finally found someone who knew Kanat.

"He used to run the glass shop over on Forge Row. But he abandoned it." The man had overheard her asking a tea shop owner and flagged her down. He was sitting at a table alone, with tea and a water pipe. Clouds of iron grass smoke streamed from his nostrils after every sentence, because he inhaled on the pipe, spoke through the smoke, then exhaled it. A thick, char-marked leather apron took up the second chair at the table. The scars on his hands and arms that matched the ones on his apron were all the clue she needed to his occupation.

"What's there now?" she asked, clasping both hands around the neck of the burlap bag of herbs to prevent herself from swiping at the air to clear the smoke.

"Nothing." He shrugged, and inhaled again. Nesrin murmured thanks, escaping before he could drown her in another exhale. His directions were simple enough, and a hill climb and two turns brought her to Forge Row. Blacksmith after blacksmith had their forges lined up and down the street. And the ring of hammers and sizzle of hot metal in water baths could be heard blocks away. At the bottom of the hill, the street led to an enormous furnace, powered by water wheels in the canal. The work of forging was a testament to the balance of the Wheel, opposition in its purest form powering creation.

She followed an alley between two of the largest forges into a shady side street, closed in at both ends by long warehouses. The glass shop was in front of her, across the street. Debris caked the stair risers, and the windows were dark and coated in soot. A sign still hung above the lintel, peeling paint depicting an ornate bottle. She thought it was meant to be colorful, but the colors were sun-bleached.

With a glance behind her, Nesrin warily crossed the street. The shop was alone, everything else on the narrow road was the back of buildings facing other streets. Midden heaps slumped along the walls, and flies buzzed in slow circles. It was not the most glamorous place to put an artisan glass shop, but perhaps he'd had no choice. She climbed the steps and tried the door. The knob turned, but the door wouldn't budge. She wedged her shoulder against it and shoved, but there was clearly something barring it. She circled to the back.

There was only a narrow space between it and the building behind it. Neither the back of the shop nor the building it faced had any windows. There was a door though. Nesrin tried it; they could not both be barred, one would have had to be locked with a key. With little chance of anyone seeing her, she was more forceful with her attempts to knock this door open. Finally, she set her bag of herbs and roots down, gathered up the hems of her caftan and entari, and kicked the door, right above the handle. Her father had broken into an old, locked shed once like that. Though the door had been considerably less sturdy. It took three hard kicks before she heard a crack and snap and the door swung inward.

Stifling an exclamation of triumph, she snatched up the burlap and went inside. It was as dark as the void and she wished she could have brought Reyhan, for some light. The open door did let in some, though it only illuminated a path into the center of a building that was much larger than it had looked from the outside. Nesrin knew nothing about glasswork. Anything glass they had in Mizraa was precious, and most of it was at the estate house. Windows and glassware and such. She did not know what she might find inside, what she even expected to stumble across in an abandoned workshop.

Three large shapes resolved in the weak light as Nesrin moved farther into the building. Furnaces, most likely, hulking against the wall to her left. As she was peering at them, she ran shin-first into something hard enough to make her yelp in pain. It was a workbench, she saw, as she stumbled back with a curse.

It took up the majority of the middle of the space, and on the far side, a standing rack held a variety of tools. Nesrin set her burlap bag on the table to free her hands, then shuffled forward with them extended. She made her way across the length of the building slowly. Her eyes adjusted enough that she was able to find the wall she thought was the front. The door she found there was not barred or locked, and when she opened it, found a smaller, narrow room that ran the length of the front.

Some small amount of light made its way in through the soot-gunked windows, so she could see the front door and the bar laid across it. A counter separated her from the very front, and she had to trace it with her hands to find a panel that lifted to allow her through.

She removed the bar and opened the door a crack for more light. There was very little to be found in the front. Just dust, some leaves that had collected in the corners, and the desiccated carcasses of insects beneath a tremendous cobweb in one corner.

The walls to either side of the door were shelves. And on those shelves were an array of abandoned bits and bobs. Decorative glassware, a pair of spectacles, small boxes. And an oil lamp.

Nesrin grabbed it, then felt along the same shelf for something to light it with. A palm-sized box held flint and steel, and she took all of it to the back, then into the alley behind for some light. She used a handful of dried leaves from a pile blown against the edge of the building to strike sparks into. When they caught, she lit the lamp wick, then extinguished the smoldering leaves with her foot and went inside. She pulled the door shut behind her and took a quick lap around the perimeter.

The workbench was clear of tools or anything, though it bore the same thick layer of dust as everything else. What was in here, or had been in here, that was worth enchanting Reyhan for? Where was Kanat? Not dead, Nesrin had to assume, unless that was the secret Reyhan was spelled to keep.

Disappointed, she held the lamp up to shelves along the walls, mostly empty, though some held more pieces, many cracked or shattered. Bowls, glasses, and a few more that appeared more decorative than functional.

"Perhaps he just hated your work that much," she muttered, kicking at a pile of debris. The distinctive clink of glass as something skittered away over the floor made her peer more closely. Just shards of something broken, perhaps a tiny bottle or jar, judging by the curve. As she turned away, the barest glint of light made her turn toward a shelf again.

She advanced, turning her head one way, then the other, to try to catch it again. It was a thin metal disk, gold, wedged behind the shelf, on the floor, buried in dust and ash. She dug it out. Nesrin set the lamp on the shelf and dusted the piece off, noting the stamped design on the front. She did not know anything about it, except that it appeared to be a crest of some kind. She slipped it into the fabric wrapped around her waist and continued past the shelves to the furnaces.

If she knew anything about glasswork, she might have known what to look for. Two of the furnaces were empty. The last one, closest to the front of the shop, looked a great deal like an oven for bread. A squat, brick-and-plaster structure with an interior chamber above a firebox.

Something whooshed in her ears. Like someone had stuffed cloth in them and now all she could hear was her own pulse. Her skin prickled. Nesrin took a step away from the thing, her fingers tightening on the lamp handle. She'd had prickles of intuition before, gut feelings she had either obeyed or ignored, but this was something different. Like a tangible assault. Reluctantly, as if something might leap out at her, Nesrin took a step closer and bent forward to look into the open chamber.

All she saw were a few scattered bits of broken glass. Something about the glass mesmerized her. She could not look away, though she also wanted to flee. She moved closer, transfixed. As she reached inside for one of the larger pieces, the lamplight caught it at an angle, and she saw something—like specks—contained inside the shard. She picked it up. It felt so viscerally wrong in her fingers that she almost threw it away again. A scream welled in her throat, but it was not hers, it was an echo. From the glass.

It tumbled from her fingers. Nesrin lurched away from the oven. The buzzing in her ears grew louder and that green haze of lightheadedness colored the very edges of her vision.

After a moment to calm down, she went to the worktable and tore away a piece of the burlap bag. Then she returned to the oven, and before she could think too hard, ducked forward and reached in, collecting up the pieces large enough to grab. She laid them out on the table. They were shards of a miniscule bottle or vial, something sized for perfume or some precious liquid. She brought the lamp closer, leaning down to examine the pieces as she swung the lamp to different angles.

Finally, its light caught in the right direction, and she saw the speckles again. Except they weren't speckles.

Her throat burned. With trembling fingers, Nesrin used the burlap scrap to pick up the largest shard of curved glass and hold it close. She knew. She could not have put into words how she knew, but the screams were in her head again as she examined the glass and the spray of inclusions. Bleached white fragments and particles.

Tears blurred her vision then traced hot down her cheeks, dripping from her chin and into the dust on the table. Terror made her eyes squeeze closed. It iced her skin. She was herself and she was not, just as when she had put her hands on the fig tree skeleton in the palace.

There were memories in trees.

As there were memories in bones.

THIRTY-FIVE

SHE RETURNED TO THE PALACE, waiting until darkness had fallen so that her filth-covered clothes and skin would be less noticeable. While attempting to find her way through gardens and less-used hallways, she got lost once.

She arrived to find the suite lit only by fading mage orbs and empty silence. She had not wanted to see anyone, especially Ihsan, but the vacant room echoed her loneliness too painfully. There was no food laid out as there usually would have been, but why would there be? The Sehzade was staying in the city, and she had not been in the palace all day.

Hunger was something she did know how to deal with. Unlike anything else from the day.

She was going to use the bath, even if she had to fill it herself. There was nothing left in her to feel guilty about Reyhan not knowing where she was; she would sort it in the morning. In fact, Nesrin did not feel ready to face Reyhan yet. Did she know about the glass? Had she been part of its making somehow? Nesrin could not bear the thought.

There was no telling what kind of bone dust had been encased in the glass fragments. It could have been animal. Even that, the very best she could hope for, was abhorrent. Life returned to the void. Its components broke down into dust to complete the circle. To trap it forever in glass… that was breaking the Wheel. And her reaction to it? The echo of the screams in her mind? It felt meaningful. It felt real.

Not a little girl playing at sensing the memories of trees. But terror and pain bound forever, suspended between death and the void. Would anyone else understand it? Were the feelings unique to her? Perhaps she was losing her mind. That would explain her nightmares.

But she could not think on it anymore. Her thoughts had been spinning in circles for candlemarks.

She folded the burlap sack open to remove her purchases. The rough weave was familiar. More familiar than anything else in the room. She'd carried countless things around Mizraa in burlap. The fibers were always catching on her calluses. She turned her palms up, then rubbed her fingers over the pads. They were nearly gone. Her skin was almost as smooth as Reyhan's now.

The last time she'd held burlap she had used it to retrieve and carry the cedar cones to her village's funeral. She curled her fingers into her palms and closed her eyes. It did not take a spell to make Nesrin Irmak disappear; she was fading, even in her own heart. Becoming something else she was not certain she wanted to be, or even could be, for that matter.

She set the bag beside a narrow table set against the wall, just to the side of the bathroom door. Before she could lay her purchases out, she had to relocate a stack of papers that Reyhan had brought for her to study and memorize. Descriptions of each Vizier in the High Council, their holdings, affiliations, and allegiances. She had yet to even look at them.

With care, she unpacked the herbs and roots from the bag. Arranging them out on the table so they would still be usable the next day took up enough concentration that she could avoid the blacker trails of thoughts in her mind. A stab of more guilt that she had not gone back to prepare the poultice for Reyhan distracted her further. In the morning she would return to the city house to make the poultice and the salve and think. Tonight, she would drown the day and its memories and revelations in a bath.

The final thing she did was take the burlap-wrapped shards of glass and tuck them into the back of one of the wardrobe drawers, behind a silk sachet of lavender meant to keep the clothes inside fresh-smelling. Nesrin took the sachet out and pressed her nose into it, inhaling deeply, hoping the scent would help to settle her. The sweet earth and medicinal smell of it filled her lungs and limbs and did make her feel more grounded. She set it back, making certain it hid the glass. She pulled the stamped gold disk from the fabric at her waist and slid it underneath as well.

Nesrin closed the drawer, then the wardrobe doors, then turned toward the bathroom. There was no hand pump on the tub pipes, to Nesrin's exasperation. But of course, there wasn't. There were probably five dozen water mages employed by the palace. She looked at the pitcher of water by the sink, but she was simply too filthy.

When she had resigned herself to hunting down help, she saw the pull bells by the door. That made sense. They were labeled as hot and cold. So Nesrin pulled both. After a moment, steaming water began to pour from the pipe over the tub. She could just barely make out the glow of magic in the water, from whichever mage was forcing water through the pipes.

Watching the tub fill mesmerized her, the sound soothing. Just when she thought she should pull the bells again to stop the fill, it stopped on its own. Depending on the power of the mage, they might be able to sense the dimension of the container. Or, they had been working so long at the job, they simply knew.

Nesrin returned to the bedroom to retrieve something clean to wear, which she hung on a hook by the door. Then she locked both the door to her room and to the main suite, to avoid surprises.

She stripped off her likely ruined clothes and stepped over the high edge of the stone tub and into the water. A basket hung on the outside of one edge, and it held a variety of soaps, oils, sponges, and cloth. She stood in the water for a long, contemplative moment, reveling in the heat as it soaked into her tired legs. Then she sat, and finally lounged backwards with an exhaled groan.

She washed her skin and hair, and thought she dozed at least once. The water had cooled completely by the time she convinced herself to leave the tub. As she patted herself dry with the softest towel she had ever touched, she examined a second assortment of bottles and pots between the two sinks.

The first pot smelled of roses, so she suspected that one was for her body. The next of honey, which all the women in her village swore on the Wheel kept a woman from aging. Likely meant for her face, then. When she withdrew the stopper from a small bottle, she found a slim wooden rod attached, and an oil smelling of rose and something else she could not name. Cedar perhaps. That one smelled like the one Reyhan often worked through her hair.

After applying each where she thought it belonged, she dressed in the clean chemise she'd selected. She opened one door a crack, and peeked through to her room. A mage orb shimmered, floating in the corner of the ceiling farthest from the bed. As if it had been driven there by an opposing force.

That opposing force was lying on her bed, one arm over his eyes, on top of the covers. He wore both caftan and salvar, though his feet were bare.

He was supposed to be in the city. He was supposed to make this easier for her. Though he did not know that. She should have told him the truth that morning. Should have relieved herself of the burden of the lies before they were silenced within her by vile, forbidden magic. Now what was she going to do? Do as Behram ordered her—let Nesrin Irmak cease to exist and marry Ihsan? Spend the rest of her life in a lie? Never see her family again?

Each path led to pain and sorrow. Clearly Ihsan wanted company. What would he do if she slept on the floor or on a couch in the common area?

She slipped out of the bathroom and crossed the room. Careful to disturb the bed as little as possible, she lay down with as much space between them as she could. He did not move, but whispered something, which snuffed the mage orb.

"Did you leave that just for me?" she said into the dark.

"No."

But she knew he had, and it made her smile and broke her heart at once. "Thank you," she whispered.

"You went to Behram Kadir's home today. Did you expect to find Mutar Charah there?" His voice in the dark was cold, as was the touch of his magic that rolled over the bed like a fog.

She shivered. She should be frightened that he knew. Frightened of the consequences of his distrust. But she was so very tired of the lies. Kadir's threats whispered in her mind, reminding her that it was not just her, and her life, at stake.

"I went"—she picked her way through a path of truth, fenced on all sides with fire—"because I make a very poor princess, and because I think you deserve better than what I have to give." She sighed, halfway in relief that she had not caused herself pain, and to shore herself up for the remainder of the conversation. "And I did not want to upset you by telling you I was going to speak with the Grand Vizier about it."

"So, you thought annulling the betrothal without my consent and sneaking back to Mizraa in the night was the solution?" His voice was wary, water washing it cold and stark. "You did not think to ask me what I thought?"

"I don't know what I thought. I thought I was coming to Narfour to marry a…" Her hesitation earned her a sharp spike of fire into her arm. "…Vizier. I was not prepared for this. Everything I do is wrong. I am an embarrassment to you, and the Princess Sultana and—"

He reached for her, both his hands closing on her wrists, and pulled her across the bed to him.

"Who told you that?" he said, low and soft. She adored his voice, all its edges, all that it carried and hid and revealed.

"It is obvious to anyone with eyes or a single wit." The words came harsh, while her mind and heart warred over whether she should move her body the rest of the way to his. She wanted to. Wanted to take comfort in him, but it felt like theft.

"You have an incredible talent for speaking insults with utter innocence," he murmured, making the decision for her by taking handfuls of the chemise and pulling her torso to his.

"Forgive me," she said, "that was not my intent."

"I know, that's why it's charming." His face and hers were at the same level, but she had hers tipped as far away from his as she could, so she could see his expression in the dark. There was little detail to it, obscured as it was.

"I don't wish to hurt you," she said. "I want you to be happy. I think you deserve to be happy." The lie that was cloaked in truth stung like thorns, making her throat raw and her eyes burn.

He was silent for so long she thought he had fallen asleep.

"What if I cannot be?" he asked, quietly. "What if my spin is this, a balance for the joy of others?"

"Do you believe that?" Nesrin asked gently. The pain in his voice hurt her, the resignation.

"I did, I…do. But you…" He shifted, releasing her and rolling to his back so he could rub his hands over his face and through his hair. "…your sunshine is contagious."

"My sunshine?" she teased.

"You are offensively cheerful," he grumbled.

"Contagiously cheerful?" she tried. "Not so contagious that I have ever seen you in a mood to be described as cheerful."

"You just don't know me well enough yet. Since meeting you I have been happy at least twice."

"When?"

"When Kuhzey told me you have been learning his language," he said. That surprised her, and she smiled. "So few have bothered to learn more than a few words." He drew in a long, slow breath, and when he exhaled, he turned his head to look at her, eyes just barely aglow with magic. If it hadn't been dark, she would not even have been able to tell. "And this morning."

His touch and kiss returned to her, overlaying all the horror of the day. No, she could not allow more of that. Nothing buried good sense like desire.

"Are you going to make me sleep without blankets?" She tugged on the edge of the covers, trapped beneath him. "It's cold."

"I believe that's me." He looked away again. "People complain I chill the air."

"It's nice," she said quickly, "just, I would like blankets. Then it would be like a lovely winter day where you have time to stay snuggled in bed where it's warm and watch the snowfall for a bit. You know?"

"No," he said. "Would it not be more like snuggling with a block of ice?"

Nesrin tilted her head back to glare at him. "Difficult man."

"It does not snow in Narfour often enough for that to happen," he relented, a grin showing in the dark.

"Oh," Nesrin said in disappointment. The first snow of every Turn, she and her sisters would snuggle close and watch the snow fall. "You could make snow, couldn't you?" she suggested, trying to bury the memory.

"Do you wish me to make it snow on you? With no blankets?" he said dryly.

"No." Nesrin stuck her tongue out at him. "I will miss the snow in Mizraa though."

Standing, he flipped the blankets back. Then he leaned over the bed and caught her by the waist, dragging her toward him. She yelped in surprise, but he was already pulling the blankets over her. Before she could speak, or move, he lifted his hand toward the ceiling and blue fractals spun up his arm. The same light sparked through the room, and a fat, cold flake landed on Nesrin's cheek.

Her indrawn breath of delight turned into a hum of wonder as more fell, clouding the air with spinning white. She slipped an arm from under the blankets and held it out to catch a few of the flakes on her palm.

"Is this difficult?" she asked, taken with the way they seemed to glow in the darkness.

"Not usually," he said, thoughtfully. "My magic has been erratic lately."

He was not in flux, not the way he had been that night she'd seen him after his nightmare. Half clothed and lit with magic. If he meant his magic was erratic now, she could not see it. He had his head tipped up, watching the snow drift through the air.

"I was promised a block of ice to snuggle with." Her words came out softened by an attack of shyness. Or guilt. They were twined together.

He dipped his chin, gaze settling with hers, that winter light spinning in his pupils. Was he going to deny her? A frightened, weak part of her hoped that he would. That he would take the choice away from her. To be strong and push him away, as was right and decent. Or to be selfish and pretend she believed she had no recourse but to live this lie.

His gaze lifted again, to the snow, then he flicked the blankets to dislodge what had collected before he tucked in beside her, on his back, hands beneath his head. He left space between them. Not much, but enough to give options.

The silence between them was comfortable, muffled and still as it would have been in real winter. Her exhaustion caught her, making her lids heavy, sleep demanding she give in. She had just shut her eyes when he spoke.

"What if I do not want you to leave?" he asked.

She was half gone to sleep, unable to think clearly. "I have nowhere else to go," she said as her eyes shut. The snowfall had subsided. She was already tumbling back into sleep when Ihsan scooped an arm down to pillow her head and pull her into the hollow of his side.

"Then stay," he murmured.

"I'll consider it," she mumbled, draping an arm over his ribs.

Sleep came, thrusting her into her nightmare anew. Was it a nightmare anymore, compared to her waking life? It was almost safe now, vacant and separate. Behram Kadir could not reach her here. But something else could. Obsidian tendrils like fingers, reaching…talons extended toward her heart. Toward the core of her.

Words came to her, as cold as Ihsan's ice. As terrifying as Kadir's fire.

Wake.

And be ended.

Thirty-Six

Tension pulled at the silence between them as Reyhan fussed at Nesrin's clothes, swiping at imaginary dust and wrinkles. Nesrin did not have energy or opinions enough to resist but stood lifeless as Reyhan pinned and primped her hair. She had added a bracelet and a ring to Nesrin's bare wrist and right hand. Reyhan did not explain and Nesrin did not ask. They were to hide the other, new jewelry, from notice. Another layer of lies. To protect them from all the pain Behram had promised them.

She was not one to hold a grudge. She never had been, her empathy had always won any battle with her anger. And anyone who could witness what she had seen done to Reyhan and not forgive the lies it birthed was heartless. That did not prevent the new reserve between them.

Ihsan had been gone when she woke. Her dream lingered, incoherent, a feeling more than a memory. As though she were waiting on a precipice to tumble over to her death. That's what she was dreaming of, wasn't it? The void. The end. It had been the only clear thought she'd had, right after she startled awake and Ihsan murmured something soothing, arranging her so he was curled at her back as if he were a shield.

When a knock came at the hall door, Reyhan left to answer it. She returned carrying an armload of something wrapped beautifully in cloth and paper and bound with ribbons.

"It must be the clothes you commissioned from Mutar Charah." Reyhan set the packages on the bed, and Nesrin moved to her side as the fire mage unwrapped the first one. The clothing within was green, silk and brocade, layers of shades that complemented each other. Nesrin had never seen any clothing more beautiful, she was afraid to even touch it, let alone believe it was meant for her. She was still staring at it when Reyhan opened the second package.

"What—" But she did not finish as her fingers stroked the red fabric with yellow stitching. Her dark eyes were wet, and fat tears spilled over when she looked up at Nesrin. "You cannot."

"Why not?" Nesrin pulled the clothing from its wrapping and held it up to Reyhan's body. "You said it was my money. You deserve something beautiful. Consider it my thank-you, for all you have done to help me. I saw you lusting after this fabric in Mutar Charah's shop." Nesrin laid the entari and matching caftan next to hers.

"They do not match at all," Reyhan complained at the red next to the green.

"No." Nesrin smiled sidelong at her. "But they complement each other, I think."

Reyhan sniffed, swiping at her tears as she gave a little laugh. "Somehow, yes, they do."

They hung the clothes up together, and Nesrin was happy for the bit of reprieve from her heavier thoughts.

But when they finished, Reyhan inadvertently brought them crashing back.

"The Council will be discussing Mizraa and the Blight this afternoon." Reyhan's voice had gone dull. Nesrin's hands curled into fists at her sides. Despair choked out all her other emotions. Even with the generous allowance from the palace, her family would starve with no food available. Were they even receiving the stipend? It would be sent to Bardakci Pasha, and what reason would he have to give it to them? He had never struck her as benevolent.

"Nesrin?" Reyhan said.

She looked at her. "What?"

"I asked if you had thought about what you might say if they wish for you to speak."

"I doubt they would want me to speak again." Nesrin cut her gaze away from Reyhan's. Even if they did wish for her to speak, it was unlikely the Grand Vizier would allow it to go on for too long. Too much risk.

Risk. There was so much, now. Navigating around the many lies she was telling. Protecting her family, herself, and Ihsan. *If you attempt to defy me again, then my only other option is to kill him. And you. Then everyone you love.*

She could no longer stay ignorant; she could not ignore the peril of failing to fit this new role. The many people she had put in harm's way. It did not matter if she was not meant to be this person—there was nothing else to be done.

"We have some time." She pointed to the stack of Vizier profiles. "Help me study."

Nesrin's hand tightened on Ihsan's arm. He responded with a squeeze of his. They entered the Council Hall together like that, arm in arm. It was a world removed from the first, and even the second time she had attended the Council Hall. She had been alone, then. Frightened. Overwhelmed.

She was still the latter two.

Was she alone? Ihsan was beside her. There was…care between them. Something fragile, and new. Something she wanted to nurture, to tend to. But knew she should not. When she cast a furtive look at him, trying not to turn her head in the process, the corner of his mouth ticked up in acknowledgment. Nesrin immediately cast her gaze forward again. It was too easy to think of more kisses. More moments of him as she thought he might have once been. Thoughtful, and sweet.

Ihsan strode forward over the tiles, Nesrin keeping pace and counting the patterns as she did, though she needn't have. Ihsan guided her, giving subtle signals with his body for when she should stop, and they bowed together. It was proof of something she already knew. People were not meant to walk alone. The give and take of knowledge, confidence, joy, and sorrow were vital to every soul.

The Princess Sultana sat on the dais where Ihsan had when Nesrin previously attended the hall. Her clothes and hair were in perfect order, her expression smooth and emotionless.

This close, Nesrin could see the exhaustion dulling the Sultana's eyes, the layers of grief. *Do not let them see you care.* She knew what it was like to have to bear through with the day-to-day while shouldering grief. But not the way the Sultana did. Not when that day-to-day was the weight of an entire country, its people, a war, a father near death. Navigating a relationship with a Grand Vizier who was so obviously an enemy but who had so much political shielding, he was nigh untouchable. That the woman could sit there and look even a fraction as put-together and capable as she did awed Nesrin. This was not the silly, young, fluff-headed princess the old men in Mizraa imagined. That she had imagined.

This was a Queen.

They straightened together and Ihsan led her to the bench to the left of the dais. He sat closest to Naime, and Nesrin beside him. Viziers arrived in a trickle after them, murmuring as they took their seats. The mood in the room was less combative than the last time she had attended, when she had so thoroughly botched her performance. Was that all it was? A performance? It felt that way. Her entire life was a performance, now. Instead of earning coins, she earned safety.

For herself, for her family. She glanced at Ihsan once more. Safety for everyone she cared for.

The murmurs continued as others entered and found their seats. Nesrin thought of the map Reyhan had drawn for her. Of the names and titles carefully inked into each space. There was Yavuz Pasha, Governor of the Northern valley. Rival to Balik Pasha, who governed from most of what lay north of Narfour. Nesrin fiddled with the beading on her entari as she scanned the faces and named those she could. But her attention strayed repeatedly to Enver Balik. Nearly twice her age, rotund with the indulgence of wealth and the softening of age. What if he had not rejected her? What if she were sitting beside him, instead of Ihsan? Would he even have allowed her to attend? Reflexively, she reached for Ihsan's hand. Perhaps she should not have.

He turned his hand over, lacing his fingers between hers. The touch was noted by others in speculative whispers and a few dismissive chuckles. Embarrassed, Nesrin tugged to free her hand but Ihsan tightened his grip and lifted her hand to press his lips against her knuckles, the ice in the gaze he cast around the room as loud as any proclamation.

The Viziers quieted, gazes flicking away from Ihsan's. Nesrin could not help but look to Naime, wondering. The Princess Sultana watched with a whisper of a smile, eyes just beginning to tighten at the edges with a true smile. Was there a world where they could be friends? Or allies at the least.

Nesrin's heart squeezed as Ihsan lowered her hand back to his knee, still entwined in his. When he met her eyes, she beamed, and the severity of his mien softened. He held her gaze a moment more, until Behram Kadir tapped his staff against the tiles to draw attention. When he looked away, Nesrin felt set adrift but for the anchor of his fingers in hers, the coolness of his palm.

"By now you are all aware that the Blight has reached Mizraa," the Sultana said without preamble. The gravity in her voice, the wisp of airy magic that pressed the words into everyone's skin, silenced the hall. The Sultana did not need to elaborate what that would mean. Within a handful of small turns, there would be no food sources in Tamar. They would be completely dependent on trade with Menei. With the Sultan's wealth turned toward the war in Sarkum, and the looming Republic forces, they had very little to trade with.

Nesrin thought of her family. Of their neighbors, of all of Mizraa. How desperate they had been before the Blight had arrived in Mizraa. How long could they last? How long would Narfour last? How long before the word spread to the people in the city, and in their panic, they attacked each other, and the refugees?

"I will require an accounting of each of your governances sooner than I had asked for at the beginning of the season, so we may assess how to best distribute—"

She was cut off by outcries from several of the Viziers, some launching from their seats to stand. Nesrin could not put the shouts to faces; everything mingled together in chaos. The Sultana drummed the fingers of her right hand on the arm of her seat, her expression showing nothing of whatever she thought of the interruption. Beside Nesrin, Ihsan's fingers flexed, his whole body tensing to stand, but the Sultana gave the tiniest shake of her head, though she did not look at them. Ihsan relaxed, breathing a curse.

"Are they always so disrespectful?" Nesrin leaned close to whisper.

"Only on six days of the small turn," Ihsan murmured back, his face irritated despite the jest. Nesrin did not have it in her to smile either. Circumstances were dire enough without them turning against the Sultana, who appeared to be the only level head in the room at the moment.

Nesrin cast a look at the Grand Vizier. He, too, watched the outburst, but his silence was more obviously calculating than the Sultana's.

"Gentlemen," the Sultana said, with a more forceful push of magic in her voice, "when there is silence, we may work on a solution."

"Solution?" someone choked. Nesrin looked in that direction but could not pick the speaker from a cluster of flustered Viziers across the aisle from her. Again she named them in her head, based on the seats where each stood. Each controlled small areas near Narfour. The Viziers who controlled the Northern valley, Yavuz, Dogan and Balik Pashas, were silent. Yavuz Pasha respectfully so, Balik sitting as though forced to, red-faced, and glaring. Dogan Pasha's attention was fixed on the Grand Vizier. "What solution is there to the circumstances *you* have brought upon us?"

Nesrin was able to pinpoint the speaker then. She could not remember his name but knew that he controlled a narrow governance north of Narfour, alongside Balik Pasha's much larger holdings. Stuck between Balik Pasha and the coastline, his land had little to offer in the way of cultivation of necessary foodstuffs. Olives were his main contribution, Nesrin thought. She despaired of how much there was to remember. How her memory was already ejecting bits and pieces that had been clear when Reyhan was drilling her.

"This is clearly the work of destruction mages, whom you have let into Tamar," a man behind him shouted. Ihsan clicked his tongue, and when Nesrin turned to look at him, her gaze caught on the Grand Vizier instead, and a smirk disappeared from his face. He caught her looking, and held her stare, one eyebrow lifting. The arrogance of the challenge, the way he bled confidence from every pore, made fury wind up her spine and around her throat. And the answering fire in his eyes made her shrink in fear.

Nesrin had never hated anyone. Disliked, certainly. But never this. This coiled tension. This ugly, angry, violent repulsion. She had never felt it a day of her life. But it consumed her now. Spreading from her core to her limbs, blossoming as heat in her skin and teeth and eyes.

Like she was burning from the inside out. It stretched and pushed as though trying to break free of her body.

Someone snapped a challenge at the Vizier who had levered blame on the Sultana. Others rose in defense of both, their prattle becoming insults and shouted incriminations.

The Grand Vizier smiled as he watched Nesrin, as if he could see her struggle and wished to provoke her more. What could she do after all? She was his, leashed and muzzled. The noise and voices around her became a buzz, a synchronized movement of sound like a cordon of starlings, shifting in unison through her awareness. Swooping once in favor of the Sultana, and back, swinging to repudiation.

Nesrin's hate wound tighter and tighter, fed by the look in the Grand Vizier's fervent gaze. And it seemed to her that if she opened her mouth, it would pour forth, made physical. Wheel, if she could choke him with it, she would. The scar around her body ached and crawled, itched as if it would peel away from her in one piece.

Vaguely, Nesrin was aware that the Viziers had lost control, were nearly to the point of physical brawling, and that the Sultana was on her feet. Ihsan rose, the air around him and Nesrin plummeting in temperature. Her next exhale was frosty. Ice shot away from Ihsan in ragged lines, and he staggered a step forward with a grunt. The men shouting at each other suddenly cried out in fear as that ice climbed their legs and froze benches. A vase on the far side of the hall shattered, the sound so loud in the cavernous room that it silenced everyone.

"Enough!" the Sultana said, her voice made a klaxon by her magic, so loud it left Nesrin's ears ringing. Naime's dark eyes flared in surprise, her mouth closing abruptly. Then she turned her appalled gaze on Ihsan. He shook his head, closing his hands into fists. The magic scintillating on his skin winked out, and the ice melted.

For a moment, all Nesrin could hear was the echo of buzzing voices in her ears. She had stood, but did not remember when, and her head was pounding. She sat abruptly, dizzy. Ihsan lowered himself beside her, though the Sultana remained standing.

Wheel, she was suddenly so tired. She could barely think.

"This outrageous behavior will solve nothing. We need plans, not recriminations."

"And what of Bardakci Pasha? Why have you not called him to the Council? Where are his reports?" Balik Pasha asked, though the tenor of his voice told Nesrin he was shaken by Ihsan's display of power. Nesrin touched Ihsan's elbow. He glanced at her. His confusion was plain on his face. He had not meant to exert that much force. That is what he had meant by it being erratic.

"I have already drafted a summons for him," the Sultana said, as she sat down once more. "It will go out today."

"Is summoning him away from his duties, now, when they are more important than ever, the wisest choice, Efendim?" Behram Kadir suggested, his expression devoid of any hint of the many lies he was attempting to preserve. If looking at him did not make her so furious, she might have admired his ability.

"Then his daughter should be able to speak to the condition of Mizraa, should she not?" Balik Pasha said. Kadir turned a scathing look on him, and the man closed his mouth and dropped his gaze. Dread dried Nesrin's mouth but made her palms clammy. When the Sultana looked to her, Nesrin thought she might faint backwards off the bench.

"What can you tell us of the state of affairs in Mizraa?" Her steady voice was Nesrin's lifeline, and she clung to it as she stood. All Reyhan's lessons and admonishments tumbled into chaos in her mind as the entire room stared at her. Nesrin folded her hands in front of her and released a breath, which loosened her shoulders. This was something she knew, as well as she knew herself. She was the daughter of Temel Irmak.

Fiery razors of pain shredded up her arm, and it was all she could do to hold herself steady and silent.

Her vision swam and she could not help but look at Behram. The full force of his attention was on her. All his threats burned in his eyes, turning her stomach to lead. The ring and bracelet itched on her skin, as though their spells were spurred by their master's focus. But all she had to do was speak about crops. She needn't say anything that would engage the enchantments or make anyone suspect her. Or put anyone she loved in danger.

When Nesrin spoke, her voice tremored. "There was no Blight when I left Mizraa." She wanted to close her eyes to ward off the antagonistic stares. The expressions that suggested she had nothing of import to say. The taunting silence. What did they want to hear? Platitudes? Lies? They seemed to devour the ones Behram told them. Should she tell them more?

Her own breaths were loud in her ears, drowning out the susurrations of the men around her.

"So you said. Or perhaps you did not notice its encroachment," said a Vizier who she could not place by name or remember where he governed. The man beside him scoffed in agreement.

"No," Nesrin blurted. Embarrassment singed her neck and cheeks.

The same Vizier, whose small eyes against his broad face gave him a porcine countenance, shook his head and waved a patronizing hand. "This is pointless. She has nothing to tell us. I certainly would not trust my daughters to give a proper accounting of my estate." There were quiet laughs of agreement.

"No," Nesrin repeated, her anger giving her voice more power. "Mizraa was my home. I know every corner of it. Every field, every orchard, every stream and wildflower patch. There was no Blight in Mizraa when I left."

"Useless information that means nothing now," he shot back. More agreed with him.

"It means"—*now* her voice echoed around them, so they were forced to listen—"that the Blight arrived after I left. Which also means it is spreading faster. Much faster than it was at the beginning of the Great Turn. It means this winter, you would have had a full season to harvest what you could and salvage the fields. It means you now have a few turns, at most, to do the same." It was both terrifying and exhilarating to stand up to them. "But I'm certain you did not need a woman who spent her whole life on the estate to tell you that," she added.

"Let us keep ourselves civil," Behram said, with a tap of his staff against the tiles. The sound startled Nesrin out of her temper and she sat. She fumed. She had been no less civil than the Viziers.

"What might be salvageable?" the Sultana asked.

Nesrin curled her hands together, then apart as she thought. "The winter wheat would not be dry enough to harvest for storage yet." She thought of her father, how he would calmly face the dire circumstances, thinking of ways to save as many as he could. "But we needn't worry about storing any with so much shortage. It will likely be consumed right away if it is rationed out." She looked at the Sultana. "There were a dozen fields planted. And a dozen more just set with summer crops."

Naime offered Nesrin a tip of her head in acknowledgment, her mouth barely suggesting a smile of approval. "Is there any chance the new crops will mature?"

"If the Wheel is turning miracles," Nesrin said. The Sultana shifted, her lips pressing together as she surveyed the room.

"Your reports of stores still available in your holdings will be compiled for the Sehzade. All arable land is to be converted to the purpose of crops. All Viziers with holdings in Narfour will turn their attention to trade assets and connections. They will also provide reports on stores they have, as well as fishing assets. If you have ships not currently engaged, consider whether they might be refitted."

"Refitted?" The man who scoffed was thin as a stalk of wheat, with prominent teeth that put Nesrin in mind of a rat. "You cannot mean for merchant galleys to be used as fishing vessels?"

"I mean to feed the people of Tamar by whatever means we can muster," the Sultana replied.

He blundered forward, deaf to her marble mask and harsh tone. "That is your solution? Why not pull what stores are left in the villages into Narfour? Are there not stores in Mizraa already, to be shipped?" He turned from the Sultana to Nesrin. It took her a heartbeat to realize he expected her to answer.

There were stores. But they were what was left of the rations for her village. Her family.

"Tell me"—Nesrin stood again, filled with a strange, sizzling energy she wished she could hurl out at them—"how you mean to harvest the wheat when the workers are dead from hunger? Who will drive the wagons to deliver it? You, Pasha? And what will you do when there is nothing but cadavers left to pour your wine?"

Behind her, Reyhan drew in a hissing breath, but that was her only reaction, and Nesrin could not bring herself to look at Ihsan, though he seemed relaxed, not angry.

The rat-faced Vizier drew up in astonishment, glancing around him as his companions muttered and chuckled in discomfort. "That is enough, Mistress Bardakci," Behram ordered. "You will address this Council with the respect it is due," and the open warning in his face only angered her more.

"You want solutions that deprive you of nothing, but those no longer exist. You cannot sacrifice the men and women who break their backs to give you ease without dooming yourselves, and Tamar." Nesrin tried to keep her face neutral, instead of letting it twist up in disgust, but by the answering expressions of anger on theirs, she had not succeeded. The ring and bracelet were hot in warning, as she edged too close to the chasm that separated her from them. Peasant, and noble. The truth of who and what she was. "You are supposed to govern the people. Not starve them to save yourselves. You should be ashamed."

"That is *enough*." Behram slammed the staff on the tiles, the crack like the sound of a whip.

The other Vizier, emboldened by Behram's outburst, shot to his feet. "How dare you speak to me like that, you b—"

"Have a care how you address my consort, Pasha." Ihsan's voice was as cold and hard as deep winter ice, as dangerous as Nesrin had ever heard him. "And you, Grand Vizier." He stared across the aisle, the two men's gazes meeting like crossed swords. "If the truth she speaks is too difficult for you to hear, then perhaps you do not belong in Council."

My consort. The words were cold from his lips, but warm in her heart. He had not spoken loudly, but the hall fell silent, nonetheless.

"The princess consort is correct," Naime said, meeting Nesrin's startled stare with a smile that felt like an anointing. "We will not starve the many to save the few. Yavuz, Dogan, and Balik Pasha, I require an updated account of your stores."

"Forgive me, Efendim, but would it not be more expedient, and more likely to succeed, if you recalled the armies?" The Grand Vizier masterfully applied a respectful tone to words of mutiny. "It is the war that had drained us of food and supplies that might have sustained us through this Blight. A Blight that I remind you *came* from Sarkum. Whom you invited into Tamar."

A hush muffled the room, the tension in every body pulling the air tight.

"Grand Vizier," the Sultana said, smooth as silk, "perhaps you were unaware that men require food, whether they are at war, or at home. So, I do not see how your suggestion solves the problem of impending starvation."

The Grand Vizier smiled as though she were a child, but the Sultana continued on even as he opened his mouth to respond. "The Sehzade will travel with Mistress Bardakci to Mizraa to accomplish an accounting."

"I have already dispatched men to do so in my holdings, Efendim," Yavuz Pasha said. Nesrin barely heard him. If Ihsan went to Mizraa… could she make him understand what was happening? Her family would not know all the lies she was keeping, surely, and would reveal her.

But her hope withered when she looked at Behram. His expression was as placid as the Sultana's. But Nesrin saw the same threat in his gaze now that had accompanied his words when he'd promised her the consequences of revealing herself.

"I can leave by tomorrow," Ihsan said.

Behram's glare bore into Nesrin. Mechanically, her conscience buzzing through her muscles, Nesrin put her hand on Ihsan's arm. When he looked at her, she forced a worried expression. Though she thought it likely came across as sorrowful, since she was very nearly in tears.

"But the trip could take turns," she murmured, "and the Sultan…" Her voice failed at the end. At the vile use of his pain to protect herself. It felt as if she could not breathe. Behram had said marrying Ihsan would be a mercy. But this…this was not mercy. Or kindness. She felt sick.

Ihsan's brow knitted, his pale hazel eyes going hard as he searched her face. The glimmer of mistrust was there. And she wanted to scream for him to listen to it. Instead, she squeezed his arm as though to comfort.

"Forgive me, Sehzade, but I agree with your consort," Behram said, with the most genuine look of concern painted on his face. "Now is not the time for you to leave Narfour. Let someone else shoulder that task. It is merely accounting." He shrugged at the insignificance. As Nesrin watched him expertly implant doubt, it occurred to her that her secrets might not be the only ones he was protecting in Mizraa. Why was Osman Bardakci his creature, as he had put it?

Ihsan looked to the Sultana, whose eyes were sorrowful.

"It is your decision," she said.

"You have neglected another important matter, Efendim," Behram said. The Sultana looked at him as if bracing for a blow. Nesrin might have imagined it, but her complexion seemed to pale a fraction. "There is a rumor"—he grinned regretfully—"that the Agassi has fallen."

Nesrin did not understand, but everyone else did. The hall erupted with voices. They were worse than the gossips in Mizraa, like upset hens, clucking and crowing. Naime's fingers clawed at the bench arms, a tremor crackling through her visage. She blinked away a shimmer in her eyes.

"You were misinformed, Grand Vizier, and I would be interested to know where you heard this rumor?" the Sultana said, her voice nearly as icy as Ihsan's. The cacophony died back. "You do not usually fall prey to gossip."

"A reliable source." He smiled apologetically, and she returned it, stiffly.

"I spoke face to face with the Agassi only a few turns ago, Grand Vizier," Ihsan said. "Are you suggesting he simply disappeared in the intervening time?"

"I am suggesting the man is at war, and war does frequently result in people dying," Behram retorted calmly.

Only because Nesrin was still watching Naime did she see the flinch of the princess's expression.

"Perhaps, a compromise, in light of this rumor." Behram had not noticed Naime's distress, and Nesrin thought that a mercy. "You might consider pulling the armies back to the Engeli, to regroup, and reallocate supplies. After all, you cannot win a war without a general." The condescending look he leveled on her would make any sane woman want to end him.

"If the Agassi falls"—Naime's composure remained, but Nesrin knew, somehow, she was crumbling to pieces beneath it—"I will consider consulting you for military strategy. But until that time, and until I have proof that such a thing has occurred, Rahal Agassi and Elder Attiyeh are my military advisers."

"The armies are a significant drain on our now unreplenishing food supply," Behram continued. There were murmurs of agreement.

"I am aware, Grand Vizier." The Sultana stood. "And you should remember that the Republic has armies converging on the northern border of Sarkum, and a fleet of war galleons constructed and ready to launch into the Sun Sea. We cannot huddle in Narfour and pretend we are invisible. They are coming for us, as I warned you they would."

The ominous words sliced through Nesrin like a blade, severing her from thinking of her own worries. War. In Tamar itself?

Behram drew himself up, readying to speak again, but the Sultana cut him off with a flick of her hand. Flames pulsed and died out in his eyes. "I dismiss all of you to the tasks assigned. As I am provided updates, I will share them." She gave no one else a chance to speak, but descended from the dais and strode toward the doors. Her maids scurried after, Samira in the lead, close at her mistress's heels.

Ihsan stood. Nesrin followed suit. Behram watched Nesrin. She felt the heat of his magic. He came down from his place on the dais steps, angling toward her, but was stopped by Doruk Caliskan dashing to his side.

Nesrin followed Ihsan, though she wanted to bolt from the hall. From all of them.

Thirty-Seven

Naime stood, paced to the window, then returned to her chair. Ihsan sat with his own thoughts, though they seemed to return again and again to Nesrin. To the way Kadir had stared at her. Her hand on his arm had been warm, but her words had caused fissures in his magic. Lies. In her eyes, rounded and worried. Lie. He gritted his teeth and waited for Naime to say something that would convince him he was paranoid. Inventing enemies where there were none. Not her. Not Nesrin. He needed her to be who she seemed. To be kind. He needed it so much that it ached to even consider any other truth.

"He's protecting something," Naime finally said. She stood again, moving to the glass doors to look out at the garden. She clasped her hands tightly in front of her, the tension in her expression pulling Ihsan taut.

"Then I will go to Mizraa." Ihsan started to stand, but Naime turned a commanding look on him. He sank back into his seat on the couch.

"He was also right. You cannot leave now." Her throat worked, a sheen coming over her eyes, and she turned her head away. When she spoke again her voice labored around controlled tears. "The Wheel slows for my father with every breath. You must go see him, or I am afraid you will lose your chance." Her voice was as kind as she could make it, but there was also recrimination.

It was deserved. And she was right that Ihsan should see him. But he did not know if there were enough pieces left of his heart to bear seeing Omar half swallowed by the void. Not him. Whose strong shoulders had held Ihsan high enough to pick the best figs from the tree. Whose firm, gentle voice had led him through lessons of magic and life. Whose care had been there when his own father's was not.

Omar was all Ihsan had left of his stolen childhood. To accept that he was leaving… Ihsan felt set adrift in a vast sea of pointlessness. He wanted to say, *I cannot. I am afraid. Afraid the only parent I have left does not know me.*

But he was a grown man, and Naime was losing Omar too, her actual father. So, he said nothing. Naime stared at him, as though her will alone would make him rise and walk through the doors to Omar's bedroom. His death bed. He had not risen since his trip to the library. Had barely spoken. Except to sometimes murmur an imagined conversation with Dilay.

A lance of pain pierced Ihsan's heart, and he turned his face away from his cousin.

"San." The coaxing in her voice was too much.

"What do you wish to do about Kadir? You cannot let him choose who to send."

"Perhaps I can persuade Mutar Charah," Naime said. Her vexed expression meant he had not ended the previous conversation with the subject change.

"He'll never agree to let her go. He hates her almost as much as I hate him."

"I'll have to outmaneuver him." She sounded as tired as a swordsman returning to the battlefield. Which was not far from the truth. Kadir was wearing her down, aided by her father's wasting death, her city's descent into civil unrest, and a war turning in favor of the enemy. And the fear for Makram she could not hide from Ihsan. They'd heard nothing more from Sarkum, and he could only imagine the burden of anxiousness she bore. "I only need frame it as an issue for the Merchant Guild."

"But even they are split in their loyalty." This would be easily solved if Amara were willing to turn the considerable force of her magic on Kadir. But not only was that illegal and likely to spark a civil war, magic in opposition was tricky. Kadir would be able to null her power, even if it cost him dearly. Ihsan briefly entertained the idea of Kadir as a puppet of Amara's, but it disturbed him as much as it pleased him. "Yavuz Pasha could send some of his men to do an accounting. It would make sense if we simultaneously called for an audit of his own holdings."

Naime tipped her head. "I need to consider." She regarded him, and he wanted nothing more than to escape. He could not take another lecture, not when he already knew she was right. "San, there is something between Kadir and your betrothed. I cannot name it, or guess at its nature—"

"I know." The admittal cut open the bruised place on his ego. "I'll be here tonight, if you need me." He stood, turning his back on her and the rebuke in her eyes and ready on her lips. Her softly huffed exhale was her only answer.

When his hand closed on the handle of the door to the garden, she spoke again. "Be careful, San."

He had meant to return to the city. Instead, he stood by the fig tree, listening. At the far end of the garden, the doors to his suite were open to the evening air. Laughter and voices drifted to him. He recognized the rhythm of Nesrin's, and the tick of fire in Reyhan's.

That was an odd sensation, looping in coils around his chest, a wish, a hope, that the sound and feeling might become normal for him. Mundane. She had a knack for that. For hope.

Hope that he might not be doomed to isolation all his life. Hope that there were still people in the world who were kind, and giving, and that those acts were as contagious as the Blight.

The incessant chittering of a flock of birds broke him from his thoughts and he looked up. They were massed in the branches of the fig, darting and picking at whatever insects must have taken up residence in the tree's bones. There were more birds than he had seen in Turns. They were everywhere he looked, lately. More bees too. Their hum filled the cracks in every hush, everywhere he went.

Strange. Sometimes the weather of a winter changed the hatch rates of creatures. But this Turn was the most fertile he could ever recall. He'd even seen servants frequently chasing snakes out of the palace, which had been a rare occurrence before. They tended not to congregate in places so busy with traffic. An odd counterbalance to the Blight. But perhaps that was exactly what it was, the Wheel's attempt to balance the destruction.

The grass was greener and taller than usual for this early in the summer, and plants were blooming already. Nesrin must appreciate that, reminders of the rural home she missed. She did not speak of it often, but he could see how it hurt her, how she struggled to fit in to this mold demanded of her. At least she was trying. Could he say the same?

On a whim, he stepped out of his shoes. The grass tickled his skin. He stared down at his feet. What did she get from this? He did not feel immediately more grounded or connected to the earth. But that could just be a trick of his affinity. Perhaps voids more easily resonated a bit with each element, since they did not harmonize strongly with one, as a mage did.

"Dear oh dear"—Cemil's voice danced with edged humor—"what has that little country mouse done to our Ice Prince?"

What small peace had started in him was strangled immediately at the sound of Cemil's singsong. Ihsan turned his gaze sideways and up, to where Cemil stood framed by one of a line of arches along the outer edge of the far walkway. If he had been there long, he would have had to be purposely damping his fire, or Ihsan would have sensed him.

Ihsan dropped his gaze to the grass, contemplating whether he wanted to scurry back into his shoes. But this weakness was already revealed, so what did it matter? What vexed him most was that Cemil was able to get into the Sultan's garden at all. It was closed off and guarded at most entries. Except, of course, Cemil had been playing in the palace since he was a child, alongside Naime, Samira, and Ihsan, and knew as many secret halls and corridors as they did.

There was a pull, deep in his heart, to miss his friend. To miss the closeness that he had not had with anyone else since the fire. To have someone other than Naime to trust. But he could never trust Cemil again.

"I can have the guards escort you out of the garden, or you can find your own way." Ihsan stepped toward him. "Now."

"So prickly," Cemil admonished. He did not move to leave, or come closer, and they stood, not looking at each other, in silence. Like two ibex with horns locked, stalemated on how to break apart only to attack again.

Cemil managed first. "I never thought I would see the day you actually fell for someone."

No. Ihsan had always tried hard to be the exact opposite of his father. Who could not keep his hands, or other parts, to himself. Ihsan scowled at the ground. "Even if that was your business, I am not falling for anyone. We are betrothed. I am fulfilling my duties." The not-quite truth of that was loud and obvious even to his own ears.

Cemil cast his gaze at Ihsan's bare feet. "I see. Your duties seem quite friendly?" He tipped his head toward the sound of laughter coming from Ihsan's suite. "But we both know you never had much sense in choosing your friends."

Ihsan flicked his gaze up to meet Cemil's challenge. He could not interpret the stiff smile and hard look in Cemil's gold eyes. "Last warning, Master Kadir. You are not welcome here."

"I was reminded recently of that time you stole the figs off my father's desk, do you remember?"

Ihsan snorted. They'd been young. Maybe a dozen Turns. Kadir had said something in passing that Ihsan did not recall, he only remembered his anger. And in his child's brain, the greatest revenge he could come up with was to steal a handful of fruit off Kadir's desk.

"They turned out to be mealy on the inside," Ihsan recalled. Then frowned. "What made you think of that?"

Cemil shrugged, with a half-smile. "Nothing in particular. Occasionally I wonder if you learned your lesson about taking things from my father, and outward appearances." His features hardened, fire flared in his eyes as they half closed, and he turned away.

Ihsan stared at his back until he rounded a corner at the far end of the garden. He'd stopped making sense Turns ago. Between drunkenness and speaking in nonsense riddles to mock people. Ihsan thought he would be accustomed to it by now, but it still rankled. Was he telling him not to cross Kadir?

Cemil knew he did not need that warning, surely.

Ihsan bent to retrieve his shoes, and when he straightened, Nesrin was standing on the patio outside his suite, one hand on the doorframe.

He strode toward her, at a speed that made her expression tighten in apprehension. When he reached her, he dropped the shoes and pulled her into an embrace.

For an instant she was stiff, surprised, then she relaxed into him, her hands lifting to cradle his head into the slope of her neck. The way she fit in his arms, the way she gave herself fully into any contact. She was something. More grounding, more settling, than anything else he could imagine. Like an anchor into his own body.

She didn't say anything, only stroked her fingers through his hair. Her openness was her magic. Her heart…her sweetness…were more powerful than he would ever have given such things credit for. She was hope, when he held her. Hope that loss was not all he would ever feel. That he could feel other things, that he was worthy of other things. His doubts about her, about her intentions, never survived her embrace.

"You're sad," she observed. "Can I help?"

"You are," he mumbled into the warm skin of her neck. She flinched as it tickled her.

"Are you hungry?"

He took an experimental nibble of her skin, grazing lightly with his teeth. She made a little sound of pleasure, her fingers curling in his hair. Then she forced his head to turn toward the doors. Kuhzey, Reyhan, and Deniz knelt on cushions at the low table, gawking.

"Dinner is here," Nesrin whispered, with a lilt of laughter in her voice.

"Did you make it?" he teased.

She clicked her tongue. "I can make you dinner tomorrow."

Tomorrow. A pang for the idea of that, of something easy and simple. Amidst everything else, all that threatened to unravel. He needed the reprieve of simplicity.

Ihsan let her lead him inside.

Thirty-Eight

"No," Reyhan corrected, again.

Nesrin closed her eyes, trying to will away the urge to throw her trowel down in frustration. "Then it is Caliskan Pasha," she tried again.

"Yes." Reyhan paced away, shuffling through the papers she held, then drew another. "And?" She turned back.

Nesrin shoveled a bit more dirt into the pot that she steadied between her knees. She sat on the front steps of Ihsan's city house, working on the neglected rose that bothered her every time she entered. She'd come to fulfill her promise to make Ihsan dinner, but the drooping rose had seemed like a project that would take her mind off of everything else.

She set the trowel down and picked up a pair of snips. "He sits in the"—she squinted as she visualized the side of the room across from her seat in the Council Hall—"third bench, fourth seat, middle row."

People passed by on the street, only a few taking notice of the two of them. At the top of the hill, a boisterous group of young noblewomen laughed and gossiped, ambling toward them. Everyone gave them wide berth, bowing as they passed.

"Yes," Reyhan said, bringing Nesrin back to her tasks. Reyhan lowered the entire stack with a snap against her thighs to glare at Nesrin. "You know this well enough. We should work on political alliances, or trade agreements."

"Or." Nesrin sat as she swung the trowel up and pointed to the west, slinging dirt that scattered over Reyhan's shoes. "I could walk into the sea and not have to worry about any of this."

Reyhan shook one foot, then the other to dislodge the dirt. "I will remind you that it is *you* with the sudden interest in learning your duties."

Nesrin pressed the heel of her palm to her brow, then remembered how dirty her hands were. As she lowered her hand to look, a burst of feminine laughter snapped her attention to the street. The noblewomen, five of them, were passing by. She recognized two from her betrothal ceremony, candidates to marry Ihsan.

Every single one wore a tiraz marking them a mage, so Nesrin set her trowel down and stood, bowing to them. When she rose, she smiled, but they were looking at her in disdain. One whispered something, and they burst into laughter. For a moment, shame wound in her belly. But her mother had told her that the best way to disarm a potential enemy was kindness.

"Would you like a flower?" Nesrin asked Hazal Yavuz, who was closest to her, who had not joined in the whispering. The younger woman's eyes flared in surprise, then she smiled shyly and broke away from the group. Nesrin snipped one of the healthier blooms from the rose and held it out. "Hazal, yes?" Nesrin said. The girl nodded. Behind her, the others had stopped, laughing expressions fading. "We should have tea, sometime." Nesrin swiped a loose hair from her face. "I hardly know anyone here."

A fleeting wince of shame flashed over the woman's mien, then she smiled. "I would like that."

"Here," Nesrin said, breaking the thorns off the stem, "now it is harmless."

Hazal gave a soft, resigned laugh, and nodded as she took the bloom. "Thank you, Princess Consort."

Nesrin startled at the title, but recovered quickly, and when Hazal returned to the group, Nesrin clipped and held out another bloom. One by one they came forward to accept. All but Ekim Bahar, whose father had called Nesrin backbred at the betrothal ceremony. The two of them met gazes. Ekim's was hard and hostile. She pressed her lips into a line, dropping a disdainful glance up and down the length of Nesrin. "You'll have no blooms left and just a bedraggled, empty plant."

It would have been easy to snipe back. Ekim was an easy target. But Nesrin knew where that path led. And she had enough enemies already. "Roses are like people, they give back what they are given. If I give it care, it returns the kindness with beauty."

"Oh? You think all people give back? What of the Sarkum thieves up in the camp? What are they giving back for the coin you stole from the coffers to feed them?"

The ferocity of Ekim's belief in her own words left Nesrin momentarily stunned.

"Ekim," one of her companions chided, "now is not the time."

Ekim ignored her. "You, and sympathizers like you, that steal from hardworking men like my father, make me sick." Ekim stalked away. The others hesitated, then followed, heads down. A small swarm of servants hurried behind.

Something wet struck the stones at Nesrin's feet. When she looked up in confusion, she saw a man dressed as a steward, mouth in a sneer. He had spit at her.

Reyhan was quicker. "How dare—"

She was interrupted by a shriek from behind them. Deniz was a streak of movement down the steps, knocking Nesrin sideways. She smashed into the steward like a charging ram.

"Did you just *spit* at the princess consort?" she howled, hands balled into fistfuls of her apron and caftan. When the man glowered at her, Deniz produced a wooden spoon from her apron pocket and brandished it.

Reyhan dashed forward, grabbing Deniz's arm and hauling the woman back.

"Your mistress is more concerned about outsiders than she is her own people!" the steward shouted.

"Enough," Ekim snapped at him as she marched back toward them. "You'll be relieved of your position for this kind of public display." With an expression like it caused her physical pain, she bowed to Nesrin. "Forgive me, I would never condone such behavior."

Nesrin shook her head, unable to speak. She hid her trembling hands by clasping them together and forcing a stiff smile. She made herself stand there until the group had faded into the crowd at the bottom of the hill, and the rest of the people on the street had gone about their business. Then she spun, without looking or speaking to Deniz or Reyhan, and fled inside.

WHEN IHSAN RETURNED TO THE house after a day receiving and organizing accounts of food stocks, Deniz leapt up from the common room couch like a lion in wait, ambushing him the moment he walked in.

There wasn't any patience left in him to give anything, even the appearance of being held together and fine for her or anyone else. He wanted solitude.

No, not solitude. He wanted Nesrin. He wanted the way he felt when she was near. She had a knack for quiet company when it was needed.

"You tell that vile Vizier that his daughter and her servants are no better than wild animals!" Deniz demanded, her usually sullen face animated and red-cheeked. He regarded her dispassionately as he yanked at the buttons of his entari, the light of the setting sun bleeding too much fire into the room for his peace of mind.

"Could you be more precise?"

"He spit at her!" Deniz cried. "He should have been beaten in the street for all those busybodies standing around staring to see what happens."

"Deniz," Ihsan growled. "What are you talking about?"

"Some hackneyed, dilapidated old steward that belongs to Ekim Bahar or her father, *spat* at Mistress Bardakci, right there"—she pointed past him toward the front of the house—"in the street."

"What?" Ihsan's fingers stilled, halfway through the buttons.

A knife struck wood with a thunk beyond them in the kitchen. Deniz put her hands on her hips and pointed. "She's been holed up in there since. I've told her she needs to report him to the palace guards, and she refuses. Go talk some sense into her."

Ihsan raised an eyebrow at Deniz's incensed, protective bossiness, but the woman ignored him, spinning around to stomp up the stairs. He finished undoing the buttons of the entari. The idea of someone spitting at Nesrin turned his exhaustion into impotent anger, wishing he had been there. Ekim, like her father, was spineless when she wasn't backstabbing. And he would happily have frozen the steward to the cobbles.

Shrugging out of the entari as he strode between the seats in the common area, he then tossed it over the back of a chair before turning into the dining room. When he took a careful peek into the kitchen, he saw her, standing at the prep table in the center of the room. She wore an apron dusted with flour, and a cloth wrapping her hair, though some curled strands of russet were free. She swiped at one with the back of her wrist and a murmured curse, her hands sticky with flour. Balls of plump dough sat up to one side of the table. She rolled another into a thin log, and deftly braided three together. She tucked the ends and set the loaf aside.

"Are you just going to stare at me?" she bit out.

"I did not wish to interrupt. Or have your ire turn from the dough to me."

Her eyes narrowed a fraction, then she returned to her work.

"Why are you angry?" he said, cautiously approaching. She flicked a look at him.

"Deniz did not tell you? Was she not sitting out there like a vulture, waiting for you to return?"

"That is harsh," Ihsan said. Though it was true, he did not think Nesrin understood that Deniz was angry on her behalf.

"In the valley, people listened to me"—she drove the heel of her palm into one of the chunks of dough—"they trusted me with their loved ones. They did not correct my every move, judge me in every way possible. Start rumors about my body, about me. They did not attack me with whips, spit on me in the street, or yell accusations in my face." Each sentence was accompanied by a violent movement. Grabbing more dough, or slapping it against the table, whipping it into braids.

The declaration took some of the heat out of her. She bent forward to plant her elbows on the table and press the heels of her hands against her eyes.

"I hate the Council. I hate the way they make me feel. I hate the way I let them make me feel. I hate that nothing I do here is correct, that no matter what I do, I anger or offend someone."

"Of course you feel that way," he said, going to her side. She lifted her head, turning to look up at him. "Any sane person would."

"Mizraa was already suffering. People will die." She lowered her hands. "And I am here. Useless. Trimming roses and making bread." She shoved a dough ball away from her as she straightened.

"What would you do there, that you cannot do here?" he asked, staying near the corner of the table instead of sidling up to her. Her slurry of emotions played across her face and in her handling of the bread. Quick, hard anger, slower sorrow. Each a ping within the well of his power, a shimmer of disquiet. She shook her head as she shaped another loaf.

"I would be even more useless there." A sharp smile flitted across her face but was gone the moment he saw it. "At least here I can speak for them." Her brow dipped as she stared at the tidy row of bread. Then, she reached for and set the last of the dough in front of her. Her work was more careful this time.

Ihsan let the meditative sight of her hands at work coax and calm him. Unconsciously he shifted closer, until her right arm brushed his as she moved. Nesrin slid a look at him, bumping her hip against his.

"You want attention, hmm? You're as bad as a cat."

"Am I?" he said. "Maybe you should pet me, then." The words were out before he'd considered them, and he flinched inwardly when she went still. "I did not mean…" He closed his teeth around the rest.

Nesrin wiped her hands on her apron. She drew a towel over the resting loaves and crouched down to a bucket of water beneath the table, where she rinsed her hands without a word. As she rose and dried them by swiping them over the back of her caftan, Ihsan tried to make his thoughts align into some kind of sense. Had he offended her and now she was leaving?

Nesrin crossed the room and rose on tiptoe to pull down a small ceramic jar topped with wax cloth from one of the shelves on the wall. Then she returned. Ihsan put his back to the table, leaning on the edge as she stopped in front of him. She held the jar in her palms between them.

"You reminded me, I made this for you." Her voice was unsteady, her face downturned. "It's a balm, for your scars."

When he would have told her *no thank you*, she hurried on. "I put some things in it so the smell won't trouble you." She held it up, close to his face, her hazel eyes worried, but hopeful. Ihsan forced himself to sniff, braced for the hit of nausea, of panic.

Instead, something warm, cinnamon, and clove, reminded him of the welcoming scents of the kitchen. Of Nesrin, cloaked in the smell of her cooking. The yeast scent of the rising bread intertwined with this new one. He looked at her over the little pot, and she offered a hesitant smile.

"It smells good," he managed, though the simple words did not encompass that it brought her to him. Her smile beamed. He wanted to push her hands aside and draw her close, to bury his face in the curve of her neck and write the feel of her skin alongside the scent of the kitchen. To find the same comfort in this moment that he found sleeping beside her. But he did not move.

Nesrin lowered the pot to the table beside him. He clutched the edge, pressing backward to feel it dig into him, so he did not reach for her. "Would you like to try a little?" She lowered it and her gaze, untying the string and removing the cloth from the top. The salve within was a warm yellow, not the fatty, pale color of the burn salve that still made immediate revulsion overtake him.

This was kindness. Nesrin's kindness. He should at least appear grateful.

He collected the smallest amount he could on a fingertip. "Do not be too disappointed," Ihsan said as he swiped the unctuous mixture along the scarring on his jaw. "The palace doctors have tried everything to make them—" He didn't finish. Palatable? Bearable for others to look upon? They'd done what they could for his comfort, now treatment seemed more aimed at the comfort of others.

Her head lifted, revealing her scrunched brow. "Scars fade or they do not, it is different for everyone. But there are no creams or spells to make it happen. This is not to erase your scars." Nesrin swirled a finger through the salve and held it toward him with a seeking expression. He nodded permission. "I made it to help with the pain, and the itching." She moved a step closer and stroked the salve onto his jaw, too softly, too hesitantly. Petting him.

With a pang of irritation and disappointment at her hesitation, he wrapped his fingers around her wrist to stop her. "You do not have to, if it troubles you."

She stared at him, her face still, but the expression in her eyes changing rapidly from hesitancy to sadness, to consternation. "You're daft. It only troubles me because I know you do not wish to be touched."

"You are the only person I will allow to call me daft," he grumbled, "and only this once." He should have told her he did want to be touched. By her.

"What will my punishment be if I call you daft again?"

"Prison," he said as sternly as he could. She formed her mouth into a little *o*, her eyes widening in mock surprise.

"Then who will you have to pick on?" She waggled the jar of salve in front of his face. He shoved down the urge to grab it from her and pull her to him for the connection he wanted. He loved the teasing, but it was not enough anymore.

"I think it's the other way around," he said as she dabbed a bit more of the medicine on her finger.

"I think you enjoy it." She resumed her work, dabbing and rubbing in a businesslike manner that he wished was something else.

He made a noncommittal noise and tried not to pull away from her as she worked, not very gently, over the skin on his jaw and neck. But she noticed.

"Does it hurt?"

"Sometimes." He tipped his head to the left to give her better access. "Sometimes it is fine, but I never know which it will be. And your bedside manner is lacking."

"Mmm." She dipped her fingers again. The small, firm circles she rubbed into his skin were more rough massage than caress. His muscles relaxed by degrees, his mind emptying of aggravations and thoughts. The smell enveloped him, spices that made him languid.

"Who spit at you?" Ihsan said when she scooped another fingerful of salve. The briefest pause in her movement indicated her hesitation. "If I do not learn it from you, I will learn it from someone else."

"And what will you do?" Nesrin lifted her gaze to his.

"Supply the palace with an ice sculpture for their next celebration," he said, without smiling. It was what he wanted to do, to anyone who would dare do such a thing to her.

Her eyes crinkled as she lifted her hand to swipe a bit of hair away with the back of her wrist. He reached up and tucked it behind her ear. He lingered too long, so he could trace the curve of it. Her lashes fluttered and she dropped her gaze. "A servant of Ekim Bahar's. He claimed I was stealing from Tamar, to give to thieves from Sarkum."

"There are balances in these decisions, hardships that you could not have understood with no training at court." He did not want her to regret her kindness. Or to lose it, to become anything other than what she was. "I can have him punished."

"No," she said, quietly. "Do not go to battle on my behalf. You will only diminish me further in their eyes. I can fight my own battles, if I choose to."

"You want me to stand quietly aside while someone disrespects you, and me?"

"Punishing him will not make him remember their humanity, or mine." She finished applying salve to his jaw and the slope of his neck. She touched her finger to the throat of his caftan, distracting him from the burdensome truth of her words. "More? Or I can leave it for you."

There were walls between them that he did not want there. She was not being honest with him. Embarrassed, he suspected. But also something else. Angry?

"I cannot reach all of them, so it is you, or it is Kuhzey," he said. That was a lie. If she did not want to, then he would leave the rest. He was not going to order Kuhzey to rub him all over with oily salve.

"I'll hand it off to him then, shall I?" The repressed smile on her mouth cried to be kissed away, and certainly eased some of his worry. He released his grip on the table, catching the front of her apron in one hand and flicking open the top loop of his caftan's neck with the other. It was invitation that made his gut twist in apprehension. They had kissed, yet…it all felt so veiled, and uncertain.

He tugged, and she fell against him with a small grunt. He wanted things to be certain. Wanted to cement where they were, and where they were going. Wanted her to let him stand up for her.

Nesrin's shoulders squared, nothing on her face to indicate her mind was anywhere near where his was. "Stop that, you pest," she admonished.

Maybe their physical closeness meant something different to her than it did him. Maybe he was misreading everything, and her kindness and closeness with him was nothing more than that. Ihsan stared at her, drinking in the sight of her knit brow and mouth twisted up in focus. Her touch did not hurt. Was too firm to tickle or set his skin on fire with burning nerves. But when she unhooked the second loop of his caftan, there were nerves.

A pulse crackled down his chest and into his belly.

Her hand flattened to slide beneath the throat of his caftan, to the scars that covered his chest and right shoulder. Her face had softened, her lashes lowered, color rising up her neck and into her cheeks. He loved the russet in her hair and complexion, which allowed him to so easily see her discomposure. "You do not have to," he murmured, though he also wanted to beg her not to stop.

"I know." She lifted her gaze to his, her hand shifting to lay over his heart.

He dipped his head. "I do not want you to feel obligated."

"I know," she said again, setting the jar on the table beside his right hip. She paused, then her hands went to his sides, fingers curling, hesitant, into the fabric of the caftan. She twitched her chin up. His mind blanked, but he crossed his arms and grabbed the fabric in handfuls just above hers. They lifted the caftan free together, and when his arms were still trapped, she rested her hands on the spot between his shoulders and neck. Ihsan yanked the fabric off his arms and tossed it away.

He gripped the table again. Could she feel the hard, erratic beat of his heart? Or see the vibration through his ribs?

She took more salve on her fingers, and began working it down the front of his shoulder, and chest. All he could do was breathe, and watch, and want. They had held each other, tangled and close. But he had been clothed, and there had been peace between them. Not this loaded silence. He did not understand it.

Her work was thorough, and too medicinal to be erotic. But still a charge thickened the air between them. She avoided his eyes, both hands on him now, her thumbs pressing slow, hard circles into the scars. He hissed when she moved over tender places, and she always whispered an apology and moved her work elsewhere. But she slipped too low, her fingers on his ribs making his whole body go rigid as he twitched away with a gasp.

Her hand shifted open, the briefest of soft pets, an apology for the former offending touch as she searched his face. His irritation at the surprise of the tickle died by her stroke. All he could think was that he wanted more of that soft pet, just as she had said. Like a cat.

"I should stop."

He held her to him with a hand over her wrist, and hooked two fingers into her apron tie, pulling her even closer. Her lips parted, as he reached for her other hand and mirrored her touch on his left side.

"Nessa." He dropped his brow to hers, straightening away from the table to bring their bodies together. He cupped her neck and head, thumbs stroking over her cheeks. There was no eloquent way, not for him, to tell her what he wanted. What had started as a curiosity, and now consumed him. Her whispered name sought and gave permission.

Her fingers slotted between his ribs, her palms flattening to him. The responding rush of cold heat made his muscles tighten. Her touch continued, warm fingers drawing parallel lines as she followed the outline of muscles along his stomach. Ice cracked within his mind. His magic waking. A full-body shiver forced a breath from his lungs and prickled his skin. His body came alive for her, his magic shifting like drift ice.

She dipped her head, brushing the length of his nose with the tip of hers, then the same over his left cheekbone, then his right. The proximity of her mouth to his was lightning, the soft trace of her skin seductive and too sweet. Her gaze lifted to his, her lovely eyes wide, searching his face as she touched him.

Her thumbs traced his midline, to just above his navel. It was the barest of caresses, but it held him captive, his entire being focused on the whisper-soft pressure of her thumbs. The house and room and universe disappeared but for him, and her. His skin, and her touch. The only sound the uneven way she inhaled.

"San," she breathed, and he caught the sound with his mouth, his lips closing on her lower one. She gave a muffled mewl that unraveled his gentleness. Her hands slid up his body, leaving trails of raw sensation, and he cinched her to him with handfuls of her caftan. She retreated from the kiss for breath, but returned. First her mouth to his upper lip, then more fully, her teeth grazing him too. The tenderness of it, the way he knew she was teaching herself the feel and shape of him, calmed him. He returned the same slow exploration. Her breath shuddered in the most encouraging way.

He slid his hands down to her hips to pull them tight to his. When his arousal pressed against her, she made another purr that muddled him further. He turned them, putting her between his body and the table. When he bent and hitched her onto the flour-dusted surface, he thought she might protest or balk. Instead she hooked her legs around him and gripped his shoulders, deepening their kiss with a demanding thrust of her tongue.

His magic was too near the surface, testing his hold more than it should have. He was not an inexperienced boy, who could not maintain his control at the slightest physical distraction. What was wrong with him?

She dragged her nails down his back, yanking his worry away from his control. He nearly toppled forward, but caught himself with his hands to either side of her, magic cold and bright on his skin. A rough sound tore from his throat. Her hushed laugh broke their kiss as she drew back enough to meet his gaze. "I have not finished with the salve."

"If you want to put it on all of my scars"—he tugged the tie loose on her apron and tossed it away—"I'll have to take the rest off as well."

Her gaze turned serious. "Is that what you want?"

He thought it was more than obvious what he wanted. "Only if you do." He stroked his hands over her hair, hooking his thumbs into the cloth that bound it and pushing it free. Tangled strands fell around her face and neck. Lustrous russet. "The betrothal does not mean I would take this from you because of obligation." He twined a finger in one loose wave.

"Oh? What if I feel obligated to touch you everywhere? Thoroughly? I would hate to miss a spot." She reached for the salve jar and wiggled it playfully.

He resisted the urge to put her all the way on her back, fighting back a surge of magic and want.

"Get to it, then." He caught her wrists. He pressed her palms to the bare skin of his low belly, just above the waist of his salvar. Her lips were already kiss-swollen and her face bright with color, highlighting the brushstrokes of freckles along her cheeks and neck. When he released his hold on her so he could work the knot of his salvar loose, her fingers dug into his skin in a possessive, eager way he loved. Her teeth pressed into her lower lip, and a tumult of carnal ideas emptied his mind of anything but lust.

She leaned into him, the soft tumble of her hair brushing over his chest as she pressed kisses along his scarred shoulder. Her touch drifted in reticent increments, down, too slow, so he was aware of every fraction gained toward the too-eager ache.

"Nessa," he groaned, his hands closing on her elbows. It took everything in him not to force her hands exactly where he wanted them.

Her husky laugh on his already-too-sensitive skin made his magic a blizzard.

She gave a small shriek at the cold as it encompassed her. The ice frosted her clothes, and hair, then the table. He pressed his face into her neck, nipped her skin, and blew on it. Frost swirled in the path of his breath, and she clung to him as a shudder took her. The frost spread over his skin too, and she traced the whorls with a fingertip along the slope of his neck. A torture he was happy to endure.

"I thought I did not like the cold," she mused, her fingers chasing magic over his skin like a kitten after a feather.

"Are you about to tell me how you wish to live in the Kalspire snowpack for the rest of your days?"

"No." The warmth of her touch melted a thumbprint of frost. "But I would not mind your cold." The shyness of her declaration made bands tighten around his chest. He was afraid of that. Afraid of another person who could be taken from him. Or used against him.

"Brave. I am afraid you are too gentle to live in my cold."

She touched his mouth with three of her fingers. A ripple of tension went through his body, and he clicked his teeth together in warning. She tsked, rolling her eyes, then leaned into him. Then, she bit him, snagged his lip between her teeth. A spear of hot ice shot up his core, igniting his magic again. He caught her jaw, holding her in place, his gaze on hers as he slowly drew back, out of her grip. A raw sound escaped his throat as he did.

"You do not know me well enough to know what I am too gentle to handle," she said. Her gaze was fierce, and her beauty struck him like a blow. He pulled on her hips, grinding her to him just so he could think straight for a moment. She made a little sound that scattered his thoughts, her nails digging into his shoulders.

"You..." He kissed her throat and she let her head fall back into his hand. "...are so beautiful I cannot think straight. Come upstairs with me."

"Why?" she breathed in his ear. "I might be too gentle for whatever you have planned."

He snorted into her neck, and she laughed outright, lighting him inside with joy. That sound was powerful enough to chase away any shadow. "No, Nessa"—he kissed her below the ear, running his hand up the back of her neck and into her hair—"I think you'll be just fine."

"Oh?" Her hands stroked over his body, then her nails. "Such big assumptions."

"Thank you." He caught her behind the knees and pulled as he pressed himself harder into the V of her thighs. Her eyes slid shut, a sound slipping from her throat. "No one has ever complimented my assumptions before."

Her eyes opened as she smiled her patient amusement. Then she dragged her fingers down his chest, and belly, and into the front of his salvar. Anticipation clinched his gut. His power pulsed in time with his heartbeat, and ice frosted the floor when she wrapped her hand around him.

The air siphoned from his lungs, and when she kissed him, stroking his length and tightening her thighs around him, his sense tumbled into void.

"Upstairs?" she murmured. "Not here on the kitchen table in the flour, like a serving girl?"

He coughed a laugh, squeezing his eyes shut then opening them as he searched for coherence.

"If you keep that up," he managed, despite her exploring fingers and laughing eyes, "it will be the latter."

She sniffed haughtily. "I am Consort to a prince." She gave him a firm squeeze with her hand and his head fell into the curve of her shoulder as he groaned. "A clean table, at least."

"I'll compromise." He hitched her up, slinging his arms under her backside. She wrapped her arms around his neck. "The floor."

She broke into more giggles and squealed when he acted as though he would, in fact, lower her to the frost-covered floor, clinging with arms and legs that nearly choked him.

"They've betrothed me to a monkey," Ihsan said as he straightened, and she laughed harder, filling him with sweet elation he had not felt in a decade. It only slightly diminished at the pounding knock that interrupted from the front of the house.

Ihsan let Nesrin down, steadying her until her feet were set. Deniz called an impatient order to wait, and continued mumbling as she descended the stairs and marched to the door to answer it. Ihsan glanced at Nesrin, holding tightly to her waist when she tensed as if she would pull away.

"I am not finished with you," he admonished.

Her reply cut off when Deniz ran into the room, her face scrunched, her hands over her heart. Bashir arrived behind her.

The fact that Bashir did not even seem to notice Ihsan's state of undress, or anything else, for that matter, drowned Ihsan's joy in panic.

"Come now," Bashir said, his voice raw, "Efendim."

Thirty-Nine

They walked when he would have given anything to fly. To careen through the halls as fast as he had ever gone. But they could not. His heart leapt ahead, into the chamber with the bed so big that four of them as children had been able to jump on it at once. To the man who was father, and teacher, and Sultan. It did not help his own composure that Bashir was barely holding together his. His expression was set in stone, but that stone included a furrowed brow and hard-set mouth.

Nesrin kept pace with them despite their long strides. She was still flour-stained and mussed. The oddness of her appearance served as a kind of shield, drawing all the curious looks and whispered comments. He would spare thoughts for her discomfiture when he could, but was grateful no one noticed him or Bashir, and perhaps could not guess at what caused their urgency.

There were no more guards than usual outside Omar's suite, but a melee within. They crossed through the invisible wall of a dampening spell, which Bashir took over when they entered, freeing up the other mage who had held it in his absence. Protecting the Sultan's secret.

Nearly all the palace physicians and assistants crowded the outer suite. Body heat made the room into an oven, immediately ratcheting Ihsan's pulse. It took everything in him not to yell for them to disperse. They all tried to bow when Ihsan entered but had to shift and rearrange themselves and their tasks to make room for him to charge through to Omar's room.

It was quieter inside the bedroom, and darker, with only a few mage orbs glowing above his uncle's bed. Ceylik was there, with Havva beside him. Naime knelt on the bed beside her father, her hands on his chest, her power a bright whirlwind around her. Tears trickled down her cheeks. Samira sat beside her, with a glass of water in her hands. Sparks glittered in her hair, but when she saw Ihsan, they extinguished.

Ceylik counted a rhythm, and Ihsan understood that Naime was forcing the Sultan to breathe, and why she had not summoned him with her power. He nearly went to his knees. Nesrin's arms came around him, stronger than she looked, whispering to him. "Come," she said, "come on." She supported him until they were at the bed. Havva put her hands on his shoulders as he knelt.

"Baba," Naime pleaded. Her voice was strained with her effort to work a complicated spell to someone else's rhythm while her grief drained her energy and concentration.

"His heart beats weakly, but only while the Princess Sultana breathes for him," Havva said in Ihsan's ear. Havva's tone said more than her words.

Ihsan barely registered the strong timbre of Nesrin's voice as she murmured to Havva, asking what she could do to assist. He took Omar's hand between his own. When he was a child, he had thought it most closely resembled a bear's paw. Easily encompassing his. Strong, and broad. Enough to hold up everyone he cared for. Enough to hold up a nation.

It was frail and cold in Ihsan's now. He cradled it like a broken bird, his grief welling, a tide swelling within him until he was no longer large enough to hold it. The mage lamps extinguished as his magic took him over. Naime glowed, enough light for them to see by, like pale morning sun at dawn. His own power shimmered glacial blue alongside hers.

"Amca," Ihsan whispered, holding the cold of his power around his own body. *Not yet.* Omar's face was relaxed, as if he only slept, instead of hovering on the precipice of the void.

Nesrin sat near the head of the bed, one hip on the mattress, and laid her palm on the Sultan's brow. Havva leaned in to whisper in her ear. Rage swallowed his grief, that they could whisper and plan when everything was falling apart. But when Nesrin met his gaze, her sorrow was twin for his. She leaned forward enough to place her other hand over his. Her warmth drove out his cold. He pulled his magic back to himself and Nesrin smiled weakly. Someone cast a mage orb. Samira, or Reyhan. It scratched at his senses.

Havva rose and left the room, and Nesrin pressed her fingers to the pulse point in Omar's throat, her eyes closing. Ihsan shifted his hold on his uncle's hand so he could touch his fingers to Omar's wrist. There was barely anything to feel. An occasional, thready vibration that shimmered weakly beneath Ihsan's fingertips.

He glanced at Nesrin, who switched her hands, her right fingers to Omar's throat, her left over his heart. Ceylik asked her something, and she shook her head. Flour dusted her left cheek. Her hair was a curtain of loose curls made auburn by the mage orb. Her nose scrunched in concentration, eyes shut. Ihsan had not seen this version of her. Not seen her so confident and settled in herself. Never seen her more beautiful and vital and radiant. *Alive.* A vibrant, powerful contrast to the ebbing version of Omar. Brilliant life and fading loss.

It was painful to witness, yet also, settled him. Gave him a measure of peace to cling to. She looked at him suddenly, as if she sensed his stare. The mage orb lit the new green in her eyes, the glitter of verdance.

Her expression was sorrow, grief. And joy.

For a moment that seemed to stretch a lifetime, he saw a universe in her eyes. Birth, and death, creation…and destruction. And in that, somehow, hope. Memory. All that one had given to build them all. Everything Omar was. Everything his life had created, had nourished.

Nesrin did not speak, but it was clear to Ihsan. It was time. Omar had reached the Sixth spoke in his Turns. There was peace in that, alongside the sorrow.

Ihsan looked at his uncle's face. It was calm. Smoothed of the worry lines and confused anger that shaped his visage when he was awake.

I hope she is there to greet you, Amca. That the Wheel spins to bring you together again, in another time.

He slid one hand to rest over Naime's. Her frantic gaze went to his, read his expression. "No," she gasped, ripping her gaze from Ihsan's. "No. Baba. Please." She collapsed forward, pressing her face to her father's chest. "I need you," she wept. "Don't go."

Samira circled her arms around her friend, her own tears falling into Naime's hair. Still Ihsan could feel Naime's spell, the forced rise and fall of Omar's chest.

Ihsan stood. He could do this for Naime. Be strong when she could not. He could hold her while her world collapsed, as she, and Dilay, and Omar, had once done for him.

"Naime," he said. "It is time to stop." He took her hands and she tried to pull away, but he was stronger. He pulled her off the bed and into his embrace. "He is gone."

"No." Her mask was gone, her face an excruciating window into her torn heart, tear-stained and tortured. "I cannot do it without him. I cannot do it alone."

"You are not alone." He hugged her harder. "You have me. You have everything you have built. Everything you have yet to build. Your place is here, and his is no longer."

"I wanted him to laugh again. I wanted him to read to me again," she sobbed, burying her head against Ihsan's shoulder, and he stroked her undone hair. They had not just been father and daughter, Sultan and heir. They had been friends.

He looked at Nesrin. She sat peaceful on the edge of the bed near Omar's head, her hands folded in her lap, her eyes closed. A tear slid down her cheek. He was nothing but jagged ice on the inside. Numb on the outside.

"I can't." Naime looked at her father and her face crumpled again, her body sinking against Ihsan's as though she would drop to the floor. "I can't."

"You can," he murmured. "We can." Ihsan helped her to sit on the bed beside Omar, and she took her father's hand into her lap. She stroked the back of it, a wet sob shaking her body. Cries filled his own lungs, his held tears making his face ache. He knew the words to say, to comfort her. Somehow. The words Dilay had said to him. But he would need time for them to sink into his own belief.

Nesrin knelt in front of Naime. "Our memories," she began in a voice like warm, hopeful summer, "hold a life more truly and joyfully than a fading vessel ever will." She put her hand softly over Naime's. "This shell will nourish new life, but your father's power, and the echo of his living, will continue to spin the Wheel. In the void, and in your heart." Then she gently squeezed Naime's hand. "But first you have to let him go."

If she had not been a void, he would have sworn he heard magic in her voice. The echo of all that had been, that was, and that would be. It had to be his own grief, fighting to break free, making everything more raw, more powerful.

Samira got off the bed and came around to kneel on the floor beside Naime and Ihsan. She put an arm around Naime's waist. Ihsan stroked Naime's hair. She inhaled a long, sniffling breath. Then she wiped her eyes and rose to lean forward and kiss her father's brow. "Tell Anne I love her," she whispered. "And know that I love you, Baba."

Ihsan squeezed Omar's hand, and wished, like Naime, to hear his laugh one more time.

She touched her forehead to his. The pale glow of her magic faded, the room growing oppressively still. None of them moved, everything in the room—light and dark, sorrow and memory, eyes and hearts—focused on the last breath of Omar Sabri.

"Goodbye," Naime whispered faintly, "my Sultan."

Forty

Nesrin dove into helping Ceylik and Havva. She did not feel comfortable intruding any more on the private grieving of Ihsan and Naime, for a man who had been nothing but a title to Nesrin. The mark of a person's spin on the Wheel was the size of the hole they left in those who loved them. And it seemed he had left a chasm. Nesrin wanted to comfort Ihsan. But he had been intent on comforting his cousin. Maybe he was not ready to be consoled, and so she'd left them in privacy.

Ceylik, the palace head physician, had quickly ordered the cleanup and removal of his people and all their supplies back to the wing of the palace they practiced in. While those healers, uniformed in grey caftan and salvar with tiraz edged in green, gave her wide, judgmental berth, Havva was happy to converse. Nesrin liked Havva; she had the same no-nonsense bearing as her grandmothers. They walked together, carrying baskets of towels back to the hospital hall.

Havva did not wear a uniform, and explained to Nesrin that she was not a palace healer. Nesrin asked her about her history, and Havva told the story of becoming a mother young and putting herself through midwife training. When Nesrin thought to respond with her own midwife experiences, the ring burrowed a hot spear up her arm that drove the air from her lungs. Nesrin missed a step because of the pain, tripping on the carpet. Havva chuckled, catching her arm in a strong hand.

"Easy there. Those carpets will leap out and grab your ankles when you least expect it."

Nesrin tried to smile, but any words to brush off the incident died in her throat. Havva patted her back when she released her and turned them down a secondary hall.

"My son is the commander of the palace guard now," Havva continued on, voice bright with pride. The statement caused Nesrin to look more closely. They had similar coloring, and the husky build. But Bashir's face and unusual eyes were not hers. She did not offer up information on Bashir's father. Nesrin understood the question was off-limits.

She glanced behind her, where the apprentice healers and Ceylik were replacing supplies in a room. They did not speak once they had left the Sultan's room. Not even of mundane things. She suspected the death of the Sultan would be kept secret until the Princess Sultana was ready to announce it. Though in a palace this size, with as many nobles coming and going as Nesrin had seen, she doubted it would stay secret very long. Her head spun at all the many threads that tied to the Sultan, at the immense task Naime had ahead of her to keep them all from unraveling.

"Here," Havva said. She turned a latch on a door at the end of the hall and pushed it open with her hip. The room was large, with three sturdy wooden tables in the middle and beds lining one wall, shelves of supplies another. Havva dropped her armload on the first table and turned to take Nesrin's. Once Nesrin was inside, she saw that one of the beds was occupied.

Nesrin had never seen anyone with pale hair. Grey hair, certainly. But the man who lay in the bed had hair the color of ripe wheat. Havva saw her staring and gave a grunt of irritation.

"That is Benat," she stated, replacing supplies on shelves. Nesrin fell in beside her, though her attention stayed on him. "They cannot decide whether he is patient or prisoner. Every time he has an episode, they want to put him down in the Cliffs, and I have to remind them how long it will take me to hike myself down there to give him more draught." She shook her head.

"He isn't sleeping," Nesrin said, certain of the fact, though she could not have said why. Something fizzed along her limbs, making her scar itch and seem to writhe on her skin. She reached up to rub it. Havva watched critically, stopping to pull Nesrin's collar aside.

"This healed well, and fast," she mused. Nesrin only nodded. Havva followed her gaze to Benat. "No. He is not sleeping. Not naturally, anyway."

"Is that the Charah from the Republic?"

"It is." The answer was given with little emotional inflection.

"A woman in the market told me about him." Nesrin put another jar on the shelf.

"Rabia, I'd guess? Selling medicines and rumors on the corner of Spice Row?"

Nesrin nodded, smiling a little at Havva's irritated expression. "What is wrong with him?" She helped place cloth and tinctures back onto the shelves. It seemed the healers had emptied their stores to attend to the Sultan. Her throat tightened and she blinked away tears. She did not need to have known the Sultan to feel the pain of his absence in the people around her.

Havva let out a frustrated sound that told Nesrin almost as much as words would have. "Mutar Charah rescued him from slavery. The very simplest thing wrong with him is that he is addicted to poppy."

Nesrin knew, even without Havva's sarcastic tone, that it wasn't simple at all. They did not have much access to poppy in Mizraa, but occasionally traders came through selling it or addicted to it themselves. Her grandmothers had told her one especially troubling tale about trying to help someone break their poppy habit. But could not.

"He is also a mage who came into his powers in adulthood."

Nesrin glanced at him. Mages usually came into their power before their bodies began adolescence. There were occasional late bloomers, who had to deal with learning their magic at the same time they were dealing with new emotions and bodies. But a mage whose power was dormant until adulthood was dangerous. Power became symbiotic with its wielder over Turns of careful practice, growing in strength as the mage did. To be inundated with a Charah's power so late in life…

"Is he dangerous?" Nesrin asked quietly. Havva nodded.

"He attacked Mutar Charah before she subdued him and brought him here. And we have not allowed him to wake since he arrived. We are waiting for instructions from the Princess Sultana. But of course, she has been preoccupied." Her voice dropped, her face mournful. Then she shook it off. "You seem to know a great deal about healing. Unusual for a noble, unless they've gone through the University for it."

Nesrin turned away from Havva to hide her wince as the ring lashed her with fire. "We had very good healers in Mizraa," she said, and hoped it was enough. Havva did not press. While she finished putting away the baskets, Nesrin approached Benat. It was the absolute stillness that had tipped her off that this was more than sleep. The blanket was tightly, smoothly tucked around him, undisturbed from even a twitch. Not a single wrinkle. His breathing was even, though a fraction shallow, for her comfort.

His skin was pale, perhaps from the effects of withdrawal but also, she suspected he naturally lacked the more golden shading of those from Tamar, Sarkum, and surrounding. Likely from the same heritage that gave him his washed-out hair. He was handsome in a foreign kind of way, but that thought brought Ihsan to her mind, and that she had been gone from his side longer than she would have liked. But it felt intrusive to insert herself in the middle of the family grief. It also made her long for her own family.

Were they worried about her? Had Bardakci Pasha told them anything? Or had they suffered in silence and ignorance of her fate, afraid to give away her duplicity? She focused on Benat again so her emotions did not spiral into places she would struggle to escape from.

"What House is he?" she asked, without turning. Most mages wore their Houses in their face and bodies, their features marking them. But perhaps because he slept, she could not guess.

"Earth," Havva said. "Sometimes, when the sedatives wear off, he dreams and the whole palace shakes." Between Ihsan's ice dreams and Benat's earthquakes, it seemed a wonder the palace was still standing.

"Are you in charge of his care?" Nesrin sat on the stool pushed against the bed near his head.

Havva snorted. "That old goat would not allow me to claim such a thing, but he certainly listens to me when it comes to this one. They don't deal with poppy as much up here in the palace as we do down in the slums."

"You mean Ceylik?"

"Pompous blowhard," Havva grumbled under her breath as she crouched to organize a shelf. Nesrin pressed her lips together to avoid her smile and looked at Benat again. The talk was that the Republic hated magic. That it hunted down mages within its borders and murdered them. Some of the merchants who frequented Mizraa said they had seen mages—or their parts—hung as warnings on the main roads leading to the capital, Corsyra. What had this man been through? His magic had been dormant his whole life. It would be terrifying to have magic suddenly awaken in your body if you were not raised among mages. And as an adult.

"Does the poppy suppress his magic?" Nesrin pondered out loud as she smoothed a hand over the blanket on his chest.

"It does. But at a cost. We have been trying to wean him off the poppy and on to other herbs that aren't so dangerous. But his body..." She hummed a sad sound.

His heart beat strong beneath Nesrin's hand. So different to the fading feel of the Sultan's. Life, and death. The cycle spun in Nesrin's thoughts.

Wake.

She flinched. That echoing voice. One, and many. It whispered in her convoluted dreams, frightened her and beckoned. Seemed to draw her toward it, pulling at her energy, her breath and pulse.

Beneath her hand, Benat's heart sped, its rhythm becoming fluttery. He twitched, his eyes slitting. Pain, like the looter's fire whip wrapping her anew, spun up her body, so intense she thought she might split open. Then the ring sent its vile, burning magic up her arm, and Nesrin would have screamed, but it stole her voice, and she only sucked in a searing breath.

Something clattered when Havva dropped it, then the older woman was at Nesrin's side, shaking a stoppered bottle in one hand.

"Benat, can you hear me?" Havva said. Light flickered beneath his lashes. Nesrin nearly bolted back off the stool as molten lines of magic dripped red and black over his face. "Lift his head," Havva ordered, and Nesrin did without hesitation as Havva plucked the cork from the bottle.

The pungent, offensive scent of valerian made Nesrin cough. The voice of her dreams quieted, and the pain in her scar dissipated. Havva measured a dose of the concoction in the bottle into a spoon and dribbled it into Benat's mouth. He made a feeble attempt at moving away, but Nesrin held him, and he groaned in protest as she laid his head back down.

"Miri," he said, followed by an unintelligible string of hard syllables that sounded like stuttering. Havva shushed him and shook her head when his lashes fluttered and he quieted, the magical lines fading from his skin.

"Of course he wakes up when she isn't here. Poor woman was at his side almost every moment," Havva tutted.

"Who?" Nesrin retreated from Benat, rubbing her arms to try to make the prickles calm down.

"Mirari. She came from the Republic with Mutar Charah. This one's friend. Or more, if you ask me." Havva winked at her. Nesrin smiled wanly. More? With a man confined to drugged sleep and fighting powerful magic? It made her entanglement with Ihsan seem so simple.

"I should return," Nesrin suggested, and Havva nodded. "Unless you need more help?"

"Off you go." Havva waved her away like she was shooing a bug. The door opened and a young woman stuck her head in as Nesrin headed for the hall.

"Havva, Attiyeh Charah was looking for you."

"Me? Or Bashir?" Havva asked. The girl shrugged and disappeared again. Havva squinted at the door. "Cycles I have on most of them. But you'd think I was a clueless child the way they speak to me."

"Well, I know who I would choose to heal me." Nesrin smiled coyly at Havva, who shook the spoon she'd used on Benat at Nesrin.

"You are welcome," Havva said, then hoisted herself off the stool with a push on her knees and a groan. She bowed, and Nesrin swallowed her protest at the movement, nodding stiffly instead. She headed into the hall.

WHEN SHE ARRIVED AT THE Sultan's suite, it was quiet in the hall, the guards doing a good job of maintaining neutral expressions.

Just past them, and the door to the rooms, Commander Ayan stood with Attiyeh Charah, speaking quietly to each other. When Nesrin approached the doors, both of them looked up. A flash of something transformed Attiyeh Charah's mien, something watchful. Nesrin's hands spasmed into fists and she entered the Sultan's rooms when one of the guards pushed the door open for her. She'd imagined that suspicion in Attiyeh Charah's stormy eyes, hadn't she?

The common area of the suite was empty. It had been so close and bustling when she'd arrived with Ihsan. Now its quiet was reflective, and too melancholy. The door to the garden stood open, allowing in a breeze. Nesrin couldn't see him, but she was certain Ihsan was out there. She stepped out onto the patio stones and waited for her eyes to adjust to the darkness. No mage orbs hung in the fig tree, and it broke her heart open again.

Ihsan stood just beyond the light from the door, cloaked by night, staring toward the palace rooftops. Nesrin moved to his side. "May I join you, or would you rather be alone?" She tried to keep her voice low and unobtrusive.

He did not look at her or speak, only swung an arm around her shoulders and drew her into his body. He buried his face into the curve of her neck. Nesrin wrapped her arms around his waist. They stood quietly, enough that she could hear the hitching of his breath as he cried. His tears were hot on her skin, cooling quickly. She stroked his back, closing her eyes so her thoughts did not wander away. No one deserved to be alone in their grief.

"I thought I would be stronger about it," he said into her hair.

"You were strong for Naime and will be a strength for her. And I will be strong for you and hold you up." She cupped his head, tangling her fingers in his hair. "The pain of the loss is equal to the joy our loved ones brought us. Joy is quieter, steadier. Sometimes we do not notice it, until it is absent, and its hole fills with grief."

He lifted his head, touching his brow to hers, before he straightened completely. She wiped her fingers over his cheeks, brushing away the tears. Sometimes the sorrow of others was more painful to her than her own. Her entire body ached to give him comfort she knew she could not. Others could walk beside you, but this pain was a journey whose path was different for everyone. He closed his eyes and pressed his scarred cheek into her hand.

"Can I do anything?" she asked.

"You exist, and that is enough," he said, his eyes opening. The palest light glittered dimly deep within his pupils as he looked at her.

"Would you like to tell me about him?"

He shook his head. "Not yet. I cannot."

She slid her arms around his ribs once more and laid her head on his shoulder. There was comfort in the embrace for her too, and she clung.

"Sehzade." The voice that spoke from the doorway of the Sultan's rooms was female. Nesrin peeked over his shoulder. Attiyeh Charah stood just outside the doors, Commander Ayan and Reyhan beyond her, still inside. Reyhan met Nesrin's eyes with panic in hers. Nesrin stepped away from Ihsan as he turned, covering his grief quickly with a mask of anger. "May I speak with you?"

"Now is not a good time." Ice snapped in his voice. Nesrin caught a glimpse of magic that flickered and disappeared on the back of his neck.

"I know." Her gaze slid to Nesrin, hung for a heartbeat, then returned to his. "It is urgent."

"Go on then," he grated, his shoulders sagging. Nesrin touched her fingers between his shoulder blades as she moved to his side. Attiyeh Charah watched Nesrin with a quiet look. Not neutral, exactly, but guarded. As though she expected Nesrin to attack.

"It would be better if it were in private," the Charah said. Nesrin glanced up at Ihsan as he turned his head to her, and offered him a relaxed smile.

"I'll be in my room." She bowed to Attiyeh Charah as she passed, unnerved by the way the woman watched her. When she was inside and Commander Ayan moved outside and shut the door, Reyhan grabbed her hand and dragged her into her room.

"What?" Nesrin asked, niggling anxiety setting in at the look Reyhan wore, her agitation.

"What do they want?" Reyhan whispered, gaze darting to the door as though it would burst open any moment. Nesrin shook her head.

Reyhan grimaced, twining her hands together and whirling away. As Nesrin cataloged all the reasons the commander of the palace guard and a Charah might be searching for Ihsan at such a delicate time, she felt too weak and sick to stand. It was her. It was.

Nesrin sat, tipping her head into one of the decoratively carved posters of the bed. The wood was cool on her brow, and she closed her eyes. Too many emotions fought within her to feel only one. To even know what she should feel. Panic? Or fear? Relief?

All she could do was wait.

Forty-One

"Forgive me," Aysel said once Bashir had cast a dampening, with enough sincerity to ease some of Ihsan's displeasure. "If I thought it could wait, I would not trouble you." She paused, her expression softening too much. "I am sorry for the loss of the Sultan."

Ihsan forced his jaw to relax. "Why are you here?"

"Kiya returned from her investigation into those looted wagons in the North. She brought me these." Aysel held out a folded square of leather, tied with twine. Ihsan took it from her and unwrapped it.

"Glass," he stated in disbelief. She was too smart a woman to have brought him glass shards for no reason.

"The villages on the route to Golge say that wagons frequently pass this route, always at night. Every few turns or so. They are always full of crates, though no one knows what is in them, because they never stop, and they never come in the day. They always arrive from the south."

"Smuggling glass?" Ihsan suggested. He was too tangled inside to think through whatever Aysel was aiming for. To conjure enough interest to put the pieces together himself.

"Kiya went all the way to Golge. The people there claimed something similar, wagons at night, never more than two, never in the day. They say the wagons have been only a recent occurrence. Kiya also went to Koz. They described similar movement of wagons had been happening since around the time Makram returned to Sarkum. Until recently. They've stopped."

"A change of route," Bashir took mercy on Ihsan and explained.

Aysel nodded. "The glass is strange. It has inclusions, all of it does. So Kiya tried to discover where it was being made. And she learned one of the guild glassmakers, arguably the most talented guild glassmaker"—Aysel's gaze went to his—"left the guild last winter."

A merchant who left the guild was assuring they would never know work again in Narfour. Usually, they only left if they were forced to move, or change trades. Even then, they often maintained their membership, if they could afford it, for the ties to one of the most powerful entities in Narfour outside of the palace.

Ihsan lifted a piece of the glass. It was curved as though it had been part of a container. A very small bottle, or vial. He held it toward the doors, where light from inside came through. He could just make out bits in the glass. Particles. He frowned.

"His shop was abandoned, empty except for equipment he left behind. His name is Kanat. And he is promised to Reyhan. No one knows where he is." Her tone grew more reluctant as she continued, and finally she glanced at Bashir, who gave her a solemn nod. Dread sank through Ihsan like a stone plummeting into water. "Kiya has been watching the shop. And the same day I saw her visit the Grand Vizier, Mistress Bardakci later went into the shop carrying a bag and exited after about a mark's time."

"And?" Ihsan ordered, hoarse. The cold that washed him was not his power. It numbed him to the gut-wrenching revelation, so he could only stare blindly at Aysel.

"I would like your permission to question Reyhan about her promised's whereabouts." She paused, reticent, and he curled his lip at her.

"And to search Mistress Bardakci's room here, and at your residence in the city."

"For what?" He closed his hand around the leather, hard enough the glass pieces within it bit into his flesh. He knew for what. Physical proof that Nesrin was involved in some kind of smuggling operation. His heart pounded a drumbeat in his ears, his hand shaking as he squeezed the packet of glass.

Aysel paused, her jaw working.

Because he trusted Nessa. Because she was everything Behram was not, he jumped to defenses in his thoughts. Of course, she visited Kadir. The man was her father's proxy in the city. But that only made the knife of the possible betrayal bite deeper. Behram Kadir and Osman Bardakci were acquaintances. Friends, if what Kadir claimed was true. And Nessa spoke of her father with love and admiration. His magic fell over his mind like cloudshadow, dimming everything within.

"Do your search." He held the bundle of glass out to her, and when she took it, his blood left dark marks on the leather. He closed his fist around the wounds. She hesitated, searching his face, then turned and strode into the suite. Bashir released his dampening. He bowed to Ihsan then followed Aysel.

The ambient sounds of the garden were too loud and too many in the sudden absence of the spell. A breeze shifted branches; creatures rustled in bushes. Nightbirds called and insects trilled, and he hated all of it. He hated the desperation inside him that Aysel would find nothing. And feared the threat of the feelings if she found anything.

He did not want to see. He did not want to look at Nesrin or hear her protests or be there to have his heart shattered. Whether it was because he had not believed in her when he should have, or because he had ever believed in her at all. But neither could he stand out here and wait. The ice expanding inside his mind and magic would shred him. He trudged to the open door of Nesrin's room.

Nessa sat on the end of her bed, brow pressed into the wood of the corner poster, eyes closed. Her hair was down around her shoulders, her fingers white-knuckled in their grip. He could not go past the door. Reyhan stood beside Nesrin, twisting her hands together, gaze darting as Aysel moved about the room, examining bottles and drawers.

"What is this?" She held up a bottle. Nesrin's eyes opened as Reyhan answered.

"Perfume."

Aysel sniffed it and turned it one way then the other to examine the glass. Nesrin saw Ihsan. Their gazes met, and tears spilled from her eyes and down her cheeks. The shame in her face was as good as a confession, and fury built in him, brittle and choking. An easy step from grief.

Aysel moved to the wardrobe, yanking clothes out and throwing them on the floor. Reyhan protested. She crouched beside the clothes and gathered them in her arms. Aysel pulled open the drawers, tossing things as she went.

"You are not going to defend yourself?" Ihsan demanded, his voice raw, magic snapping in it. He was losing his grip on it, could see the sparkle of it coming to life in his skin. "What is this?" Only moments before she had been all he had wanted in his grief. Now…

Nessa flinched as if he'd struck her. Reyhan set the clothes on the bed and sat beside her. The fire mage dared to glare at him. Nesrin opened her mouth, then folded forward with a cry. Fire skittered along the edge of Ihsan's senses, and he glared at Reyhan. "Are you casting?"

Reyhan stared at him, eyes round as a rabbit's, her skin blanching a shade paler. Nesrin straightened.

Aysel went still, then turned from her search of the drawers, holding a small package wrapped in burlap. As she unwrapped it, the other two women watched, Nesrin with a look of resignation, Reyhan in bemusement. When Aysel revealed the glass fragments inside, Reyhan's head snapped around to look at Nesrin. She bolted up, stumbling a step back, anger bringing color back to her skin. Nesrin only stared as Aysel turned back to the drawer to finish riffling it.

"Bashir." Aysel pulled something else out of the drawer. A small gold medallion, stamped with something Ihsan could not see from where he stood. Aysel handed it to Bashir.

He turned it over, closing his eyes as he squeezed his fist around it. Golden light glowed in his hand. Not all earth mages could feel the components of earth and metal. But Bashir was powerful enough. "Another of the mocked-up ones. Just like Rifat's, and the others we found on the men that attacked the Sultana." It was Bashir's accusing gaze turned on Nesrin that broke Ihsan's hold on himself. Of all the things he imagined, that she might be of danger to Naime was not one of them.

"Say something," Ihsan barked. "What are you hiding?"

Fresh tears dampened her cheeks as she stood and stepped toward him. "I never wanted to hurt you." She reached for his hand, but he recoiled, and she stopped, her inhalation cut short. "Some lies are necessary."

His breath left him as though she'd kicked him in the gut. "She is not to leave this room," he ordered Bashir, who ducked his head. "Either of them. Find out more. Find out if she is a danger to Naime." He could not look at her as he said it, could not stomach the confirmation or denial he would find there.

Aysel strode after him on his way out. "What are you going to do?"

"I need some time." It took all his concentration to tell her politely, instead of slamming the doors closed in her face so she would not follow. Her concerned expression was framed in a pane of the glass for a moment before she returned to Nesrin's room.

All he could do was stand, holding on to the swell of feelings, tangled, and ugly. There was nowhere, no one, to turn to. No way to let them out, so instead it spread through his body, a blizzard inside him that bit like a million fragments of glass. Magic poured from him in rolling fog, freezing as it went, blackening the grass and foliage it touched as it froze and thawed.

Emotion consumed him. He wanted to scream, or rage, anything to ease the unbearable press of it. But there was nothing. The night at least, with its quiet and lack of people, demanded nothing.

Still, his thoughts spun, from his uncle and the hole of his absence, to Nessa. To picking apart everything she had said and done, picking at it like a scab, until he was bleeding grief and choking on bitterness. Every look, every smile, every touch...were they lies? Why hadn't he listened to his doubts?

He jammed his fingers into his hair, closing his eyes. But why? What did this have to do with her, with him? Glass? What did glass even matter with everything else going on? It did not feed hungry people or win battles or lose them for that matter. It wasn't even that valuable. Certainly not valuable enough for Nesrin to lie her way into a marriage.

Was Kadir somehow involved? And Cemil...

What had they been talking about that day he saw them in the hall? And in the garden...had Cemil been warning him? Why would he do that?

There were no answers for him there, in the garden, in his memories. But he knew where he could look. He could not stand around, waiting for more details from Aysel.

He took a less populated path through the palace, eschewing halls for galleries, and gathering places for gardens. He knew if he thought beyond his steps and his path, he would talk himself out of what he knew was a rash, foolish course of action. So, he did not think.

As he crossed through the last garden on his way to the courtyard, movement caught his eye. He looked up, thinking he'd simply seen a bat or nightbird slip by. But the Sultan's tower was above him, and on the long roof of the hall below it, a figure sat. There was little moon to see by, but he did not need it to know who was there.

Behram Kadir sat on the roof outside the tower window, a bottle of arak in one hand, which he lifted to his mouth. He was too drunk or too lost in his thoughts to notice Ihsan, or if he did, he did not indicate so. Ihsan's father had told him about evenings spent drinking on the roof there. Omar and him. Behram Kadir, and the brothers Yavuz. Osman Altimur.

So. Kadir knew Omar was gone. Some spy within the healer staff, perhaps. Or the guard force. Or, however unlikely, there was just enough humanity left in Behram Kadir to simply *feel* the loss of his once-friend, to sense that the Wheel was brighter tonight for the light of Omar Sabri returned to the void.

Ihsan fought with his resentment of Kadir, daring to show any sort of emotion over the loss of Omar. But the web was too tangled, too complex to unweave at the moment. He turned away and continued to the courtyard.

It was disturbingly normal. The guards manned their posts. A few carriages stood lined up to allow their passengers to disembark near the palace steps. A hoard of bats swooped and dove through the light of torches and mage orbs, feasting on insects drawn to the light. Ihsan had never seen so many in one place before. Not in all his Turns at the palace.

At the stables, grooms shoveled stalls and cared for horses. Conversations rose and fell from different directions. A boy dashed up to Ihsan when he arrived, and bowed.

"Prepare a horse for me," Ihsan told him. "For travel to the valley."

The boy straightened, mouth open, brow cinched. "At…at night, Efendim?"

"Now," he commanded.

Forty-Two

He made it to Mizraa the following evening. His horse bore the pressing pace well, as they were bred to do, but guilt for her health settled comfortably on the summit of Ihsan's piled emotions. They arrived at the estate house at a plod, the horse's head hanging, and Ihsan muzzy from lack of sleep and holding his many feelings at bay.

He swung down in the half-circle of gravel in front of the home. A young man ducked out of a small stable to the east of the house and approached cautiously. His gaunt face and bony frame reminded Ihsan of Nessa when she first came to Narfour. He pushed the thought away. Along with the stab of longing. He was furious with her, wanted nothing more than to put her from his mind. But also, he wanted the comfort of her embrace. Wanted it all to be part of his nightmares.

Ihsan held out the reins. When the youth was close enough to see Ihsan's tiraz through the dust of travel, his eyes widened, and he pelted forward in a bow so fast it startled the horse, who skittered sideways with a snort. The man cast a glance at the animal, then extended his hands palm up and spread them before he rose again. He took the reins.

"I am here to see Bardakci Pasha," Ihsan said. He suspected the stablehand had no idea who he was. He did not care, as any attempt they made to properly welcome a prince would only serve to pervert his goal.

"He's"—he looked around as though attempting to guess—"likely at his forge?"

"Are you asking me?" Ihsan prompted, eyebrows lifting.

The young man shook his head and pointed. "It's behind the house."

Ihsan looked. He patted the grey mare on her sweaty, dirt-crusted neck. "Take good care of her. She earned some pampering."

Just as the young man turned to lead the horse away, someone else came from the house. The man took the steps to the gravel quickly, then strode to stand in the young man's path. He wore an entari the color of dried blood over a black caftan and salvar, and his jet hair was combed into a knot at the base of his skull. He had the angular look of a fire mage, or at least seemed to, beneath his round cheeks and pudgy fingers.

Ihsan disliked him immediately, for the three fire sigils embroidered on his arm, and for the expression of pompous disdain on his face. How was he so well fed when Nesrin had come to Narfour starving?

"Mizraa is closed to travelers," he said in a smoky voice. "We can attend briefly to your horse to speed you on your way."

Ihsan's exhaustion emptied him of patience, too. "I am here to see Bardakci Pasha." He motioned for the stablehand to take the mare. He took a step and the fire mage put a hand on the horse's bridle to stop him.

"Bardakci Pasha is consumed by dealing with the Blight. He does not have time—"

"By order of the Princess Sultana, I am here to receive Bardakci Pasha's audit of his current stores. All Viziers with productive land have been ordered to produce numbers."

"And you are?" the mage queried.

"I am Ihsan Sabri ilr Narfour. Sehzade and Vizier of Agriculture for the Sultan of Tamar. And you?" Ihsan's polite smile was frigid.

The man's lip twitched toward a sneer, but he bowed. "Forgive my ignorance, Efendim. I am Caner Ansar, servant of Bardakci Pasha. We only mean to prevent the Blight spreading as much as we can by limiting travel through Mizraa."

"I see. I would like to discuss all those details with Bardakci Pasha."

"If I may, Efendim, I can give you everything you need, without disturbing—"

"With Bardakci Pasha," Ihsan said. He nodded to the stablehand again, and this time he went, despite the fire mage's scowl. "Would you like to escort me to him, or shall I find him myself?"

Master Ansar was not an accomplished liar. Or perhaps he was, and Ihsan was so accustomed to Behram Kadir and his mastery of untruths, that everyone else seemed amateur in comparison. He did not school his face well, or the twitch of his hands. But neither did he let his fire sit so near the surface as Kadir did.

"This way, Efendim," he said grudgingly, holding an open hand toward the house. They walked in silence, their steps on the gravel the only sound. Master Ansar led him into the house. The entrance was a broad, open foyer from the front doors. A circle in the center of the ceiling above them was open to the sky, situated over a basin in the floor to catch rainwater. It was a common way for those with wealth to balance earth, an open skylight to allow air in. Archways in a set of three paraded down the wall to the left, opening to rooms Ihsan suspected were for entertaining. A dining room, a sitting area, and one he could not see before they turned right down a hall. They passed more rooms, with closed doors, until they reached the end.

The hall opened to a circular room laid out to be a study. The outer wall was primarily windows that looked over a garden. A desk was placed to one side, with shelves of books behind. More bookshelves stood behind a semicircle of chairs and couch that faced the desk.

"If you would wait here, Sehzade, I will have refreshments brought and inform Bardakci Pasha of your arrival."

Ihsan nodded, but watched the mage as he left, closing him into the study. The man's boots echoed on the hall floor outside the door. Ihsan turned where he stood, surveying the room, then went to the open window. It allowed a breeze in, and the heady scent of roses enveloped him as he approached.

Just outside the window, an exuberant array of flowers and herbs crowded together, along with vegetables, and in among them all, roses with heavy blooms. Somehow, he knew, *knew*, that Nesrin had a hand in their vitality. That was her gift, wasn't it? Making everyone and everything around her more vital, more energetic.

Something twitched in his thoughts, but disappeared before he could grasp it. That certainty made him question his doubts. Was he letting Cemil and his riddles play to his weaknesses? But why did she have those broken glass pieces? The forged katil insignia? It made no sense if she was involved, and even less if she wasn't. And what was even happening? What might she be involved *in*?

He rubbed his fingers over his brow. He should have sent Aysel. She was the one who could sneak through a house undetected. Did he plan to rummage through drawers?

The window faced east, and he could just make out the village to the south as a series of roofs against the fields that surrounded it. Orchards to the northeast blocked his view of the lake he'd seen on his way over the pass. There was also evidence of the Blight, creeping rot from the east over fields of wheat just turning golden.

The sight made him think of Sarkum, and the windblown fields of dust and dead crops. The gaunt faces of the soldiers and the men and women who kept the camp. Of Nesrin. As gaunt as any of the soldiers.

Caner Ansar was not gaunt. Had Bardakci Pasha allowed his daughter to starve while his servant remained well fed? Why could he not keep her from his mind? She was in everything around him. Every green leaf and fragrant bloom, every face, the termination of every thought. Perhaps he would find something here that would excise her from him.

That wasn't what he wanted. He wanted a reason to hold on to her. To hold on to the man he was becoming because of her. A man he had thought was lost, with everything else that mattered to him. The gaping hole that yawned inside him at the idea of her absence was too much to bear when there were already so many pieces of him missing.

The newest fissure of Omar's death threatened to swallow him whole. He had loved his father. And the injustice of his murder haunted Ihsan. But it had been Omar who had soothed his hurts, talked with him into the night, given pride and praise for accomplishments. It had been Omar, and Dilay, who kept vigil during Ihsan's worst days.

The bright ping of a distant hammer on metal distracted him from his misery, the sound barely reaching him. He moved to another window, one that overlooked a sea of green grass that rippled to the north of the estate. The sound did not come again, and long moments passed. Then two figures crested the top of the hill behind the house. One was Caner, shorter and rounder than the other. The other was not dressed as a Vizier in Narfour would dress. No bright colors or fine fabrics. He was a tall man, perhaps as tall as Bashir. A rarity indeed.

The two men appeared to be arguing, or at least, Caner did. Gesticulating in sharp stabs of his hand, his stride more of a march than a walk. Ihsan moved away from the window when they drew close to the gravel path that wrapped the house, through the garden. He sat in a low-back chair to wait. Steps tapped in the hall a few moments later, but no voices. When the door opened, Ihsan stood.

Caner entered and stepped aside to bow as the second man came through the door.

Something about him struck as familiar, but Ihsan could not place it. Perhaps it was simply his obvious affinity for earth, which granted him a broad build that made him appear much younger and more hale than his silver-streaked beard suggested.

Osman's face relaxed, his gaze darting from Ihsan's face to his clothes and back. "Wheel's spokes," he said, "you could be his twin."

"Who?" Ihsan asked.

The man raised his eyebrows. "You are Mazhar's son?"

"I am the Sehzade's son," Ihsan bristled. Bardakci Pasha had known his father? Well enough to call him by his name. The man bowed but did not spread his hands.

"I am Osman Bardakci." He rose, and smiled. "I am surprised by the honor of having the Sehzade conduct a review that is better suited to a lesser Vizier."

Ihsan's power rippled. From a sense of fire. Or lies. It was a confused vibration. Osman stared at him, the look in his eyes intense, but nothing Ihsan could name a reason for. He did not mention Nesrin, which was an obvious reason for Ihsan to be there.

"The Princess Sultana has requested an audit of all food stores throughout the valley. And because of our tie"—Ihsan watched Osman's face for anything—"it seemed logical for me to come."

Osman's smile thinned. "Yes, of course." Then a shrewd look overtook his mien. He peered at the sun, then at Ihsan again. "You must have ridden all night. In a rush?"

"The Blight is an imminent threat." Ihsan could not interpret the meaning behind Osman's expression. But he did notice how they all stood stiff. No one moving to sit or relax. Caner hovered at Osman's side, like a handler by a skittish colt.

"Not in the next day. You should have some refreshments, and rest."

"I do not require—"

"I insist." The look in Osman's jasper eyes went hard. "Master Ansar will see to it, yes?" He cut that hard-eyed stare to Caner, whose mouth moved between a frown and a forced smile. He bowed, a quick, graceless thing, and left. He did not shut the door. Osman stood as Caner's footsteps faded down the hall, then he shut the door and sat down. Rather he slumped into a chair, gesturing lazily at Ihsan to return to his seat.

He rubbed a hand over his face, drawing attention to the soot marks along his jaw and the scars on his hands and forearms, which were bared by the rolled sleeves of his caftan. He wore no entari, but there were sweat stains in the shape of an apron across his front. Had he been at the forge, as the stable boy suggested?

"Blacksmithing is an odd hobby for a noble," Ihsan said. Osman dropped his hand into his lap and tipped his head from side to side in acknowledgment.

"There are few opportunities for hobbies here."

"When did the Blight arrive?" Ihsan sat straight in his chair, while Osman lounged, a completely different facade than when he had arrived. Than when Caner was at his side. At his question, Osman sat up, leaning his forearms on his thighs and peering at Ihsan.

"A few turns ago. It seemed to appear overnight," Osman said. Nesrin *had* just missed its arrival when she went to Narfour, then. Osman watched Ihsan intently, as though waiting for him to speak or come to some realization.

"Nesrin must favor her mother," he said, instead. Father and daughter looked nothing alike. Even their coloring was different. Osman had black hair and golden-hued skin, as was most common in Tamar. Nesrin had the ruddy look of mixed heritage.

Osman's smile was quick and stiff, and he sat straight. "My children favor their mother," he said, and barely controlled the contortion of his face like he was in pain. Fire singed Ihsan's thoughts so abruptly that he thought Caner had returned. He might have pondered it more deeply, but Osman's words had stolen his attention.

"I was not aware you had more children," Ihsan said. "But you are an anomaly at court."

"Court." He grinned wistfully. "I spent time there in my youth. But I was needed here." He shrugged, and they lapsed into silence.

Osman lifted his head. "How is the Sultan? I had heard of his declining health."

Ihsan tried and failed to control the spike of grief. Whatever passed on his face was obvious enough that Osman's expression fell. Sorrow slackened his features, and he covered his eyes with his hand for a moment. When he spoke again, it was quiet. "I could never have imagined…he was so…" Osman shook his head rather than finish with words. Then he dropped his hands and looked up. "I was sorry to hear about your father, as well."

Ihsan managed a *thank you*, but his guts twisted. His father. His mother. His stepmother. His aunt and uncle. His power, his body. Lost to him. Now Nessa, too. Naime was all he had left. And he was all she had. Her father and mother gone. Makram missing. Guilt twisted at him for leaving Naime alone with the loss.

Then grief rose up, welling like water, until he froze it. "You have not asked about your daughter."

"I assumed she was well, or I would have heard otherwise." Osman's own mask slipped into place, and he leaned back in his chair once more.

"She was half starved when you sent her to us. But you look well enough fed," Ihsan accused. Osman's brow twitched down, then smoothed. "And now she is confined to our rooms in the palace."

"Oh?" Osman's fingers tightened on the arms of the chair, his voice too calm. "Why is that?"

"The palace guard discovered her to be in possession of a suspicious item. And observed her in places she should not have been. Places that suggest she could be conspiring against the Princess Sultana."

Osman guffawed. "Nesrin?" The laugh faded behind a smile. "She would not conspire to harm a fly."

Momentarily, the man's reaction melted the ice holding Ihsan's emotions. The relief overshadowed the ripple of lies on his magic. But not for long.

"So, neither she, nor you, would know anything about the disappearance of a guild glassmaker, or night smuggling operations moving through the valley?"

Osman controlled his face and body well. Almost as well as Kadir. Better than Caner had. But earth was too near fire on the Wheel to have immunity to Ihsan's ability to detect lies. They were there, shimmering in the air between them. The plip of pebbles into still water.

Osman shot Caner a castigating look when he entered bearing a tray of tea and mezze. The fire mage said nothing, only emptied the contents of the tray plate by plate onto the circular table between Osman and Ihsan. He tucked it under his arm. "Thank you," Osman said. It was clearly a dismissal, but Caner did not move, staring at his master like the look was a tirade. Osman met his stare, and a wordless battle ensued. Ihsan picked at the food. The moment he swallowed his first bite his stomach demanded more. Which made Ihsan notice the paucity of food on the plates. He was so accustomed to the palace, to the excess, that it startled him. His appetite withered, and he sat back.

Finally, Caner left without a word. Osman looked at the tray, then Ihsan. "Please enjoy yourself. I will send someone to show you to a room, so you may rest. We can begin the accounting in the morning. I will need time to consolidate my records."

Before Ihsan could reply or even stand, Osman followed Caner. Ihsan threw the bit of flatbread he was holding back onto the tray and stood, pacing to the window. "Void and stars," he cursed.

The green grass on the hill rippled, showing gold in the dropping sun. Ihsan shoved his hands through his hair, trying to formulate a plan of some kind. Rashness had never served him. Naime was the planner. The chess master. What was he? Extraneous. He grit his teeth. What had he thought he would do here? Unravel some grand plot?

Caner and Osman appeared on the garden path, angling up the hill, clearly arguing again. But Ihsan could not hear it. He would have gladly traded his House for the ability to listen in at that moment. They crested the hill at the same time another man did so from the other direction. It was too far away for Ihsan to make out his details. But the three converged on the hilltop.

The door to the study opened. Ihsan jerked his attention behind. A maid had entered, head ducked, hands already spreading as she bowed to him. The sigil for water marked her tiraz twice.

"Forgive me, Sehzade." The lilt of water in her valley-accented voice—she spoke the same way Nesrin did. With inflection Osman and Caner did not have. Because they were not born and raised here.

She straightened. His breath left his lungs like he had been struck.

It was not Nesrin before him. But it could have been. They were the same height, the same build. The same eyes, chin, and nose. She was rail thin, as Nesrin had been, her eyes darker, her mouth thinner. Her hair was covered with a wrap of plain cloth, but a few ruddy swirls caressed her neck. Freckles were scattered over her hands and the scooped neckline of her caftan. His open-mouthed stare unnerved her, because she ducked her chin and went to work setting the dishes on a tray.

"Who are you?" he asked. She wore servant's clothing. They bore dirt and flour and were well worn, threadbare along the hem. But she looked so much like Nesrin.

"Only a servant, Efendim," she said.

"Do you…" It was a foolish question to ask, but his thoughts spun out of his control. "…have a sister?"

Her hands stopped their work, just a momentary hitch, then she continued as she shook her head. She straightened with the laden tray, bowed again as best she could over the top of it, and fled.

Ihsan grabbed the window frame. It was not uncommon for nobles to take their servants to the sheets; he knew that better than most. But the resemblance…

Was Osman trying to pass a bastard daughter off as a noble? Was that why Nesrin never spoke of her family? Why did lies shift within his awareness around her? He wanted to believe it. As complicated as it would be, he could understand that lie. He could not fault her for doing exactly what he had been doing all his life.

But Nesrin could not have managed such a lie by herself, no matter how grasping she was. Besides Osman's complicity, she would need help in Narfour.

Behram Kadir.

Ice scrawled up Ihsan's arm, feathering along the window frame and the glass, obscuring the view of the fields and the now-empty hill. What would Kadir gain? He had tried to marry her to Enver Balik. Ihsan had stepped into the marriage of his own volition, he could not blame Kadir for that.

He needed Naime to sort this puzzle. Jagged swirls of magic whipped over the visible skin of his hand. It was in flux, from his anger, but not out of control as it had been lately. As it had been when Nesrin was near. She affected him so strongly.

Perhaps this revelation answered some questions. But not all. He had more than when he arrived, certainly. Chess might not be his game but hide and seek was.

The magic faded from his skin, melted ice dripping down the window. He would wait for dark, and seek his answers.

THE NIGHT-DARK FORM LAY in front of her, coils and lashes of something in a world of nothing. Nesrin feared it. Though it did nothing but exist, inky smoke bleeding off of it. But this time, she saw that it was not just a blot of existing black within the nothingness. Something moved within it. A pulse. Voices hissed and whispered, layering over, under, and around each other. Words she did not know, sounds she could not replicate. But also, within the tumult…

Break.

Nesrin screamed in defiance. But there was no sound, no air, no movement of her constricted, curled body. Instead, she jolted awake.

Reyhan had her by the shoulders when she lunged up, panting. "Nessa?" she soothed. "Are you all right? You screamed."

"A dream," Nesrin said, her hand on her heart. "A dream I've been having since I came here. I never used to have nightmares." She pressed her hands to her face. Then it all came flooding back. The day, the night. Tears welled in her eyes. Reyhan sat on the edge of the bed, her face twisted in sympathy. "Is he here?" She knew the answer. She looked at Reyhan anyway as the other woman shook her head. "What now?"

Now Reyhan's eyes glittered, and she blinked her own tears away, turning her face toward the curtained doors. Sweat beaded on her brow, and her fingers clawed into her legs. A hard exhale. She ducked her head, squeezing her eyes shut, her body shaking as if she were trying to push something too heavy.

Nesrin put a hand on her back. "Don't," she whispered. "It's all right. I'll think of something."

Reyhan shook her head violently, launching up to pace. She wore only a tan caftan, loose over a chemise, her black hair unbound. She looked wilder than Nesrin was accustomed to. More human.

"Are you hungry? We might think better with food in our stomachs." At least that's what her grandmothers had always believed. The mind was as empty as the belly. Reyhan stopped her pacing, shoulders falling.

"No. But I will try."

THEY SAT IN SILENCE ON cushions to either side of the table in the center of the common room. There was now a guard stationed outside in the garden. He had never been there before. Nesrin suspected there were others in the hall as well. She was a dangerous criminal now, after all. Her snide thought was immediately followed by shame. She was a criminal. Even if it felt strange. Even if she wanted to fight against the label. She had lied. To Ihsan. To the Princess Sultana. To everyone.

In her deepest heart, she had not wanted to live a lie for the rest of her days. Never able to see her family. Never able to look Ihsan in the eyes or have him know her real name. Her real self. True, he would hate it now.

But neither had she wanted to go to prison, or worse.

She picked at the food, nibbling a slice of apple. The guard in the garden paced, bored. It rankled, to see him there, when he could be doing something useful like helping guard refugee supplies.

Reyhan ripped her food into pieces without eating anything, scowling, one folded leg bouncing. The agitated energy was unusual for Reyhan, but Nesrin doubted she'd ever been under polite arrest before.

Nesrin finally gave up on eating anything more than a few slices of fruit and pushed her plate away. Reyhan rose, appearing relieved to have something to do. As she collected the dishes, the door to the hall opened and Kuhzey darted in. He was more disheveled than usual, as if he had fallen out of bed and appeared in the suite. His entari was misbuttoned, his curls flat on one side, eyes wide.

He hurried to Nesrin, his hands already flying through words before he had stopped in front of her. She stood, catching his hands in hers.

"Slow down, please," she said, holding his gaze. Behind him, the doors remained open, and the guard outside peered in. So Nesrin released Kuhzey's hands and asked him what was wrong with her own stilted signs.

He responded, fingers and hands slow for her benefit, language simplified: *No Sehzade.*

She frowned. "He isn't here, if that's what you mean." It was quicker to speak to him, but she also tried to emphasize with the words she did know in Kuhzey's language. He shook his head again. He made a sign she recognized. Steepled hands. He'd made it during her first trip to the estate, just before she'd been hurt in the looting. *Home. Not Home.*

"Do you mean you don't know where he is?"

He nodded. Nesrin glanced at Reyhan, who shrugged. She leaned around Kuhzey to speak to the guard in the hall. "Do you know where the Sehzade is?" The guard shook his head.

"He is upset. He probably wanted time alone," Nesrin said. She touched Kuhzey's arm. He looked so worried, panicked. Which was a far cry from his usual lost-in-the-clouds expression.

He huffed in impatience and whipped through another series of words. She caught *Sultana*, and *sent*, then *me*.

"The Sultana sent you to find him?" Reyhan guessed, and he nodded again. "But they should be..." She glanced at the guard, then whispered, "They should be dealing with preparations. For the Sultan."

Ihsan would not shirk his duties in preparing his uncle's funeral. Nesrin could not imagine him abandoning Naime at such a time unless he was forced to. Or unless he felt there was a very good reason. But he had been so angry. Her eyes stung and her throat tightened. She had done this to him, burdened him even more during his heartbreak. When he needed her.

"Did you check the stables? If he went anywhere, he would have needed a carriage or horse," Reyhan said.

Kuhzey snapped his fingers as if to agree, then ran out into the hall again. The guard glowered as he leaned in to pull the door closed. Nesrin sank onto the couch. She could hardly think around her grief at causing him pain, at betraying him. Worry nibbled at her. Could he be hurt?

"He's managed all these Turns without your worrying, it will not help now," Reyhan said crisply. Nesrin frowned at her. Reyhan frowned back. "He was too quick to blame you," she said. "Gave you no credit, no chances."

Nesrin smiled a little. "Be careful, people might begin to think you like me."

The sadness returned to Reyhan's face, and she sat beside Nesrin on the couch. They leaned into each other.

"I will do my best for you," Nesrin said. The spells threatened at the edges of her awareness, so she did not dare to say too much.

Reyhan scoffed, then flinched. She cursed, tears springing to her eyes. Nesrin recognized the frustration. She dabbed at the other woman's cheeks with her sleeve, then wrapped her arms around her shoulders and laid her head on one.

"You are too good, Nessa," Reyhan murmured, hooking one hand on Nesrin's arm. "Too kind for this place and these people."

"There is no such thing as too kind," Nesrin said.

"It is an act of bravery here." Reyhan tipped her head to Nesrin's. They were in this maelstrom together now. "To be kind, when it is so much easier, and safer, to be cruel."

"Is it safer? To make enemies instead of allies?" Without thinking, she began to braid Reyhan's hair. It was beautiful, silky black and pin-straight. Nesrin combed her fingers through it, her thoughts drifting to her sisters, and how long it had been since she'd done this for anyone. For once, Reyhan did not protest.

Nesrin had just finished when Kuhzey returned, just as violently and energetically as he had the first time. *He took a horse*, he said, eyes huge. Reyhan gripped the edge of her seat as if to stand.

Nesrin rose. "Where would he go with a horse?" If he had not returned to his home in the city?

Kuhzey gestured, but she did not know the signs he gave her. Kuhzey pointed at her.

"Oh no." Reyhan stood abruptly. She wove her fingers together, pacing toward the garden doors, then back, her expression pained. The color washed from her face, and she spun toward Kuhzey. "Did you tell the Princess Sultana that the Sehzade went to Mizraa?"

I came straight here, he said, and Nesrin translated.

"You must." There was more. Reyhan's eyes flared as she appeared to choke on the words. Her hands clenched at her sides. The muscles in her jaw went taut.

Nesrin put a hand on her shoulder. Whatever Reyhan was trying to say, her enchantments were fighting it. "Hurry," Reyhan groaned, and a drop of blood oozed from one nostril.

"Stop," Nesrin demanded, her own enchantments punishing her with a back-bending swipe of pain. She held Reyhan's shoulders as both women went to their knees. When Kuhzey moved to help, Reyhan managed to expel one more thought.

"He's…in…danger."

Then she collapsed.

Forty-Three

Ihsan left his entari behind, using the cloth belt to bind his caftan around his waist and hips so it would not catch or flap. He had his boots in one hand, his feet bare. He had tried to sleep, knowing he could not be effective lacking two full nights' sleep. But nightmares had stalked. Screams and smoke, fear and fire. When he had bolted up from it, night had already fallen.

He could not see the moon to guess how late it was, but by the silence in the house, most, if not all, were in bed. A few dim mage orbs lingered in the hall, and he extinguished them all. If he had spent a moment at all to think before he left Narfour, he could have asked Aysel to come along. She was the spy, after all. Could all but go invisible if she wished. Meanwhile, he simply had an affinity for darkness.

The house was not so large that he was in danger of getting lost. But he did not want to go opening random doors and accidentally wake someone. Instead, he headed for the kitchen, and the door that led to the garden he had seen from the window of the study. Outside, a breeze gusted, rustling leaves. The gravel bit at his bare feet, causing a few limps and winces before he made it to the grass and the base of the hill beyond the garden. There, he put his boots on and ran up the hill.

His lungs burned by the time he reached the top. It had been Turns since running had been a frequent occurrence for him. The hill flattened at the top. The grass waved at knee level. Only a fraction of moonlight caressed it, the moon a sliver in the sky. Ihsan was likely visible to anyone awake and looking at the hill. He hurried forward, striding toward a building set back so it was not visible from the house.

It was long, resembling a run in for livestock. The building was angled so the back wall was toward Ihsan and the house behind him. As Ihsan circled to the front, he was able to see that there were only three walls, the front entirely open. A forge, each of three sections of the building divided only by the supports for the roof. As Ihsan strode the length of the building, taking in the firepit, bench, and anvil, the skitter of fire prickled his skin.

He stopped, turning a full circle. The forge was empty, and silent. When he approached the brick-lined firepit and crouched, he could tell even before he put his hand on the bricks that they were cold. Ihsan stayed as he was, crouched, arms on his knees, tipping his head up like a hound scenting. It was not unlike standing next to a fire, the way his skin sensed heat. He twisted a slow circle in his crouch, until the crawling sense of warmth made the scars on his neck and face itch.

Ihsan rose and walked forward. The feeling led him down the backside of the hill, which was significantly steeper than the side leading to the house. Thin moonlight illuminated a dirt road that curved along the base of the hill then north, a pale ribbon through fields and orchards. Likely it was the main road through the estate, for wagons and workers to move between sections and transport harvests.

When he was halfway down the hill, the lack of moonlight made itself useful. A bare red glow tinted the air at the base of the hill, near where the road curved past. He approached cautiously, angling forward and down. There was no path that he could see in the darkness, so he waded through the high grass. It shushed against his boots and salvar as he walked, a roar to his ears.

The bloom of heat on his face intensified, though he suspected he could only feel it because of his power's opposition and his sensitivity to it. Before him, a section of the hill dropped off sharply, and that minor cliff had been dug out of the hill to create a hollow. It was angled away from him, facing a bank of trees and brambles that climbed up the hill on the opposite side. The road curved in such a way that the hollow would not be visible to anyone on it.

The mouth of the hollow glowed, flaring red, then gold, then fading.

Ihsan bent low and crept forward, angling down the hill to the nearest side of the hollow. There was no place for him to hide from the gaping hole in the hill, if he wished to see inside, then he was also in jeopardy of being seen by whoever was there. And there was definitely someone inside.

A fire mage. Their magic flashed over his skin with each flare of heat inside the hollow.

If he tried to exert magic to hide in the darkness, the fire mage was likely to sense it. Unless they were too focused on their task. He weighed the risks. Being caught spying on something that was clearly meant to be a secret. Was it an important enough secret for them to attempt to silence him? It was impossible to turn back now. What was he going to do, go back to bed?

Ihsan straightened, collected his power in a firm mental grip, and walked to the mouth of the hollow.

NESRIN HANDED REYHAN A CUP of tea. Her nose had finally stopped bleeding, and her shakes were subsiding. The sun had completely fallen behind the palace walls. Because of the lack of light, Nesrin could no longer see the guard stationed outside the patio doors.

"I need you not to harm yourself." Nesrin knelt on the carpet at Reyhan's feet. Her unconsciousness had seemed like mage sleep. A short mage sleep. Had Reyhan's own magic fought the spell so hard it had rendered her unconscious, or had it simply been the pain of the enchantment? Nesrin could not voice her questions; even the thought of them had the ring and bracelet sending skeins of fire into her skull.

Reyhan thought Ihsan was in danger. The unknown threat curled in Nesrin's chest, stealing her calm. Could she escape? Go to him? Warn him. If he was in danger, did that mean her family was as well? She stood as Reyhan leaned onto the back of the couch, tipping her head back.

"I can't stay here," Nesrin said, the buzzing anxiety spreading through her limbs. She shook her hands out at her sides, trying to clear some of the feeling from her body. It didn't help.

"You cannot go. The guards will catch you before you decide which hall to turn down." Reyhan sat up to take another sip of tea.

"You've just accepted all of this," Nesrin accused her.

"I know my limits, and some of yours. And I know the guards, and the palace," Reyhan snipped back. "Go, if you like. I will see you again when they drag you back by your hair."

"You seem to know a great deal, for a maid," Nesrin replied, growing angrier. Reyhan's haughty expression flattened, and she looked into her teacup.

"I was a palace maid for most of my life."

"Then why are you working for him?"

Reyhan lifted the teacup in a mock toast. "He offered benefits that the palace could not."

"Like my benefits?" Nesrin's anxiety bloomed into anger. At everything and everyone. This had to have something to do with Reyhan's promised, Kanat. With the glass and the empty workshop. What about Enver Balik? When he had refused the marriage, had Behram subdued him with magic as well?

Puzzles had never been her strength. But there were so many consequences if she did not solve this one.

Kuhzey slipped in from the hall. Nesrin got a quick look past his slim shoulders at the two guards before he closed the door on them.

"What did the Sultana say?" Nesrin asked. Kuhzey made the motion for what Nesrin suspected was horse, or riders. "She sent someone after him?" He nodded, then tapped his throat and opened his mouth. Then he shook his head. Nesrin felt guilty she had not learned more of his language yet, that he had to pantomime so many things for her benefit. "She could not voice cast that far?"

"She has the ability," Reyhan interjected. She set her teacup down. "But I suspect her power is still drained from aiding the Sultan."

"Now what?" Nesrin asked but did not expect an answer. She turned her back on them, twisting the ring on her finger, then the bracelet. If she could get them off. If she could make someone look at them. Really look at them. But she had tried everything. And Reyhan had been fighting it for Turns. What could she unravel that Reyhan could not?

"Why are you here with us, Kuhzey?" Reyhan asked, her brows raised. Nesrin turned back as Kuhzey pointed at Reyhan.

"You fell," Nesrin interpreted his hands. "He was worried."

Reyhan frowned. "You have more important things to worry about. I'm fine."

Kuhzey frowned back. *You are my friends.* His gestures were quick and angry. *I care.*

"It's all right, Kuhzey. I've been watching her. It has been a difficult few days, sometimes people react in surprising ways to these sorts of upsets. Bodies are fragile."

He looked from one to the other, frustrated. He finally settled on Nesrin and pointed an accusing finger at her. *You are my friend.*

And Ihsan's. His hands moved in such fluid rhythm, she lagged in her understanding. *Why did you lie to us*?

Her heart ached. Tears welled as the words tumbled inside her, beating to be free, and activating the fire in the ring. Heat deadened her ability to think, and she mentally recoiled from the thoughts of the truth.

They stared at each other. Kuhzey's gaze searching her face, waiting. She tried, again. And failed again. The pain was too much. Slicing through her, and reminding her, that even if she defeated the enchantment, she could not defeat Behram Kadir. He had everything she loved in the grip of his fist.

Kuhzey crossed the distance between them and closed his hands over theirs. His features were still tight with anger, but something else was there too. He shook her closed fists gently, moving them together, then apart. Nesrin glanced at Reyhan, who only shrugged.

Kuhzey snorted in annoyance, released her hands, and signed, *I know what it looks like to be unable to speak…* He tapped his heart, brows drawing down. He drew a circle around his face and pointed at hers. *…to be trapped.*

Her breath rushed out as she understood. He pointed at her hands again. *Say it to me this way.*

Again, she looked to Reyhan. Reyhan's brows rose and she stood from the couch, stepping forward. Nesrin had not thought to try spelling out her lies with her hands. She did not know if she had the language to, and thinking around it was painful.

"Don't," Reyhan pleaded. There was so much at stake, for both of them. Even if she did succeed. What if it worked? Kuhzey could tell the Sultana. It would force Behram's hand.

Kuhzey signed, *Try.*

The cost. The cost of unburdening herself to warn them of whatever danger Ihsan was in was her family. Her life was forfeit either way, by prison or by execution. Could she trade her family for him? And Reyhan's secrets? What about her promised? Would telling Kuhzey mean his life too? Tears welled as Nesrin lifted her hands. Whatever Behram Kadir was doing that required this much magic, this many lies, this many bound people…stopping it was surely more important.

The spell still would not let her touch the ring, and if she tried to think of what she would sign to Kuhzey, the feeling of burning up inside filled her nearly to screaming. So she did not think. She closed her eyes and thought of Ihsan. Of the way he smiled when he did not want to. She thought of Sanem, laughing and happy with Anil. Of the littles, chasing frogs in the fields.

And last, she thought of seeds, and flowers, and hope, and that gave her a rush of glittering resolve.

Ring. Nesrin closed her eyes, squeezed them tight, focused on an image of the ice of Ihsan's magic swirling in circles over his skin. *Magic. Hurts.* It was hard to hold the images in her mind and also think of words she knew the sign for. *Trap.*

The fire did not come. Reyhan grasped Nesrin's arm. Nesrin opened her eyes. Kuhzey looked quizzical, but his gaze dropped from her face to her hands. To the ring. He grabbed her wrist and took hold of the bauble. When he pulled, Nesrin's knees buckled with the sheer force of the fire that filled her from head to toe. It sucked her breath and voice away, seared the inside of her skull.

Reyhan ripped Kuhzey's hand away from the ring, and he released Nesrin. She collapsed to all fours, each breath scorching.

Her eyes watered, her throat felt as though she had not had water in days. She could not answer him, could not grasp thought enough to know if she was relieved, or even more afraid.

I will tell the Sultana, he signed to Nesrin when she lifted her head and looked at him. He bolted from the room.

FORTY-FOUR

THE TWO MEN LOOKED UP when Ihsan appeared in the light from their workshop. One sat on a bench, spinning a rod with a dollop of red-hot glass bulging at the end. The other squatted in front of him with a wooden mold held open. The man on the bench, a fire mage, dropped the rod at the sight of Ihsan, and the man on the floor leapt away as the molten glass hit the dirt floor. Smoke hissed up.

The two men stared. The one on the bench rose, tense, as if Ihsan might attack.

"I'm going to give you a single chance to tell me, of your own volition, what you are doing," he said, his magic echoing glacially in his voice. The fire mage pulled his gloves from his hands, jaw tight. The other mage got up, the movement drawing Ihsan's attention to a small wooden crate, lined with a double layer of burlap, and filled with what looked like ashes. Or crushed shell.

"You aren't allowed here," the man by the crate said.

"I am allowed wherever I wish." Ihsan's words echoed in his memory, words he'd said to Nesrin, tangling her even more deeply with his confusion. "You may address me as Sehzade. Who are you?"

Both bowed, exchanging a look as they rose.

"I am Kanat," the fire mage said. That was the man Aysel had said abandoned his shop. The one promised to Reyhan. Who no one could find. He appeared to be working of his own free will.

"How do you know Nesrin?" Ihsan ordered.

Kanat shook his head. "I don't know anyone by that name."

"You?" Ihsan demanded of the other. He also shook his head. Ihsan's sleepless nights and razor-edged temper fought his logic with irrationality. He wanted to start tearing the workshop apart. To threaten them. "Your chance is running out," he said instead.

"They will not tell you anything, Sehzade." A voice came from behind him and Ihsan whirled, calling ice into his hand in the shape of a weapon, the end brutally pointed. Osman stood there, framed in the light, hands gripped behind his back. Relaxed, and smiling apologetically. "Impressive," he said. "That is not your father's power. Lalam's?"

"My powers were forged in fire." Ihsan surprised himself with his own words. Nesrin's doing as well. "I will offer you the same thing I offered them. One chance to tell me what is going on here. Refuse me, and the answer will be forced from you during your stay in the Cliffs."

Osman's smile saddened. "The Cliffs would be a welcome comfort, after these Turns."

"Who are you?" Ihsan gestured to the workshop. "What is this?"

Osman gave a dry, soundless laugh. "I am no one, now. I used to be friend to your father." His words cut off, his eyes squeezing shut.

Ihsan frowned. Was he ill? Ihsan let go of the magic holding the ice weapon in its shape against the heat in the hollow. It melted away.

"Wheel, I forgot the pain," he groaned.

"I do not know you," Ihsan said. "Yet you claim to have been a friend of my father's."

Osman sat on the bench. "Did he tell you about the goats?" He heaved the words, bending forward, fingers curling hard on the edge of the bench, face pinching. Ihsan looked to the other two men for explanation, but they both watched Osman, with manic intensity. Each moment was stranger, and that brought a looming sense of foreboding that made Ihsan even edgier than he had been.

"Goats?" Ihsan said, warily. His father had only spoken of goats during one story. One of his favorites, which he recounted at any opportunity. When he and Osman Altimur had driven a herd of dairy goats through the hall during a Council. "What about them? Were you there as well?" The name coincidence did not escape Ihsan. But as far as he knew, Osman Altimur was dead.

"No." Osman curved forward abruptly, as if he might fall off the bench. The tendons in his neck bulged. Kanat made a sound of protest, one hand out as he stepped closer, but Osman held up his own to stop him. They stood in mute horror, tensed to move if Osman fell. He forced himself straight. "Not also. It was Mazhar, and me." Each word seemed to be a battle for the man.

"Are you claiming to be Osman Altimur? He's dead." Ihsan surveyed the other two, but the bizarre conversation did not seem to be a revelation to them.

"Dead? Is that what he told you?" Osman coughed. "I might as well be." Blood welled at the corners of his mouth. His eyes closed; magic flashed briefly in jagged gold lines along the collar of his caftan. "Caner is coming," he growled in pain, hitching forward again. He slumped sideways, stretching his right hand toward Kanat. "Help me."

"I can't," Kanat said miserably.

Osman spat blood. "Take the hand if you must."

"You need a healer," Ihsan said. "What is happening to him?" he asked the other two, who did little more than stare. "Someone answer me!"

The earth mage shook his head, but Kanat set his jaw and whirled, striding to the back of the hollowed-out cliff, where mage orbs bobbed against stone carved by earth magic.

A rack of tools lined three quarters of it. With poles for the glass, pinchers, tongs, and tweezers of various sizes, wooden paddles, and a stack of molds like the one they had been using when Ihsan came in. Kanat took down an ugly, clunky blade. The kind used for cutting back brush.

"Have you lost your wits?" Ihsan stepped between Kanat and the bench, addressing Osman. Was it possible the Blight had affected them? Stealing their sanity? They had heard of nothing like that in Narfour. But that did not mean it wasn't possible.

"My wits are mine," Osman said, swiping at the trickle of blood from his nose. He looked at the smear on his wrist. "As they have not been for Turns. Move." He grabbed Ihsan's caftan and slung him sideways.

Kanat switched the blade from one hand to another, then gripped it in both. Sweat beaded at his temples as Osman spread his hand open on the bench. Three rings adorned his middle three fingers, each with a dark red stone. Kanat closed his eyes briefly, his knuckles going white. They were mad. Each of them.

Ihsan lunged for the blade, but the earth mage wrestled him back.

"Now," Osman ordered, the word a low, hollow groan that rose to a roar of pain. His arm shook as if it were controlled by someone else, his back hunching in agony as he gripped his elbow with his opposite hand. Kanat lifted the blade.

He jerked at the same time there was a wet impact. His eyes went wide, and he stumbled forward, the blade slipping out of his hands and clattering to the dirt. He went to a knee, blood spreading over his caftan. When he reached to catch himself on the bench he missed, rocking forward.

Osman caught Kanat with a curse. There was a crossbow bolt half buried in Kanat's back.

"Stop him, or he'll kill us all," Osman ordered the earth mage. The man released Ihsan to obey. A second bolt struck him in the chest, and he toppled backwards with a grunt.

The light within the hollow made the darkness outside more absolute, cloaking their attacker. Ihsan pulled all the water he could from the air, driving a sheet of ice up between them and the night. As he turned to Osman, the older man dropped Kanat's lifeless body, grabbed the blade, and lifted it. Ihsan ripped it from his grasp.

"Enough!" he roared.

"You do not understand." Osman forced a breath, sweat breaking out over his skin as all his color washed away. "I *am* Osman Alt—" The veins in his left eye burst, spilling red into the white. "Altimur." He curled an arm around his stomach, then vomited foam and blood on the bench.

"Stop." Ihsan grabbed him by his collar and dragged him to his feet. "Stop whatever this is." He was killing himself to get the words out.

"Magic," Osman said, his teeth bloodied. He gripped Ihsan's shoulders. The skin on his neck and face began to blister and his eyes fluttered as he sank toward the floor. Magic seared Ihsan's throat and scorched away his sense. "To...silence...us," Osman hissed. His head lolled, but he shook it, and blood trickled from his nostrils. "He takes everything you love"—dark blood ran from his ears—"and holds it hostage." Each word was apparent agony, crumpling him more. Osman collapsed into Ihsan, his skin breaking open and weeping.

The smell came. Blistered flesh. Singed clothing. Ihsan held his breath, leaning away, but he was trapped, while Osman burned from the inside out. Panic gnawed around Ihsan's thoughts, but he fought it away. He could not fall apart here. Another bolt slammed into the ice wall. It fissured down the middle, and Ihsan cursed. Osman's weight pulled Ihsan with him, so both men ended up on the ground.

"Who did this to you? Why?" Ihsan grabbed the man's head, and Osman's gaze fixed on his.

"She's gone," Osman forced, his gaze distant and clouded, pupils going wide. The flare of fire magic was so powerful Ihsan could feel its heat. But Osman was an earth mage, it was not his magic, though it seemed to come from him.

Osman collapsed onto an elbow, then rolled onto his back. "Mazhar is gone. To keep me. To trap me." His words were garbled around blood. "I wanted…safe." He swallowed. "My son…" His voice faded on a hiss as his body convulsed.

The ice wall shattered as the life left Osman Altimur's eyes. Ihsan spun, tearing open his salvar across his knee. Pain lashed up his leg. Caner strode out of the dark.

He looked first at Osman on the ground, then focused on Ihsan. "I have permission to kill you, and you can die knowing you caused nothing but death by coming here." He leveled the bow.

Ihsan lunged sideways, rolling awkwardly. The bow fired and the bolt struck the workbench. Ihsan charged at Caner, slamming into him with his shoulder and driving him backward. The crossbow fell from his hands. Ihsan kicked it away.

A fireball sizzled to life in Caner's hand, and Ihsan flexed his own open, then closed it around the ice that gathered there, molding it into a pike. Caner swiped at Ihsan with the fire, and Ihsan swung the ice, driving it into Caner's belly and up. It began to melt immediately, mingling with Caner's blood as he staggered back, wide-eyed. The fireball wickered out. Ihsan clutched Caner's caftan, twisting his fist in it to hold him up.

"Who is in control here?" *Say his name. Kadir.*

Caner smiled. "You cannot stop him. I already warned him you were here." He heaved a breath that sounded all wrong, then gaped like a fish. The fire mage grew too heavy to hold, slipping and pulling Ihsan to the ground again as he dropped to sit in the dirt, gasping for air that would not fill his lungs. Then Caner was gone, his eyes blank and staring. Ihsan laid him back, pressing his bloody hands to the dirt as he tried to catch his own breath on hands and knees.

He had never killed anyone. The realization made him sick. The smells, the sudden silence, his lone, panting breaths. There was more death around him in that moment than he'd ever seen in all his life. His thoughts were slow, like cold limbs, not quite in his control.

Ihsan sat back on his heels. He moved to shove his hands through his hair, but red and rust stained them in streaks. His clothes as well.

After a moment, he willed himself to his feet, and turned back to Osman, Kanat, and the earth mage whose name he had not learned. When Osman had dropped Kanat, he'd knocked over the bucket of ashes. Ihsan toed it with his boot. It crunched. Ashes did not crunch. He frowned and crouched.

Not ashes, but an uneven powder, with larger bits and shards. Ihsan took a handful and lifted it up. That sense of fire still licked at his mind, his power. He glanced behind him, but Caner was still. Ihsan's heart sped, his thoughts spinning faster, his breath matched. He'd killed him. Had caused all of the deaths. His hand closed on the powder and bits of it stabbed his palm, centering him again.

He opened his hand. There were smooth bits within the finer powder. And jagged splinters. Some had a pocked appearance.

The world slowed. Sounds dimmed, a fuzzy hum deadened the air. He picked up a fragment in his fingers, smooth on one side, pocked on the other. He looked at the pile spilled on the floor at his feet. More, like the one in his fingers, some larger, some too fine to examine. He dropped the piece into the pile. This was not powder. Or ash.

It was bone dust.

He crawled forward, to the puddle of hardening glass in front of the bench. Flecks swirled within it. Like macabre stardust. Ihsan lurched to his feet. He needed his wits, but he could not think, his mind leaping from assumption to assumption, lost. He focused on the men. First, on Kanat.

He would have to tell Reyhan. He rolled the man onto his back and swept his eyes closed with a hand, unable to look at the lifeless stare. There was a ring on his hand, but not a promise band, which he would have worn on his middle finger. The leather apron he wore interfered with Ihsan's search, but he did find a necklace with another, plain band hanging from it. Ihsan yanked it off and pocketed it.

Then he moved to the earth mage and dragged him to lay beside Kanat. He wore nothing but simple workman's clothes. And a ring similar to Kanat's. He was younger, close to Ihsan's age, at least in appearance. Dark hair, no beard. Ihsan would have thought the same of Kanat if he had not known his connection to Reyhan. Was this man missing from somewhere as well?

He tried to move Osman but could not touch him. The burns on his skin made Ihsan's stomach twist in threat and sweat break out over his body. Whatever fire had killed him had partially burned Osman's clothes. Anywhere a blister showed on his skin, the clothes were singed.

Dizziness skittered over him, tipping the world on its side, and he sat abruptly. The movement put Osman's back in view. The caftan bunched, half burned away. Most of the skin beneath was ruined. He would have looked away, could barely tolerate looking at the flesh that was so like his own had been. But he had to.

On the nape of Osman's neck, no longer hidden by the collar of his caftan, a mark like a scar marred the skin. But it was like no scar Ihsan had ever seen.

He held his breath and leaned closer, tugging the singed clothing down. Lines like spider legs radiated from a central marking. Not a scar, a sigil. A Deval's rune. Burned into Osman's skin.

He had never seen or even heard of such a thing. The strokes were far more intricate, more detailed, than any rune Ihsan had ever even read about. There were some strokes he recognized. The entire rune was centered around the shape for *burning.* Why was there a spell carved into Osman's skin? Ihsan braced, letting loose a sound of protest as he grabbed the caftan in both hands and ripped it open down the back.

The skin of Osman's back was cooked from the inside, blistered and peeling. But enough remained that Ihsan could see the marks of more runes. He pressed his bloodied palms to his brow and closed his eyes to block out the sight. His stomach cramped; his limbs shook as more sweat beaded on his skin. Panic prowled, and Ihsan fought it, trying to find a path through the labyrinth of memory and terror that tried to confound his reason.

Bones and glass. Runes in skin. He could not have conceived of anything so vile. Was someone trying to spell...people? Was that even possible? A rune did not hold power without a mage fueling it. Either Osman was powering the rune with his own magic, which made no sense, or another mage was controlling the rune. But they were not following him around day and night. Something else—the rings. He had been trying to cut them from his hands.

Only objects could hold enchantments, could hold a spell to draw on a mage's magic. But the methods were no longer taught. Enchantments were too dangerous, too uncontrolled. As far as he knew, only a Sival could work an enchantment. Why would they be using sigils, Deval magic?

What secrets were worth this?

As his thoughts paced, a different awareness slithered through him. Why did he sense fire when all the fire mages around him were dead?

He was distracted from the question by a sound. He opened his eyes and lifted his head, listening. It came again, a high trill. Then in chorus. Not a nightbird. He got to his feet and walked out of the hollow. Was it screaming? The fields beyond were quiet, and for a few moments, all he could hear was the shush of grass as the wind combed through it. But smoke rode that breeze, making Ihsan gag. Then the sounds came again, a scream, no longer muffled by the stone of the cliff. Ihsan jogged up the hill. A muddy orange light pulsed beyond the hill, and the sight nearly shattered his control of his magic.

First, he saw the remains of the forge, burned to the ground. The supports holding the roof had collapsed, and flames skittered insipidly over the tiles, seeking more fuel.

The house came into view, stopping Ihsan mid-stride. Flames roared from the windows and doors. The plaster would not burn, but everything inside was. Slowly, he crested the hill. All he could hear was his ragged breath, somehow the same sound as the rush of flames.

Caner had set the house and forge on fire to hide whatever secrets this place held. Ihsan fought his body, every fiber screaming to flee, his hands unsteady and clammy. Black clung to the edge of his vision, and thoughts, trying to squeeze him out. He could not breathe or think. The heat from the house touched his face and a feral cry rose in his throat.

Then he saw her. The woman who looked so much like Nesrin, on her hands and knees in the gravel drive, frantically drawing runes in the dirt, two others with her, one doing the same as her, the other standing behind them. She was in sleeping clothes, pale in the moonlight, her feet were bare. Her hair hung loose and blocked her face, and all he could see was Nesrin. How she had leapt onto a wagon to save strangers. How she had done her best at everything put in front of her, with no magic, and no experience.

He could not do less than that. Not when he had the power to help.

He surged into a run. He ran fast enough to outrun his thoughts, to outpace his own panic as the fire roared above him from the windows. The roses were wilted and browned from their proximity to the heat. He hit the gravel driveway at a sprint and staggered to a stop beside the others. One was the stablehand, the other was an older man who appeared to be another servant. The woman did not look up when Ihsan arrived, whispering her spell as she traced the outline of a water rune that was pulling water from the ground to pool at the surface.

The house slumped oddly, one of the walls beginning to buckle. A booming crack made the woman flinch. She swiped her hand through the rune, called a word, and a lash of water struck the front of the house. And did nothing. She sobbed as she swiped the rune away and began again.

"They'll come from the village," the older man said, putting his hands on her shoulders. "We need more help."

"It will be too late," she wailed, and caught sight of Ihsan. Her eyes widened. "Please. Sehzade, please, our family is in there. My sisters. My mother and brother. Can you help them?"

Ihsan's vision tunneled. His heart thumping, his ears filled with the crack and snap of wood exploding in the heat of the flames. His lungs were closing, the acid scent of smoke and the heat of the flames driving him into the feral memory of being trapped in fire. He had to escape.

A spiral of magic twined through his body, the cold spreading through his limbs, pushing the heat away. Leaving ice and clarity. The air around him chilled, and their breath billowed white. Frost spread away from his feet.

The cold swirled in him, the magic waking on his skin. It numbed everything. The fear. His thoughts. His body. Sparks and still-glowing bits of ash floated through the air, and any that came near him snuffed before they reached him.

Had he noticed that before? Or had it been so long that he was near enough fire that he had never seen his magic do that? Shield him physically, as it did emotionally. *It saved you*. Nesrin's awestruck voice in his memory woke him from his paralysis.

It had not failed him. It was not twisted, or damaged. No more than he was twisted, or damaged. His magic was scarred, like his skin. Because they had survived.

Ihsan had the overwhelming urge to apologize to his magic, as if it were a friend he had wronged.

"Where are they?" As he asked, the western end of the roof collapsed inward. The woman shrieked, pressing her hands to her mouth.

"This floor. We were staying in the servants' quarters." The older man indicated the west-facing side of the building. Ihsan grabbed the stablehand by the arm.

"You are Fifth House?" It was common practice to have a fire mage employed in stables, exactly because all the fodder was such a hazard and they could often sense and stop any fires before they went wild.

The young man gave a mute nod. "Only an Aval."

"I only need you to help me clear a path and show me where to go."

"I'm coming." The woman got to her feet, and the man stepped forward as she did.

"No, I cannot keep everyone safe and find your family. You can help by staying out here." That was the truth, but he also did not want the pressure of more people with him. More people there to see him fall apart or fail.

"We can bring you water." She indicated their buckets and the water still pooling on the ground from her spells. Ihsan scowled but pointed.

"To the steps, no farther."

Her nose scrunched, brows drawing down. Just like Nesrin. He looked away, toward the house. He wrapped his fear in a cage of rime and will. There was no alternative. He would not let people die if he could save them.

They moved forward in a cluster, across the gravel, and up the stairs. The woman and older man each carried two buckets of water, and its presence gave him something to hold in his thoughts other than fear.

Magic whipped over his skin, winter-bright, as ice and frost spread from each of his steps, melting the moment he moved away. In the crystal shell of his magic, the heat was kept at bay. The woman and man set the buckets on the top step.

The door was ruined, the wooden frame falling in on itself, the door crumpling. The incredible heat pushed like a weight into the opposition of his magic. The stablehand began his spell, coaxing fire away from the doorway. There would be no moisture in the air inside the house; Ihsan would be unable to call ice inside.

He hefted a bucket, threw its contents toward the burned-out doorway, then quickly shoved a hand away from his chest. The water blasted forward, freezing as it went, creating a tunnel of ice into the center of the home. The fire licked at it, battling Ihsan's will as if it had one of its own. The tunnel glowed orange with reflected flames. The concentration it took to hold the ice against the fire emptied his mind of anything else, even fear. He hefted another bucket and brought it with him as he entered the tunnel of ice.

"I will hold this spell as long and as far as I can, you have to search for them," he directed the stablehand. The two of them moved forward through the dripping tunnel, shoulder to shoulder. The young man slipped twice, falling to his hands and knees once. Ihsan hoisted him up. The boy called, and they both listened, though the hiss of fire on ice muffled anything they might hear. The flames roared, sucking air away and leaving them both tired and breathless before they'd moved halfway through the central room.

"I hear something," the stablehand said, stopping in front of Ihsan. They listened together, and Ihsan heard it too. A weak cry to the left. The stablehand glanced around, trying to find his bearings. "The servants' quarters would be that way." He pointed northwest of where they were. Ihsan only remembered a vague outline of the central room and many doors. He had not spent enough time to know which they were aiming for. But he released his magical grip on the ice to his left, and the young man swept another path clear with his own spell, though it cost him. Ihsan could sense how much weaker the spell was from the first.

"There." He pointed toward a door half open, where a pile of collapsed supports blocked it from opening farther.

The cry came again. Smoke rolled in ponderous, black swirls; the only thing holding them away from suffocating the two of them was the fire mage's weak control. Ihsan lifted the bucket of water and repeated his own work, slinging it toward the door and freezing a new tunnel. They slipped and collided together as they tried to hurry to the door.

The fallen supports still smoldered, too hot to touch, for Ihsan anyway. His magic wound tighter, stronger, holding the ice around them and his panic at bay, but siphoning his energy at a frightening rate. "Is there anyone in there?"

"Yes," a small, raw, voice cried, "help!" A child. The stablehand shoved the tangled pile of supports, budging them sideways. He threw his entire body against them, his clothes burning away in places but his skin untouched. Finally, they shifted, and he grabbed the charred door with both hands, ripping it open. A young girl crouched just inside, covered in soot and ash, and beyond her a man held another girl in his arms. She was dead or unconscious. A woman lay at his feet, unmoving.

"Can you walk?" Ihsan asked of the man in the room. He nodded, fatigue dragging his expression.

"Can one of you take her?" He indicated the woman on the floor. The stablehand did so, though he was of a similar size as the woman. Ihsan lifted the conscious girl into his arms. She went without protest, though tears streaked through the soot on her face. She coughed and dropped her head on Ihsan's shoulder. The man inside the room slung the girl he held over his shoulder, and as he crept out of the room, trying to stay beneath the swirling wall of smoke, Ihsan saw he was missing an arm.

He took an assessing look at Ihsan's ice tunnel, eyes bleary and smoke-burned. Then he moved forward without a word.

"I cannot hold the fire any longer," the stablehand said, straining under the dead weight of the woman he carried. As soon as he said it, Ihsan felt the fire close in on his tunnel, the heat melting it faster than he could freeze it.

"Run," he ordered. Holes opened around them, windows to the flames, and smoke rushed in to fill the space. It stung his eyes, blinding him and poisoning his breath. Everyone tripped and stumbled, bumping into each other. "Right!" he bellowed when they reached what was left of his first tunnel. It was gone, leaving a swiftly drying, wet path to the door. He blinked to clear the tears streaming from his eyes, saw the one-armed man stumble and jump aside as a burning support dropped from above to crash beside them.

"Catch!" the woman shouted from outside. Ihsan saw her move as he had, throwing a bucket of water toward the man holding the unconscious girl. His lips moved, shaping the water into a comet that shot toward Ihsan. Ihsan shaped it into an arch of ice, just strong enough to hold as he and the stablehand raced beneath it, more ceiling crumbling above them. The pieces smashed into the arch, spraying sparks and shards into their backs as they dove outside. He curled his body around the girl he held, landing on his side and sliding through the gravel.

"Anne?" the woman outside pleaded, kneeling and embracing the other woman as the one-armed man laid her on the gravel then collapsed beside them. Ihsan released his hold on the girl, who scrambled to the others. He groaned, forcing himself to his hands and knees, then rolled to sit. He coughed, trying to wipe the lingering sting of smoke from his eyes. His lungs burned. They felt too small for the breaths he wanted to take.

The house shuddered and leaned, collapsing from the middle inward, pouring smoke and flame into the black sky.

Ihsan looked up when a person stopped in front of him. It was the older man who had waited outside. He crouched in front of Ihsan. "I am Temel Irmak," he said. "I owe you the lives of my family."

"Are they all right?" Ihsan's voice was rougher than the gravel beneath him, scraped raw and weak by smoke. Temel looked behind him, where the woman and girl tended to the others, sisters, Ihsan guessed.

"They will be. They are breathing. Metin prevented them getting burned." He gestured at the younger man, whose face was soot-stained. Then he looked at Ihsan. "Who are you?"

"Ihsan," he said. He did not have energy for more. The lack of sleep and expenditure of magic was too much. There was a tug in his mind, in his bones, to sleep. But he could not.

"He's the Sehzade," Nesrin's lookalike said. "He was visiting the Pasha."

"Oh." Temel managed a strange, head-only bow from his crouched position. "Have you seen Bardakci Pasha?"

Ihsan closed his eyes as a wave of dizziness nearly tipped him sideways. "He's dead. Caner Ansar is dead."

"In the fire?" Temel sat, face drawn, voice hollow.

"No," Ihsan said. He did not know what else to say. He did not know who was an ally of Ansar's. Who was tangled in whatever this was. "Is this your family?" he asked instead. Temel nodded.

"Your daughter looks remarkably like..."

Temel's expression turned fierce. The woman looked up from tending her mother, who was coughing. She left her mother's side to come to Ihsan's. "Who? Who do I look like?"

"My wife," Ihsan said. The words were out, put together by a mind barely functioning, before he considered they were not perfectly true. Though it felt right to say it. He still wanted it. Wanted her. The woman's eyes filled with tears.

"Oh," she said, dropping beside her father, taking Ihsan in with a wary look. "My sister was taken to Narfour. And we do not know her fate. But obviously she isn't your wife. She's only a servant, like us."

"Taken?" Ihsan repeated. The woman's eyes welled. Temel checked over his shoulder at the others.

"She took my place. I was supposed to go, to be betrothed. She took my place because I was promised to someone here. She left in the middle of the night...she..." The words died.

"Nesrin," Ihsan said. It could be no one else. He almost laughed. Not a criminal. A loving sister.

Her expression transformed with hope. "You do know her! Is she all right? Bardakci Pasha told us not to speak of her. Told us she was in danger."

"What danger?" Ihsan asked. If there were any danger besides the consequences of lying about her nobility.

"Only that if anyone found out who she was, and what she had done, he would kill her."

"Who?" Ihsan growled. "Osman?"

She shook her head. "The Grand Vizier."

Kadir had tried to pass Nesrin off as a noble. And Osman had upheld the lie. Why? Because he had to. Because the spells written on his body would kill him for revealing the lies he was made to tell. But why all of that—certainly not only in order to hide Nesrin's identity.

Osman Altimur had disappeared from Narfour before Ihsan and Naime were born. Had he been out here all those Turns? Trapped by Kadir? With magic? Or threats? He'd mentioned a woman, and a son. Where were they?

If Kadir was willing to do that to a man of his same rank, was able to do it to a Sival of the Fourth House, he could surely do it to a void, a woman naive to him and everything about Narfour. But he could not trap her with an enchantment, could he? Not if she was a void with no magic to power an enchantment.

Panic chased away all Ihsan's exhaustion, all his nausea. The image of Osman burning himself alive to tell his secrets. The look on Nesrin's face when Ihsan had asked her for the truth.

Wheel curse him, he'd left her there. Alone. With Behram Kadir aware that his secrets were being stripped away. He jumped to his feet. "I need my horse."

Forty-Five

Kuhzey had not returned by the next morning. No one had come except for a lone maid, who had brought a tray of food and tea before the sun rose, which was now tepid. Nesrin poured some anyway and tried to drink it. There were many reasons why Kuhzey would not have returned immediately. And none of them put her at ease.

Reyhan paced to the garden doors, then sat, picked her cup up, forgot to take a sip before replacing it. She stood, fingers worrying the bracelet on her wrist. Occasionally she would work her way through a series of the signs she could make. Nesrin's only guess was that she was attempting to piece together her story with the few words she knew. She recognized the sign for "magic" repeated frequently.

"What is keeping them?" Reyhan dropped her hands to her sides in exasperation.

Nesrin was more concerned with questions she could not ask and Reyhan could not answer. What danger did Ihsan face in Mizraa? And would it encompass her family, because he was there?

Now she had to stand as well, needing movement to slow her spiraling thoughts. The sleepy guard at the garden doors had his head tipped back, staring into the grey sky, mostly turned away from them.

Occasionally he gave a slow blink. If he fell asleep, could she sneak out? She abandoned the idea immediately.

Then the door opened, and Reyhan drew in a strained breath. Nesrin spun.

The hall guard stood framed in the doorway, his face twisted with panic.

Red bloomed across his throat then spilled down the front of his uniform. His dazed gaze fixed on Nesrin's as he dropped to the floor, hands going to his throat. The red spilled over them too as he pitched forward. Nesrin's breaths came raw and ragged, her mind unable to grasp and make sense of what was happening before her. Nausea twined with fear, vines circling her throat.

She heard Reyhan inhale, and the thick compression of a dampening fell into place as Reyhan released her scream. Nesrin's gaze traveled up from the guard and the red spreading on the white tile. Red blood. On the guard, and the black clothes of the man standing over him. And the crimson figure at his side. Fire and blood.

She was a little girl, holding her older brother between her legs while she tightened a tourniquet around the stump of his arm. His screams in her ears. The man beneath the horse was red. With blood, flesh, and white bone. Red clothes stained black. Fire had burnt a charred ring in the grass around him, had cooked the flesh of the horse that lay atop him. The smell…

The blood. Always he was covered in blood. Her gaze met fire as she dropped to the floor, on her knees. The empty dream pulled at Nesrin, trying to yank her away from the twisted spiral of present and memory, but she resisted, curling her fingers into the wool of the rug beneath her. She sobbed a breath as a curved knife dripped red from the stranger's fingers.

Beside him, Behram made a dismissive sound as the man in black wiped the blade clean on the soldier's clothes. Behram flicked a hand in signal as he stepped aside. Mahir came from behind him, striding into the room, with Kuhzey in his grasp. Kuhzey tried to bolt toward

Reyhan and Nesrin and Reyhan stepped forward to help. Mahir closed a hand on Reyhan's throat as he grabbed the back of Kuhzey's caftan and turned, throwing Kuhzey with an earth mage's strength. Kuhzey slammed into a chair, toppling it, and collapsed in a heap on the floor. He gagged for air.

"Because of you and your meddling"—Behram crossed to Nesrin as Mahir shoved Reyhan onto a couch and the man in black closed and locked the hall door—"that mongrel of a prince has run off to Mizraa and destroyed everything."

He crouched in front of her, taking hold of her wrist. Nesrin slapped him with her free hand, all her fear and fury in the strike. The sound fell flat inside the dampening.

Fire burst open in his eyes. "I should kill you." He closed his fingers in Nesrin's hair and yanked her forward. "But you are too useful to me, to a war I can no longer prevent." Standing, Behram pulled her up by her hair. Grabbing for his wrist, she shrieked, but the sound was swallowed by the dampening and he was unmoved by her clawing hands and kicking legs.

The guard from the garden opened the doors and bowed as Cemil strode into the room. That single point of hope shriveled. Cemil stopped, appearing agitated, gaze jumping from one direction to another. It touched Nesrin's and skittered away.

Behram shoved her into a pile at Cemil's feet. "Bring her."

Cemil led them across the garden and into a windowless hallway meant for servants. He kept a firm grip on one of Nesrin's arms, dragging her along as he peered around corners and moved from hall to hall.

Nesrin hoped someone would cross their path, someone would notice the oddity of their formation. But Cemil navigated the entirety of the palace unseen. The early mark was not their ally either, as Nesrin had noted that the palace was not a place where much took place before midmorning.

None of them spoke, or fought, because the guard from the garden had Kuhzey at knifepoint, and the man in black had Reyhan the same. But they hardly needed that. Between Cemil, Behram, and Mahir, there were a variety of instantaneous deaths awaiting them.

Eventually the servant halls Cemil seemed so familiar with set them out in a main hall, which they followed through a portion of the palace Nesrin had never seen. Cemil opened a door in an alcove, and the daylight spilled in.

They stepped outside into the warm, thick air. The Kalspire speared the sky to the east. They had come out north of the palace, then. A path broke away from the door in three directions, east, west, and north. Only the north led away from the palace, the other two hugged its outer wall as they curved away.

Cemil tugged Nesrin forward, along a path of gravel through a grove of oak trees. She thought briefly of running, but while she might have chanced the consequences on her own, she could not bring herself to risk Kuhzey and Reyhan.

The stones cut at her feet. Not so long ago they had been accustomed to walking bare everywhere, but turns in shoes and on carpets had softened them. She flinched and stumbled, Cemil pulling her each time with a little yank.

The grove path wound through a scattering of boulders, which grew in size as they neared the edge of the trees. They were moss-covered, some taller than the people that walked between them.

"See if Banu left the horses where she said she would," Cemil ordered the man who had stood guard at Nesrin's room. He handed Kuhzey off to Mahir, then jogged ahead. They continued on, Mahir dragging Kuhzey, the other guard forcing Reyhan forward with a grip on her wrists and hair, and Cemil with Nesrin.

If they had horses waiting, where did Behram mean to go?

The guard returned and gave a breathless report. "There are only five horses. We'll have to double up."

"That will slow us too much," the man in black said to Behram.

"Indeed. If you do not wish for the Sultana's storm mage to do to you what she did to Rifat, I suggest you find a solution to that problem."

"Yes, Efendim," the man in black said. He drew the same blade he'd murdered the hall guard with and crossed the three steps between him and the other guard. Before the man understood what his intent was, the blade was buried to the hilt in his gut. He slumped to the gravel path. The man in black bent and snapped the other man's neck. Nesrin's vision swam, bile stinging in her mouth. More blood. More death. Something inside her spun. Faster.

There was death. Natural. Given for life, to feed, or to finish. But this...murder. Thoughtless, senseless, uncaring. Twice. Her repulsion bloomed into anger. Heat like sun unfurled along the scar that circled her body, blazing across her cheek. Her eyes went dry and hot.

The man in black straightened, gaze on Reyhan.

"Don't you touch her," Nesrin snarled, and her voice was strange, layered, like in her dreams. She lunged for the man but came up against Cemil's hold. Cemil tsked, yanking her backwards against him, cinching an arm around her shoulders.

"Try not to be stupid," he said in her ear. She tried to twist free, but he was much stronger than she would have guessed. "This is *not* the time."

Nesrin stilled. Her blood thumped in her body, in time with something else. Another thrum she did not know. Her scar ached, her head pounded. Between her anger and her fear, she was nothing but nerves and frantic energy.

"I would rather die than go anywhere with you," Reyhan said in a voice shifting from hard edges to near tears. The murderer stepped over his comrade's body and toward Reyhan.

"Your cooperation is appreciated," Behram sneered. "Do not fret. Your love will be with you soon, if he has not preceded you." His expression flickered to amusement, even as Reyhan's flashed to despair.

Reyhan spit at his feet.

Behram's magic came fully alive. Fire poured off him, his eyes lit with it, it danced over his skin. Flame whips lashed across his face and hands, crimson flares curling and snapping. He went for Reyhan.

Kuhzey and Nesrin both lunged at once. Mahir held Kuhzey easily, but Nesrin managed to break free of Cemil's grip, charging into Behram's side. He fell backwards against a massive oak trunk. Nesrin grabbed for his face, raking her nails over his cheek and neck. He caught her wrists, squeezing hard enough she thought the bones would crack.

"You stupid bitch. I only need you alive. I do not need you walking, or talking, or with your hands. Do you understand? Never touch me again."

He shoved her so hard she reeled back, stumbling and falling against one of the boulders, the back of her head ricocheting off stone. Lights burst over her vision, and she slumped, dizzy, sick. Someone pulled her up, roughly, and her head lolled as she fought to see straight. The trees and skyline spun and shrank. She tried to hold herself upright, but her legs might have been made of cheese for all the weight they would bear.

Someone called her name. Darkness swallowed the grove. Had the sun set? In the middle of the day? Her thoughts looped strangely. Incoherent.

No…she was dreaming. Trapped, again. Unable to move. Unable to escape her fate in life or in dreams. Hopeless.

Hope.

Wake.

Fire flickered in her peripheral and she was conscious, staring into Cemil's face. Her thoughts were slow; stringing them together was like trying to wade through a muddy river bottom. "Wake up, damn you." He gave her a little shake.

Wake.

She fell into blackness again. She screamed into the void. Her voice fell away into the utter stillness, or never came at all. She was not alone. Just outside of arm's reach, something made of twilight lay like a flipped mirror image of her. Curled around itself, head pointed toward her feet, feet level with her head. As her words died in the dark, it opened eyes she had not been able to see.

A head lifted from the ground. Then a body rose. But it was not human. Shaped like a human but made of ephemeral obsidian. Solid black against empty nothing. It reached for her. Nesrin wanted to run from it but could not even twitch.

Death. She knew it now. The end. It had been stalking her in her dreams.

Reach for me.

Inky fingers reached across the space, shadows trailing like smoke.

Nesrin woke from the dream gasping. This time it was Behram hauling her to her feet, from where she had collapsed against the boulder face.

"You've given her a concussion," Cemil said from behind his father. "Will you carry her, or shall I?"

"My need for you is quickly waning. Watch your mouth," Behram snarled.

She was cold. Her teeth chattered. Her body shivering. Reyhan and Kuhzey huddled together, Mahir standing ready with dagger and sword if they attempted to flee.

"You will either be a live asset to me, or a useless corpse to them, and your chances for the former are dwindling," Behram said, the flames still twisting like angry snakes over the skin she could see.

Walk. She commanded her body. Instead, her legs buckled, and she sank again. Behram caught her by the throat and drew the dagger from his belt. She fell into darkness even as her hands closed on his wrist in a feeble attempt to fight him. Reyhan's scream faded in her perception.

The shape reached for her. Death. She could feel her body fighting for air, but that feeling was far away, and this felt safer than waking again to that terror. This emptiness was not so terrible.

What was death but fuel for life? She had never feared it before. Why should she now?

Be ended, and be born.

She reached back, her fingertips meeting no resistance as the shadow's fingers eclipsed hers. Then black tendrils spun up her arm and enveloped her. Briefly the amorphous face became whole, a man. Black hair and black eyes widened in surprise to look at her. They knelt in front of each other, him coalescing out of the darkness, hands raised, and fingers entwined.

Who... Her question drifted without sound.

An ally. Break. You must. He squeezed her fingers, and his black light, claws of night and nothing, swept around her. *And this.* There was no ring on her in the nothingness, but the man tapped it with a fingernail, his eyes going black from pupil to sclera. A metallic clink sounded in her mind. Then he was gone. Leaving only the magic.

Only death.

Wake.

Charah.

The voice drummed in her bones. A mirror image of herself appeared before her in the dark, a featureless copy, on its knees as she was. A twinkle of green light glittered at its hip, then spun upward, leaves and curls of vines made of green light sprouting outward as the vine grew around its body, ending in a coil about its neck and blazing across its cheek. The figure's eyes opened, and they glowed with light the color of new grass. A sound like a stone cracking filled the nothingness and Nesrin's eyes opened.

White-hot agony blazed over her skin and through her skull. As if she were simultaneously being filled with energy and drained of it. Roasted alive. She tried to scream, but Behram's hand was on her throat, cutting off air and sound. Fire rippled over him in patches, his face contorted in effort. The ring was attacking her, its fire inside her muscles, winking in and out of existence, as if chased away. The others cried out, and fire exploded away from Reyhan and Cemil. The boulder at Nesrin's back cracked in half with a shudder.

Her scar burned ice cold, then hotter than the fire whip that had made it, starting at the base near her hip and spiraling up her body. Behram cursed as green light flooded the grove. He raised the dagger in his free hand. Nesrin released her grip on the wrist that held her throat and pinned her to the stone and held the dagger at bay with both hands.

Something terrible built inside her, from her very center, swelling and swelling until it was going to kill her. Behram pressed down with the dagger, commanding something of Cemil and Mahir that Nesrin could not hear because roaring filled her ears.

The thing inside her burst. Green light and raw energy raced away from her, over the people that surrounded her, through the trees and rocks, a green dome into the sky and over the palace. Mahir bellowed as it threw them all to the ground and broke apart his dampening. The man in black struck his head and did not move from where he lay.

The ring and bracelet exploded into glittering bits.

Green light rained in twinkling shards all around them, and where it touched, new growth erupted. Nesrin heaved breaths in great gulps.

She was alive?

Somewhere behind Behram, Cemil groaned and the sound warped into a deranged bark of a laugh.

Her ears rang, and tears filled her eyes, blurring her vision. The air tasted of copper as she tried to free her lungs.

Behram managed to keep his feet, his magic raging in streaks white with his rage. He drove his dagger toward her again, but Nesrin fought to hold him off. He was not expecting her strength. A peasant's strength. Their gazes locked, and he bared his teeth.

"Look at you." His eyes held manic fire. "Do you fathom what you could do? Empower armies. Win wars. We could be nearly invincible."

The green magic twined down her arms and around her fingers, pale leaves of light opening across her skin. A twig and leaf sprouted from the wooden handle of Behram's dagger, breaking it apart as it became a branch. The blade tumbled to the ground as Nesrin dug into herself for enough strength to shove him away.

She pushed away from the rock, and swept the blade up in her hand, holding it by the tang.

Nesrin lunged at Behram, but he swatted the dagger out of her hand. "You think you're going to kill me? You have never harmed a man in your life, even I can guess that."

The magic whispered in her veins, power she could call. Command. If she knew how. But she didn't need it for this. For a man of flesh and blood.

"No, I haven't," Nesrin said as she picked the blade up again. "But I have gutted plenty of pigs"—she pointed it at him—"what's one more?"

Mahir grabbed the hilt of his yataghan, but Reyhan reached at the same time, hands closing on the blade, heating it with her magic. Mahir howled as his flesh melted on the hilt. Cemil sighed as if the entire thing made him impatient, and drew his own weapon.

"No," Nesrin ordered when Kuhzey moved as if he would confront Cemil.

"I will not be undone by a filthy mongrel peasant," Behram barked as he nodded for Cemil to advance. But when Cemil took a step toward her, ice swept up his legs, over his waist, and down his arm.

"Then me," Ihsan said as he strode around a curve in the path. He stopped, and six guards, including Bashir Ayan, gathered behind him. Cemil laughed as he tossed his sword to the ground and laced his fingers behind his head.

In the moment it took Behram to understand what had happened, Nesrin crossed the path and swung her fist, hitting him squarely in the scar that bisected his cheek. He reeled back.

She wilted with relief, sinking to the gravel.

"If you move…" Bashir's voice rumbled through the stone around them. "…I will take great pleasure in making you a permanent feature of this boulder garden."

"Ah. The whore's brat has arrived," Behram spat. Then tipped his head back. If Bashir heard Behram, Nesrin could not tell, because he was staring at her. Everyone was staring at her. She looked down at herself. Roots and vines reached from where she sat, growing outward, a corona of new life. Green light drew soft, curling shapes along her wrists and hands, unfurling into the suggestion of leaves then whispering away.

She knew it was hers, the way she knew her fingers and toes and freckles were hers. But it did not make any sense. Nesrin raised her gaze again as Ihsan came to stand in front of her.

"San." The simple word wobbled. The hard set of his expression relaxed. Her composure crumbled, her lip quivering and tears flooding her eyes. "I think…I think I have magic." It was the most nonsensical thing in the world to say, but the corner of his mouth twitched in mirth.

"I think you might." He crouched, pressing his fingers to the back of her head. She winced as a lancet of pain bit into her skull. His fingers came away bloody. Ihsan turned his head toward Behram. Ice spread over the gravel and up Behram's legs. He bared his teeth, and heat blasted away from him. But the ice did not melt, creeping higher.

"You are like a cockroach that will not die," Behram said in disgust to Ihsan. Cemil snorted. It broke the standoff like a spell, and the guards moved, taking hold of Cemil and Mahir. Ihsan's ice melted away.

"Hold his fire," Bashir ordered as his men went for Behram. They led him away first.

A guard finished wrapping Cemil's wrists with a chain and pushed him back toward the palace. Cemil looked back. "San," he said.

Ihsan returned the look, his hand finding Nesrin's. His breath hitched, and she tightened her grip on his.

Cemil winked at him, with a grin that held both sadness and taunt.

Ihsan exhaled but said nothing. Cemil's smile fell, as did his gaze, and he let the guard pull him around.

"Burn bright, little fire," Ihsan said to his retreating back. Cemil glanced over his shoulder with another grin and raised his bound wrists to give Ihsan a little salute. Ihsan sank to the stone beside Nesrin. "Go," Ihsan told Bashir when he hesitated. "I'll bring her."

Bashir bowed and the rest of them left, leaving Ihsan and Nesrin alone but for the trees.

"I thought you were in Mizraa?" she said, her voice uneven. He scrubbed a hand over his face. She saw it was filthy. As were his clothes. And he smelled of smoke.

"I came to save you." He lifted her hands, searching for something.

"Oh," Nesrin said. "Thank you."

"The ring?"

"It broke," she said, reflexively touching the now-bare finger, then her wrist.

"Clearly my help was unneeded." He shook his head at her, casting a gaze from her head to her feet and the magic still bleeding from her and fueling the vines that were beginning to spiral around the trees. Petals drifted down over them, and when they looked up, saw that a small almond was dropping its flowers. Had it bloomed because of her?

"You have no idea how to stop, do you?" he said, gently.

The tears came again, and she shook her head. He caught her face gently in his hands and kissed her brow.

"It's all right," he said. "We will figure it out, and it will be all right."

She rose to her knees and put her arms around his neck. "See? I do need your help." She shook, trembling like she was cold, but she knew it was weakness and the aftermath of everything that had happened.

"I thought I failed you. I was so afraid…" His voice faltered. He stroked a hand over her hair. "Nessa, forgive me."

"I'll consider it," she whispered, smiling when he pulled back to give her a look. Then he leaned in as if to kiss her. But Nesrin reared. "Are you going to forgive me?"

"I'll consider it. If you kiss me."

She pursed her lips. "You still don't know who I am, do you?"

"Nesrin Irmak, daughter of Temel and Pembe Irmak, sister to Sanem, Metin, Nimet, and Nuray. Who are all safe and well, thanks to me. Does that earn me a kiss?" He cocked a brow.

"You met them? And they're all right?" Nesrin's hands covered her mouth as tears filled her eyes.

"I met them. I brought them here." He brought her hands down and tried again to kiss her, but she put her hands over his mouth with a frown. "They're here? And you can't...you can't kiss me. I'm not... we can't be—"

He wrestled her against him. "We can be whatever I say we are. And you are mine. Nesrin Irmak, Charah of the Third House. My betrothed. My consort. Mine."

She started to gasp, but he caught her mouth in his. Nesrin closed her hands into fists and tapped them half-heartedly against his shoulders, but he only kissed her harder. He pulled away, pressing her brow to hers and shaking his head.

"And now I also have to tell you that you are under arrest," he said, grumpily.

Forty-Six

Nesrin stood in the hall, her hands tucked between her and the wall. Attiyeh Charah was with her. Nesrin wished for her sister, or mother. Or Reyhan and her harsh critique.

Attiyeh Charah was there in her capacity as Lieutenant Commander, as Nesrin's guard. Technically, Nesrin was also on trial today. The Council Hall would serve as Tribunal. And since she had not been pardoned, she was a prisoner.

They had allowed her to stay in Ihsan's rooms, instead of the Cliffs. Because in truth, she had already told her story a dozen times.

This Tribunal was only for the benefit of the Council, and those who would oppose the Sultana's plan to put Behram Kadir to death.

The petite guard paced. She was like bottled lightning, too energetic for her small frame, and was entertaining to watch, at least.

"I don't know what you're grinning at, I'm not the one leaving a ruddy mess everywhere I walk." She stepped to Nesrin and plucked a leaf from the braid curled around her head. She spun it in her fingers. "You are the least frightening Charah in existence. Oh no, don't make flowers grow in my fields." She flicked the leaf at Nesrin, but it was clearly teasing.

"I have spent a lifetime without magic. You cannot expect me to master it in two days, Attiyeh Charah."

"It's Aysel. And it's the creatures that bother me. Not you," she said. A butterfly found its way through one of the open windows of the hall and flitted to land on Nesrin's hair. Aysel watched its path with wary eyes. "It's unsettling."

"It could be snakes," Nesrin said. "Or mice. Or pigeons." She shrugged when Aysel recoiled. It did not bother Nesrin. Animals had always been comfortable with her. Now there were just more of them—drawn by her slow leak of magic. But it did not lend her much gravitas, the way Aysel's stormy eyes did, or how Amara's supreme command of herself made others pay attention. Nesrin was still herself. Just a woman more at home in a field than a palace. The butterfly, bright green with emerald-framed wings, fluttered away again.

Behram had said she could win wars, but so far all she did was leave a trail of growing things behind her. And make everyone's magic react too strongly to their intentions. She'd always thought creation mages had been healers. And perhaps they were. Chara'a were different than other mages of their House. Just as Aysel was the only air mage who could summon storms.

"This Tribunal is called to order," a male voice announced inside the hall. Aysel's teasing demeanor turned serious, and she tipped her head toward the doors.

They entered side by side. Six guards flanked the doors, facing the dais at the end of the aisle. Three men and one woman sat in chairs at the base of the dais, and the Princess Sultana sat on her usual gilded bench, above them on the platform. Nesrin tried not to look at Ihsan, where he sat to the Princess Sultana's left and below the dais.

Looking at him would stir her emotions and make what was to come even more difficult to bear. She only briefly looked to the Sultana's right, where the Grand Vizier, Cemil, Mahir, and Reyhan sat, each with a guard whose magic was in opposition to their own. Their hands and feet were bound, their mouths gagged, their eyes covered.

Nesrin counted the tiles as they approached, out of habit. She kept her back straight and her eyes fixed on the circular, wooden platform that had been placed before the judges and the dais. Aysel delivered her there, then stepped back. The urge to bow to the judges and Princess Sultana was physically painful to ignore. It still did not feel like the truth, this new self.

Most of the Viziers of the Council were present. Nesrin did note some gaps. Associates of Behram's? Every face was more serious than they had ever been when she was previously present.

Each of the judges represented one of four Houses. She supposed since she was the only creation mage she had ever heard of, there could not be six. Their blank expressions made Nesrin even more nervous.

"Nesrin Irmak, you stand accused of impersonating a noblewoman," the woman, an earth mage, said, her voice clear and neutral. "Contriving to break the Wheel with a lie in marriage, stealing money from the Sehzade, and palace. Conspiring with an alleged criminal and possible enemy of the Sultanate. And involvement in a smuggling operation with the supposed end goal of insurgence." The judge looked up from the list she had read aloud. The dry tone and emotionless delivery were what caught in Nesrin's throat like a burr. It all sounded so…terrible.

Her scar ached as her emotions flared up, and the magic followed its path, curling lines and leaves lighting over her skin. Nesrin closed her eyes, trying to take slow breaths. There had been no time for lessons. She only had what she could remember from her siblings learning their magic and control.

"You are expected to control yourself in this Tribunal," one of the men said. Nesrin opened her eyes. She was not going to grow accustomed to being stared at like a creature from a fable. So many in the hall were turned toward her as green light ebbed and flowed across her skin and in her eyes. Two birds flew in from an open window to land near her feet, hopping and pecking.

"The Tribunal will excuse Irmak Charah. Her power is newly awakened," the Princess Sultana said. Nesrin looked at her in gratitude, and she gave the tiniest of smiles in response.

"What do you say to the charges, Irmak Charah?"

"They are true," Nesrin said. "I did all those things."

That started the murmuring, a hum that surrounded her. Rising and falling in time with her heartbeat. But she had promised herself that this time, she would not fall apart. In her short time in Narfour she had seen life taken and traded and thrown away. With or without magic—these people were not better than her. They had no right to look down on her.

"Do you intend to defend yourself?" the woman asked.

"I would like to explain," Nesrin answered, her voice more unsure than she meant it to be. The judge nodded, and Nesrin clasped her hands together.

This part she feared the most. The beginning. "When I was a child, a noble visited the estate from Narfour. They said he was looking for his wife. But I never knew for certain why he came." She started to wring her hands, then forced them to her sides. "He went riding in the barley field. His horse bolted, and he fell, but was tangled in the stirrup and was dragged." Nesrin looked at Ihsan, and his frozen expression nearly killed her resolve. But she steadied herself and looked away. "My father and brother were riding the irrigation channels and I was walking behind. My father chased the horse. My brother managed to jump from their horse to the man's, but it threw him, his arm tangled in the reins, and it"—she had to stop to swallow as the visceral memory overtook her—"he lost his arm, but managed to bring the horse down in one of the canals."

"I trust this recounting has relevance to the current charges?" one of the other judges said impatiently.

Nesrin ducked her chin. "My father and I had to free the rider and my brother, and we were able to save the rider. Bardakci Pasha informed us that the man we had saved was the Grand Vizier."

As the room reacted, Nesrin met Ihsan's gaze. Magic turned his eyes glacial blue, his features strained, his fingers gripping the edge of the bench too hard. Her logical mind knew she had not caused Ihsan's suffering. That she and her father could not have known what their kindness would result in. But it hurt, nonetheless, to see the understanding fall over Ihsan's expression.

"For the purposes of the Tribunal, you will refer to Bardakci Pasha as Altimur Pasha. His identity was confirmed," one of the men, a fire mage, said.

She had not had time to speak with Ihsan. They had been forced to stay apart, so that Ihsan could not "taint" her testimony. She only knew a few details that were shared when he had come to the rooms to inform Reyhan that Kanat had been killed.

"We saved the Grand Vizier's life, and so, he owed us a life debt," she said. That sent the room into a rush of conversation. A small, ugly part of her rejoiced in seeing the truth of Behram Kadir's Wheel-breaking loosed in the Council. One of the judges banged a staff until everyone quieted, and Nesrin continued, recounting how she came to be in Narfour, the switch of betrothals, the lies.

"You did not know that you were a mage?" the earth mage queried. Nesrin shook her head. The judge appeared unconvinced, but continued. "You went into the marriage intending to deceive the Grand Vizier and your future husband."

Nesrin flinched. She could not help but look at Ihsan. But his expression was verglas. "Yes."

"Your family had no knowledge of your deception?"

"No."

The judges conferred again.

"Did you ever attempt to tell the truth to the Sehzade, or to anyone?"

"I did. I told the Grand Vizier I would not lie anymore. He attacked me. Held me down and put an enchanted ring on my hand. He was going to carve a rune into my skin. But Master Kadir told him the Sehzade would see it. He put a bracelet on instead, which had what I guessed were runes to control the enchantment."

"Do you have these items?"

"They were destroyed when my magic woke. But while I wore them, I could not speak of anything involving my identity, or his lies, any truths without the ring causing me excruciating pain."

"But enchantments? Is her word enough proof?"

Aysel stood. "I have also witnessed Kadir Pasha's ability to enchant. In his home, he had locks that exploded when tampered with."

The woman judge nodded thoughtfully, and Aysel returned to her seat.

Amara stood. Nesrin had not noticed the Water Charah until that moment. She held out a small velvet bag. "These stones were part of a bracelet *gifted* to me by the Behram Kadir. I suspect they might also hold such an enchantment."

A judge nodded to a guard, who took the bag from Amara and gave it to the judges. Each took a moment to look through the red stones within.

"May I address the Tribunal?" Ihsan asked. The judge closest to him made a gesture of invitation. Ihsan stood. "When I went to Mizraa to investigate Irmak Charah, I met Altimur Pasha. He revealed his identity to me, but doing so activated similar enchantments, and those spells killed him. They burned him alive." Ihsan's gaze settled on Nesrin, and for a moment the frost retreated so she saw the horror that haunted him. Ihsan sat.

"Thank you, Sehzade," the judge said, then looked to Nesrin. "But you were able to inform the Sehzade's steward of this enchantment?"

"Kuhzey cannot speak with words," Nesrin said. "He uses his hands. I had been learning some of it. I can only assume the Grand

Vizier did not think to prevent that method of communication in his runes."

The judge closest to Behram scoffed. "Spells cannot be so specific as that."

"They can," the Princess Sultana interjected. "If the rune is complex enough, and the mage well enough versed in intention." She gave an edged smile. "There is no mage in Tamar more gifted at intention than Behram Kadir. My mother often spoke of his prowess at that tenant of magic."

Behram shifted, a rise of heat filling the room. The Second House guard assigned to him set hands on his shoulders, suppressing his magic.

Naime continued, "And no one more likely to overlook a servant who speaks in gestures as a threat to him."

"Thank you for your insight, Efendim," the woman judge said. She addressed the prisoners. "Reyhan Malas, please join Irmak Charah on the stand."

Reyhan stood. Her guard took her arm to lead her to Nesrin's side. She was dressed only in plain caftan and salvar. The guard removed her blindfold and gag.

They had thought Nesrin would be able to break Reyhan's enchantments, since she had broken her own. But she had so far been unable to. No one could determine if it was simply that she did not know how to control her power, or if it had been something else—the sheer force of her magic waking, or that Behram had never carved his spells into her skin that had allowed her to break the enchantment. There was also the figure in the void. The destruction magic that had woken her power. It had touched the ring.

So Reyhan remained as she was, a prisoner in her own body. And now, for nothing, as Nesrin suspected it had been Kanat's life that Reyhan was protecting. Whatever he was doing in Mizraa, with glass and bone. Reyhan did not know enough of Kuhzey's sign language to speak to the subject that way, and it would be long hours of tutoring before she would.

The judge nodded to the guard, who then turned Reyhan's back toward the dais.

"No," Nesrin ordered. They meant to bare Reyhan's back to a room full of strangers. "I tried that, and even attempting to look activates the spells. Please."

"There is no need to make a spectacle of a victim," the Princess Sultana said, her voice ferocious with cold power.

"She has kept secrets from you, Efendim," one of the male judges said, rising to address her, "aided an enemy of the Sultan."

"What will seeing the marks that Irmak Charah says are there do for this Tribunal?" the Sultana asked. All four judges remained silent.

Tears wet Reyhan's cheeks, and Nesrin dabbed them away. Then she wrapped her arms around the other woman and tipped her brow against Reyhan's temple. Reyhan leaned into her.

The men of the Council whispered disapproval of the display. Nesrin did not care.

"If you require evidence of these runes, I will make sketches of the ones I saw on Osman Altimur," Ihsan said. That seemed to satisfy the judges. Nesrin held onto Reyhan until the guard led her away, back to her seat.

"Were you aware of what Mistress Malas's enchantments prevented her from saying?"

"I tried to find out," Nesrin explained. "That was why I went to the glassworks. Why I had shards of the glass."

"What did you discover there?"

It was still difficult to believe that she had power. Magic. And that it was her magic that had let her understand what was in the glass. What was in the trees. Creation led to death, as death led to life. "There were bone shards in the glass. I believe"—she shut her eyes, then opened them, her magic vining upward again as her sorrow swelled—"they were human." She could not tell them how she knew that. How she had felt the screams and the pain and the fear.

The judge looked at Ihsan. "You said you found bone dust in Mizraa, in a secret glasswork? Do you suspect they were purposefully incorporating the bone into the glass?"

"They were creating bottles," Ihsan answered. "Which fits with what was found at a site in the North where a wagon carrying glass was attacked and the bottles destroyed."

"Do you have anything final to say, Irmak Charah?" the judge asked. Nesrin glanced at Ihsan, and he dipped his chin to her. All the things she had to say to him…this was not the place.

"No," she said.

"Thank you, Irmak Charah. You may be seated."

Aysel motioned Nesrin to the bench beside Reyhan, and Nesrin stepped down.

"Kadir Pasha, Master Kadir, please take the stand."

Nesrin sat beside Reyhan, putting her hand over her friend's bound ones, as father and son were guided to the platform. Their gags and blindfolds were removed. The precautions seemed more for show than any actual control of either man's magic. A thought was all they needed to burn the palace down. But water mages stood ready beside them, in case they tried such a thing.

The judge began to speak, but Behram cut her off.

"Save your breath. I will not be interrogated by this farcical excuse for a Tribunal."

"If you will not submit to questioning, then the evidence will be reviewed in lieu of your testimony. You will be given no other opportunity to defend yourself. Is that your intent?"

Behram sneered, his gaze fixed on the Princess Sultana. Fire flickered in his irises. If looks were poison…

Nesrin's hand tightened on Reyhan's.

"Everything I have done, I have done for the good of Tamar. If you want more from me, you will have to take it."

The Princess Sultana's face remained serene. When she said nothing, Behram scoffed. "My lies should not be the ones of concern to this Tribunal, to anyone in this room." He continued to taunt Naime with his stare, and she sat like stone, unmoved.

"The Tribunal requires a list of all whom you have enchanted, and that you undo those enchantments."

"No," Kadir said.

Naime's expression shifted a fraction toward resignation. "Do so, and you will be granted leniency."

"You will let me live, if I give you more power by revealing a lifetime of work and study?" He smiled in resignation. "You can hang me, little girl. And show all of Tamar you are as incompetent and immoral as your father."

Naime canted her head at him, then Cemil.

"Is that your wish as well, Master Kadir?" the judge continued, unperturbed by Behram's vitriol.

Cemil's gaze fixed behind Naime. On her servant, Samira. Nesrin caught the movement when Samira mouthed, *please.* The desperation in her eyes made tears well in Nesrin's. She looked away in time to catch Cemil wink.

"I am my father's son, so I will follow his lead," he said.

"Then this court finds you guilty of sedition, practicing illegal magic, contriving to deceive the Sultan and his heirs, and attempted murder. You are stripped of your titles and holdings, and sentenced to death by the laws upheld in this Tribunal. Restrain them," the judge said to the guards, "and return them to the Cliffs."

As a guard moved to replace the gag in Behram's mouth, the Grand Vizier shot a look at Naime. "The Wheel knows your hypocrisy, and its balance will be my revenge."

Forty-Seven

FOR THE FIRST TIME since his father's death and the fire, Ihsan approached his rooms in the palace and felt peace. Settled in his body, in his heart. Finally he existed in one place and time, instead of being pulled apart by memory and anger. For a moment, at least.

It was peaceful within, but it was also chaos with so many people inside, everyone talking over everyone else. He fought the urge to leave again.

Kuhzey stood pressed into the corner of the outside wall like a cornered rabbit. Nesrin sat in the center of the room, the table pushed aside, her family around her. The two young girls were in her lap, tangled together like gangly fawns. Her older sister brushed her hair. Her brother, father, and mother sat cross-legged in front of her, recounting the fire. One of Nesrin's grandmothers slouched in a chair, overseeing the reunion by sleeping.

Reyhan was there as well, but she sat in the other chair, staring out the window at the garden. Nesrin's other grandmother stood behind Reyhan, a hand on her shoulder. She was speaking to the younger woman, but her words were drowned out by the other chatter in the room. There were more questions for the fire mage, but Naime had insisted she be given time to process her grief. He wished he had words for her. Closure. He had been reluctant to give her any detail at all, but she had wanted to know.

Nesrin saw him first, her smile bright and beautiful. Green glowed through the hazel of her eyes. The same green he had seen countless times and been too self-absorbed to recognize or understand. The others noticed her silence and all their gazes turned at once to him. Nesrin shooed her younger sisters off her lap then stood. She wore only her caftan, a pale green that suited her immensely, her hair undone, everything about her soft and welcoming, and shyly hopeful.

It had not been his rooms that made him feel peaceful, but knowing she was here. Anywhere she was became a sanctuary for him.

"Kuhzey, have a carriage take Irmak Charah's family to the city estate so they may settle in," Ihsan said. Her family had followed him to Narfour when he had left Mizraa in a panic. They'd arrived the next morning, causing a stir at the gate with their demands to see Nesrin. She deserved this reunion with them, but he had not had any time with her, in privacy, since he found her. He just wanted her, for a moment.

Sanem popped up like an angry gopher out of its hole, fists on hips. "And what about Nesrin? How long is she to be a prisoner? How dare—"

Nesrin clapped a hand over Sanem's mouth and whispered something in her ear. Her sister shook her off. Kuhzey herded the family together and toward the door with a distinct air of desperation. Reyhan followed them, closing the door softly behind her.

Nessa spoke first. "You saved my family." Earnest eyes searched his. "You went into a fire to save them." She swallowed. "I cannot imagine what it cost you. Thank you. I don't know what I would have done if…if—"

"I know," he said. He wanted something to do with his hands, but there was nothing. He squeezed them into fists, then released them.

"Can you forgive me? For everything I have done to you? Everything I caused? I wish I had never laid eyes on Behram Kadir. What if he lived because of my magic?" Tears made her eyes gleam even brighter. Green like peridot. The green of new life, and hope.

He caught her chin and jaw in his hand. "Never apologize to me for who you are. Never apologize to anyone. If you and your father had not saved Kadir that day, I would never have met you. I would still be chasing shadows and hatred. I do not want the life that would have been without your kindness. I do not want a life without you." He lowered his fingertips to touch the scar that twined up from beneath her caftan over her neck and jaw, to her temple.

The magic followed its lines, like a vine of green growing around her. Magic from pain. Life from sacrifice. "Can you forgive me? I wanted you to be a lie. I wanted to stay where I was. Wallowing. I doubted you when I should have believed in you."

"Can you believe in me now? After all this?" Her brows knit.

"I don't think there is anything I believe in more," he said. The way she looked at him unwound everything. Softened edges and thawed ice. She looked at him with trust, and fascination. He dropped his mouth to hers, desperate.

Her hands closed in his entari, meeting his desperation with her own, but only for a moment. Then she pulled back abruptly, her brow furrowed.

"Can a prince marry a farmworker?"

"If a commoner is good enough for the Sultan of Tamar, then certainly the only Creation Charah in existence is good enough for an extraneous prince."

"You are not extraneous." She flicked an angry, glowing green gaze up to his.

"I can marry anyone I want."

Nesrin worried at the clasps of his entari. "I thought you had to marry a noblewoman." Her gaze had dropped from his, and she had the top clasp undone, her fingers tucking into the collar. They were warm, magic thrumming erratically. His thoughts slipped to lying tangled with her in bed, to the many times he had wanted her.

"I do. You are a Charah." He forced his thoughts back to the moment. "You *are* a noblewoman."

"I am also a criminal," she protested. He did not think she was aware that she was stroking the backs of her fingers over his neck. As if to soothe her anxious energy. It was not soothing for him. It was waking up every nerve in his body.

"The Tribunal pardoned you. And Reyhan. They understood you were both under duress. Naime will ask you to stand in the Circle of Chara'a. You are not a criminal."

"But I—"

"Nessa," he demanded.

"SaaAAaan," she mocked.

"Fine," he said. "Then the punishment for your crimes is a lifetime of me."

Her expression went sly. "How terrible for you." She set her fingertips on his jaw. He curved his hand around the back of her neck and took a fistful of her caftan in the other, pulling her to him. "Bound to a criminal for all your days?"

Her skin held that warmth that was an addiction for him. Heat like life. He wanted more of it. He wanted all of her, her brightness chasing away the frost.

She slid her hands back, fingers digging into his hair. "Shall I comfort you?" she murmured, soft lips tracing a smile as she tugged gently on his hair, arching into his body. Desire coiled at the base of his spine, a warm ache that consumed his thoughts. He lost capacity to reply with something witty as he battled with the onslaught of wanting.

When he did not say anything, she nudged his chin with her nose, canting his head down with her grip in his hair. Then she touched his lips with her own, a whisper, barely any contact at all. "Kiss me?" she asked.

He slid his fingers into her loose hair to gather it all around one hand then twisted it into his grip. He tipped her head back and to the side. Vines of green magic coiled and blossomed over her, drawing tempting paths that led under her caftan. But he began with her bared throat, and neck, in a series of devouring kisses. Nesrin went soft against him, her breath a flutter of warmth into his own neck. When he grazed her skin with his teeth, wanting to bite hard but resisting, she turned her head into his with a pleading moan.

She reciprocated his kisses, wet and warm, with teeth, her hands fumbling in between them to claw at his belly, then tug at the clasps of his entari once more. It rooted him where he was, the world falling away to nothing but the ache spreading through him. She tried to direct him with a push of her head, the pressure of her hands, but he did not want to give up her skin, even if it meant her mouth.

"Let's see what your magic can do, hmm?" he breathed, pressing another frosty kiss to her neck. She trembled. He had intended to carry her to the nearest bed. But Naime chose that moment to let herself in.

Ihsan twisted enough to see as Samira, Bashir, Amara, and Aysel followed Naime into the room. He pressed his face into the warm, pliant give of Nesrin's skin and kissed her throat with a groan before he straightened.

"Welcome." He gave an unenthusiastic wave toward the seats. Nesrin stifled a giggle that came out as a snort as she quickly fixed the toggles of his entari. He turned as Naime crossed the sitting room and chose a chair, her gaze fixed firmly away from his.

Amara barely held a smile in check as she did the same, and Aysel slapped him on the back as she went by and flopped onto the couch. Bashir remained by the door to cast a dampening spell.

Ihsan swallowed back any sharp comments he would have made when he met Naime's gaze. There was no kind way to phrase that she looked terrible. Drained and heartsick. There had been no time to grieve the loss of her father. The possible loss of Makram. They may have finally put Kadir in prison, but that did not solve the dying crops, the vandalism, looting, and random attacks in the city. It did not stop the Republic massing on the northern border.

"What do you need?" Ihsan asked. Naime offered him a weak smile. Nesrin left his side to kneel at the table between the women and began pouring tea.

Samira gasped, rushing to take over the task.

"Please let me," Nesrin said. "It makes me happy."

Samira looked at Ihsan, and he shrugged. "Chara'a are inexplicable, I have discovered," he said as he sat beside Aysel. She grinned slyly at him, and he rolled his eyes away from her.

"And Irmak Charah most inexplicable of all," Amara said. "As I have mentioned to the Princess Sultana, I believe it was her presence in Mizraa that held the Blight off for so long." She took a cup of tea from Nesrin. "And I believe she is now doing the same for Narfour."

"Could I cure it?" Nesrin asked, looking at her palms. The magic had quieted somewhat, though occasional flickers of green moved through her eyes or drew a creature near.

"It was explained to me by the Suloi that those with creation magic were more passive," Amara said, "that it did as it willed. I have seen healing magic." Her lashes lowered, a flicker of emotion crossing her face. "But it was weak."

"There are more creation mages?" Nesrin asked, hope bright in her face. Sorrow quieted Amara's expression.

"Only two, that I could find. The rest were taken captive or killed by the Republic's mage hunters."

"Without more creation mages to draw power from, I cannot imagine you can push back a Blight that has taken two nations," Naime said. Though she had the distant look in her eyes that told Ihsan she was combing through her knowledge. She blinked whatever thoughts there were away. "But, I would ask you to stand in the Circle of Chara'a. Your power and the balance you create by simple existing will surely have some positive effect."

"Even if I cannot do anything with my magic?" Nesrin curled both hands around her teacup, and her gaze went to Ihsan's. He gave her a reassuring smile.

"You can learn. You will learn," Naime said, gently, "because your unintentional amplification of the magic of others is not only useful, but potentially dangerous."

They had only briefly discussed what Kadir had intended to do with Nesrin by kidnapping her. Naime had even, momentarily, considered trying to have the information forced from Kadir. But they both knew there was unlikely any method on the Wheel outside a Veritor's power that would break open Behram Kadir. What he might do with a mage that could potentially vitalize an entire army was a frightening rabbit hole of possibilities.

"Being bound to the Circle does not require any spells on your part," Naime continued.

"Of course I will," Nesrin said, though the apprehension had not left her face. "I will do my best."

"Yes." Naime gave Nesrin a true smile. "I have no doubt."

"Can you tell us how your magic woke?" Amara asked.

Nesrin turned her teacup around and around. Ihsan got up and settled beside her on the floor, unable to leave her isolated in her discomfiture. She smiled at him as Aysel muttered something to herself, crossing her arms over her chest and one leg over the other. She gave him a smug grin.

"I have been dreaming," Nesrin began, her gaze dropping. "Of...I suppose it was the void. But I didn't realize it."

Naime's gaze became razor sharp.

"There was a voice. Or many."

"We have all touched the void," Amara said, glancing at Aysel, who nodded. "You will connect with it once more during the binding."

"When you did, was there someone else there? There was something, or someone else with me. Death. Or destruction," Nesrin said. Ihsan glanced to Naime in time to see her expression flash to hope, then fear. "It kept telling me to wake up. And finally, I touched it in the dream. And I think it broke the ring."

"An avatar of the Sixth House?" Naime mused. "Each of the others has reported a similar encounter. But not of a different House, and not corporeal enough to touch."

"I think"—Nesrin hesitated, then squared her shoulders—"I think I needed destruction magic for my own magic to wake up or it might have stayed locked away all my life. Like the cedar cones."

"The what?" Ihsan asked, as the others looked at Nesrin in confusion.

"The cones of the Tamar cedar. They only open when heated by fire, or they lie dormant, sometimes for Cycles." Nesrin frowned. "You did not know? Are you not the Vizier of Agriculture?"

Ihsan huffed. "Cedar trees are not agriculture, they are forest."

She pulled a face at him then turned her attention to Naime, who was rubbing her fingers over her brow.

"Of course," Naime said, eyes closing. "The Third House is not gone. It is dormant."

The realization settled over each of them, in fragments. Ihsan thought of Dilay. How she had always called voids seeds of potential. She may have been more correct than she ever imagined.

"No other House requires its opposition to wake to its magic," Amara countered.

"No," Naime said. "But creation and destruction are uniquely linked, one feeding the other in an infinite loop."

"Then does each creation mage need to be exposed to destruction magic to wake?" Aysel asked. "Where would we even begin with such a task?"

"I do not know," Naime said. "I've seen nothing in my reading that even hints at this. It was possible no one knew, because there had never been an event like the Sundering War before."

Nesrin laced her fingers with Ihsan's, seeking grounding, he thought. He squeezed, and she smiled, though she did not look at him.

"I don't think it was an avatar," she began. "It looked…seemed like a man to me," Nesrin said. "Just as confused as I was. He had black hair and black eyes, and when he spoke"—she looked at Aysel—"he had an accent like yours."

Aysel drew back, then met Naime's eyes across the table.

"Makram," Naime said his name as if it were a spell to summon him. The steadiness of her expression faltered. "What does that mean?" The question she did not complete Ihsan heard anyway. If he was appearing in dreams, was he alive, or dead?

Amara touched Naime's shoulder. "The void is conduit to the magic of Chara'a. It is how I can call the Sehzade's power to me to speak across distances. If he is there, it could mean any number of things."

A glow ringed Naime's irises, her hands clenched into fists. "What else do you remember?"

"He said…" Nesrin scrunched her eyes shut. "…he could not come to me, I had to reach for him. He seemed stuck. Or trapped?" Nesrin opened her eyes and made an apologetic face.

Naime expelled a hard breath, cutting her gaze away to hide the bloom of tears in her eyes.

"What could trap a Charah?" Ihsan asked.

"A Destruction Charah, for that matter," Amara added. "Certainly nothing physical."

Nesrin bit her lip, her gaze touching Ihsan's as if asking permission. He squeezed her fingers.

"Benat is a Charah," Nesrin said, gently, the look she leveled at Naime sympathetic. But when the implications hit Naime, her skin went pallid, and magic flashed white in her eyes.

"Drugged?" Aysel snarled. The smell of ozone wafted from her and she tensed like a hound who had scented prey.

Naime's fingers dug into the arms of the chair as she turned her glowing eyes on Aysel.

"Find him."

Forty-Eight

The Tomb of Sultans sat northeast of the palace. It was only accessible from the palace, or by acrobatic feats of cliff climbing from the western face of the Kalspire. The ritual ground for funerals was a field in front of the tomb. The Sultan, carried by Ruslan and five other stewards, was led by a contingent of twelve guards arranged in a circle around the stewards and their burden.

It was little different than the funerals in the valley, except for the sheer number of people involved. If there were a single servant or courtier left in the palace Nesrin would be surprised. Naime and Ihsan followed behind the gilt wooden platform upon which the Sultan rested. Nesrin walked with Kuhzey, Reyhan, Samira, and the handful of other maids and stewards that accompanied Naime and Ihsan. Behind them, the Viziers and their families, then everyone else followed, a trail of people that stretched back into the palace grounds, moving at a somber pace.

The Sultan's platform was set on a stone table, and the men who carried it bowed to it before fading back into the crowd. All those attending formed a circle around the stone structure and the cloth-wrapped body atop it. The cloth was white, with ribbons laid across it in the color of each House, ending in black. The Sixth. Her hand went to Reyhan's as a woman dressed in black and charcoal grey approached the Sultan's head. They did not intend to burn the Sultan's body, but to use the old ways.

"That is Attiyeh Charah's mother," Reyhan murmured, "Dilara Attiyeh." If the audience was shocked to see a destruction mage present, no one was brave enough to voice it.

Aysel approached her mother and set something in her outstretched hands as they murmured the funeral prayer to each other. Then Aysel set her gift on the stone beside the Sultan, a flower yet to bloom, and took a place to her mother's left. Amara did the same, moving to Aysel's left to form the beginning curve of a circle around the Sultan's pyre.

Nesrin bit her lip, glancing to Reyhan, who smiled encouragement, and Nesrin stepped forward, brushing her fingers along Ihsan's as she passed him. Her nervous energy seeped from her in green tendrils. The grass beneath her feet and around her path perked and turned a deeper green, and pink and white clover bloomed in her footprints, leaving a flower trail behind her.

Whispers were a gauntlet, and stares. As if she were the Wheel itself, rolling along in front of them. She wore the custom caftan and entari that Amara had made for her, all of it in shades of green that stood out among the other colors. Alone.

Nesrin circled the stone pedestal bearing the Sultan's body and approached Aysel's mother. The destruction mage was nothing like Nesrin would have imagined a death mage to be. She looked like any other woman, any other mother. Petite like her daughter, with hair of salt and pepper and a measured bearing that came from whatever hardships she had endured to end up in Narfour.

There was an itchy sensation in Nesrin's skin, something that set her on edge. Like a force pushing on her when she did not wish to be pushed. The opposition of Dilara's magic.

Dilara Attiyeh stared back at Nesrin with eyes welling with tears. "I never thought, in my lifetime—" she whispered, but cut herself off with a shake of her head. Then she held her hands out. Nesrin lifted her palms, scratched and sticky with pitch, despite Reyhan's valiant efforts, and set the cone she had retrieved into Dilara's hands.

Dilara smiled a breathy laugh, her fingers curling to grip Nesrin's and the cedar cone. "From dawn, to dark," she began, and Nesrin echoed. "Winter, to summer." She paused, lifting her gaze to Nesrin's and murmuring, "Birth, to death"—words Nesrin knew had been excised from the prayer after the Sundering War.

Tears filled her own eyes as she repeated them. "We walk the circle. We spin the Wheel."

"Will you open the cone?" Nesrin whispered. Dilara traced a tiny, simple sigil on the cone's tightly closed scales. The echo of the magic made Nesrin shudder, but the discomfort was forgotten the moment the cone cracked open, spilling waxy seeds into Nesrin's palms. She closed her fingers around them and went to stand at Amara's left. Bashir Ayan walked the circle of them to repeat the prayer, then stood to Nesrin's left. Then Samira did the same.

Naime went next. She bent to kiss her father's cloth-wrapped brow. She set a single downy feather beneath the rope colored the blue of the First House. Ihsan followed, then a slow procession of nobles and their families.

When all the gifts were piled around the Sultan and everyone had moved a respectful distance away, Dilara let the silence linger for a moment.

"From void—" She pricked her palm with a slim blade, and used the blood to draw a sigil on her skin. Inky shadows twined around her fingers as she looked at Aysel. Aysel whispered a word, and lightning snapped in her hair, lifting her braids away from her body. Then Amara, whose skin awoke with silver like moonlight.

Nesrin's breath quickened as Amara looked to her with an opaque silver gaze. Nesrin closed her eyes, tightening her fingers around the seeds. *Grow*, she said, pouring all her love, and hope, and belief into the wish. When she opened her eyes, green swirled in vines and drifting shimmers of leaves over her hands, and a single cedar seed had sprouted open, unfurling in her palm. She nearly sobbed in disbelief.

Bashir went next, his skin lighting with golden fractures, and finally Samira, igniting a cloud of sparks and drifts of crackling embers over her skin.

"—to void." Dilara stepped forward and laid her palm on the Sultan's brow. The obsidian magic swept over his body in the same manner that the tendrils had reached for Nesrin in the dark of her dreams.

The body, and gifts, crumbled, collapsing inward, sifting to dust. Dilara silenced her spell by closing her fist.

Barely muffled sobs scattered through the gathered nobles. Nesrin met Dilara's gaze across the stone, and Dilara ducked her head.

Death…

Nesrin stepped forward and opened her cupped palms to reveal the cedar seedling, which she set on the stone. Of its own will, a thread of green magic trailed from her fingers as she stepped away.

…and life.

The seedling stretched taller, roots trailing down over the stone, branches unfurling to reveal branchlets with miniscule green scales.

Naime and Ihsan buried the Sultan next to his wife and planted the cedar tree at their feet. And when everyone else had left but for the mages who had formed the circle, Naime and Ihsan still knelt beside the graves of Omar and Dilay Sabri.

All of them rejoiced in stories that made them smile, and laugh.

And they mourned.

Forty-Nine

The walls of the Hall of Chara'a sang, and screamed. Magic, trapped forever within stone and glass. Voices of mages long past, perhaps the same that had murmured in Nesrin's dreams. There was wonder and creation in the hall, and sacrifice. She clutched the fabric over her heart, staring around the room.

Room was too small a word for the vastness of the space before her. The hall was circular, surrounded on all sides by stone risers that met the walls at windows open to views in every direction, allowing in the midmorning sun. The floor itself was the Wheel, depicted in great tiles of white marble and pale sandstone, with semiprecious stone at the outer edge for each House.

In the center, a white sun whose curved rays marked the boundaries between Houses shone in the light. Naime stood in its heart, one hand on a staff covered with a cloth. Samira stood beside her mistress. She held an opalescent sphere which seemed to glow. Both women appeared untroubled by the ghost whispers that bounced from wall to wall, slithering from and between the mages gathered, and mages that had been before. Or perhaps they could not hear them.

Aysel stood on the white marble of the First House spoke, and Amara on the turquoise of the Second. They both ducked their heads in greeting as Nesrin took her place on the polished malachite of the Third House. Her gaze swept across the floor to the obsidian spoke across from her. She did not know Makram, but did she imagine she felt a strand of connection between where she stood and his place? An empty pull?

Her family sat in the risers behind Amara. Her mother and Sanem clutched hands, both in the throes of snuffling tears. Metin picked at a thread on his caftan, and the littles fought each other in hissed whispers. Her father gave Nesrin a somber nod as she turned to Naime.

Naime welcomed her with a genuine smile as she lifted the cloth from the scepter. It was wooden, set into a socket in the floor, with six twisted fingers like roots. Naime traded the cloth for the orb and placed it into the grip of the scepter. It was a solid, polished stone, iridescent.

When the stone was set, Naime approached Nesrin, and set the scepter in another socket between the sandstone and the malachite. Nesrin reached to touch it, drawn by the light scintillating in its depths. But Naime gave the barest shake of her head.

"Nesrin Irmak ilr Mizraa, named Princess Consort of the Sehzade, Charah of the Third House..." Naime's voice wavered, and she met Nesrin's gaze with joy in hers. "...to be bound to the Circle you must choose the manner in which you will serve it."

Aysel and Amara had explained what had happened to them, how it felt, and so Nesrin was not afraid when she placed her hands beside Naime's on the stone. Naime's magic came to life, a pale glow like the silver-gold ring of dawn light around the mountains. It was beautiful, and mesmerized Nesrin until Naime gently tapped her finger to hers, reminding Nesrin that she too had to release her grip on her magic.

Though, she did not have a grip on her magic. It did as it willed. She closed her eyes, and a bright thread of Naime's magic pulled her into nothingness.

The Hall of Chara'a fell away. She could no longer feel Naime, or the stone, see or hear the people who were all around her. Now that she knew what it was, she wasn't afraid, only curious.

She could not move, she understood, because she did not truly exist here. Not physically. This was a place for magic. The beginning, and the end.

Aysel and Amara had spoken of figures that came to them. Of points of light in the dark, but Nesrin saw nothing. No sign of the shadow figure that had helped to wake her magic. She hoped he was all right.

Are you here?

There was no answer. Perhaps because she was the only one, there was no figure to greet her.

But as she thought it, a point of fluttering green light coalesced, and bobbed toward her.

A butterfly. Was it lost?

The butterfly hung in the space before her, more brilliant green than any worldly butterfly. Its luminescence could not travel far beyond it, for the black of the void consumed it.

Are we lost?, it seemed to mimic, its language as understandable to her as Kuhzey's was.

A House cannot be lost. Its memory is held in the land, in the dust, and the bones. In every leaf, and seed.

Wake them.

Then the butterfly was gone, a glowing green point of light taking its place before her.

A seed.

The hope of a House in slumber.

And Nesrin understood.

In her mind's eye, she touched the seed. A thread of green light spun out from it, connecting point after point within the void. And one by one they lit. Each uncurling like a sprout, to rise as a mage, each a new thread tied to her, every breath giving and taking, like roots to leaves and leaves to roots. Mages reborn, as she was. Each the joy and promise of that which could be, to balance that which was lost.

Creation.

The selfless giving of one thing to another. The warmth of spring after winter, the anticipation of a flower yet to open its petals, an egg to hatch, a mother to birthe. The magic of a seed, waiting inside its shell to push its way bravely and blindly into the light. Growth from pain, life from death, the unbreakable, unstoppable force that was hope.

Brilliant light pushed back the void, and Nesrin opened her eyes to see Naime before her. The Sultana glowed like the sun, the moonstone echoing it.

"Hope," Nesrin said. "The Third House serves by hope."

Her magic spun away from her in a flurry of green light, filling her with undulating energy and joy, and touching each person present with its vitality. Butterflies came through the windows in droves, alighting along the paths of her power as Nesrin's magic sank into the malachite floor and pulsed outward, following the lines of the spoke toward the center of the Wheel and tracing the Circle there.

"Hope of the Circle," Naime said, her magic glowing so brightly Nesrin had to squint to see her. "You are bound to its service, from this day, until your last."

The magic retreated, swirling up and climbing Nesrin like vines, and the butterflies and birds that had come flitted away, moving to higher, safer perches as Nesrin's magic quieted. And in her heart, there were more. Countless heartbeats fluttered within her magic now. Awake. Alive.

Tears filled her eyes as she met the Sultana's gaze. At the contact, something like a pin's prick sank deep into Nesrin's awareness, and a tension pulled taut between Naime, and Nesrin. Naime's magic faded, and as it did, the stone glowed brighter. Her skin was pale, her breath shallow. But she smiled.

Because Nesrin was touching the stone, she felt something disturbingly like the spells Behram had captured in garnet and ruby flicker and fade. She drew her hands away, gaze questioning. But Naime was barely keeping her feet, her pupils nearly swallowing the cinnamon of her irises.

"Are you all right?" Nesrin murmured. Naime withdrew her hands from the stone, wiping them on her caftan as she squeezed her eyes shut. She nodded once. The stone's milky light looked suddenly threatening to Nesrin, and she took a step away. Naime did the same, steadying herself before she bowed.

"Irmak Charah," she said.

One by one, each person in the hall stood, and bowed, hands spreading to her. Nesrin stared, turning a slow circle as she looked, half panicked, at the number of people. As her gaze passed over the Fifth House risers, Reyhan lifted her head enough to catch Nesrin's eye. She tapped her own chin, motioning for Nesrin to stand straight.

Nesrin breathed a laugh, and obeyed, straightening her spine and lifting her chin. Then her gaze fell on Ihsan as he rose from his bow.

Everyone else began to leave their seats. Some left immediately, some lingered, chatting, or perhaps waiting for her. But Ihsan held her gaze as he came to her side.

He dipped his head to put his mouth near her ear. "You do not make such a terrible princess after all." He brushed her cheek with a kiss then twined her arm with his to stand beside her as people gathered to speak with her, or gawk.

She greeted and met as many people as she could before Ihsan led her away, following Naime back to her rooms.

"I will have to send Ihsan to Mizraa to settle things there," Naime said as she entered her room. "Did Altimur Pasha have any children?" Naime turned to face them once she reached the doors to the garden.

"He mentioned a son, but I know nothing beyond that," Ihsan said.

"If he did, they were never in Mizraa, or it was a secret," Nesrin added. Naime turned her back to them to look out the window. She stiffened. Then fumbled for the door handle and hurried outside.

Ihsan glanced at Nesrin, then they followed.

Naime went to her hands and knees at the base of the fig tree. "San," she breathed, and sat back on her heels, revealing what had drawn her outside.

A single, perfect leaf stretched wide from a new shoot at the base of the tree. Ihsan crouched beside Naime and touched the shoot reverently.

He lifted his gaze to her, and she smiled. "Perhaps it liked the apple core," Nesrin said, quietly. He grinned, and Naime did too, then swiped her fingers over her eyes.

Nesrin hoped this new tree would bear witness to happier memories than its predecessor.

Fifty

"Nesrin." Ihsan stalked into the study and swung the door shut with a thump behind him. Nesrin looked up from her spot curled in one of the chairs, reading a book the Sultana had lent her on magical control. He stood for a moment, fingers caught in his hair, staring at the carpet in front of him as though he had just seen the edge of the void.

"Yes?" She closed the book around her finger to hold her place. He had returned that morning from Mizraa, but they had not seen each other yet. This was not the way she had expected he would greet her.

Ihsan pinched the bridge of his nose. "There is a goat in my garden."

Nesrin opened her book again and returned to reading, trying to keep her face from cracking into a grin. "That is Duru. Nimet's milk goat."

"They brought a…" He shook his head. "My home is not a stockyard."

"You said she was in the garden, not the home." Nesrin gave him a coy smile. He glowered at her. Buse, who perched on the arm of the chair next to her, gave a pleasant meow of greeting and flicked his bushy tail. Ihsan groaned in despair as he crossed the room to flop onto his back on the couch.

"Are you aware"—he closed his eyes, unhooking the toggles of his entari as he spoke—"that your brother sleeps without any clothes?"

"Mmhmm," Nesrin said, catching her lips between her teeth to stifle a giggle.

"I crossed his path this morning when I returned. It was not unlike encountering a great shaven bear trundling through my foyer."

Nesrin burst into laughter. "I am sorry, I should have warned you." To be fair, she had not expected Metin to make himself quite so at home. Though she had been at the palace for the days Ihsan had been gone. Her family had made his home their own in short order. "Is this how you greet me after days apart? I missed you," she said. He opened his eyes and tipped his head to look at her.

"Come here," he said. Nesrin briefly considered denying him to tease, but she set her book down and moved to sit on the edge of the couch beside his hip. He lifted himself just enough to catch her hands in his to pull her forward onto him as he lay back down. She held the arm of the couch as she peered down into his face.

"Welcome back." There was more. But she could not find words to express the way her heart filled to see him. That she was happy just to look at him. He stroked his hands down her arms.

"You want a proper greeting, do you?" he said as he tucked his head into the curve of her neck and kissed below her ear. His lips were deliciously cold, raising gooseflesh along her right side.

"You have…" She paused breathlessly as his hands skimmed her sides, cold even through the fabric of her caftan. "…on several occasions, greeted me properly but not finished the job."

His hands stilled, and he pressed his head back into the cushion so he could look at her with narrowed eyes.

"Not my fault," he grumbled.

"Oh?" Nesrin sat up over his thighs. He followed, his fingers digging into her hips, legs flexing beneath her. She pushed his entari off his shoulders, and he released her long enough to shrug out of it. "I suppose it was my fault we are always being interrupted."

"That sounds correct, yes," he said, pressing a too-quick kiss to her mouth, then coming back for a deeper one. Nesrin moaned quietly, too aware that her family filled the house to the brim. Ihsan rolled her hips into his, grinding himself against her in a way that made her whimper.

"My fault?" she said against his lips. "You were the one groping me. You started it."

"No," Ihsan rumbled, tugging at her caftan to pull it free from beneath her hips. "I distinctly remember you groping me, and I very much want you to do it again." His hands found their way beneath the caftan, to her skin. Like his lips, they were cold, pebbling her skin and making her gasp again. He spread the fingers of one hand over her low back to draw her toward him. With his other he massaged her leg, fingers digging, gently, into her muscles as he worked his way up her thigh.

"I like this," he said, running his hand up and down her thigh again, fingers curved along the inside, so sensation bolted up her leg and into her stomach. "The way you feel. The shape of you." He stroked his hand up under her caftan to her belly and brought the other around so he could coast them up her torso in unison, thumbs hooking beneath the weight of her breasts.

Her body, already alight and sensitive, tensed in anticipation of the touch. Her breath caught as she waited, and hoped, for him to unwrap the cloth that bound her chest.

Magic flurried in his eyes.

"I want to see you," she said. "Your magic?" She hoped it was all right to ask.

"I am willing to give you almost anything you ask for at this moment."

"Hmm"—Nesrin tugged at his caftan—"apples?"

He issued a growl and took her by the waist as if to move her off his lap. Instead, she gasped as his fingers found ticklish places, and when she flinched away he tried to hold her and they both tumbled off the couch and landed in an awkward heap. He cursed as she laughed.

He rolled to his back with a groan, then wrestled himself out of his caftan. Nesrin settled herself on his hips again.

"That," Ihsan said as he squeezed his eyes shut, "might kill me."

Nesrin pulled her own caftan over her head and tossed it aside, then leaned forward, placing her hands to either side of his head. "Better?"

"Marginally." Blue shifted beneath his skin like winter wind, fractals and flakes tracing pale streaks. She stretched out on top of him, settling her hips between his knees. Her own magic fluttered warmly, pulsing in and out of her novice grip of it.

"Don't hold it," Ihsan said, folding one arm beneath his head so he could watch her. "I want to see yours too."

Nesrin scrunched her face, still trying to learn what it felt like to hold it, or let it go.

"Relax," he coaxed, dragging his free hand through her hair.

"What if I make a plant grow out of your chest?" Nesrin wasn't very worried about such a thing. As far as she could tell she could not create out of nothing. She could only empower what was already there. But the idea of her magic completely unleashed and emboldened by the throes of passion made her wonder if she might collapse the house under the weight of a vigorous rose bush.

"The only thing you're making grow isn't in my chest," Ihsan said, grinning when she turned a wide-eyed look of surprise on him.

"Was that a joke?" She laughed.

"Not entirely, no."

Nesrin hid a smile by dropping her head to kiss his belly, just above his navel. His muscles tightened beneath her, his legs pressing close and his hips lifting a fraction. She drew a line with the tip of her finger from her kiss to the top of his salvar, then followed the waistline to his right side.

With a quick glance at his face, she flattened her hand and stroked it up his side, over skin mottled and pocked, textured by pain and healing. His brows knit together, lids lowering, his hand in her hair closing into a grip. She took the touch all the way up his side, over the same scars on his chest, to hook her fingers behind his head.

She rose on her hands and knees, so she could brush her lips along his jaw, the uneven skin that marked him there, and followed it down his neck.

"It's all right?" she whispered into his ear before she touched another kiss to the hook of his jaw. She retraced her touch, her hand roving back down his side.

Ihsan lifted his head to free his arm, both hands bringing her head to his to answer her question with a kiss that opened her magic and his. Winter met summer in a swirl of blue and green, ice and vines. Frost spread away from him, over the places their bodies met, and melted at the warm touch of her body and her magic.

"It's all right," Ihsan breathed between kisses. "You are. You are right. Perfect. Everything I've ever wanted, needed, and did not think I deserved."

"Deserved?" She made a thoughtful noise even as she fought back a rise of emotion that threatened tears. "You are very frosty"—she touched him as she spoke—"but luckily for you, I love winter."

"Liar," he said.

"Fine," she murmured, touching her nose to his as her heart and magic spilled open. "Perhaps it is not winter I love." At her pause, his gaze locked to hers and blue light rimed his eyes, his breath catching. She swallowed the shyness that wanted to silence her, the part of her that was still a servant void, small, and unnoticeable. "Perhaps it is you."

"Perhaps?" he replied, hands on her arms, winter in his skin. "And what if I loathe summer, but love you? What if…" His magic-lit gaze perused her face. "…I cannot imagine how I lived before I knew you?"

"Then you should not live without me again."

"Agreed." He bent his knees around her hips. "You should marry me."

Nesrin gave a soft laugh as she nodded. "I'll consider it."

He held her arms, rolling her carefully to her back to rise above her. Then he hooked his fingers into her salvar and pulled them to her ankles. She wriggled free, and he returned to her on hands and knees, pressing a line of kisses up the inside of her leg. Beneath each touch of his lips a wisp of green magic glowed and disappeared, warmth curling and climbing up her body. His fingertips stroked up the outside of her thighs, paused at her hips, dug into the curve there, as he drew a half-circle of kisses from one hip bone to the other.

Frost bloomed where he touched, cold counterpoint to the warmth of her body and her magic and served to make her feel each touch more keenly. By the time he had wandered a lazy trail of kisses to her ribcage, she could think of nothing but wanting him. He rose all the way up, knees bracketing her sides, and Nesrin tugged on the ties of his salvar.

They sagged, and she pushed them down past his hips. He braced himself on his hands and kicked them the rest of the way off.

She had never seen a man completely naked. The trysts she had were all conducted half clothed, too rushed to have time for stripping clothes. She could not take her gaze from him.

"I hope you always stare at me that way," he said.

"What way?" Embarrassment flushed her face and neck. Ihsan made a sound, dipping his head to her breastbone.

"As though I amaze you," he murmured to her skin, his fingers brushing along her collarbone.

"You do," she whispered back. "You are beautiful."

His jaw flexed, and despite the slivers of frosty blue flurrying over his skin, she was certain she saw a faint flush on his neck.

"These freckles," he said in a low hum, his hand sliding to the swell of her breast beneath the cloth of the wrap. "I wonder if I could count them."

She spluttered. "Not likely. They're everywhere." She supposed that a princess probably shouldn't have freckles, but that hardly mattered now. She could be the first.

"Oh really?" Ihsan's head bobbed up, and he gripped her waist and flipped her like a flatbread. Nesrin squealed in surprise, and tried to escape, but his hands clasped her hips to hold her to the carpet.

"San," she demanded as she tried to push herself up, but she was laughing, as he pinned her legs between his knees and kneaded handfuls of her backside.

"Shh." He ran his hands up her back. "I'm counting."

She dissolved into more giggles, her forehead pressed to the carpet as his fingers reached her neck and dug into her hair. He stretched out on top of her, kissing her neck and a line across her shoulders.

She was distracted from those touches by the press of his erection, making her squirm. She turned her head to look at him over her shoulder, propping her chin in her hands. "Are you finished yet?"

"If you keep wiggling like that I will be," he mumbled as his fingers worked free the cloth around her chest. She grinned, then gasped when his chilly hands slid to her breasts. He murmured something into the back of her neck, then rolled her abruptly onto her back.

"You take your time, don't you?" Nesrin said as she bent her knees up to either side of him to try to urge him on top of her. He hovered over her on all fours, and at her words he ferried a hand down her inner thigh.

"In a rush?" he asked, fronds of frost masking his face as he slid a soft touch between her thighs. If she could have dissolved into a million tiny bits she would have. Her fingertips clawed into the carpet beneath her, and her eyes slid shut as his fingers teased and promised but did not deliver.

"I am now," she groaned when he lifted his hand away, dragging damp fingers up her thigh. Her hips followed the motion, lifting in demand.

"Good," he said as he moved up over her, taking a moment to acquaint each of her breasts with his mouth and tongue. The cold of his magic made her feel made of lightning, and she was undone and desperate by the time he brought his face level with hers. She clasped his head in her hands.

"Enough," she pleaded.

THERE WAS SO MUCH MORE he wanted to do. He would have happily spent the rest of the day getting to know every bit of her. Lost from the world, where nothing mattered but how many times he could make her whimper or plead his name. But he also wanted to see her come apart for him, and that desire won over the others.

"You are very demanding, Princess Consort." He lowered himself to his elbows, his hips aligned to hers. She squeezed her thighs, soft and strong, in desire. The damp heat at her core made all his plans and rational thoughts fracture into shards.

"I believe you feel the same," Nesrin murmured, hooking her legs over his back and reaching down to grip him. A charge surged through him, and he barely held back a wave of unleashed frost, though the air chilled around them. She squeezed her arms around him and pulled her body tight to his with a shiver.

Ihsan nuzzled her hair. "All right?" He didn't want the cold to hurt her.

"Not yet." Nesrin bit his shoulder. The zing of pain turned to pleasure by the time it reached his hips, a knife to his restraint. He tucked a hand beneath her to tilt her up and fit his hips to hers with a push.

Her nails clawed into his back as she moaned, the sound amplifying the burst of relief and need that tightened every muscle in his body. His plans for a long, slow lovemaking evaporated when she pressed her head back, her body arching beneath his, a vine of green zipping in a spiral up her scar. Leaves and tendrils of magic drifted beneath her skin, pulsing with every push and pull of their bodies.

He followed the green spiral with reverent fingers, over her belly and the dip of her waist, and picked it up again where it curved around her neck to her jaw and up to her temple. He kissed her there, and she turned her head to his, fingers locking in his hair as she kissed him.

Her magic stretched in and around him, like a bolt of energy, or pure sunlight, filling him to overflowing with his own power.

It broke from his control moments before she cried out beneath him and dragged him with her as every muscle in her body contracted. Lights burst behind his eyes, and ice shot out in every direction with such force that he heard something shatter, and something else tumble to the ground.

The entire room filled with the green starburst light of Nesrin's magic, her eyes wide in disbelief, clinging to Ihsan as he fought his charged power back under his control.

Somewhere, distantly, someone screamed, and Ihsan winced as he collapsed on Nesrin.

Something pounded on the floor, from below. Nesrin groaned, the puff of air directed at a spiraled strand of hair that had fallen over her face.

"In the middle of the day?" a voice cried from beneath them. Ihsan lifted his head, one eyebrow cocked as he looked down at Nesrin. She grimaced.

"That's anneanne. They're not…my family has never been very discreet." She blushed.

"Considering"—Ihsan glanced around the room, slightly dizzy and still bleeding frosty magic into the air—"that I might have frozen the entire house"—he brushed her hair away from her face—"I will forgive them this once."

She suppressed a laugh, a look of satisfied fatigue making her more beautiful than ever.

"I see no reason to leave the room." He let his head fall between her shoulder and neck.

"Oh, you will." Nesrin reached above her head and tugged one of their caftans close, sweeping it over them like a blanket.

"Absolutely not," a woman's voice barked from the sitting room.

"She is my sister, and I don't need your permission," another voice, which proved to be Sanem's when she marched into the room, argued.

"Honestly," Nesrin groused. Ihsan sat up, holding the caftan over as much of himself as he could, and Nesrin did too, huddling into his side.

"If you're finished with your very loud endeavors"—Sanem folded her arms over her chest—"then you can come help clean up the absolute disaster that all that ice has caused."

"I don't have to," Nesrin said, "I'm a princess." She stuck her tongue out.

Sanem scoffed and moved as if to come haul Nesrin naked from the room.

"Don't you dare. At least let me dress," Nesrin shrieked. The sound pierced Ihsan's ear and he grimaced.

Sanem sniffed and stormed back out. Reyhan bowed, twice, stumbling through an apology as she pulled the door shut behind them.

"When are they returning to Mizraa?" Ihsan growled. He'd thought growing up in the palace had not afforded him any privacy. Clearly, he had been horribly incorrect.

"Not soon enough," Nesrin said. She looked at him from the corners of her eyes, a small, mischievous smile on her lips. He had not seen that smile before but knew instantly it would be his favorite.

"Shall I lock the door?"

He grinned, pulling her into his lap.

"NESSA," Sanem howled from the sitting room.

"Wheel and spokes," Nesrin pouted. Then she kissed Ihsan and rose to hunt for her clothes.

He watched her as she dressed, letting tranquility sink into his bones and heart that had been too long absent.

"I love you," he said, as she made for the door. Nesrin turned and flung herself into his arms.

"Yes." She pulled back to cup his face in her hands. "Yes." Green spun a curl in the depths of her hazel eyes. "I love you."

"Prove it," he said, "and go tame your family."

"Yes, Sehzade." She kissed his brow, then stood.

"Nessa," he said as she crossed the room to go. She paused. He forced the next words out, though he knew it was the right decision. "Have Reyhan light the central brazier."

Her lips parted, her soft exhale the only evidence that he had surprised her.

"You're certain?"

He dipped his chin. Fire had been as important in his life as water. He could not ignore that balance because of fear. Her prideful smile made it worth it. Even if it caused him some discomfort. Nesrin rushed from the room, excited.

Ihsan pulled his salvar on but did not rise from his place on the floor, leaning against the couch. He let her words blanket him, warm and safe and truer than anything he'd felt in a long time. There was so much left to do, problems to solve, dire, hard decisions to be made.

But Nesrin was here.

Creation was awake on the Wheel once more, and he could feel that new vitality, in his heart, and in his magic. Could feel her.

Strong enough to hold them all.

Fifty-One

It was too warm a night for the hooded ferace she wore. Perhaps it was an unnecessary thing to do, but she had very little time and could not afford to be recognized or have her whereabouts whispered back to the palace. She'd ridden a horse instead of taking a carriage. It was not unusual for her to leave the palace at night, when her duties were finished for the day. But she was not visiting family tonight.

She doubted she would ever visit them again, after this.

The City Guard operated from a building in the northwest section of the Water District. It included a barracks, kitchens, a common hall, and offices. It took up the better part of a block, separated from the businesses and homes around it by a sprawling practice yard. It was too late at night for anyone to spar or drill, so the yard was quiet.

She secured her horse at one of the posts made for the purpose. For a moment she stood, eyes closed, feeling the night air and listening to the sounds of a sleepy city. This was the threshold, the moment where two paths remained open to her. Always two. She'd spent so many Turns choosing between these two directions. It had always been the nobler one. The one for the greater good.

Tonight, it could not be.

She stepped away from the horse, taking the path around the east side of the building where the note had directed her. That note was folded in her pocket, worried nearly to transparency. It lay beside the small purse of gold coins she carried. The path took her past the outside of the barracks. The windows there were narrow and high, so they let in air, but did not allow for the distraction of sight-lines. It meant she passed underneath them without notice. At the north end she turned the corner to the backside of the building. A single door led into the back of the barracks, and the guard captain's office.

Her knock was quiet. Too quiet, she thought when it went unanswered. But as she lifted her hand to try again, a man's voice called for her to enter. She turned the knob and stepped inside.

The room was dimly lit by an oil lamp instead of mage orbs. That was often a clue that something illicit was happening, since oil lamps required no fire mage to light, and therefore one less person who might be aware someone was in need of light in the middle of the night. It was sparely furnished, a simple square with a bed in one corner, a desk in the other, and a wardrobe. Captain Akkas sat behind his desk, feet propped on its surface. He wore only salvar and boots, and a dark glass bottle of alcohol sat within easy reach. There was another door behind him, presumably into the barracks interior.

He said nothing when she entered, watching her with dark eyes bearing the unfocused look of someone well into their drink. He laced his fingers over his belly. When she had closed the door behind her, he gave her a sly smile that made her skin crawl. But she had been too long in Naime's service to let something like that fluster her. She knew a bully when she saw one.

"Good evening, Mistress Azmeh."

"Do you have it?" Samira asked. He canted his head, then unfolded his hands, dropped his feet to the floor, and leaned forward on his desk.

"I do. And the payment?" He leered. He had the look of a boar, a barrel-shaped body, a nose with prominent, upturned nostrils, and fleshy cheeks that rounded when he smiled. She despised him. But she dug into her pocket and pulled out the purse and tossed it on the table. The heavy sound of it was loud in the cramped room. He dragged it toward him and opened it, digging a finger inside to count the coins. "Very nice," he purred. He shifted to the side and dug in his salvar pocket to fish out a key, which he used to open a drawer in his desk. He retrieved a small box before he closed and locked the drawer again.

Then, to her dismay, he stood and walked around the desk to approach her. He stank. Of sweat, and alcohol. His intentions, or at least the drunken lust that fueled them, echoed in her magic. The strike of steel to flint.

He took hold of her wrist to turn her hand up and place the box in her palm. Samira's fire sparked awake, but she did not move to shake him off. Instead, she turned the box around in her hand and opened it. The item inside was unremarkable, considering all that it would ruin.

"I knew having that mold would be useful someday," he continued in a murmur, gaze coasting her face and down. Samira snapped the box closed. His face was so close to hers that the moist heat of his breath touched her skin. He swept her hood off her head. She twitched away from his touch.

"Goodnight, Captain Akkas," Samira said. But when she tried to move away, his other hand closed on her arm.

"I don't think we're done."

"We are." Fire snapped in her voice.

"You don't get to command me, servant girl. I can end your plans right now by turning you in. You may stay of your own accord, or I can arrest you for whatever treason you have planned for tonight." He smiled. That smile. Wheel, she loathed it. Every man who thought he had bested Naime. Who was so comfortable in their unearned power they believed themselves invincible. Who looked at others and saw less. How he looked at her and saw, not a person and a mage capable of turning him into a human torch, but something to be used for his pleasure.

"You can take your hand off me, or I can burn your office to the ground."

"And kill all these men?"

"No," Samira bit out, and the bottle of alcohol on his desk burst into flame, exploding in a shower of glass and splashes of blue and red fire to ignite his desk and papers. "Just you."

He cursed, leaping toward the desk to slap at the flames. Samira left. As she turned the corner of the building, she drew the hood back up. Captain Akkas was right about one thing, that she would not burn a building full of innocent people. But the need to burn something in her fury billowed in her, undeniable. When she mounted her horse, she did not spur it back to the palace, as she had intended, but toward the Fire District.

The home was unchanged from the memory of her first and last time ever setting foot in it. She tied the horse at a post up the hill, far enough away that it would not panic when she did what she intended. She followed the creeping growth of the firecress all the way to the balcony with her gaze. He had stood there sometimes. Her heart wanted it to be because he was watching for her. But her head was too practical for that, after everything.

She erased the vision of him from her mind's eye and climbed the steps. The front door was unlocked, so she went inside. At the far end of the central room, her gaze fell on the unused fountain. She crossed the space and put her hands on it, staring into the empty, dry basin. It represented everything wrong, every corrupted, rotting fiber of the Kadir line. Her fury ignited, sparks snapping away from her, floating away and burning themselves out as she climbed the stairs.

Her memory supplied the image of Behram and Cemil, standing side by side just inside the balcony doors, denying her. A brazier stood there now. Samira went to it, the heat of her anger and her fire igniting the carpet as she walked. When she grabbed the edge of the brazier, the coals inside lit, and she shoved it over, spilling embers across the floor. The curtains kindled. Then a chair leg.

She turned her back on the brazier and spread her arms out at her sides, calling swirling ropes of flames to her hands. All magic was fueled by a mage's energy, but fire, more than any other power, was shaped by the emotion of its wielder, to warmth, or destruction.

And there was nothing in Samira's heart at that moment but heart-broken rage. She released the flames in bolts of heat that beat into the walls to either side, so hot it splashed, raining sparks and whisps of fire across the room. Everything caught.

Wheel fire was indiscriminate, burning through fuel as well as emotion. She lifted her arms, commanding it to engulf the molding. When she was caged by her own scorching magic everywhere, she lowered her hands. There was no water here. Not even a memory of it in the fountain. Her creation spread with gleeful abandon.

For a moment she watched it, and wished everything else in her would turn to ash. But fire would not consume her, even if she wished for it to.

Downstairs, she flicked her fingers at furniture and paintings, at the rugs. All she wanted was to erase Behram Kadir from existence. But as always, he had made it impossible. She fled the house, trailing fire in her steps. Then she turned to touch a flaming finger to the firecress vine. Its leaves withered, the flowers drooping and shrinking, then finally ignited.

Samira took off the coat and slung it into the fire then walked away. She was already at her horse's side when the inferno was noticeable on the street and neighbors began to gather. They had begun shouting when she guided the horse into an alley, cutting through side streets until she felt safe to spur him back to the palace.

The Council Hall was silent, and dark. It was so late at night that not even the servants were still awake. She took soft steps over the tiles, rounding the dais and the lattice screen to either side of it. At the back, she knelt and pulled a dagger from the back of the fabric that wrapped her waist. She unsheathed it then jammed the blade into the crack between tiles. It took a moment to lever the stone tile high enough that she could get her fingers under it. She lifted it free. The stone was thick and heavy and hard to set down without scraping or knocking.

The hole beneath it was as black as the void. She returned the dagger to its sheath and into the cloth wrap, then descended the ladder into the tunnel. She conjured the tiniest mage orb possible once she was on the ground, then followed the tunnel. Since Makram had conducted his now-famous infiltration of the palace, the tunnel beneath the palace was no longer a secret.

Samira had only walked this way once before when Makram had guided Naime through it. Still, she had to determine which branch of the cavern she needed. That might be the easiest part of all. Easiest in execution, but most difficult to force herself to do. When she arrived at the far end of the enormous cavern lit by luminous moss, she extinguished her orb and closed her eyes.

My fire to yours. Always.

She dropped mentally into the firestorm of her magic, and as she had first done as a child, reached out with tendrils of power. Tracing a thread of feeling that always led to the same place. One she could follow, even if she were blind. The thread drew taut, and a pulse of awareness opened within her. She opened her eyes and followed the feeling which led her down the middle tunnel.

When she arrived at the cell, Cemil was sitting, alone, his back against the stone wall. They kept fire mages in cells carved completely of stone, but for the door, which was made of tungsten. Tungsten was rare and required both fire mages and earth mages to form into anything usable. It had very few uses, except to make bars that a fire mage could not melt.

It was not so different than the first time she had ever seen him, and the lonely ache flared.

"Hello, Spark," he said without moving or opening his eyes. Her heart stuttered, a crucible of emotions igniting so quickly she could barely breathe.

"Are you the Charah of fire?" There were so many small things that had made her wonder. And his secrets. Secrets he had kept even from her.

His eyes opened, golden with fire. "The Fire Charah does not exist," he said. "Is that why you're here? I wondered if you could bring yourself to come say goodbye." He cut his gaze away. "I wish you hadn't."

His voice held nothing but the warmth she had known it for in all the Turns of their childhood and time in the University. There was also exhaustion. Resignation. It came to her, like Blight from one crop to another, sucking her strength. *Yours*, he had said. *I am nothing but yours*. It had been a promise he broke only turns later.

She wrapped her fingers around the bars and tipped her forehead against the cold metal. Her breath was ragged, though she tried to keep it steady, to hold her tears a few moments longer. But she did not have that kind of power. Not like Naime. The tears came, evaporating in the heat of her sorrow before they traced her cheeks. The strength in her knees gave as a sob tore from her lungs. But he was there, arms through the bars, around her, holding her up.

"No," he cajoled, "not for me."

She reached between the bars to his face. She missed him. Missed him like her heart had been torn from her chest. His eyes closed and his head dropped forward to the bars. She slid one hand to press over his heart. "Tell me these were not your decisions. Tell me it was not you who burned his closest friend. Tell me that monster spelled you like he did the others."

His eyes closed, head pressed to the bars. "No enchantment could make me do what I have done. No spell." He slid a hand up to her neck, his arm reaching through the gaps. "I would never change the choices I have made," he said. "Not a single one."

She let go of him, gripping the metal instead, her grief ripping her to pieces.

"Go home, Spark," he said. "You do not belong here." His gaze met hers, all the fire gone from his eyes, so they were the true color that so few actually got to see. Jasper. Like golden stone in morning sun.

Samira reached into her pocket and withdrew the box. She opened it, revealing the key within. She held it up between them. The look of grievous denial that contorted his face made everything inside her go still. She had not even considered that he might tell her no. She pressed the cell key toward him, but he lifted his hands and stepped away.

"No," he said, backing all the way to the back of the cell and sliding down the wall to sit where he had been when she'd found him.

"Cemi," she choked. "Please." The tears came again, the sorrow and confusion pouring out of her. "I cannot watch you die. Please don't make me watch you die."

"I will not trade your life for mine," he barked. "Get out before I summon a guard."

Samira fumbled the key toward the lock, but he was up and on her instantly, reaching to snatch it from her hand. She stumbled back as his arm shot through the bars at her, falling backwards against the cell behind her.

An arm snaked around her neck from behind, cinching her so hard against the bars that she cried out in pain as the metal ground into her shoulder blades and back.

Panic suffused Cemil's face, and her own body, as she tried to breathe past the crushing pressure on her throat. She could not. Neither could she make a sound. She clawed at the arm, grabbing hold and releasing her power to burn the person holding her.

He laughed. "Hello, Samira, dear. I know you are not foolish enough to try to burn a fire mage?" Kadir murmured in her ear. Fire erupted from Cemil in a torrent, blazing up and out as he roared a denial. But Mahir must have been in a cell nearby, because a dampening cut the sound off abruptly.

Samira clawed at Kadir's arm, kicking and twisting, trying to get a foot backwards between the bars to kick him. Holding the key as far away as she could so he could not take it from her. He yanked at her sleeve, trying to get the key. Samira threw it away from her, into the darkness of the stone tunnel beyond.

"That was foolish. I only want to help. Let me out, and I'll make certain your beloved comes with me. You cannot make him, because you do not have what he wants," Kadir whispered, "but I do."

Her vision dimmed, her lungs aching for air, her thoughts whirling. Cemil had hold of his bars, and they glowed red and white with heat. His face twisted in agony. He dropped to his knees, falling sideways and scrunching around himself with a scream she could not hear.

Samira's legs failed, her weight pulling her harder into Kadir's choking grip. He released her and she crumpled to the stone, sucking in a searing breath of air. There was nothing in her awareness for a moment but her animal need for breath, deep, burning heaves that slowly brought her back into her body. She crawled to Cemil, reaching through the bars to his hand.

"Cemi." The air shimmered as the dampening fell away. Cemil was conscious, lying curled on his side, eyes closed, breathing hard. When her hand went to his, he opened his eyes, revealing they were bloodshot. He rolled to his elbows, crawling close enough that he could reach through to cup her face. "You're all right?" she begged.

"Wheel damn you," he rasped. "The one time I want you to choose her, you finally choose me." He closed his hands over hers on the bars. Warm. And gentle. He had always been gentle. Behram Kadir had broken what was most precious to her in all the world, and its loss was going to kill her.

"I always chose you," she murmured, holding onto his wrists. "You just couldn't see it."

"I will not let you do this."

"I know." It took all her will, all her self-control, to pull away from his grip and stand. He watched her, until he realized what she was doing.

"Samira," he said her name like a curse.

But she walked into the dark tunnel and retrieved the key. She could not allow herself to think or feel. Because no matter what she chose, she was losing a piece of herself. She stopped in front of the cell that held Behram Kadir. "If I ever see you again," she said, "I will kill you. No matter what it takes. No matter what it costs."

"I think we both know the likelihood of that happening, under any circumstances." He smoothed the sleeves of his caftan and flicked his gaze at the lock. Samira unlocked it. Behind her, Cemil smacked his fists against the door. She could not look at him as she handed the key to Kadir. He freed Mahir first, then returned to open Cemil's cell.

"I'm not going anywhere," Cemil said, teeth bared like he'd gone feral. The liquid fire of his magic pulsed erratically in his skin, and his fists clenched and unclenched, his teeth grit.

"Are you intent on a battle of wills, or shall I remind you what I still control in this city? What I am capable of doing?" Kadir said. "Your impotent temper tantrum is only going to end in more pain. For everyone." He made a gesture and Mahir advanced, casting another dampening as he did. Cemil lunged at him, but Mahir made a grabbing motion, and a hunk of rock snapped off the wall of the cell, crashing into the back of Cemil's skull.

Samira cried out as he fell to his hands and knees. "Bring him," Kadir ordered Mahir. Cemil tried to fight as the earth mage hauled him up, but even an earth mage Mahir's age had strength like stone.

"Don't hurt him!" Samira wailed.

Kadir cast her a disdainful glance. "If you were not here, he would not be fighting me. It is not I that is hurting him, but you."

"You vile monster," she spat.

Mahir dragged Cemil out of the cell. His head lolled. She would have run to him, but his father stood between them.

"I am only the monster that Dilay Akar and Omar Sabri made."

"No," Samira said, "you are the monster you chose to be."

He gave a wry smirk. "We are all what we have to be to survive." He turned his back on her, dropping the key on the rock floor. Then he limped toward the entrance to the Cliffs, Mahir wrestling Cemil after him. Her last glimpse of Cemil was his frantic backwards glance before the darkness of the passage swallowed them.

Half her heart went with him. And the other beat too slowly in her chest. She entered the cell where Cemil had been and pulled the door shut behind her.

She sat in the middle of the floor and waited.

She did not know how many marks passed before she heard anyone approach. But she knew who it was before they arrived. The cold wind that smelled of winter and roses. The schism of ache that went through her chest at what was to come.

Samira looked up and met Naime's gaze.

Naime gripped the bars, her eyes aglow with winter sun. "What have you done?" she breathed.

Samira did not answer, only stood and walked to meet Naime at the bars.

"What have you done?" she repeated, more forcefully. "I cannot spare you. I cannot save you." Tears welled in her eyes and her next breath was a sob.

"I know," Samira said. She was abandoning Naime when Naime needed her most. It hurt to breathe when she saw the anguish in her friend's face. She could not ask for forgiveness from Naime that she could not give herself. She had known what she was choosing, when she came to free Cemil.

Naime reached through the bars to clasp Samira's neck, and Samira did the same, their brows touching.

"I love you most in all the world," Samira whispered. Another sob shook Naime's body.

Except for Cemil.

The End

Author's Note

THANK YOU FOR READING! Ihsan and Nesrin were where this whole series began, and they went through many incarnations before they arrived at this one. I went through several incarnations as well, from mom of one to mom of two. A move across the country, a move across a city, a pandemic. I lost myself, I found myself, and then I was finally ready to write this book.

I hope it speaks to you.

If you enjoyed this book, you can continue on in the series, follow me on social media, and sign up for my newsletter (for fun FREEBIES!) here:

Acknowledgments

I WON'T LIE. THERE were MANY, many times I thought this book was not going to get written. It was so many things, it was stuck in my brain in its original form—the seed of an entire series.

I struggled. I slogged. I cried, A LOT. I fought the haze of motherhood. I wanted to write it so badly, I pushed. It did not come until it was ready. Until I was. Until the nights weren't sleepless anymore with baby number two. Until there was kindergarten, and day-to-day schedules that were predictable. Then it trickled.

I had to learn how to write in bits and pieces, instead of bigger chunks of time. It was so, so hard.

But it is here, and I hope you love it. I hope, for those of you who have been with me, waiting so patiently since the beginning, that it is worth the wait.

The fact that this book is in your hands at all really comes down to the people who hustled when I could not. When every word had to be forced from me. My sister, as always, is the reason I ever published. My cheerleader, the one who smacks me about when I get down on myself. The one who reminds me that yes, I felt like this during the last book too. Thanks, Squish.

Anka, who was an ARC reader for Reign & Ruin. Who inexplicably lived in the same city and had a kiddo the same age as mine. Who became a friend and a vital writing partner. Thank you for the sprints, and the advice, and the enthusiasm. I miss you, Lady.

Michelle, my editor, who takes my terrible time management in stride and is kind and patient and has a sharp eye for all the details.

Terry Roy took the brunt of it this time around. She designs my interiors, and dustjackets, lays out my covers and formats my books. I handed her a doorstop of a book at the absolute last minute, and she made it happen. I could not do this without each and every one of these folks, and I am so grateful for them and their incredible talents.

Tatiana Anor, as ever, whose iconic artwork has made my books unmistakable. And a new artist this time around, Liz at Raven Pages Designs, did the case linework for the hardbacks and I couldn't be more in love with them.

I'd like to extend a special thank you to Dr. Manthe, who helped me with some medical questions. And Dania, who was kind enough to answer my questions about some of the Turkish words I used.

And as always, my readers. Thank you for believing in me, and in the books, and taking this bookish ride with me, even when it takes a bit of a break.

ABOUT THE AUTHOR

J. D. EVANS WRITES epic fantasy romance. After earning her degree in linguistics, J. D. served a decade as an army officer. She once spent her hours putting together briefings for helicopter pilots and generals. Now she writes stories, tends to two unreasonable tiny humans, knits, sews badly, gardens, and cultivates Pinterest Fails. After a stint in Beirut, J. D. fell in love with the Levant, which inspired the setting for her debut series, *Mages of the Wheel*.

Originally hailing from Montana, J. D. now resides in North Carolina with her husband, two attempts at mini-clones gone awry, and too many stories in her head.

Made in United States
Orlando, FL
08 April 2024

45597694R00332